Dear Reader,

Welcome to the seco... ...ls
Conner and Brody, ...the
Montana Creeds an... ...ttled
down in Stone Creek, Arizona, ...
five-year-old son and a new bride, Melissa. Back in Lonesome
Bend, Colorado, where Steven and the twins were raised as
brothers, the lovely Tricia McCall catches Conner's eye. Will
he be able to resist her charms? Or can this rancher tame
himself into a happy domestic life with a beautiful bride of
his own?

I also wanted to write today to tell you about a special group
of people with whom I've become involved in the past couple
of years. It is The Humane Society of the United States
(HSUS), specifically their Pets for Life program.

The Pets for Life program is one of the best ways to help your
local shelter—that is, to help keep animals out of shelters in
the first place. Something as basic as keeping a collar and tag
on your pet all the time, so if he gets out and gets lost, he can
be returned home. Being a responsible pet owner. Spaying or
neutering your pet. And not giving up when things don't go
perfectly. If your dog digs in the yard, or your cat scratches
the furniture, know that these are problems that can be
addressed. You can find all the information about these—and
many other common problems—at www.petsforlife.org.
This campaign is focused on keeping pets and their people
together for a lifetime.

As many of you know, my own household includes two dogs,
two cats and six horses, so this is a cause that is near and
dear to my heart. I hope you'll get involved along with me.

With love,

Paula Reid Miller

LINDA LAEL MILLER

CREED'S HONOR

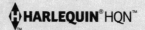

Recycling programs
for this product may
not exist in your area.

ISBN-13: 978-0-373-77580-4

CREED'S HONOR

Copyright © 2011 by Linda Lael Miller

All rights reserved. Except for use in any review, the reproduction or utilization of this work in whole or in part in any form by any electronic, mechanical or other means, now known or hereafter invented, including xerography, photocopying and recording, or in any information storage or retrieval system, is forbidden without the written permission of the publisher, Harlequin HQN, 225 Duncan Mill Road, Don Mills, Ontario M3B 3K9, Canada.

This is a work of fiction. Names, characters, places and incidents are either the product of the author's imagination or are used fictitiously, and any resemblance to actual persons, living or dead, business establishments, events or locales is entirely coincidental.

This edition published by arrangement with Harlequin Books S.A.

For questions and comments about the quality of this book, please contact us at CustomerService@Harlequin.com.

® and TM are trademarks of Harlequin Enterprises Limited or its corporate affiliates. Trademarks indicated with ® are registered in the United States Patent and Trademark Office, the Canadian Trade Marks Office and in other countries.

Printed in U.S.A.

www.Harlequin.com

Also available from

LINDA LAEL MILLER

and Harlequin HQN

To some of my favorite Laels:
Mike and Sara and Courtney and Chandler

CREED'S HONOR

CHAPTER ONE

Lonesome Bend, Colorado

TRICIA MCCALL WAS NOT THE TYPE to see apparitions, but there *were* times—especially when lonely, tired or both—that she caught just the merest flicker of a glimpse of her dog, Rusty, out of the corner of one eye. Each time that happened, she hoped for the impossible; her heartbeat quickened with joy and excitement, and her breath rushed up into the back of her throat. But when she turned, no matter how *quickly,* the shepherd-Lab-setter mix was never there.

Of course, he wasn't. Rusty had died in his sleep only six months before, contented and gray-muzzled and full of years, and his absence was still an ache that throbbed in the back of Tricia's heart whenever she thought of him. Which was often.

After all, Rusty had been her best friend for nearly half her life. She was almost thirty now, and she'd been fifteen when she and her dad had found the reddish-brown pup hiding under a picnic table at the campground, nearly starved, flea-bitten and shivering.

She and Joe McCall had debugged him as best they could, fed him and taken him straight to Dr. Benchley's office for shots and a checkup. From then on, Rusty was a member of the family.

"Meow," interrupted a feline voice coming from the general vicinity of Tricia's right ankle.

Still wearing her ratty blue chenille robe and the pink fluffy slippers her best friend, Diana, had given her for Christmas many moons ago as a joke, Tricia looked down to see Winston, a black tom with a splash of white between his ears. He was a frequent visitor to her apartment, since he lived just downstairs, with his mistress, Tricia's great-grandmother, Natty. The separate residences were connected by an inside stairway, but Winston still managed to startle her on a regular basis.

"Meow," the former stray repeated, this time with more emphasis, looking earnestly up at Tricia. Translation: *It's cat abuse. Natty McCall may* look *like a harmless old woman, but I'm being starved, I tell you. You've got to* do *something.*

"A likely story, sardine-breath," Tricia replied, out loud. "I was there when the groceries were delivered last Friday, remember? You wouldn't go hungry if we were snowed in till spring."

Winston twitched his sleek tail in a jaunty, oh-well-I-tried sort of way and crossed the small kitchen to leap up onto Tricia's desk and curl up on a tidy stack of printer paper next to the keyboard. He watched Tricia with half-closed amber eyes as she poured herself a cup of coffee and meandered over to boot up the PC. Maybe there would be an email from Hunter; that would definitely lift her spirits.

Not that she was down, exactly. No, she felt more like someone living in suspended animation, a sort of limbo between major life events. She was marking time, marching in place. And that bothered her.

At the push of a button, the monitor flared to life and there it was: the screensaver photo of her and Hunter, beaming in front of a ski lodge in Idaho and looking like—well—*a couple*. Two happy and reasonably attractive people who belonged together, outfitted for a day on the slopes.

With the tip of one finger, Tricia touched Hunter's square-jawed, classically handsome face. Pixels scattered, like a miniature universe expanding after a tiny, silent big bang. She set her cup on the little bit of desk space Winston wasn't already occupying and plunked into the chair she'd dragged away from the dinette set.

She sat very still for a moment or so, the cup of coffee she'd craved from the instant she'd opened her eyes that morning cooling nearby, her gaze fixed on the cheerfully snowy scene. Big smiles. Bright eyes.

Maybe she ought to change the picture, she thought. Put the slide show of Rusty back up. Trouble was, the loss was still too fresh for that.

So she left the ski-lodge shot where it was. She and Hunter had had a good thing going, back in Seattle, in what seemed like a previous lifetime now even though it had only been a year and a half since the passion they'd been so sure they could sustain had begun to fizzle.

As soon as she sold the failing businesses she'd inherited when her dad died—the River's Bend Campground and RV Park and the decrepit Bluebird Drive-in theater at the edge of town—she could go back to her *real* life in the art world of Seattle. Open a little gallery in the Pike Place Market, maybe, or somewhere in Pioneer Square.

Beside her, Winston unfurled his tail so the end of it brushed the back of Tricia's hand, rolled it back up again and then repeated the whole process. Gently jolted out of her reverie, she watched as wisps of black fur drifted across her line of vision and then settled, with exquisite accuracy, onto the surface of her coffee.

Tricia shoved back her chair, the legs of it making a loud, screeching sound on the scuffed linoleum floor, and she winced before remembering that Natty was out of town this week, visiting her eighty-nine-year-old sister in Denver, and therefore could not have been disturbed by the noise.

Muttering good-naturedly, she crossed to the old-fashioned sink under the narrow window that looked out over the outside landing, dumped the coffee, rinsed the cup out thoroughly and poured herself a refill.

Winston jumped down from the desktop, making a solid thump when he landed, as he was a somewhat rotund fellow.

Leaning back against the counter, Tricia fortified herself with a couple of sips of the hot, strong coffee she knew—even without Natty's subtle reminders—she drank too often, and in excessive quantities.

Winston had been right to put in his order for breakfast, she reflected; it was her job to feed him and empty his litter box while her great-grandmother was away.

"Come on," she said, coffee in hand, heading toward the doorway that led down the dark, narrow stairs to Natty's part of the house. "I wouldn't want you keeling over from hunger."

You're not even thirty, commented a voice in her head, *and you're talking to cats. You seriously need a life.*

With a sigh, Tricia flipped on the single light in the sloping ceiling above the stairs and started down, careful because of Winston's tendency to wind himself around her ankles and the bulky slippers, which were a tripping hazard even on a flat surface.

Natty's rooms smelled pleasantly of recent wood fires blazing on the stone hearth, some lushly scented mix of potpourri and the lavender talcum powder so many old ladies seemed to favor.

Crossing the living room, which was stuffed with well-crafted antique furniture, every surface sporting at least one intricately crocheted doily and most of them adorned with a small army of ornately framed photographs as well, Tricia smiled. At ninety-one, Natty was still busy, with friends of all ages, and she was pretty active in the community, too. Until the year before, she'd been in charge of the annual rummage sale and chili feed, a popular event held the last weekend of October. Members of the Ladies' Auxiliary—the organization they'd been auxiliary *to* was long defunct—donated the money they raised to the local school system, to be used for extras like art supplies, musical instruments and uniforms for the marching band. And while Natty had stepped down as the group's chairperson, she attended every meeting.

Natty's kitchen was as delightfully old-fashioned as the rest of the house—although there was an electric stove, the original wood-burning contraption still dominated one corner of the long, narrow room. And Natty still used it, when the spirit moved her to bake.

Without the usual fire crackling away, the kitchen seemed a little on the chilly side, and Tricia shivered once as she headed toward the pantry, setting her coffee mug aside on the counter. She took a can of Winston's regular food—he was only allowed sardines on Sundays, as a special treat—from one of the shelves in the pantry, popped the top and dumped the contents into one of several chipped but still beautiful soup bowls reserved for his use.

Frosty-cold air seemed to emanate from the floor as she bent to put the bowl in front of him. Tricia felt it even through the soles of those ridiculous slippers.

While Winston chowed down, she ran some fresh drinking water and placed the bowl within easy reach. Then, hugging herself against the cold, she glanced at the bay windows surrounding Natty's heirloom oak table, half expecting to see snowflakes drifting past the glass.

A storm certainly wouldn't be unusual in that part of Colorado, even though it was only mid-October, but Tricia was holding out for good weather just the same. The summer and early fall had been unusually slow over at the campground and RV park, but folks came from all over that part of the state to attend the rummage sale/ chili feed, and a lot of them brought tents and travel trailers, and set up for one last stay along the banks of the river. The modest fees Tricia charged for camping spots and the use of electrical hookups, as well as her cut of the profits from the vending machines, would carry her through a couple of months.

Some benevolent soul could still happen along and buy the properties Joe had left her, but so far all the For Sale signs hadn't produced so much as a nibble.

Tricia sighed, watched Winston eat for a few moments, then started for the stairs. Yes, it was early, but she had a full workday ahead over at River's Bend. She'd already let the seasonal crew go, which meant she manned the registration desk by herself, answering the phone on the rare occasions when it rang and slipping away for short intervals to clean the public showers and the restrooms. After the big weekend at the end of the month, she would shut everything down for the winter.

A lump of sadness formed in Tricia's throat as she climbed the stairs, leaving the door at the bottom open for Winston as she would the one at the top. As a child, she'd loved coming to River's Bend for the summers, "helping" her dad run the outdoor theater and the campground, the two of them boarding with Natty and a series of pampered cats named for historical and/or political figures the older woman admired.

One had been Abraham; another, General Washington. Next came a redoubtable tabby, Laurel Roosevelt, and now there was Winston, for the cigar-smoking prime minister who had shepherded England through the darkest hours of World War II.

Tricia was smiling again by the time she reached her own kitchen, which was warmer. She was about to sit down at the computer again to check her email, as she'd intended to do earlier, when she heard the pounding at the back door downstairs.

Startled, Winston yowled and shot through the inside doorway like a black, furry bullet, his trajectory indicating that he intended to hide out in Tricia's bedroom, under the four-poster, maybe, or on the high shelf in her closet.

Once, when something scared him, he'd climbed straight up her living room draperies, and it had taken both her *and* Natty to coax him down again.

The pounding came again, louder this time.

"Oh, for pity's sake," Tricia grumbled, employing a

phrase she'd picked up from Natty, tightening the belt of
her bathrobe and moving, once more, in the direction of
the stairs. She followed the first cliché up with a second,
also one of Natty's favorites. "Hold your horses!"

Again, the impatient visitor knocked. Hard enough,
in fact, to rattle every window on the first floor of the
house.

A too-brief silence fell.

Tricia was halfway down the stairs, steam-powered
by early-morning annoyance, when the sound shifted.
Now whoever it was had moved to *her* door, the one that
opened onto the outside landing.

Murmuring a word she definitely *hadn't* picked up
from her great-grandmother, Tricia turned and huffed
her way back up to her own quarters.

Winston yowled again, the sound muffled.

"I'm coming!" she yelled, spotting a vaguely familiar and distinctly masculine form through the frosted
glass oval in her door. Lonesome Bend was a town of
less than five thousand people, most of whom had lived
there all their lives, as had their parents, grandparents
and *great*-grandparents, so Tricia had long since gotten
out of the habit of looking to see who was there before
opening the door.

Conner Creed stood in front of her, one fist raised to
knock again, a sheepish smile curving his lips. His blond
hair, though a little long, was neatly trimmed, and he
wore a blue denim jacket over a white shirt, along with
jeans and boots that had seen a lot of hard use.

"Sorry," he said, with a shrug of his broad shoulders,
when he came face-to-face with Tricia.

"Do you know what time it is?" Tricia demanded.

His blue eyes moved over her hair, which was

probably sticking out in all directions since she hadn't yet brushed and then tamed it into a customary long, dark braid, her coiffure of choice, then the rag-bag bathrobe and comical slippers. That he could take a liberty like that without coming off as rude struck Tricia as— well—it just *struck* her, that's all.

"Seven-thirty," he answered, after checking his watch. "I brought Miss Natty a load of firewood, as she wanted, but she didn't answer her door. And that worried me. Is she all right?"

"She's in Denver," Tricia said stiffly.

His smile practically knocked her back on her heels. "Well, then, that explains why she didn't come to the door. I was afraid she might have fallen or something." A pause. "Is the coffee on?"

Though Tricia was acquainted with Conner, as she was with virtually everybody else in town, she didn't know him well—they didn't move in the same social circles. She was an outsider raised in Seattle, except for those golden summers with her dad, while the Creeds had been ranching in the area since the town was settled, way back in the late 1800s. Being ninety-nine percent certain that the man wasn't a homicidal maniac or a serial rapist—Natty was very fond of him, after all, which said *something* about his character—she stepped back, blushing, and said, "Yes. There's coffee—help yourself."

"Thanks," he said, in a cowboy drawl, ambling past her in the loose-limbed way of a man who was at ease wherever he happened to find himself, whether on the back of a bucking bronco or with both feet planted firmly on the ground. The scent of fresh country air clung to him, along with a woodsy aftershave, hay and something minty—probably toothpaste or mouthwash.

Tricia pushed the door shut and then stood with her back to it, watching as Conner opened one cupboard, then another, found a cup and helped himself at the coffeemaker.

Torn between mortification at being caught in her robe with her hair going wild, and stunned by his easy audacity, Tricia didn't smile. On some level, she was tallying the few things she knew about Conner Creed— that he lived on the family ranch, that he had an identical twin brother called Cody or Brody or some other cowboy-type name, that he'd never been married and, according to Natty, didn't seem in any hurry to change that.

"I'm sure my great-grandmother will be glad you brought that wood," she said finally, striving for a neutral conversational tone but sounding downright insipid instead. "Natty loves a good fire, especially when the temperature starts dropping."

Conner regarded Tricia from a distance that fell a shade short of far enough away to suit her, and raised one eyebrow. Indulged himself in a second leisurely sip from his mug before bothering to reply. "When's she coming back?" he asked. "Miss Natty, I mean."

"Probably next week," Tricia answered, surprised to find herself having this conversation. It wasn't every day, after all, that a good-looking if decidedly cocky cattle rancher tried to beat down a person's door at practically the crack of dawn and then stood in her kitchen swilling coffee as if he owned the place. "Or the week after, if she's having an especially good time."

"Miss Natty didn't mention that she was planning

on taking a trip," Conner observed thoughtfully, after another swallow of coffee.

The statement irritated Tricia—since when was Conner Creed her great-grandmother's keeper? All of a sudden, she wanted him *gone,* from her kitchen, from her house. He didn't seem to be in any more of a hurry to leave than he was to get married, though.

And he was using up all the oxygen in the room.

Did he think she'd bound and gagged Natty with duct tape, maybe stuck her in a closet?

She gestured toward the inside stairway. "Feel free to see for yourself if it will ease your mind as far as Natty is concerned. And, by the way, you scared the cat."

He flashed that wickedly innocent grin again; it lighted his eyes, and Tricia noticed that there was a rim of gray around the blue irises. He had good teeth, too—white and straight.

Stop, Tricia told her racing brain. Her thoughts flew, clicking like the beads on an abacus.

"I believe you," he said. "If you say Miss Natty is in Denver, kicking up her heels with her sister, then I reckon it's true."

"Gee, that's a relief," Tricia said dryly, folding her arms. Then, after a pause, "If that's everything…?"

"Sorry about scaring the cat," Conner told her affably, putting his mug in the sink and pushing off from the counter, starting for the door. "Truth is, the critter's never liked me much. Must have figured out that I'm more of a dog-and-horse person."

Tricia opened her mouth, shut it again. What did a person say to that?

Conner curved a hand around the doorknob, looked back at her over one of those fine, denim-covered shoulders of his. Mischief danced in his eyes, quirked up one corner of his mouth. "If you wouldn't mind letting me in downstairs," he said, "I could fill up the wood boxes. There's room in the shed for the rest of the load, I guess."

Tricia nodded. She had an odd sense of disorientation, as if she'd suddenly been thrust underwater and held there, and on top of that had to translate everything this man said from some language other than her own before his meaning penetrated the gray matter between her ears.

"I'll meet you at Natty's back door," she said, still feeling muddled, as he went out.

She stood rooted to the spot, listening as the heels of Conner's boots made a rapid thunking sound on the outside steps.

Winston crept out of the short hallway leading to the apartment's one bedroom and slinked over to Tricia, purring companionably while he turned figure eights around her ankles.

Wishing she had time to pull on some clothes, fix her hair and maybe even slap on a little makeup, Tricia went back down to Natty's place, bustled through to the kitchen, turned the key in the lock and undid the chain, and wrenched open the door.

Conner was already there, standing on the porch, grinning at her. After looking her over once more in that offhand way that so disconcerted her, he shook his head slightly and rubbed the back of his neck with one hand.

"Thanks," he said, his tone husky with amusement. "I'll take it from here."

Tricia felt heat surge into her cheeks, spark in her

eyes. He knew she was uncomfortable and not a little embarrassed, damn him, and he was *enjoying* it.

"I'll come back in a few minutes to lock up behind you," she replied, ratcheting her chin up a notch in hopes of letting Conner know he wasn't getting to her.

Well, maybe he was, a little, she admitted to herself, terminally honest. But it wasn't because of the invisible charge buzzing around them. She wasn't used to standing around in her bathrobe talking to strange men, that was all.

"Fine with me," Conner answered, lifting the collar of his jacket against a gust of wind as he turned to descend the steps of Natty's back porch. His truck, large and red, with mud-splattered tires and doors, was parked alongside the woodshed.

Possessed of a peculiar and completely unreasonable urge to slam the door behind him, hard, Tricia instead shut it politely, turned on one heel and fled back upstairs to her apartment.

There, in her small bedroom, she hastily exchanged her robe and pajamas for jeans and a navy blue hooded sweatshirt, replaced the slippers with sneakers. Advancing to the bathroom—she'd had larger *closets,* she thought, flustered—Tricia washed her face, brushed her teeth and whipped her renegade hair into a tidy plait.

Intermittently, she heard the homey sound of wood clunking into the boxes beside Natty's fireplace and the old stove in the kitchen.

She nearly tripped over Winston, who was lounging in the hallway, just over the bedroom threshold.

"That," Tricia sputtered, righting herself, "is a *great* place to stretch out."

"Meow," Winston observed casually, flicking his tail

and giving no indication that he planned on moving anytime soon. He was quite comfortable where he was, thank you very much.

Tricia took a moment to collect her wits—why *was* she rushing around as though the place were on fire, anyway?—smoothing her hands down the thighs of her jeans and drawing in a deep, slow breath.

Consuming a carton of low-fat yogurt for breakfast, she stood on tiptoe to look out the window over her kitchen sink, which afforded her a clear view of the backyard.

And she forgot all about reading her email.

AFTER HE'D FILLED Miss Natty's wood boxes, making sure she had plenty of kindling, Conner unloaded the pitch-scented pine—a full cord—stacking it neatly in the shed. With that done, he could check the delivery off his mental to-do list and move on to the next project—stopping by the feed store for a dozen fifty-pound bags of the special mix of oats and alfalfa he gave the horses. When he finished that errand, he'd head for Doc Benchley's office to pick up the special serum for the crop of calves born that spring. Doc had served as the town's one and only veterinarian since way back.

Unlike a lot of people in his profession, Hugh Benchley didn't specialize. He treated every animal from prize Hereford bulls to Yorkshire terriers small enough to fit in a teacup, and had no evident intention of retiring in the foreseeable future, even though he was well past the age when his fellow senior citizens preferred to spend their days fishing or patronizing the flashy new casino out on the reservation.

"I won't last six months from the day I close my practice," Doc had told Conner more than once.

Conner understood, since he thrived on work himself—the more physically demanding, the better. That way, he didn't have time to think about things he wished were different—like his relationship, if you could call it that, with his twin brother, Brody.

Dusting his leather-gloved hands together, the last of the wood safely stowed for Miss Natty's use, he started for the driver's-side door of his truck. Something made him look up at the second-story window, a feeling of prickly sweetness, utterly strange to him, and he thought he saw Tricia McCall peering through the glass.

Wishful thinking, he told himself, climbing into the rig.

He'd seen Tricia lots of times, usually at a distance, but close-up once or twice, too.

How was it that he'd never noticed how appealing Natty's great-granddaughter was, with her fresh skin and her dark, serious eyes? She had a trim little body— he'd figured that out right away, her sorry bathrobe notwithstanding—and just standing in the same room with her had put him in mind of an experience when he and Brody were kids. Nine or ten and virtually fearless, they'd dared each other to touch the band of electric fence separating the main pasture from the county road that ran past the ranch.

It had been raining until a few minutes earlier, and they were both standing in wet grass. The jolt had knocked them both on their backsides, and once they'd caught their breath, they'd lain there laughing, like the pair of fools they were.

Because any memory involving Brody tended to

be painful, the good ones included, Conner avoided them when he could. Now, as he shifted the truck into gear and eased out of Miss Natty's gravel driveway, his thoughts strayed right back to Tricia like deer to a salt lick.

He signaled a right turn at the corner, heading for Main Street, and the feed store.

As a kid, he recalled, Tricia had spent summers in Lonesome Bend with her dad. Shy, she'd kept to herself, sticking to Joe's heels as he went happily about his business. Even then, the run-down drive-in theater, with its bent screen, had been a losing proposition, and the campground hadn't been much better.

Like all his friends, Conner had gone swimming at River's Bend every chance he got, but he didn't remember ever seeing Tricia so much as dip a big toe into the water. She'd sit cross-legged and solemn on the dock, always wearing a hand-me-down swimsuit, with a towel rolled up under one arm, and watch the rest of them, though, as they splashed and showed off for each other.

At the time, it was generally agreed that Tricia McCall was a little weird—probably because her parents were divorced and lived in different states, an unusual situation in those days, in Lonesome Bend if not in the rest of the country.

Since his older cousin, Steven, split his time between the ranch and a mansion back in Boston, neither Tricia nor her situation had struck Conner as strange—she was just quiet, liked to keep to herself. He'd been mildly curious about her, but nothing more. After all, she always left town at the end of August, the way Steven did, turning up again sometime in June.

Drawing up to the feed store, Conner pulled into the parking lot and backed the truck up to one of two loading docks. He shut off the engine, got out of the rig and vaulted up onto the platform to help with the bags, stacked and waiting to be collected.

And still Tricia lingered in his mind.

As a teenager, Tricia continued to visit her dad every summer, and she went right on marching to her own private drumbeat, too. The popular girls had declared her a snob, a snooty city girl who thought she was too good for a bunch of country kids. But she was wearing some guy's class ring on a chain around her neck, Conner recollected, and he'd steered clear because he figured she was going steady.

And because he'd been bone-headed crazy about Joleen Williams, the platinum blonde wild child with the body that wouldn't quit.

Somebody elbowed Conner, and that brought him back to the here and now, pronto. Malcolm, Joleen's half brother and a classmate of Conner's since kindergarten, grinned as he pushed past with a bag of horse feed under each arm. "Clear the way, Creed," Malcolm teased, his round face red and sweaty with effort and a penchant for triple cheeseburgers and more beer than even Brody could put away. "People are trying to *work* here."

Conner grinned and slapped his friend on the back in greeting. The day was cool and crisp, but the sun was climbing higher into a sky blue enough to make a man's heart catch, and the aspen trees, lining the streets of Lonesome Bend and crowding the foothills all around it, were changing color. Splashes of bright crimson and gold, pale yellow and rust, and a million shades in between, blazed like fire everywhere he looked.

"How've you been, Malcolm?" he asked, because in small towns people always asked each other how they were, even if they'd seen each other an hour before at the post office or the courthouse or the grocery store. Moreover, they cared about the answer.

"I was fine until you showed up," Malcolm answered, tossing the feed bags into the bed of the pickup and turning to go back for more. "What kind of fancy horses are you keeping out on that ranch these days, anyhow? Thoroughbreds, maybe? This stuff costs double what the generic brand runs, and I swear it's heavier, too."

Conner laughed and hoisted a bag. "Maybe you ought to sit down and rest," he joked. "It would suck if you had a heart attack right here on the loading dock."

"It would suck if I had a heart attack *anyplace*," Malcolm countered, continuing to load the truck. "Hell, I'm only thirty-three."

Conner, sobered by the picture the conversation had brought to mind, didn't answer.

"You heard about Joleen?" Malcolm asked, when they'd finished piling the bags in the back of the truck.

Conner jumped down to level ground and put up the tailgate on his rig with more of a bang than the task probably called for. He'd been over Malcolm's sister for years, but any mention of her always stuck in his craw. "What about her?" he asked, looking up at Malcolm, who stood rimmed in dazzling sunlight on the loading dock like some overweight archangel.

"She's coming back to Lonesome Bend," Malcolm answered. His tone was strange. Almost cautious.

"No offense, Malcolm," Conner replied, "but I couldn't care less."

Malcolm was quiet for a moment. Then, in a rush of words, he added, "You want this feed put on your bill, as usual?"

"That'll be fine," Conner said, opening the door of his truck and setting one booted foot on the running board, about to climb behind the wheel. "Thanks, Malcolm."

"Conner?"

Halfway into the rig, Conner ducked out again. Malcolm had shifted his position, and his features were clearly visible now. He wasn't smiling.

"What?" Conner asked.

Malcolm sighed heavily, swept off his billed cap and dried the back of his neck on one shirtsleeve. "She's with Brody," he said, as though it pained him. "I guess they've been—seeing each other."

Everything inside Conner went still. It was as if the whole universe had ground to a halt all around him.

Finally, he found his voice. "I guess that's their business," he said, flatly dismissive, "not mine."

CHAPTER TW0

THE WIND RUFFLED THE SURFACE of the river, placid enough where it nestled in the tree-sheltered bend, the stony beach curving easy around it, like a cowboy's arm around his girl's shoulders, but wilder out in the middle. There, the currents were swift and, a mile downriver, there were rapids, leading straight to the falls.

Every so often, some hapless soul would be swept away in a canoe or even an inner tube, and find himself rushing at top speed toward a seventy-five-foot drop over the waterfall and onto the jagged boulders below.

It was a miracle nobody had been killed, Tricia thought, pulling her jacket more tightly around her and surveying the rocky shore in front of her. The area was littered with crushed beer cans, cigarette butts and fast food wrappers—kids had been partying there again.

Sighing, Tricia pulled a pair of plastic gloves from her pocket and snapped them on, then unfolded the large trash bag she'd tucked into the waistband of her jeans. There were No Trespassing signs posted, of course, but they seemed to have no more effect that the ones that read For Sale.

She picked up all the aluminum cans first—those were destined for the recycling bin—then collected the rest of the trash, using a smaller bag.

Tricia liked being outside, chilly as it was, under

that blue, blue sky, breathing in the singular scents of autumn, though cleaning up after thoughtless people wasn't her favorite chore. It would be a nice day for a bonfire, she reflected, bending to retrieve a potato chip bag that looked as though it had been chewed up right along with its contents.

It was then that she made eye contact with the dog.

Nestled beneath the very same picnic table where she and Joe had found Rusty all those years ago was a painfully thin mutt with burrs and twigs caught in its coat and sorrow in its liquid brown eyes.

"Hey," Tricia said, dropping to her knees.

The dog whimpered, tried to scoot out of her reach when she moved to touch him.

"It's okay," she murmured. She tried to harden her heart a little, but it remained tender. "I won't hurt you, buddy."

Resting on her haunches, her hands on her thighs, Tricia studied the animal carefully. He was probably yellow under all that dirt, she concluded, though there would be no way to know for sure until he'd been cleaned up a little. Since he wasn't wearing a collar, let alone ID tags, Tricia never seriously entertained the idea that some anxious pet owner was out there somewhere, searching frantically for the family dog.

She extended one hand cautiously, still wearing the plastic gloves, though they wouldn't protect her from a bite. The poor creature snarled feebly in warning.

Tricia drew back. "No worries," she said gently. "Wait here, and I'll bring you something to eat."

She got to her feet and headed for the log building that housed the office and a couple of vending machines, tossing the trash bags into a Dumpster as she passed it, the gloves following quickly behind.

Inside the tiny space, measuring no more than twelve by twelve in its entirety, a fire burned in the Franklin stove, exuding pleasant warmth, and the varnish on the front of the big rustic reception counter bisecting the room reflected the dancing flames.

For just a moment, Tricia paused, feeling a pang of regret at the prospect of moving away. This place had seen a lot of happy times in days gone by—families eager to camp out in a tent, cook their meals under the sky, swim in the calm inlet of the river. As eager as she was to sell everything and return to Seattle for good, letting go would be hard.

Shaking off the spell, she rounded the counter, took her purse from one of the shelves underneath it and scrabbled around in the bottom of the bag for the change she continually tossed in. Maybe she'd get one of those little plastic coin holders, the kind that gaped open like a grin when you squeezed either end. For now, though, the slapdash method had to do.

When she had a palm full of quarters, dimes and nickels, Tricia approached the vending machine. Chester, the man who ran the route, dropping sandwiches and candy bars and snack-size bags of chips into the slots, hadn't been around recently. It was the end of the season, and the pickings were slim.

She finally decided on a ham sandwich, sealed inside a carton with a see-through top—the edges of the bread were curling up—dropped the appropriate number of quarters into the slot and pushed the button. The sandwich clunked into the tray.

Tricia studied it with distaste, then sighed and

marched herself toward the door. Outside, she peeled back the top of the container, and walked back to the picnic table.

A part of her had been hoping the dog would be gone when she got back, she realized as she knelt again, but of course he was right there where she'd left him. He raised his head off his outstretched forelegs and sniffed tentatively at the air.

Tricia smiled, broke half the sandwich in two and held out a portion to the dog.

He hesitated, as though expecting some cruel trick—the world clearly hadn't been kind to him—then decided to chance it. He literally wolfed down the food, and Tricia gave him more, and then more, in small, carefully presented chunks, until there was nothing left.

"Come out of there," Tricia coaxed, fallen leaves wetting the knees of her jeans through and through, "and I'll buy you another sandwich."

The dog appeared to consider his—or her—options.

Tricia stood up again, backed off a few feet and called for a second time.

A frigid wind blew in off the river and seeped into her bones like a death chill. She longed for hot coffee and the radiant coziness of the fire in the Franklin stove, but she wasn't going to leave the dog out here alone.

It took a lot of patience and a lot of persuasion, but the poor little critter finally low-crawled out from under the picnic table and stood up.

Definitely a male, Tricia thought. Probably not neutered.

"This way," she said, very softly, turning and leading the way toward the structure her dad had euphemistically referred to as "the lodge." The dog limped along behind her, head down, hip bones and ribs poking out as he moved.

Tricia's heart turned over. Was he a lost pet or had someone turned him out? Dropped him off along the highway, thinking he'd be able to fend for himself? That happened way too often.

The dog crossed the threshold cautiously, but the heat of the stove attracted him right away. He teetered over on his spindly legs and collapsed in front of it with a deep sigh, as though he'd come to the end of a long and very difficult journey.

Tears stung Tricia's eyes. There was no animal shelter in Lonesome Bend, though Hugh Benchley, the veterinarian, kept stray dogs and cats whenever he had room in the kennels behind his clinic. His three daughters, who all worked for him, made every effort to find homes for the creatures, and often succeeded.

But not always.

Those who didn't find homes ended up living on the Benchleys' small farm or, when they ran out of room, in one of the shelters in nearby Denver.

This little guy might be one of the lucky ones, Tricia consoled herself, and wind up as part of a loving household. In the meantime, she'd give him another vending machine sandwich and some water. Most likely, he'd been drinking out of the river for a while.

While the dog ate the second course, Tricia called Dr. Benchley's office to say she was bringing in a stray later, for shots and a checkup. It went without saying that a permanent home would be nice, too.

Becky, Doc's eldest daughter, who kept the books for her father's practice and did the billing at the end of the month, picked up. Fortyish, plump and happily married to the dairy farmer on the land adjoining the Benchleys', Becky had a heart the size of Colorado itself, but she sighed after Tricia finished telling her what little she knew about the dog's condition.

"It never stops," Becky said sadly. "We're bulging at the seams around here as it is, and at Dad's place, too, and Frank says if I bring home one more stray, he's going to leave me."

Frank Garson adored his wife, and was unlikely to leave her for any reason, and everybody knew it, but Becky had made her point. Bottom line: there was no room at the inn.

"Maybe I could keep him for a little while," Tricia said hesitantly. Then she blushed. "The dog, I mean. Not Frank."

Becky laughed, sounding more like her old self, but still tired. Maybe even a little depressed. "That would be good."

"But not forever," Tricia added quickly.

"Still not over losing Rusty?" Becky asked, very gently. As a veterinarian's daughter, she was used to the particular grief that comes with losing a cherished pet. "How long's it been, Tricia?"

Tricia swallowed, watching as the stray got to his feet and stuck his muzzle into the coffee can full of water, lapping noisily. "Six months," she said, in a small voice.

"Maybe it's time—"

Tricia squeezed her eyes shut, but a tear spilled down her right cheek anyway. "Don't, Becky. Please. I'm not ready to choose another dog."

"We don't choose animals," Becky said kindly. "They choose us."

She couldn't possibly be expected to understand, of course. As soon as a real-estate miracle happened—and Tricia had to believe one *would* or she'd go crazy—she'd be moving away from Lonesome Bend, probably living in some condo in downtown Seattle, where only very small dogs were allowed.

She swallowed again. Dashed at her cheek with the back of her free hand. The canine visitor knocked over the coffee can, spilling what remained of his water all over the bare wooden floor. "Be that as it may—"

"How's eleven-thirty?" Becky broke in, brightening. "For the appointment, I mean?"

Tricia guessed that would be fine, and said so.

She hung up and hurried into the storage room for a mop, and the dog cowered as she approached.

Tricia's heart, already pulverized by Rusty's passing, did a pinchy, skittery thing. "Nobody's mad at you, buddy," she said softly. "It's all ok."

She swabbed up the spilled water and made a mental note to stop off at the discount store for kibble and bowls and maybe a pet bed, preferably on sale, since the trip to the vet was bound to cost a lot of money. The dog—he needed a name, but since giving him one implied a commitment she wasn't willing to make, *the dog* would have to do—could live right here at the office until other arrangements could be made.

Taking him home, like naming him, would only make things harder later on. Besides, Winston would probably take a dim view of such a move, and then there was the matter of seeing another dog in all the places where Rusty used to be.

She did wish she hadn't been in such a hurry to give Rusty's gear away, though. She could have used that stuff right about now.

The dog looked up at her with an expression so hopeful that the sight of him wrenched at something deep inside Tricia. Then he meandered, moving more steadily now that he'd eaten, over to the vending machine. Pressed his wet nose to the glass.

Tricia chuckled in spite of herself. "Sorry," she said. "No more stale sandwiches for you."

He really seemed to understand what she was saying, which was crazy. The similarities between finding Rusty and finding—well, *the dog*—were getting to her, that was all, and it was her own fault; she was letting it happen.

She brought him more water, and this time, he didn't tip the coffee can over.

Gradually, they became friends, a three steps forward, two steps back kind of thing, and while Tricia doubted he'd tolerate being scrubbed down under one of the public showers, he did let her remove the twigs and thistles from his coat.

At 11:15, she hoisted him into the backseat of her secondhand blue Pathfinder without being bitten in the process. A good omen, she decided. Things were looking up.

Maybe.

Doc Benchley's clinic was housed in a converted Quonset hut left over from the last big war, with an add-on built of cinder blocks. As buildings went, it was plug-ugly, maybe even a blight on the landscape, but nobody seemed to mind. Folks around Lonesome Bend appreciated Doc because he'd come right away if a cow fell sick, or a horse, whether it was high noon or the middle of the night. He'd saved dozens, if not hundreds, of dogs and cats, too, along with a few parrots and exotic lizards.

He drove his ancient green pickup truck through snowstorms that would daunt a lesser man and a much better vehicle, and once or twice, in a pinch, he'd treated a human being.

Distracted, Tricia didn't notice the other rigs in the clinic's unpaved parking lot; she wanted to borrow a leash and a collar before she brought the dog inside, in case something spooked him and he took off. And she was totally focused on that.

She fairly collided with Conner Creed in the big double doorway; his arms were full of small boxes and he was wearing a battered brown hat that cast shadows over his facial features.

"Sorry," she said, after gulping her heart back down into its normal place. Nearly, anyway.

He said something in reply—maybe "Excuse me"—but Tricia had already started to go around him, unaccountably anxious to get away.

Becky stood behind the counter, wearing colorful scrubs with pink cartoon kittens frolicking all over the fabric, holding out the leash and collar without being asked. Her eyes sparkled as she looked at Tricia, then past her, to Conner.

"Thanks," Tricia said.

She turned around, and Conner had disappeared. Her relief was exceeded only by her disappointment.

All for the best, she told herself firmly. *It's not as if you're in the market for a man. You've got Hunter, remember?* Never mind that she hadn't seen or even spoken to Hunter lately.

Outside, Conner was just turning away from his truck, where he'd stowed the boxes he'd been carrying before. He adjusted his hat, giving her another of those frank assessments he seemed to be so good at.

"Need help?" he asked, at his leisure.

Tricia realized that she'd stopped in her tracks and made herself move again, but color thumped in her cheeks. "I can manage," she said.

Conner approached, nonetheless, and when she opened one of the Pathfinder's rear doors, he eased her aside. "Let me," he said, taking the leash and collar from her hand. He lifted the panting dog out of the vehicle and set him down, offering the leash to Tricia. "What's his name?"

"I call him *the dog*," Tricia said.

"Imaginative," Conner replied, with another of those tilted grins.

Tricia bristled. "He's a stray. I found him hiding under one of the picnic tables at River's Bend, just this morning."

What all this had to do with naming or not naming the animal Tricia could not have said. The words just tumbled out of her mouth, as though they'd formed themselves with no input at all from her brain.

"So you're leaving him here?" Conner asked. His grin lingered, but it wasn't as dazzling as before, and his voice had a slight edge.

"No," Tricia said. She'd just gotten her feathers smoothed down, and now they were ruffled again. "He'll be staying at the office until I can find him somewhere to live."

She'd hoped that would satisfy Conner and he'd go away, but he didn't. He dropped to his haunches in front of the dog and stroked its floppy ears.

"A name doesn't seem like too much to ask," the rancher said mildly.

Tricia tugged at the leash, to no real avail. "We'll be late," she fretted. As if she had anything to do for the rest of the day except clean restrooms at the campground. "Come on—dog."

Conner stood up again. He towered over Tricia, so her neck popped when she tilted her head back to look into his face.

She liked shorter men, she reflected, apropos of nothing. Hunter, at five-eight, was tall enough. *Perfect,* in fact. He was the perfect man.

If you didn't mind being ignored most of the time.

Or if you set aside the fact that he didn't want children. Or that he didn't like animals much.

"He'll be here at the clinic awhile," Conner said, ostensibly referring to the dog. "Have lunch with me."

Tricia blinked. She didn't know what she'd expected, if indeed she'd expected anything at all, but it hadn't been an invitation to lunch. Was this a date? The thought sent a small, shameful thrill through her.

"Natty's a good friend of mine," Conner went on, adjusting his hat again. "And since you and I seem to have started off on the wrong foot, I thought—"

"We haven't," Tricia argued, without knowing why. The strange tension between them must have made her snappish. "Started off on the wrong foot, I mean."

Again, that slow grin that settled over her insides like warm honey. Agitated, she tugged at the leash again and this time, the dog was willing to follow her lead. Relieved, she made her way to the doors.

But Conner came right along with her. He was a persistent cuss—she'd say that for him.

"My, my," Becky said, rounding the desk to take the leash from Tricia but looking all the while at the dog. "I see a bath in your future," she told him. Then, meeting Tricia's gaze, she added, "We're looking at an hour and a half at the least. More likely, two. Dad's schedule is packed."

The dog whined imploringly, his limpid gaze moving between Tricia and Conner, as though making some silent appeal. *Please don't leave me.*

She'd better toughen up, Tricia thought. And now was the time to start.

"Mr. Creed and I are going to lunch," she heard herself say, in a perfectly ordinary tone of voice, and was amazed. "I'll check back with you later on."

"Good idea," Becky agreed, with a little twinkle.

Just as Conner had done earlier, the woman crouched to look into the dog's eyes. "Don't you be scared, now," she said. "We're going to take good care of you, I promise."

He licked her face, and she laughed.

"Hey, Valentino," Becky said. "You're quite the lover."

Valentino, Tricia thought.

Oh, God, he had a name now.

But as Becky rose and started to lead the dog away, into the back, he made a sound so forlorn that Tricia's eyes filled.

"We have your cell number on file, don't we?" Becky turned to ask Tricia, who was still standing in the same place, feeling stricken. "You haven't changed it or anything?"

"You have it," Tricia managed to croak. She felt Conner take a light hold on her elbow. He sort of steered her toward the doors, through them and out into the parking lot.

"Lunch," he reminded her quietly.

Her cell phone chirped in her purse, and she took it out, looked at the screen, and smiled, though barely. There was a text from Diana's ten-year-old daughter, Sasha. "Hi," it read. "Mom let me use her phone so I could tell you that we're on a field trip at the Seattle Aquarium and it's awesome!"

Tricia replied with a single word. "Great!"

"No sense in taking two rigs," Conner commented.

The next thing Tricia knew, she was in the passenger seat of his big truck, the cell phone in her pocket.

It's just lunch, she told herself, as they headed toward the diner in the middle of town. Except for the upscale steakhouse on the highway to Denver, Elmer's Café was the only sit-down eating establishment in Lonesome Bend.

All the ranchers gathered there for lunch or for coffee and pie, and the people who lived in town liked the place, too. It was continually crowded, but the food was good and the prices were reasonable. Tricia occasionally stopped in for a soup-and-sandwich special, sitting at one of the stools at the counter, since she was always alone and the tables were generally full.

Today, there was a booth open, a rare phenomenon at lunchtime.

Tricia wondered dryly if the universe *always* accommodated Conner Creed and, after that, she wondered where in the heck *that* thought had come from.

Conner took off his hat and hung it on the rack next to the door, as at home as he might have been in his own kitchen. He nodded to Elmer's wife, Mabel, who was the only waitress in sight.

Mabel, a benign gossip, sized up the situation with a good, hard look at Tricia and Conner. A radiant smile broke over her face, orangish in color because of her foundation, and she sang out, "Be right with you, folks."

Conner waited until Tricia slid into the booth before sitting down across from her and reaching for a menu. She set her cell phone on the table, in case there was another communiqué from Sasha, or a call from Doc Benchley's office about Valentino. Then she extracted a bottle of hand sanitizer from her bag and squirted some into her palm.

Conner raised an eyebrow, grinning that grin again.

"You can't be too careful," Tricia said, sounding defensive even to herself.

"Sure you can," Conner replied easily, reaching for a menu.

Tricia pushed the bottle an inch or so in his direction.

He ignored it.

"There are germs on everything," she said, lowering her voice lest Mabel or Elmer overhear and think she was criticizing their hygiene practices.

"Yes," Conner agreed lightly, without looking up from the menu. "Too much of that stuff can compromise a person's immune system."

Tricia felt foolish. Conner was a grown man. If he wanted to risk contracting some terrible disease, that was certainly his prerogative. As long as he wasn't cooking the food, what did she care?

She dropped the bottle back into her purse.

Mabel bustled over, with a stub of a pencil and a little pad, grinning broadly as she waited to take their orders.

Tricia asked what kind of soup they were serving that day, and Mabel replied that it was cream of broccoli with roasted garlic. Her own special recipe.

Women in and around Lonesome Bend were recipe-proud, Tricia knew. Natty guarded the secret formula for her chili, a concoction that drew people in droves every year when the rummage sale rolled around, claiming it had been in the family for a hundred years.

Tricia ordered the soup. Conner ordered a burger and fries, with coffee.

Then, as soon as Mabel hurried away to put in the order, he excused himself, his eyes merry with amusement, and went to wash his hands.

Tricia actually considered making a quick exit while he was gone, but in the end, she couldn't get around the silliness of the idea. Besides, her SUV was still over at the veterinary clinic, a good mile from Elmer's Café.

So she sat. And she waited, twiddling her thumbs.

DAMN, CONNER SAID SILENTLY, addressing his own reflection in the men's-room mirror. It was no big deal having a friendly lunch with a woman—it was broad daylight, in his hometown, for God's sake—so why did he feel as though he were riding a Clydesdale across a frozen river?

Sure, he'd been a little rattled when Malcolm told him Brody and Joleen were on their way back to Lonesome Bend, but once the adrenaline rush subsided, he'd been fine.

Now, he drew a deep breath, rolled up the sleeves of his shirt and hit the soap dispenser a couple of times. He lathered up, rinsed, lathered up again. Smiled as he recalled the little bottle of disinfectant gel Tricia was carrying around.

Of course there was nothing wrong with cleanliness, but it seemed to Conner that more and more people were phobic about a few germs. He dried his hands and left the restroom, headed for the table.

Tricia sat looking down at the screen on her cell phone, and the light from the window next to the booth rimmed her, caught in the tiny hairs escaping that long, prim braid of hers, turning a reddish gold.

Conner, not generally a fanciful man, stopped in midstride, feeling as though something had slammed into him, hard. Like a gut punch, maybe, but not unpleasant.

Get a grip, he told himself. Out of the corner of his eye, he saw Mabel and everybody at the counter looking at him.

Pride broke the strange paralysis. He slid into the booth on his side, and was immediately struck again, this time by the translucent smile on her face. He'd never seen anybody light up that way—Tricia's eyes shone, and her skin glowed, too.

"Good news?" he asked.

She didn't look at him, but he had a sinking feeling the text was from a guy.

"Very good news," she said. Her gaze lingered on

the phone for a few more moments—long ones, for Conner—and then, with a soft sigh, she put the device down again.

Conner waited for her to tell him what the good news was, but she didn't say anything about it.

"Do you have a dog?" she asked Conner.

Momentarily tripped up by the question, he had to think before he could answer. "Not at the moment," he said.

"Maybe you'd like one?"

Mabel arrived with their food, and Conner flirted with the older woman for a few seconds. "Maybe," he said, very carefully, when they were alone again. "Sometime."

"Sometime?"

"We're pretty busy out on the ranch these days," he told her, picking up a French fry and dunking it into a cup of catsup on the side of his plate. "A dog's like a child in some ways. They need a lot of attention, right along."

Belatedly, Tricia took up her spoon, dipped it into her soup and sipped. He could almost *see* the gears turning in her head.

"Dogs are probably happier in the country than anywhere else," she ventured, and her eyes were big and soulful when she looked at him. He felt an odd sensation, as if he were shooting down a steep slope on a runaway toboggan.

"Plenty of townspeople have dogs," he said, once he'd caught his breath. He knew damn well what she was up to—she wanted him to take Valentino off her hands—but he played it cool. "Even in big cities, you see every size and breed walking their owners in the parks and on the sidewalks."

Some of the color in her cheeks drained away, and he could pinpoint the change in her to the millisecond—it had happened when he said "big cities."

"I wouldn't want to keep a dog shut up in an apartment or a condo all day, while I was working," she said. Even though she spoke casually, there was a slight tremor in her voice. "Not a big one, anyway."

He thought of that morning, when he'd poured himself a cup of coffee in her kitchen above Miss Natty's place. Her apartment *had* looked small, but he didn't think she'd been referring to her present living quarters.

Suddenly Conner remembered all those For Sale signs. Of course—Tricia was planning to leave town when she finally sold the campground and the RV park and that albatross of a drive-in theater. These days, when folks wanted to see a movie, they downloaded one off the net, or rented a DVD out of a vending machine. Or drove to Denver to one of the multiscreen "cinaplexes."

Conner cut his burger in half and picked up one side. He'd been hungry—breakfast time rolled around early on a ranch, and he hadn't eaten for hours—but now his appetite was a little on the iffy side.

"You planning on leaving Lonesome Bend one of these days?" he asked, when he thought he could manage a normal tone of voice. As far as he knew, the properties she'd inherited from her dad weren't exactly attracting interest from investors—in town or out of it.

She glanced at her phone again, lying there next to the salt and pepper shakers and the napkin holder, and a fond expression softened her all over. A little smile crooked one side of her mouth. "Yes," she answered, and this time she looked straight into his eyes.

"When?" he asked, putting down his burger.

"As soon as something sells," she said, her gaze still steady. "The campground, the RV park, the drive-in—whichever. Of course, I'd like to get rid of all three at once, but even one would make it possible."

"I see," Conner said. Why should it matter to him that this woman he barely knew was ready to get out of Dodge? He couldn't answer that, yet it did matter.

Then she smiled in a way that turned his brain soft. "Now, about the dog..."

CHAPTER THREE

TRICIA WAS GETTING NOWHERE with Conner Creed and she knew it. The dog wasn't going to have a home on the range—not the *Creed* range, anyway.

"I'd better get back to the clinic and pick up my car," she said, watching as Mabel removed their plates and silverware from the table and hurried away at top speed as though she thought she was interrupting something. "I have things to do while Doc Benchley is treating Valentino."

It was dangerous, saying the name, actually giving voice to it. She might start caring for the dog now, and where would that lead? To another fracture of the heart, that's where.

Conner paid for their lunches, shaking his head in the negative when Tricia offered to chip in, and they left the diner, headed for the parking lot where his truck was parked. He held the door for her while she climbed in, like the gentleman he probably wasn't.

He was quiet during the drive back to the clinic, even a little cool.

"Thanks for lunch," she told him when they drew up alongside her Pathfinder, getting her keys out of her purse and unsnapping her seat belt.

Conner was wearing his hat again; he simply tugged at the brim and said, "You're welcome," the way he might have said it to the meter reader from the electric company or a panhandler expressing gratitude for a cash donation.

Tricia got out of the truck, shut the door.

Conner nodded at her and waited until she was behind the wheel of her own rig, with the engine running. Then he backed up, turned around and drove away.

Why did she feel sad all of a sudden? To cheer herself up, Tricia pulled her phone from its special pocket in her purse and pressed one of the buttons. Hunter's smiling face appeared on the screen, along with the message he'd texted earlier.

I miss you. Let's get together—soon.

Tricia waited to be overtaken by delight and excitement—hadn't she been missing Hunter for a year and a half, yearning to "get together" with him?—but all she felt was a strange letdown that seemed to have more to do with Conner Creed than the man she believed she loved. Weird.

There was no figuring it out, she decided with a sigh. She put the phone away and went over her mental shopping list as she headed for the big discount store where a person could buy pretty much anything.

The dog beds weren't on sale, but she found a nice, fluffy one for a decent price and wadded it into her cart. On top she piled a small bag of kibble, two large plastic bowls, a collar and a leash and, because she didn't want Valentino to feel lonely when she left him at the office for the night, she sprang for a toy—a blue chicken with a squeaker but no stuffing—to keep him company.

There were a few other things Tricia needed to pick up, but none of them were urgent and her cart was full, so she wheeled her way up to the long row of checkout counters and got in line.

Twenty minutes later—a woman ahead of her paid for a can of soup with a credit card—she drove back to the campground office with her purchases, arranging the bed in front of the woodstove and hauling the kibble to the storeroom, where she opened it and filled the bowls—one with food and one with water.

She set them carefully within reach of the dog bed, adjusted everything and was finally satisfied that the arrangement looked welcoming. As the finishing touch, Tricia removed the price tag from the blue chicken and laid the toy tenderly on the bed, the way she might have set out a teddy bear for a child.

"There," she said aloud, though there was nobody around to hear. Talking to herself—she had definitely been alone too much lately, she decided ruefully, especially since Natty had left to visit her sister.

Conner popped into her mind, but Tricia blocked him out—with limited success—and told herself to think about Hunter instead. In the end, she had to bring up the phone picture again just to remember what Hunter looked like.

And even then the image didn't stick in her mind when she looked away.

NOT GOOD, CONNER THOUGHT when he pulled in at the ranch and saw Davis, his uncle, waiting in the grassy stretch between the ranch house and the barn. Davis's expression would have said it all, even if he hadn't been pacing back and forth like he was waiting for a prize calf to be born.

"What?" Conner asked, once he'd stopped the truck, shut it down and stepped out onto the running board.

Davis was an older version of his son, Steven, with the same dark blond hair and blue eyes. He was a little heavier than Steven, and his clothes, like Conner's, weren't fancy. He was dressed for work.

Steven had a ranch of his own now, down in Stone Creek, Arizona, not to mention a beautiful wife, Melissa, a six-year-old son named Matt and another of those intermittent sets of twins, both boys, that ran in the Creed family.

In fact, if Conner hadn't loved Steven like a brother—had the same strong bond with his cousin that he'd once shared with Brody—it would have been easy to hate him for having more than his share of luck.

"Did you get the serum?" Davis asked, as though Conner were on an urgent mission from the CDC, carrying the only known antidote to some virus fixing to go global.

Conner gave his uncle—essentially the only father he'd ever known, since his own, Davis's older brother, Blue, had died in an accident when Conner and Brody were just babies—a level look. "Yeah," he answered, "I got the serum. Didn't know it was a rush job, though."

Davis sighed, rummaged up a sheepish smile. "We've still got plenty of daylight left," he said. "Kim and I had words a little while ago, that's all. She put my favorite boots in the box of stuff she's been gathering up to donate to the rummage sale. I took issue with that—they're good boots. Just got 'em broken in right a few years ago—"

Conner laughed. Kim, Davis's wife, was a force of

nature in her own right. And she'd been a mother figure to her husband's orphaned twin nephews, never once acting put upon. It was a shame, Conner had always thought, that Kim and Davis had never had any children together. They were born parents.

"I reckon it would be easier to buy those boots back at the rummage sale than argue with Kim," Conner remarked, amused. The woman could be bone-stubborn; she'd had to be to hold her own in that family.

"We won't be here then," Davis complained. "I've got half a dozen saddles ready, and we'll be on the road for two weeks or better."

"I remember," Conner said, opening a rear door and reaching into the extended-cab pickup for the boxes of serum he'd picked up at Doc Benchley's clinic. There were still a few hours of daylight left; if they saddled up and headed out right away, they could get at least *some* of the calves inoculated.

So Conner thrust an armload of boxes at Davis, who had to juggle a little to hold on to them.

"You'll be here, though," Davis went on innocently. "You could buy those boots back for me, Conner, and hide them in the barn or someplace—"

Conner chuckled and shook his head. "And bring the wrath of the mom-unit down on my hapless head? No way, Unc. You're on your own with this one."

"But they're lucky boots," Davis persisted. "One time, in Reno, I won $20,000 playing poker. *And I was wearing those boots at the time.*"

"We're doomed," Conner joked.

"That isn't funny," his uncle said.

Davis and Kim lived up on the ridge, in a split-level rancher they'd built and moved into the year Brody and

Conner came of age. Because Blue had been the elder of the two, the firstborn son and therefore destined to inherit the spread, the ranch belonged to them.

Conner occupied the main ranch house now, and since Brody was never around, he lived by himself.

He hated living alone, eating alone and all the rest. He frowned. There he went, thinking again.

"Everything all right?" Davis asked, looking at him closely.

"Fine," Conner lied.

Davis was obviously skeptical, but he didn't push for more information, as Kim would have done. "Let's get out there on the range and tend to those calves," he said. "As many as we can before sunset, anyhow."

"You ever think about getting a dog?" Conner asked his uncle, as they walked toward the barn. "Old Blacky's been gone a long time."

Davis sighed. "Kim wants to get a pair of those little ankle biters—Yorkies, I guess they are. She's got dibs on two pups from a litter born back in June—we're supposed to pick the critters up on this trip, when we swing through Cheyenne."

It made Conner grin—and feel a whole lot better— to imagine his ultramasculine cowboy uncle followed around by a couple of yappers with bows in their hair. Davis would be ribbed from one end of the rodeo circuit to the other, and he'd grouse a little, probably, but deep down, he'd be a fool for those dogs.

Reaching the barn, they took the prefilled syringes Conner had gotten from Doc Benchley out of their boxes and stashed them in saddlebags. They chose their horses, tacked them up, fetched their ropes and mounted.

Once they were through the last of the gates and on

the open range, Davis let out a yee-haw, nudged his gelding's sides with the heels of his boots, and the race was on.

VALENTINO LOOKED LIKE a different dog when Becky brought him out into the waiting area, all spiffy. His coat was a lovely, dark honey shade, and when he spotted Tricia, he immediately started wagging his tail. She'd have sworn he was smiling at her, too.

"See?" Becky bent to tell him. "I told you she'd come back."

Tricia felt a stab at those words—she was only looking after this dog temporarily, not adopting him—but when she handed over her ATM card to pay the bill, she got over the guilt in short order.

Good heavens, what had Doc done? Performed a kidney transplant?

Taking Valentino's new collar and leash from her bag, Tricia got him ready to leave. While she was bending over him, he gave her a big, wet kiss.

"Eeeew," she fussed, but she was smiling.

"Looks like we're due for a change in the weather," Becky commented, nodding her head toward the big picture window looking out over the parking lot and the street beyond. She sighed. "I guess it's typical for this time of year. Winter will be on us before we know it."

Tricia had noticed the dark clouds rolling in to cover the blue, but she hadn't really registered that there was a storm approaching. She'd been thinking about Valentino, and Hunter's text message—and Conner Creed.

"Let's hope the snow holds off until after the big rummage sale and the chili feed," Tricia said, her tone deceptively breezy. If the weather was bad, the campers and RVers wouldn't show up for that all-important final weekend of the season, and if *that* happened, she was going to have to dip into her savings to pay the bills.

"Amen to that," Becky said, but her old smile was back. She leaned down to pat Valentino's shiny head. "Aren't you the handsome fella, now that you've had a bath?" she murmured.

A light sprinkle of rain dappled the dry gravel in the parking lot, raising an acrid scent of dust, as Tricia and Valentino hurried toward the Pathfinder. She opened the rear hatch and was about to hoist the dog inside when he leaped up there on his own, nimble as could be.

"You *are* pretty handsome," Tricia told him, once she'd gotten behind the wheel and turned the key in the ignition. She'd just buckled her seat belt when the drizzle suddenly turned into a downpour so intense that the windshield wipers couldn't keep up, even on their fastest setting.

Thunder boomed, directly over their heads, it seemed, and Valentino gave a frightened yelp.

"We're safe, buddy," Tricia said gently, looking back over one shoulder.

The dog stood with his muzzle resting on the top of the backseat, looking bravely pathetic.

"Now, now," she murmured, in her most soothing voice, "you're going to be fine, I promise. We're just going to sit right here in the parking lot until the storm lets up a little, and then we'll go back to the office and you can eat and drink out of your new bowls and sleep on your new bed and play with your new blue chicken—"

Tricia McCall, said the voice of reason, *you are definitely losing it.*

Another crash of thunder seemed to roll down out of the foothills like a giant ball, and that was it for Valentino. He sprang over the backseat, squirmed over the console and landed squarely in Tricia's lap, whining and trembling and trying to lick her face again.

That was the bad news. The good news was that even though there was more thunder, and a few flashes of lightning to add a touch of Old Testament drama, the rain stopped coming down so hard.

After gently shifting Valentino off her thighs and onto the passenger seat, Tricia put the SUV in gear and went slowly, carefully on her way.

Valentino, panicked before, sat stalwartly now, probably glad to be up front with Tricia instead of all alone in the back.

"You're not going to make this easy, are you?" she asked the dog, as they crept along the rainy streets with the other traffic.

Valentino made that whining sound again, low in his throat.

"I'll take that as a no," Tricia said.

They got back to River's Bend in about twice the time it would normally have taken to make the drive, and by then, the rain was pounding down again. Tricia parked as close to the office door as she could, but she and Valentino both got wet before they made it inside.

Shivering and shedding her jacket as she went, Tricia headed straight for the stove and added wood to the dwindling fire inside.

Valentino sniffed his kibble bowl and drank some water, then went back to the kibble again. There was more thunder, loud enough to raise the roof this time, and flashes of lightning illuminated the angry river out past the safety ropes that were supposed to keep swimmers within bounds.

Tricia wondered how Winston was faring, back at the house; he didn't like loud noises any more than Valentino did, and the poor cat was all alone at home, probably terrified and hiding under a bed. He'd want his supper pretty soon, too, she thought, biting her lip as she stood looking out at the storm. Winston liked his routine.

She turned from the window and smiled as Valentino gulped the last of his kibble ration, washing it down with the rest of the water. Then he inspected the bed, sniffed the blue chicken, and turned three circles before giving a big yawn and curling up for a snooze.

Tricia refilled his water dish at the restroom sink and put it back in place, then checked the office voice mail, hoping for a few reservations for the last weekend of the month, but there had been no calls.

Resigned, she fired up the outdated computer she used at work, and waited impatiently while it booted up. The black Bakelite office phone with a rotary dial rang while she was waiting.

Over by the fire, Valentino began to snore.

Smiling a little, Tricia checked the screen on her phone, saw Diana's number and answered with a happy "Hello!"

"You'll never guess," said Diana. A smashing redhead, Diana had been the most popular girl in high school and probably college, too. She was smart and outgoing, then as now, and she was the best friend Tricia had ever had.

"What?" Tricia asked, leaning on the back of the counter and grinning. "You won the lottery? Paul's been elected president by secret ballot? Sasha is bored with fifth grade and signing up for law school?" Paul was Diana's husband; the two had been happily married since they were nineteen.

"Better," Diana replied, laughing. "Paul got that promotion, Tricia. We'll be moving to Paris for *at least two years*—Sasha will *love* it, and we've already found the perfect private school for her." Diana, a teacher, home-schooled Sasha, not to keep her out of the mainstream but because the child had a positively ravenous capacity for absorbing information. "The French school is famously progressive. Of course, we have to go over there as soon as possible, to look for an apartment…"

It was a dream come true, and Tricia was happy for her friend, and happy for Paul and Sasha—she truly was. But Paris was so far away. She could hardly get to Seattle these days. How was she supposed to visit France?

"That's…great…." she managed.

"You'll come over often," Diana said quickly. She was perceptive; that was one of the countless reasons she and Tricia were so close.

"Right," Tricia said doubtfully.

Valentino's snores reached an epic crescendo and then started to ebb.

Diana went on. "Paul and I were hoping—well—that Sasha could stay with you while we're away, checking out real estate. Paul's folks would look after her, but they're traveling in Australia, and mine—well, you know about my parents."

Diana's mother had a drinking problem, and her dad went through life on autopilot. Letting them babysit Sasha was out of the question.

Tricia closed her eyes. She loved Sasha but, frankly, the responsibility scared her to death. What if the adventurous ten-year-old got hurt or sick or, God forbid, *disappeared?* It happened; you couldn't turn on the TV or the radio without hearing an Amber alert. "Okay," she said. "Sure."

"Don't be too quick to agree," Diana said, with a smile in her voice. "We'll be gone for two weeks."

Tricia swallowed. "Two weeks?" The words came out sounding squeaky. "What about her schoolwork? Won't she get behind?"

"Sasha is way ahead on her lessons," Diana assured her. "Two weeks will be a nice break for her, actually."

"You don't want to take her to Paris?"

Diana chuckled. "It's a long flight, especially from the West Coast. We'd rather she didn't have to make that round-trip twice. Besides, we don't get that many opportunities for a romantic, just-the-two-of-us getaway."

"Two weeks," Tricia mused aloud, then blushed because she'd only meant to think the words, not *say* them.

This time Diana laughed. "Feel free to say no," she said sincerely. "I know you're busy with whatever it is you do down there in Colorado. Paul can go to Paris alone—he's perfectly capable of choosing an apartment that will suit us—and I'll stay here in Seattle with Sasha."

Affection for her friend, and for Sasha, warmed Tricia from the inside. Made her forget about the driving rainstorm she had to drive through to get home, for the moment at least. "Nonsense," she said. "Paul is real-estate challenged and you know it. Remember the time he almost bought that mansion with the rotting floors and only half a roof? I'll be *glad* to have my goddaughter visit for two weeks." She paused. "Unless you'd rather I came over there."

"Sasha's never been to Colorado," Diana said gently. "She'll love it. You do have room for her, don't you?"

The apartment had one bedroom, but the living room couch folded out. "Of course I do," Tricia responded.

"It's settled, then," Diana said.

"It's settled," Tricia agreed, already starting to look forward to Sasha's visit. The child was delightful and Tricia adored her.

"So what do you hear from the biggest loser these days?" Diana asked.

Tricia sighed. That was Diana's nickname for Hunter, whom she had never liked, though, to her credit, she'd always been polite to him. "I had a text from him today, as a matter of fact," she replied lightly. "He misses me."

"I'll just bet he does," Diana said dryly.

"Diana," Tricia replied, good-naturedly but with the slightest edge of warning.

"When were you planning to rendezvous?" Diana asked, with genuine concern. "Are Paul and I messing up your love life by dumping our brilliant, well-behaved and incomparably beautiful child on you, Trish?"

What love life? Tricia wanted to ask, but she didn't.

"Hunter and I have waited this long," she said practically. "A few more weeks won't matter. And I can't wait to see Sasha."

"You're a good friend," Diana said.

"So are you," Tricia replied. Okay, so Diana wasn't Hunter's greatest fan. She didn't really know him, that was all. She was protective of all her friends, especially the ones who had been painfully shy in high school, like Tricia.

"Trish—"

Tricia tensed, sensing that Diana was about to say something she didn't want to hear. "Yes?"

Diana sighed. "Nothing," she said. When she went on, the usual sparkle was back in her voice. "Listen, I'll make Sasha's flight arrangements and email her itinerary to you. I suppose she'll fly into Denver. Is that going to be a problem for you? Getting to the airport, I mean?"

Tricia smiled. "No, Mother Hen," she said. "It will *not* be a problem."

Diana really *was* a mother hen, but not in an unhealthy way. She liked taking care of people, but she knew when to back off, too. She'd learned that the hard way, she'd once confided in Tricia, courtesy of her profoundly dysfunctional parents. "All right, then," Diana said. There was another pause. "By the way, do you have plans for Thanksgiving? Paul doesn't have to start his new job until after New Year's, so you could join us in Seattle—"

Valentino stretched, got to his feet and went to press his nose against the door, indicating that he wanted to go out.

Point in his favor, Tricia thought. *He's house-trained.*

"Thanksgiving is Natty's favorite holiday," she reminded Diana, crossing to open the door for Valentino. "We always spend it together."

Standing on the threshold, Tricia noted that the rain

had slowed again, but the sky looked ready to pitch a fit.

Valentino went out, showing no signs of his previous phobia.

Tricia remained in the doorway, keeping an eye on him, the phone still pressed to her ear.

"I knew you'd say that," Diana said.

Tricia laughed. It was still midafternoon, but thanks to the overcast sky and the drizzle, she had to squint to see Valentino. "It's always good to be invited," she said.

The dog lifted his leg against one end of a picnic table and let fly.

The conversation wound down then, to be continued online, with email and instant messaging.

Tricia said goodbye to her friend and put down the phone before going back to the open door and squinting into the grayish gloom.

There was no sign of the dog.

"Valentino!" she called, surprised by the note of panic in her voice.

Just then, he rounded the row of trash receptacles, trotting merrily toward her and wearing a big-dog grin.

By the time Tricia left for home an hour later, Valentino was sound asleep on his new bed. She carefully banked the fire, made sure he had plenty of water and an extra scoop of kibble in case he needed a midnight snack. She'd been dreading the moment she had to leave him, but he didn't seem concerned.

She promised she'd be back first thing in the morning and, apparently convinced, Valentino stretched on his cozy bed and closed his eyes.

DAVIS AND CONNER RODE BACK toward home with a hard rain beating at their backs and soaking their clothes. They'd managed to rope and tie at least a dozen calves, injecting each of them with serum before letting them up again.

In the barn, they unsaddled their horses and brushed the animals down in companionable silence.

"You sure you won't buy those boots back for me?" Davis asked, with a tilted grin that reminded Conner of Steven and made him feel unaccountably lonesome. "At the rummage sale, I mean? You're not really all that scared of a little bitty thing like Kim—"

Conner rustled up a grin. "Nope," he admitted. "I'm not scared of Kim. But I *do* have some pride. You think I want the whole town of Lonesome Bend knowing I bought your broken-down old boots?"

Davis chuckled, sweeping off his hat and running a wet shirtsleeve over his wet face. "Since when do you give a damn what the 'whole town' thinks about anything?"

Conner rested a hand briefly on his uncle's shoulder. "You go on home," he said. "Change your clothes before you come down with pneumonia or something. I'll finish up here."

"Kim thought you might want to come over for supper tonight," Davis ventured. He and Kim worried about him almost as much as they did Brody. "She's making fried chicken, mashed potatoes and gravy—"

Conner's mouth watered, but the idea of cadging a meal from the people who'd raised him, though it was an offer he would have gladly accepted most times— especially when his favorite foods were being served—

didn't sit so well on that rainy night. "No, thanks," he said.

He wanted a hot shower, a fire in the wood-burning stove that dated back to homestead days, and something to eat, the quicker and easier to cook, the better.

Those things, he could manage. It was the *rest* of what he wanted that always seemed just out of reach: a woman there to welcome him home at night, the way Kim welcomed Davis. Not that he'd mind if she had a career—that would probably make her more interesting—as long as she wanted a family eventually, as he did...

"Conner?" Davis said.

He realized he'd been woolgathering and blinked. "Yeah?"

"You sure you don't want to have supper with us?"

"I'm sure," Conner said, turning away from Davis, silently reminding himself that he had horses to feed. "Go on and get out of here."

Davis sighed, hesitated for a long moment and then left.

Moments later, Conner heard his uncle's truck start up out front. He went back to thinking about his nonexistent wife while he worked—and damn if she didn't look a little like Tricia McCall.

WINSTON SAT ON A WINDOWSILL in the kitchen, looking out at the rain. The wind howled around the corners of Natty's old house, but the cat didn't react; it took thunder and lightning to scare him.

And there hadn't been any since Tricia had arrived home, taken a quick shower to ease the chill in her bones and donned sweatpants and an old T-shirt of Hunter's.

Every light in the room was blazing, and she'd even turned on the small countertop TV—something she rarely did. That night, she felt a need for human voices, even if they did belong to newscasters.

Tricia couldn't help thinking about Valentino, alone at the office, and when she managed to turn off the flow of *that* guilt-inducing scenario, Conner Creed sneaked into her mind and wouldn't leave.

"I know what you're thinking," she told Winston, opening the oven door to peer in and check on her dinner, a frozen chicken potpie with enough fat grams for three days. "That I should be eating sensibly. But tonight, I want comfort food."

Winston made a small, snarly sound, and his tail bushed out. He pressed his face against the steamy glass of the window and repeated insistently, *"Reowww—"*

Tricia frowned as she shut the oven door. And that was when she heard the scratching.

Winston began to pace the wide windowsill like a jungle cat in a cage. His tail was huge now, and his hackles were up.

Again, the scratching sound.

Tricia went to the door, squinting as she approached, but there was no one on the other side of the glass oval.

"What on earth—?" She opened the door and looked down.

Valentino sat on the welcome mat, drenched, gazing hopefully up at her.

"How did you get here?" Tricia asked, stepping back and, to her private relief, not expecting an answer.

Valentino's coat was muddy, and so were his paws.

He walked delicately into Tricia's kitchen, as though he were worried about intruding.

Winston, to her surprise, didn't leap on the poor dog with his claws bared, despite all that previous pacing and tail fluffing. He simply sat on his sleek haunches as Tricia closed the door and began grooming himself.

Valentino plunked down in the middle of the floor, dripping and apologetic.

Tricia's throat tightened, and her eyes burned. Somehow, he'd gotten out of the office, and then found his way through town and straight to her door.

She bent to pat his head. "I'll be right back with a towel," she told him. "In the meantime, don't move a muscle."

CHAPTER FOUR

WITHIN THREE SHORT DAYS, during which the rainstorms dwindled and finally passed, leaving the scrubbed-clean sky a polished, heartrending shade of blue, Valentino charmed his way into Tricia's affections and even won Winston over.

Of course she was still telling herself the Valentino arrangement was temporary that Saturday morning, and she wrote her festive mood off to her lifelong love of autumn and the fact that she would be meeting Sasha's plane in a couple of hours. She'd been in regular contact with Hunter, though mostly by email, because he was so busy getting ready for a big show at a new gallery on Bainbridge Island. Also, it didn't hurt that virtually every camping spot and RV space was booked for the following weekend—*plus* a big group had reserved the whole campground for a Sunday barbecue.

The deposits had fattened Tricia's bank account considerably, and thus it was with figurative change jingling in her jeans that Tricia loaded Valentino into the back of the Pathfinder a few minutes after 10:00 a.m. and set out for the Denver airport.

She put on a Kenny Chesney CD as soon as she cleared the city limits—this was the only context in which Lonesome Bend, population 5,000, was ever referred to as a "city"—so she and Valentino could rock out during the drive.

Kenny's voice made her think of Conner Creed, though, and she switched it off after the third track, annoyed. Shouldn't it be *Hunter* she had on her mind? Hunter she imagined herself dancing with slow and close to the jukebox in some cowboy bar? After all, she hadn't seen Conner since their lunch date.

Hunter, on the other hand, had invited her to join him on a cruise to Mexico the week between Christmas and New Year's, going so far as to buy the tickets and forward them to her as an attachment to one of his brief, manic emails.

Remembering that, she frowned. She was—thrilled. Who wouldn't be? It was just that he hadn't consulted her first, had just assumed she'd be willing to drop everything—or worse yet, that she didn't have any holiday plans in the first place—meet him at LAX on Christmas night, and board the ship the next morning.

She knew a sunny, weeklong respite from a Colorado winter would be welcome when the time came and, besides, all that merry-merry, jing-jing-jingling stuff always gave her a low-grade case of the blues. Sure, she had Natty to celebrate with, but the music and the decorations and the lights and the rest of it made her miss her dad so keenly that her throat closed up, achy-tight. Joe McCall had loved Christmas.

To her mother, Laurel, December 25 was a nonevent at best and an orgy of capitalistic conspicuous consumption at worst. A skilled trauma nurse, too-busy-for-her-own-daughter Mom was always in the thick of some international disaster these days—floods in Pakistan, earthquakes in China, tsunamis in the Pacific, mudslides in South American countries whose names and borders changed with every political coup.

Suffice it to say, Laurel and Tricia weren't all that close, especially now that Tricia was a grown-up. To be fair, though, except for her parents' quiet divorce when she was seven, and all the subsequent schlepping back and forth between Colorado and Washington state, her childhood had been a fairly secure one. Until Tricia started college, Laurel had stayed right there in Seattle, working at a major hospital, making the mortgage payments on their small condo without complaint, and showing up for most of her only child's parent-teacher conferences, dance recitals and reluctant performances in school plays.

If there had been a coolness, a certain distance in Laurel's interactions with Tricia, well, there were plenty of people who would have traded places with her, too, weren't there? So what if she'd been a little lonely when she wasn't staying with Joe and Natty in Lonesome Bend?

She'd had a home, food, decent clothes, a college education.

Not that Laurel considered a BA degree in art history even remotely useful. She'd recommended nursing school, at least until one of those Bring Your Kid to Work things rolled around when Tricia was thirteen. Laurel had been in charge of Emergency Services then, and it was a full moon, and Tricia was so shaken by the E.R. experience, with all its blood and screaming and throwing up, that she'd nearly been admitted herself.

Even now, though, on the rare occasions when they Skyped or spoke on the phone, Laurel was prone to distracted little laments like, "It would be different if you were an *artist*—your degree would make some kind of *sense* then—" or "You *do* realize, don't you, that this Hunter person is just using you?"

Tightening her hands on the steering wheel, Tricia shook off these reflections, determined not to ruin a happy day by dwelling on things that couldn't be changed. Better to concentrate on the road to Denver, and Sasha's much-anticipated visit.

Valentino, meanwhile, sat quietly in the back, watching with apparent interest as mile after flat mile rolled past the Pathfinder's windows. He was good company, that dog. No trouble at all.

When they reached the airport, and she rolled a window down partway and promised she'd be back before he knew she'd even been gone, he settled himself in for a midmorning nap.

Tricia locked the rig and headed for the nearest bank of elevators, checking her watch as the doors slid open and she stepped inside. Sasha was scheduled to land in less than half an hour.

So far, so good.

THE BIG TOUR BUS ROLLED UP the dusty road to the Creed ranch house just before noon, and the sight of it made Conner smile. The monstrosity belonged to Steven's wife Melissa's famous brother, the country-western singer Brad O'Ballivan, and there was an oversize silhouette of his head painted on one side, along with the singer's name splashed in letters that probably could have been read from a mile away, or farther.

Davis and Kim had postponed their own road trip as soon as they learned that the Stone Creek branch of the family had decided on a spur-of-the-moment visit, and they were standing right next to Conner, grinning from ear to ear at the prospect of seeing their three grandchildren.

Conner, just as pleased as his aunt and uncle were, had nevertheless been waiting for the proverbial other shoe to drop ever since he'd learned that Brody was headed home, with Joleen Williams in tow. Several days had gone by since Malcolm had broken the news on the loading dock at the feed store, and there'd been no sign of David and Bathsheba in the interim, but Conner remained on his guard just the same. Brody *would* show up in Lonesome Bend, if not on the ranch, that was a given; it was only a question of when.

The Bradmobile came to a squeaky-braked stop in between the main ranch house and the barn, and the main door opened with a hydraulic *whoosh*. Six-year-old Matt and his faithful companion, a dog named Zeke, if Conner recalled correctly, burst through the opening.

Sparing a grin for his "Uncle Conner" as he dashed straight past him, the little boy hurtled off the ground like a living rocket, and Davis, laughing, caught the child in his arms.

"Hey, boy," he said.

Steven got out of the bus next, turning to extend a hand to his spirited wife, Melissa, a pretty thing with a great figure, a dazzling smile and a law degree.

"Where are those babies?" Kim demanded good-naturedly.

Smiling, Melissa put a finger to her lips and mouthed the word *Napping*.

Steven approached, shaking his father's hand and then turning to look at Conner. "Any word from Brody?" Steven asked.

Conner stiffened, a move that would have been imperceptible to most people, but Steven knew him too well to miss any nuances, however subtle. "Now, why would you ask me that, cousin?" Conner retorted.

Steven's nonchalant shrug didn't fool Conner, because the nuance thing worked two ways. "He told Melissa and me he might be headed this way," he said. "That was a week ago, at least. I figured he'd be here by now."

"He might be in town someplace," Conner allowed, his tone casual. "Staying under the radar."

Steven gave a snortlike chuckle at that. "As if Brody Creed has *ever* stayed under the radar," he replied. His eyes were watchful, and gentle in a way that made Conner wary of what would come next. "You know he and Joleen hooked up somewhere along the line, right?"

Conner cleared his throat, watching as Kim and Melissa crept into the tour bus for a glimpse of the six-month-old twins, Samuel Davis, called Sam, and Blue, named for Conner and Brody's dad. Davis, Matt and the dog were headed for the barn, because Matt had a serious addiction to horses.

"Yeah," Conner said belatedly, and his voice came out sounding huskier than he'd meant it to. "I heard." He displaced his hat, shoved splayed fingers through his hair and sighed. "Why does everybody seem to think I'm going to have to be talked in off some ledge because Brody and Joleen are up to their old tricks?"

Steven rested a hand on Conner's shoulder and squeezed. "'Everybody' doesn't think any such thing," he said quietly. "It's a long way in the past, what happened. Maybe far enough that you and Brody could lay the whole thing to rest and get on with it."

Conner made a derisive sound. "I'm sure that's what he wants, all right," he said sarcastically. "Why else would he be bringing Joleen with him?"

Steven sighed. Dropped his hand from Conner's shoulder. "This is Brody we're talking about," he reminded his cousin. "My guess would be, he figures bygones are bygones after all this time."

Kim and Melissa emerged from the bus, each of them carrying a bundled-up baby and beaming. Conner wondered if Kim had "accidentally" awakened the twins from their naps.

"That is some bus," he said, shaking his head. "If I didn't know better, I'd think you wanted to attract as much attention as possible, cousin."

Steven laughed. "We've stirred up some interest at gas stations and rest stops between here and Stone Creek," he admitted. "But as soon as folks realize Brad O'Ballivan isn't going to pop out and strum a few tunes on his guitar, they leave us alone."

Kim and Melissa went on by, headed for the house with the babies, and Steven ducked into the bus, returning moments later with a fold-up gizmo that might have been either a portable crib or a playpen.

The sight gave Conner a pang, and he wasn't very proud of himself, knowing that what he was feeling was plain old envy.

Steven had a ranch and a wife and, now, kids. Pretty much everything Conner had ever hoped to have himself.

Steven read Conner's expression as he passed. "Let's get inside," he said easily. "It's colder than a well-digger's ass out here and, besides, we've got a lot to catch up on."

A FEMALE FLIGHT ATTENDANT ESCORTED SASHA out into the arrivals area.

"That's her!" Sasha whooped, pointing at Tricia and practically jumping up and down. "That's my Aunt Tricia!"

Beaming, Tricia opened her arms. The flight attendant smiled, watching as the child, bespectacled and pigtailed, clad in a pink nylon jacket, a sweater and little jeans with the flannel lining showing at the cuffs, left her carry-on bag and ran into Tricia's hug at top speed.

"I got to sit in first class!" Sasha announced, when Tricia and the flight attendant had had a brief exchange, the purpose of which was to verify Tricia's identity. "I was next to a man who kept clearing his sinuses!"

Tricia chuckled. "Yuck," she commented.

Sasha grasped the handle of the carry-on and jabbed at her smudged glasses where the wire rims arched across her tiny, freckled nose. "We don't even have to stop at baggage claim," she informed Tricia proudly. "All my stuff is right here in this suitcase. Mom said I didn't need to bring my whole wardrobe since you probably have a washer and dryer."

"There's a set downstairs, in my great-grandmother's section of the house," Tricia said, taking Sasha's free hand and leading her toward the first of several moving walkways. "Do you need to use the restroom or anything?"

Sasha shook her head, making her light brown pigtails fly again. "I did that on the plane," she said. "There wasn't even a line in first class."

"Wow," Tricia said. "What about food? Are you hungry?"

Sasha grinned up at her. Her permanent teeth were coming in, too big for her face. She'd be a beauty when she got older, Tricia knew, just like Diana, but right now, she was headed into an awkward stage. "Aunt Tricia," she said patiently, "I was in *first class*."

Tricia laughed again. "So you mentioned," she teased.

On the way to the parking garage, Sasha chattered on about the upcoming move to Paris, and how she'd be attending a *real* school over there, with other kids and different teachers for different classes and everything, because her mom and dad had been able to find one that could provide "the necessary academic challenges." Homeschooling was okay, she stressed to Tricia, but it would be fun to ride buses and have a school song and all that stuff.

Tricia listened in delight, though a part of her was already missing Sasha and Diana and Paul, which was silly, when they hadn't actually moved yet.

When they reached the Pathfinder, Valentino was standing with his nose pressed to the window on the rear hatch, steaming up the glass.

"You *have a dog!*" Sasha crowed, obviously thrilled by the discovery. "You actually got another dog!"

"Not exactly," Tricia said, but Sasha didn't hear her. She was totally focused on Valentino.

Tricia unlocked the doors and lifted the hatch, fielding Valentino with one hand, so he wouldn't jump out of the vehicle and hurt himself, and hefting up Sasha's surprisingly heavy bag with the other.

Sasha tried to scramble into the back with Valentino, and Tricia stopped her. It was only then that she realized she didn't have a booster seat for the child to ride in. Feeling incredibly guilty, she helped Sasha onto the backseat and waited while she buckled up.

"In Washington," Sasha informed her cheerfully, "I have to use a booster seat. It's against the law not to."

It's against the law here, too, Tricia thought ruefully, rummaging up a smile. "We'll stop and buy one first thing," she said.

"What's the dog's name?" Sasha asked, straining to pat his head, when Tricia was behind the wheel, belted in, and ready to head out.

"Valentino," Tricia answered, wondering if she ought to explain that she was just keeping him until she could find him a good home and deciding against the idea in the next instant. Sasha wouldn't understand.

When the time came, Tricia thought sadly, neither would Valentino.

"Doesn't he need to get out of the car before we go?" Sasha inquired, ever practical. She got that from her dad; Diana was smart, but impulsive.

"We'll hit the first rest stop," Tricia promised.

"What if he can't wait?" Sasha fretted.

"He's a good boy," Tricia said, driving slowly along the aisle leading to the nearest exit. "He'll wait."

"Not if he *can't,*" Sasha said.

"Sash," Tricia said gently. "He'll be okay."

"He doesn't look anything like Rusty," the little girl observed, after a short silence, while Tricia was stopped at the pay window, handing over her ticket and the price of parking.

The remark gave Tricia a bittersweet feeling, a combination of affection for the child and grief for Rusty. "No," she said softly, as they pulled away. "He's not Rusty."

"That's okay," Sasha said earnestly, evidently addressing Valentino. "Rusty was a *really nice dog,* but you're nice, too."

Tricia smiled, though her eyes stung a little.

They stopped at the first shopping center they passed and took Valentino on a little tour of the grassy dividers in the parking lot before settling him in the Pathfinder again and dashing into a chain store, hand in hand, to buy a proper booster seat.

Though Tricia was at a loss, Sasha knew the layout of the store from visiting the branch nearest her home in Seattle, and she went straight to the section with car seats. Once the purchase was made and they were back at the car again, they wrestled the bulky seat out of its box, laughing the whole time, and it was Sasha who showed Tricia how the various straps and buckles worked.

She had a booster seat just like it, she said.

A store employee, rounding up red plastic shopping carts, took charge of the empty box, and they were good to go.

"Now we're legal," Sasha said. "Valentino and I would be stranded if you got arrested."

Tricia drove out of the lot and onto the highway. "The most important thing is that you're safer now," she told her goddaughter. "But even if something did happen, you wouldn't be left to manage on your own."

"But who's going to use this seat when I'm in Paris?" Sasha asked. "It cost a lot of money."

There it was again—her practical side. How many kids troubled their heads about such things?

"Not to worry," Tricia answered, wanting to reassure

the child. "It'll come in handy now, and when you visit again."

Sasha sighed. "But it might be a long time before that happens," she said. "I might be too big to even *need* a booster seat next time I come to Colorado. I might even be a *teenager* by then." From her tone, she didn't find the idea of being a teen completely unappealing.

"It'll be a while," Tricia said, though she knew Sasha would be grown-up long before anybody else—Diana and Paul included—was the least bit ready for that to happen.

Mercifully, Sasha moved between subjects like a firefly flitting from branch to bough, and her concern over the expense of the booster seat was apparently forgotten. "Are we going to do fun stuff while I'm staying with you?" she asked.

Tricia reached up and adjusted the rearview mirror just far enough, and just long enough, to catch a glimpse of Sasha's face. Valentino, living up to his name, rested his muzzle against the little girl's cheek.

"Yes," she said. "We are going to do fun stuff."

"Like what?"

"Well, we could go out for pizza. And rent some DVDs at the supermarket—"

Tricia couldn't help thinking how ordinary those activities must sound to an urban child, and she stumbled a little. "And there's a barbecue at River's Bend tomorrow afternoon. We're invited."

The mysterious Sunday reservation had been made under the name "Stone Creek Cattle Company," and Tricia had regarded the invitation as a formality, never intending to attend as a guest. Now that she had a child to entertain, it sounded like a good idea after all—the sort of Western shindig one might expect to see in Lonesome Bend, Colorado.

"Will it be like a party?" Sasha piped up, clearly intrigued. "With music and sack races and games of horseshoes and stuff?"

"I don't know," Tricia confessed, mildly deflated. Good heavens, she was really batting a thousand here.

"You're invited, but you don't know what kind of party it's going to be?"

Sasha, Tricia thought wryly, would probably grow up to be a lawyer.

"The people are from out of town," she said. "I had the impression that it's a pretty big gathering."

"They're strangers?"

"I guess so, but—"

"A barbecue might be fun. They have them in people's backyards sometimes, in Seattle, but I'll bet cookouts are pretty unusual in France."

Tricia smiled. "Probably," she agreed. "But the French are very good cooks."

"My friend Jessie," Sasha remarked, "says the French don't like Americans."

"Jessie?" Tricia countered, stalling so she could think for a few moments.

"Jessie's mom homeschools her and her brother, the same way my mom does me," Sasha said. "She's ten, just like me—Jessie, I mean—but she doesn't have to sit in a booster seat anymore because she's taller than I am. A *lot* taller." She paused, drew a breath. "What if I don't grow any bigger? What if I'm as old as you and Mom and I still have to ride in a stupid booster seat, like a baby, because I'm *short?* Jessie says it could happen."

"Jessie sounds—precocious," Tricia said. "You aren't

through growing, kiddo—take it from me. Your dad is six-two, and your mom is five-seven. What are the genetic chances that you'll be short?"

"Grandma is short," Sasha reasoned.

"I've met your grandmother," Tricia responded. "And you don't take after her at all."

"But she is short," Sasha insisted.

"I guess," Tricia allowed, picturing Paul's sweet mother, who was indeed vertically challenged. "Care to make a wager?"

"What kind of wager?" Sasha asked, sounding eager.

"I'll bet that when you come home from France, you'll be at least five-five."

"What if I win? I mean, suppose I'm still four-six-and-a-half?"

"I'll buy you a whole season, on DVD, of whatever shows your mom will let you watch."

"Mom *hates* TV," Sasha said. "But I get to watch an hour a day when we live in Paris, if I have all my homework done, because that will help me learn the language."

Tricia barely kept from rolling her eyes. Sometimes Diana, who had been adventurous in the extreme before Sasha came along, overdid the whole responsible-parenting thing. "Okay," she said. "What would work for you?"

"The *Twilight* series," Sasha answered, with a marked lack of hesitation. "*All* the books in it."

"Deal," Tricia said, hoping she wouldn't have to pay up before Sasha was old enough to read about teenage vampires in love.

"What do you get if I lose?" Sasha wanted to know.

Tricia considered carefully before she replied. "Well, you could draw me a picture."

"I'd be willing to do that anyway," Sasha said, sweet thing that she was. "Your prize has to be something better than *that*."

"Let's think about it," Tricia suggested.

"Pizza for supper tonight?" Sasha asked.

"Pizza for supper tonight," Tricia confirmed.

"Yes!" Sasha shouted, punching the air with one small fist. "Mom *never* lets me eat real pizza, but Dad and I sneak it sometimes."

Valentino, caught up in the excitement of the moment, barked in happy agreement.

THE STONE CREEK CATTLE COMPANY, Tricia discovered the next day, when she and Sasha arrived at the campground to attend the barbecue, was owned by none other than Steven Creed.

There were Creeds everywhere—Davis and Kim, whom Tricia liked very much, were in attendance, each of them carrying a duplicate baby, dressed up warm. Conner was there, too, looking better than good, hazy in the heat mirage rising from the big central bonfire.

"Hello, Tricia," Steven said, when she stopped in her tracks. Suddenly, all her youthful shyness was back; she might actually have fled the scene if Sasha hadn't been with her, all primed for a Wild West experience she could brag about when she started school in Paris.

"Steven," she said, with a polite nod. "How are you?"

"Fantastic," Steven replied. "Married, with children." His blue gaze shifted to Sasha, who was staring at him in apparent fascination, probably thinking, as a lot of people did, that he looked like Brad Pitt. "Is this lovely young lady your daughter?"

Sasha gave a peal of laughter at that, as if it was totally inconceivable that her honorary aunt could be somebody's mother.

"No," she answered. "Aunt Tricia is my mom's best friend. I'm visiting for *two whole weeks* because we're moving to Paris in a couple of months—"

"Nice to see you again, Steven," Tricia said, after laying a hand lightly on Sasha's small shoulder to stem the flow.

He looked around, probably for his wife, and when his eyes landed on the friendly woman bouncing one of the matching babies on one hip while she chatted with some other guests, they softened in a way that moved Tricia deeply and unexpectedly.

Had Hunter ever looked at *her* that way? If he had, she hadn't noticed.

"Looks like Melissa is caught up in conversation," Steven mused, smiling. "Don't take off before I get a chance to introduce you two."

"Sure," Tricia answered, blushing. "I'd like that."

Steven nodded, excused himself and walked away. Sasha had wandered off to play with some of the other kids, but Tricia wasn't alone for long. She followed him with her gaze, and when she looked back at the space he'd occupied before, Conner was there.

"Hi," he said.

She smiled up at him, even though she felt incredibly nervous. The dancing-to-a-jukebox fantasy from the day before, when she'd had to turn off Kenny Chesney, filled her mind.

"Hi," she replied. Oh, she was a sparkling conversationalist, all right.

"I'm glad you're here," Conner said. She wouldn't have known that by his expression; he wasn't smiling. In fact, he looked as though he were trying to work out some complex equation in his head. "How's the dog?"

"Valentino's fine," she answered. She'd thought she was over her childhood shyness, but here it was, back again. "He's at home, with Natty's cat."

Could she sound any more inane?

Conner finally grinned, a spare, slanted motion of his mouth. "He's going to be big when he's full grown, you know," he remarked.

Was it possible that Conner Creed was shy, too? Nah, she decided.

"That's why I'm hoping to find him a home in the country someplace," she said. "Where he can run."

Conner merely nodded at that.

Tricia blushed, wishing the tension would subside. It didn't, of course, and she couldn't stand the brief silence that had settled between them, at once a bond and a barrier, so she burst out with, "He was supposed to live here, in the office, but he wouldn't stay put. He managed to escape somehow, and showed up on my doorstep in the middle of that last big rainstorm—"

Stop babbling, she ordered herself silently.

Conner frowned. "How could he have gotten out?" he asked, and when he walked over to examine the office door, Tricia followed right along. The rest of the world seemed to fall away, forgotten. "You locked up, right?"

"I forget sometimes," Tricia said, enjoying his apparent concern for her personal security more than she probably should have. "And the lock is old, like the rest of this place, and it doesn't always catch. A gust of wind could have blown it open."

"Or somebody could have broken in," Conner said, taking the dark view evidently. "Did you call Jim Young and report what happened?"

"No," Tricia said. "I drove over here and checked things out myself, after I got Valentino dried off and settled at the apartment. Nothing was missing, or anything like that."

Just then, Steven's attractive wife joined them, baby tugging happily at a lock of her bright hair.

"I'm Melissa Creed," she said, smiling at Tricia, putting out her free hand.

Tricia took the other woman's hand and smiled back. "Tricia McCall," she said.

Melissa slanted a mischievous glance at Conner, who was just standing there, contributing nothing at all. "Of course I might have expected you to introduce me," she told him.

He shoved a hand through his hair, sighed. He looked mildly uncomfortable now, as though he might bolt. "Clearly," he said, "that wasn't necessary."

Melissa laughed at that, and her eyes shone as she turned her attention back to Tricia. "The food is almost ready," she said. "Women and children get to be first in line."

By tacit agreement, they started toward the picnic area, where the huge grill was emitting delicious aromas, savory-sweet.

Tricia called to Sasha, who came reluctantly. She'd already made friends with some of the other kids, though they'd only been there a few minutes.

Melissa stayed at Tricia's side while they waited their turns.

"What's the occasion?" Tricia asked, taking in the crowds of people. She recognized most of them, but there were some strangers, too. "For the party, I mean?"

Melissa smiled. "My husband likes to bring people together," she said. "The more, the merrier, as far as Steven's concerned."

"Oh," Tricia said, at a loss again.

Just then, Melissa spotted some new arrival and waved, smiling. "Excuse me," she said. "I might have to referee."

With that, she hurried away.

Tricia turned her head, and there was Brody Creed in the distance, looking so much like his brother that it made her breath catch.

CHAPTER FIVE

BRODY.

Conner couldn't have claimed he was surprised to see his brother; he'd been warned well ahead of time, after all. But he still felt as though he'd stepped through an upstairs doorway and found himself with no floor to stand on, falling fast.

Careful as Conner was to keep a low profile, Brody's gaze swept over the crowd and found him with the inevitability of a heat-seeking missile. It was, Conner supposed, the twin thing. He'd nearly forgotten that weird connection between him and Brody, they'd been apart for so long. As kids, they'd been a little spooked by the phenomenon sometimes, though mostly it was fun, like scaring the hell out of each other with stories about escaped convicts with hooks for hands, or swapping identities and maintaining the deception for days before anyone caught on.

Brody narrowed his eyes. His hair was longer than Conner's, he hadn't shaved in a day or two, and his clothes were scruffy, but for all that, seeing him was, for Conner, disturbingly like looking into a mirror.

Where was Joleen? Conner wondered, subtly scanning Brody's immediate orbit. There was no sign of her—which didn't mean she wasn't around somewhere, of course. Like Brody, Joleen had a talent for turning up unexpectedly, in his thoughts if not in the flesh; she probably enjoyed the drama of it all. Joleen had always been big on drama.

Now Brody made his way through the clusters of people, smiling and speaking a word of greeting here and there, but he was headed straight for Conner. Pride made Conner dig in his boot heels and stay put, though he didn't feel ready to deal with Brody just then. He folded his arms, tilted his head to one side, and waited. If he bolted, Brody and whoever else was looking might think Conner was afraid of his brother—and he wasn't. It was just that there was so damn much going on under the surface of things, and Conner had trouble maintaining his perspective, at least as far as Brody was concerned.

"Hello, little brother," Brody drawled, when the two of them were standing face-to-face. He'd been born four minutes ahead of Conner, as the story went, and he'd always enjoyed bringing it up.

Like it gave him some advantage or something.

Conner gave a curt little nod, realized his arms were still folded across his chest, and let them fall to his sides. "Brody," he said, in gruff acknowledgment that the other man existed, if nothing else.

Brody indulged in a cocky grin, his mouth tilting up at one corner, his blue eyes mischievous, but watchful, too. Despite all his folksy affability, Brody was on high alert, just as Conner was. Maybe it had slipped his mind that they'd always been able to read each other like bold print on a billboard, but Conner definitely remembered.

"I'm just passing through," Brody said, and while his voice was easy, his eyes gave the lie to the impression he was doing his best to give. Whatever his reasons for returning to Lonesome Bend might be, they were important to him. "So there's no need for you to get all bent out of shape or anything."

"Who says I'm bent out of shape?" Conner asked, sensing that he had the upper hand. Since they'd always been so evenly matched that all either of them ever gained from a fistfight, for instance, was a lot of cuts and bruises but no clear victory, the insight came as something of a revelation.

"Just going by past history," Brody replied, raising both eyebrows. "Last time we ran into each other, at that rodeo in Stone Creek, you landed on me before I could get so much as a *howdy* out of my mouth."

Conner felt a twinge of shame, recalling that incident, though he wasn't about to concede that he'd started the row—it had been a mutual, and instantaneous, decision. And, as usual, it had ended in a standoff.

"What do you want, Brody?" he asked now. His arms were folded again. When had that happened?

"Just a place to hang my hat for a while," Brody replied, sounding sadly aggrieved.

"How about on Joleen's bedpost?" Conner asked, and then could have kicked himself, hard. Not because the remark had been unkind, but because of the way Brody might interpret it.

That slow, Brody-patented grin spread across his brother's beard-stubbled face. "So *that's* the way it is," he said, hooking his thumbs in the belt loops of his jeans, like some old-time cowpuncher surveying the herd. Next, he'd probably turn his head to one side and spit. "I don't mind telling you, little brother—I didn't figure you'd give a damn what Joleen and I might do together, after all this time."

The old rage seethed inside Conner, but glancing past Brody, he caught a momentary glimpse of Tricia McCall, sitting at one of the picnic tables, in the midst of a crowd of other diners, and something shifted inside him, just like that.

It hurt, like having a disjointed bone yanked back into its socket, but there was an element of relief, too. What the hell?

"You're right," Conner told his brother stiffly, finally paying attention to the conversation again. "The two of you can join the circus and swing from trapezes for all I care."

Brody put one hand to his chest, his fingers splayed wide, and feigned emotional injury. "Then you shouldn't have a problem with me bunking out at the ranch for a couple of weeks," he said. "Especially since the place is half mine anyhow."

By that time, Davis had worked his way over to them, probably dispatched by Kim. She wouldn't want any fights breaking out, with all those kids and women around, and if anything happened, the gossip wouldn't die down for years.

"You two are bristling like a couple of porcupines," Davis observed dryly, his Creed-blue eyes swinging from one brother to the other. "I don't need to tell you, do I, that this is neither the time nor the place for trouble of the sort you're probably cooking up right about now?"

Conner let out his breath, rolled his shoulders again.

Brody grinned at their uncle. "Just saying hello to my brother," he said, sounding guileless, but unable to resist adding, "and meeting with the usual hostile response, of course."

"Where's Joleen?" Davis asked quietly, watching Brody.

Brody rolled his eyes and flung his hands out from his sides. "Why the hell does everybody keep asking me that?" he wanted to know. Fortunately, he didn't raise his voice; that would have been like dropping a lighted match into a puddle of spilled kerosene. "I'm not the woman's keeper, for God's sake."

Just her lover, Conner thought, automatically, and waited for the rush of testosterone-laced adrenaline. It didn't come. And that threw him a little.

Brody thrust out a dramatic sigh, looking like a man who'd bravely fought the good fight, heroic in the face of great tragedy, won the battle but lost the war. "Look," he said, still careful to speak quietly, since half the town was present and watching out of the corners of their eyes. "Joleen and I met up by accident, at a rodeo in Lubbock, that's all. She'd just split the sheets with some yahoo, and she was too broke to even buy a bus ticket back home, so I brought her, since I happened to be headed in this general direction anyway. End of story."

Conner leaned in until his nose and Brody's were almost touching. "You've obviously mistaken me," he growled, "for somebody who gives a rat's ass why you and Jolene came back to Lonesome Bend."

"That's enough," Davis said sternly, as in days of old, when Brody and Conner had been even more hotheaded than they were now. "*That will be enough.* This is a party, not some dive of a bar in Juarez. If you want to beat the hell out of each other, be my guests, but do it at home, behind the barn. Not here."

A brief and highly incendiary silence fell.

"Sorry," Conner finally ground out, insincerely.

"Me, too," Brody added, lying through his teeth. "Fact is, I've lost my appetite anyhow, so I'll just be heading home to the ranch—if nobody minds."

Like he cared whether or not anybody minded anything, ever. Brody had always done whatever he damn well pleased, and people who got in his way were just expected to deal.

"Kim and I will be hitting the trail right after Steven and Melissa and the kids leave tomorrow," Davis said, watching Brody. "I'd offer to let you stay at our place and look after things while we're gone, but Kim's already made other arrangements."

Brody raised both hands, palms out, like the not-too-worried victim of a stick-up. "No problem," he said, after a pointed look at Conner. "I've got a yen to sleep in my own bed, in my own room, anyway. 'Course I'll have to sleep with one eye open, since I'll be about as welcome as an unrepentant whore in church."

Davis leveled a glance at Conner, put an arm around Brody's shoulders and steered him away, toward the barbecue area, where the grill was smoking and food was being handed out. "Don't say anything to Kim," the older man began, his voice carrying back to Conner, "but there's this pair of boots she donated to the rummage sale—"

In spite of everything, Conner chuckled. If Davis Creed was anything, he was persistent—some would say stubborn—just like the rest of their kin.

After giving himself a few moments to cool off,

Conner made his way to Kim's side. She immediately turned to face him.

"Thanks for not making a scene," she said, not unkindly but with the quiet directness they'd all come to expect from her. "This get-together means a lot to Steven. It's his way of showing off his wife and kids to the hometown folks, and I'd hate to see that get ruined."

"I hear you, Kim," Conner replied. Brody and Davis were in line for grub by then, each of them holding a throwaway plate and jawing with folks around them. "But if anybody ruins this shindig, it won't be me."

Real pain flickered in Kim's eyes. Conner's biological mother had died soon after giving birth to him and Brody, leaving Blue alone and grief-stricken, with no clue as to how to look after two squalling, premature newborns, and this woman had stepped up, loved them like her own. She'd been firm, even strict sometimes, Kim had, but there had never been a single moment when Conner had doubted her devotion, and he was pretty sure Brody would have said the same.

They'd been lucky to have Kim in their lives, and even luckier to have Davis, because their uncle had run the ranch for them after Blue's death, and guarded their interests with absolute integrity. On top of that, he'd been a father to them.

"If only you and Brody could get along," Kim said sadly.

"That requires trust," Conner replied, his voice quiet. "And Brody and I don't have that anymore." Without conscious effort, he sought Tricia again, with his eyes, found her, and he was heartened by the mere sight of her.

Why was that?

Kim, typically, had followed Conner's gaze, registered that he was watching Tricia, even though he would have preferred to keep that particular tidbit of information to himself. "Tricia McCall?" Kim asked, her voice very soft, pitched to go no further than Conner's ears. "My faith in your judgment is restored, Conner Creed. Frankly, it's a mystery to me why a woman like that is still single."

"Maybe she likes being single," Conner suggested.

"The way *you* like being single, Conner?" Kim immediately retorted.

His hackles didn't exactly rise, but they twitched a little. "What is that supposed to mean?"

"You know perfectly well what it means," she answered, but she rested a hand on his forearm and squeezed. "Even without these two eyes in my head, I would still have known how much you want somebody to share your life. Whenever you so much as look at Steven, or Melissa, or any of those kids—even the dog, for heaven's sake—it's right there in that handsome mug of yours. A sort of lonely hunger."

"'Lonely hunger'?" Conner asked, with a lightness he didn't feel. "You read too many of those romance novels."

"It wouldn't hurt you or Brody or, for that matter, Davis, to read a few romances," Kim said, undaunted. "That way, you might know how a woman likes to be treated."

Conner let out a huff. "My point," he said, "is this— don't get carried away—Tricia's involved with some guy in Seattle. Keeps his picture on her computer monitor as a screen saver."

Kim smiled. "You've been to Tricia's place?"

Conner felt his neck go warm. "Yes," he answered. "I took Natty a load of firewood, as I do every fall and right on through the winter, and since the old gal was away, I needed somebody to let me in so I could fill the wood boxes. Tricia lives upstairs, above Natty's."

Kim was musing now. Thoughtful, but still amused. "Maybe the guy in that picture is her brother or just a good friend. He might even be gay."

"Right," Conner said dryly. "And Santa Claus might come down my chimney on Christmas Eve and stuff a Playboy bunny into my stocking."

Kim arched an eyebrow, but she was smiling again, full-out. "Bitter," she said. "Conner Creed, you are a bitter man. And in the prime of your life, too."

"I'm not bitter," Conner retorted, knowing that what his stand-in mom said was true. He *was* bitter, over what he perceived as Brody's betrayal of his trust, over the way he'd never met the right woman, as so many of the guys he knew had—Steven in particular.

"Don't try to B.S. me, Conner," Kim said. "I know you better than you know yourself. You're taken with Tricia, and there's not a darn thing wrong with that. Man up, why don't you, and ask her out?"

"To do what?" Conner scuffed, strangely unsettled by the idea of making a move on Tricia. What if she said no? What if she said *yes?* "Go to a hoedown? Or maybe that rummage sale slash chili feed? Anyway, she has company, a little girl."

"Sasha," Kim clarified knowledgeably. "She's Tricia's best friend's daughter, and she's ten years old. Also, she's horse crazy, like most girls her age."

"Meaning?"

"Meaning, you thick-headed cowboy," Kim replied, with exaggerated patience and wry affection, "that if you invite Sasha to go riding on the ranch, Tricia will automatically come with her. That's how Davis and I fell in love, you know. We were on a trail ride together, with a bunch of friends, and the first night, we got to talking by the campfire, and it was happy trails from then on. We've been traveling side by side ever since."

"In that case," Conner answered, his tone dry, "I'll take care to avoid trail rides."

Kim quirked a smile. "Don't give up your day job," she whispered, before turning to walk away. "You'd never make it as a comedian."

Conner watched her go. And he steered clear of the chow line, since his stomach felt all tensed up, as if it were closed for business. If Steven and Melissa's visit hadn't been such a short one, he would have gotten into his truck and gone home.

Maybe saddled a horse and headed up into the green-and-gold-and-crimson foothills, where the aspens whispered, where the streams tumbled over rocks and, except for the occasional call of a bird, those were pretty much the only sounds.

Up there, in the spectacular hills, a man could hear himself think. Get some kind of handle on the stuff that was—or wasn't—happening in his life.

But he was stuck, for now anyway.

Might as well make the best of it, and join the party.

TRICIA HELPED WITH THE CLEANUP, telling herself that she ought to leave the barbecue now that she'd put in a cordial appearance, but the bonfire was nice and people were having fun, especially the children, and somebody was tuning up a banjo. The thought of going home, even though Sasha would be with her, was an intensely lonely prospect.

Carolyn Simmons, perhaps the only person in Lonesome Bend who was even more rootless than Tricia, helped, too. A gypsy with no apparent home, Carolyn joined in with the other women and a few men, gathering paper plates and cups and plastic flatware from the ground and the tops of the picnic tables, stuffing the detritus into garbage bags.

"Are you volunteering at the rummage sale again this year?" Carolyn asked Tricia, her tone and manner at once casual and friendly.

"Natty's been trying to pin me down for kitchen duty," Tricia said, smiling in response. "I think she only wants me to guard the family chili recipe, though." Like just about everyone in Lonesome Bend, Tricia was curious about Carolyn, who was always ready with a cheerful hello or a helping hand, but extremely private, too. She kept a roof over her head by housesitting, mainly for the reclusive movie stars, corporate execs and other famous types who bought or built enormous homes outside town but rarely used them. Besides that, her only known income was from the original clothes she designed and sold online or through consignment boutiques.

Carolyn chuckled at Tricia's answer. She had shoulder-length hair, streaked blond but somehow very natural-looking, and her eyes were wide and green, surrounded by thick lashes. "I don't blame Natty one bit," she said warmly. "That chili is so good it ought to be patented."

"Amen," Tricia agreed. The chili recipe was closely

guarded indeed; only Natty and her sister, the one she was visiting in Denver, knew how to make it. The single written copy in existence was brought out of some secret hiding place every October, on the Thursday preceding the rummage sale, and carefully protected from prying eyes.

Even Tricia, a true McCall, had merely managed glimpses of that tattered old recipe card over the years, with its bent corners and its spidery handwriting slanting hard to the right, though Natty had intimated that it might be time to think about "passing the torch." That remark never failed to alarm Tricia, who adored her great-grandmother, and couldn't imagine a world without her in it.

"How is Natty, anyway?" Carolyn asked, dropping a full garbage bag into one of the trash containers and dusting off her hands against the thighs of her black jeans. "I usually run into her at the grocery store or the library, but I haven't seen her around lately."

Tricia explained about the Denver trip, and quickly realized that Carolyn wasn't listening. Her gaze had snagged on Brody Creed, laughing with friends on the other side of the campground, and she seemed powerless to jerk it away again.

Intrigued herself, Tricia watched Brody for a few moments, too, thinking in a detached way that while he and Conner *did* resemble each other closely, there were obvious differences, too.

Conner moved with quiet purpose, for example, while Brody was loose-limbed, ready to change directions at any given moment, if it suited him to do so. There were other qualities, too—some of them so intuitive in nature that Tricia would have had a hard time putting names to them. She knew, somehow, that even if the Creed brothers *tried* to look as alike as possible, she would still know Conner from Brody in an instant. And that was puzzling indeed.

Carolyn snapped out of her own reverie a bit before Tricia did, and when their eyes met, a sort of understanding passed between them—empathy, perhaps. Or maybe just the silent admission that some questions didn't have answers. Not obvious ones, at least.

And then Carolyn surprised Tricia by saying calmly, "What a fool I was, way back when."

This time, it was Hunter who popped into Tricia's mind. She shook off the image and smiled reassuringly. "Weren't we all?"

Carolyn's gaze strayed back to Brody, but didn't linger. When she looked at Tricia again, it was clear that a door had closed inside Carolyn. It reminded Tricia of the way people board up a house when they know there's a category 4 hurricane on its way. "Some of us," she said sadly, with one more glance at Brody, "knew *exactly* what they were doing."

Carolyn had a history with Brody Creed?

Whoa, Tricia thought, hoping Carolyn hadn't noticed the way her eyes had widened for a second or two there. She'd lived part of every year in this small, close-knit community, starting with that first summer after second grade, when Joe and Laurel had called it quits and filed for a divorce, and for the better part of a year and a half since her dad's death.

None of which meant that she was any kind of insider when it came to the locals and their secrets, but, still, she usually had a *glimmer* of what was going on, if only because of things Natty and her friends said in passing, when they got together to sip tea around the old woman's kitchen table. In many ways, Lonesome Bend was like a soap opera come to life, and everybody kept up with the story line—except her, evidently.

Carolyn gave an awkward little laugh. "I'm sorry," she said, embarrassed. "That came out sounding pretty bitchy."

Tricia decided not to comment. Then she remembered that she was still holding her own bag of after-barbecue trash and tossed it into the bin.

"I'm going to be staying on the Creed ranch for a while," Carolyn said, as she and Tricia walked away from the line of garbage cans. "Looking after things for Davis and Kim, I mean. It's a great house, and they have horses, too. I have permission to ride the gentler ones, and I was wondering—"

Her voice fell away, perhaps because she'd seen something in Tricia's face.

Tricia *had* felt a hard jab to her middle when Carolyn announced her next housesitting assignment, given that, living on the ranch, the other woman would be in close proximity to Conner, and, recognizing the emotion for what it was, she was ashamed. Yes, Carolyn was an attractive woman, presumably available. But she, Tricia, certainly had no business being jealous and, anyway, if Carolyn *was* interested in one of the Creed men, it was Brody, not Conner.

Her relief was undeniable.

"What?" she asked belatedly. "What were you wondering?"

"Well, if you and your niece might like to go trail riding sometime," Carolyn said, almost shyly.

"I've never been on a horse in my life," Tricia replied.

It wasn't that she didn't *like* horses, just that they were so big, and so unpredictable.

Diana was an accomplished equestrian, and because of that, Sasha was comfortable around the huge creatures.

"Well, then," Carolyn said, spreading her hands for emphasis and grinning a wide, Julia Roberts grin, "it's time you learned, isn't it?"

"I don't know—"

Just then, Sasha rushed over. Sometimes Tricia thought the child had superpowers—particularly as far as her hearing was concerned. Just moments before, she'd been on the other side of the campground, playing chasing games with other kids and several dogs. Let the word *horse* be spoken, though, and she was Johnny-on-the-spot.

"I want to go riding," Sasha crowed. "Please, please, *please*—"

"Do you read lips or something?" Tricia asked.

"Matt's uncle Conner is going to ask us to go riding, with a bunch of other people. Matt heard him talking about it, and he told me, and *you've got to say yes,* because I honestly don't know how I'll go on if you don't!"

Tricia chuckled and gave one of Sasha's pigtails a gentle tug. "When is this big ride supposed to take place?" she asked, hoping nobody would guess that she was stalling.

"Next Sunday, after the chili feed and the rummage sale are over," Sasha expounded, breathless with excitement. "It'll be the last of the good weather, before the snow comes."

"We'll see," Tricia said.

Carolyn was still standing there, smiling.

"Please!" Sasha implored, clasping her hands together as if in prayer and looking up at Tricia with luminous hope in her eyes.

"I have to ask your mom and dad first," Tricia told her, laying a calming hand on the little girl's shoulder. "I'll send them a text, and when they land in Paris, they'll read it and we'll probably have our answer right away."

"They'll say yes," Sasha said confidently, beaming now. "I ride with Mom *all the time*." The smile faded. "We mostly just ride in arenas and stuff, because Seattle's such a big city. In France, we probably won't get to do it at all. But this is *real* riding, on a *real* ranch, just like in that movie, *City Slickers*."

Tricia and Carolyn exchanged looks, both of them smiling now.

Somehow, they'd gone from being acquaintances to being friends.

"Not *too* much like it, I hope," Tricia said. "And that's what we are, isn't it? A pair of city slickers?"

"Speak for yourself," Sasha joked, folding her arms decisively in front of her little chest and jutting out her chin. "I might *live* in a city, but I know how to ride a horse."

"Yes, you do," Tricia conceded. "Now, what do you say we head for home? Valentino probably needs to go out for a walk, and Winston likes to have his supper early."

"Can we give Winston sardines?" Sasha asked. "It's Sunday, and he always gets sardines on Sunday. That's what you said."

"It is indeed what I said," Tricia answered, nodding to

Carolyn as the other woman waved goodbye and walked off. "And I am a woman of my word."

"Good," Sasha said, in a tone of generous approval.

Tricia took the little girl's hand. "Let's go thank Matt's dad and mom for inviting us to the barbecue," she said. "Then we'll go home and walk Valentino and give Winston his sardines."

Sasha yawned widely and against her will, politely putting a hand over her mouth. It was still fairly early in the day, but she'd been running around in the fresh air for a couple of hours now, laughing and playing with a horde of energetic country kids, and she probably wasn't over the jet-lag of the trip from Seattle.

By the time Sasha had had a warm bath and watched part of a Disney movie on DVD, she'd be asleep on her feet.

"Can I send the text to Mom and Dad?" she asked, when goodbyes and thank-yous had been said, and the two of them were back in Tricia's Pathfinder, headed toward home. "I know how to do it."

Tricia smiled, remembering the message she'd received from Sasha before, from the aquarium in Seattle. "Sure," she said. She pulled over to one side of the road, just long enough to extract the cell from her purse and hand it to Sasha. "Remember, your mom and dad's plane didn't leave Sea-Tac until this morning, so they're still in transit."

Sasha sighed in contented resignation. "And that means they won't get the message until they land. I *know* that already."

"I did mention it before, didn't I?" Tricia admitted, in cheerful chagrin.

"That's okay, Aunt Tricia," Sasha said, already

pushing buttons on the phone like a pro. "You're probably tired, like me."

Love for this child welled up in Tricia, threatening to overflow. "Probably," she agreed, her voice a little husky.

By the time they pulled into the driveway alongside Natty's venerable old Victorian, Sasha had finished transmitting a fairly long text message to her parents and put the phone aside.

They could hear Valentino barking a welcome-home from the bottom of the outside stairway, and he was all over Sasha with kisses the moment Tricia unlocked the door.

She was about to reprimand the dog when Sasha's delighted giggles registered.

They were having fun.

"I'll get the leash," Tricia said, stepping around the reunion on the threshold. She set her purse and phone on the counter and glanced at her computer monitor, across the room, wondering if Hunter had sent her any emails. There would be plenty of time to check later, she decided, collecting Valentino's sturdy nylon lead from the hook on the inside of the pantry door.

Sasha and Tricia took the dog for his much-needed walk, bringing along the necessary plastic bag for cleanup, and Winston was waiting when they got back, prowling back and forth on his favorite windowsill and meowing loudly for his dinner.

Sasha fed the cat an entire tin of sardines from Natty's supply downstairs, while Tricia gave Valentino his kibble and freshened his bowl of water.

Since both Sasha and Tricia were still stuffed from all they'd eaten at the barbecue, supper would be contingent on whether or not they got hungry and, if they did, it would consist of either leftover pizza from the night before or cold cereal, sugary-sweet.

They watched a movie together, then Sasha went into the bathroom to bathe, don her pajamas and dutifully brush her teeth, all of these enterprises closely supervised by Valentino. In the meantime, Tricia folded out the living room couch, retrieved the extra bed pillows from the coat closet and fluffed them up so Sasha would be as comfortable as possible.

The little girl insisted on checking Tricia's cell phone, just in case there had miraculously been an answer from Diana and Paul, and seemed mildly disappointed when there wasn't. "Missing your mom and dad?" Tricia asked softly, sitting down on the hide-a-bed mattress while Sasha squirmed and stretched, a settling-in ritual she'd been performing since she was a toddler.

"A little bit," Sasha admitted wisely. "But I like being here with you and Valentino and Winston, too."

Tricia kissed her forehead. "And we like having you here," she said. "In fact, we love it."

Sasha snuggled down in her covers, while Valentino took up his post nearby, eschewing his dog bed for a hooked rug in front of the nonworking fireplace. "And you love *me,* too, right?"

Tricia's throat tightened again, and she had to swallow a couple of times before she replied, "Right. I love you very much."

Sasha's eyes closed, and she sighed and wriggled a little more. "Love—you—" she murmured.

And then she was sound asleep.

CHAPTER SIX

BRODY AND CONNER STOOD IN THE side yard of the main ranch house that blue-skied morning, keeping the length of a pitchfork handle between them, watching as two shiny RVs pulled out onto the county road, one after the other. Both horns tooted in cheery farewell and that was it. Melissa and Steven and the kids were on their way back to Stone Creek, Arizona, in the Bradmobile, while Davis and Kim were heading for Cheyenne, where they intended to pick up their just-weaned Yorkie pups.

And Conner was alone on the place with his brother, which was the only thing worse than being alone on the place *period*. Brody served as a reminder of better times, when they'd been twin-close, and instead of assuaging Conner's loneliness, it only made him feel worse, missing what was gone.

Since country folks believe it's bad luck to watch people out of sight when they leave a place, especially home, Conner turned away before the vehicles disappeared around the first bend in the road and made for the barn. He'd saddle up, ride out to check some fence lines and make sure the small range crew moving the cattle to the other side of the river, where there was more grass, was on the job.

The crossing was narrow, through fairly shallow

water, and the task would be easily accomplished by a few experienced cowpunchers on horseback, but Conner liked to keep his eye on things, anyhow. Some of the beeves were bound to balk on the bank of that river, calves in particular, and stampedes were always a possibility.

Conner was surprised—and *not* surprised—when Brody fell into step beside him, adjusting his beat-up old rodeo hat as he walked.

"So now that the family is out of here," Brody said mildly, "you're just going to pretend I'm invisible?"

Conner stopped cold, turning in the big double door-way of the barn to meet Brody's gaze. "This is a working cattle ranch," he reminded his brother. "Maybe you'd like to sit around and swap lies, but *I* have things to do."

Brody shook his head, and even though he gave a spare grin, his eyes were full of sadness and secrets. "Thought I'd saddle up and give you a hand," he said, in that gruff drawl he'd always used when he wanted to sound down-home earnest. He came off as an affable saddle bum, folksy and badly educated, without two nickels to rub together, and that was all bullshit. No one knew that better than Conner did, but maybe Brody was so used to conning people into underestimating him, so he could take advantage of them when they least expected it, that he figured he could fool his identical twin brother, too.

Fat chance, since they had duplicate DNA, and at one time they'd been so in sync that they could not only finish each other's sentences, they'd had whole conversations and realized a lot later that neither of them had spoken a single word out loud.

"Thanks," Conner said, without conviction, when the silence became protracted and he knew Brody was going to wait him out, try to bluff his way through as he'd do with a bad poker hand, "but it's nothing I can't handle on my own." *Like I've been doing all these years, while you were off playing the outlaw.*

Of course, Conner had had plenty of help from Davis along the way, but that wasn't the point. The ranch was their birthright—his and Brody's—and Brody had taken off, leaving him holding the proverbial bag, making the major decisions, doing the work. And that, Conner figured, was a big part of the reason why he didn't have what he wanted most.

Brody sighed heavily, tilted his head to one side, as though trying to work a kink out of his neck, and looked at Conner with a mix of anger, amusement and pity in his eyes. Then he rubbed his stubbly chin with one hand. "This place," he said again, and with feigned reluctance, "is half mine. So are the cattle and the horses. While I'm here, I mean to make myself useful, little brother, whether you like it or not."

Conner unclamped his back molars. "Oh, I remember that the ranch is as much yours as it is mine," he responded grimly, forcing the words past tightened lips. "Trust me. I'm reminded of that every time I send you a fat check for doing nothing but staying out of my way. That last part, I did truly appreciate."

Brody chuckled at that, but his eyes weren't laughing. "God damn, but you can hold a grudge like nobody else I ever knew," he observed, folding his arms. "And considering my history with women, that's saying something." He paused, taking verbal aim. "You want Joleen back? Go for it. I'm not standing in your way."

Conner spat, though his mouth was cotton-dry. "Hell," he snapped. "I wouldn't touch Joleen with *your* pecker."

Brody lifted both eyebrows, looking skeptical. "You know what's really the matter with you, little brother? You're *jealous.* And it's got nothing to do with Joleen or any other female on the face of this earth. It's because I went out there and *lived,* did everything you wanted to do, while you stayed right here, like that guy in the Bible, proving you were the Good Son."

Conner's temper flared—Brody's words struck so close to the bone that they nicked his marrow—but he wasn't going to give his brother the satisfaction of losing it. Not this time. "You're full of shit," he said, turning away from Brody again and proceeding into the barn, where he chose a horse and led it out of its stall and into the wide breezeway. Brody followed, selected a cayuse of his own, and the two of them saddled up in prickly silence that made the horses nervous.

As usual, it was Brody who broke the impasse. He swung up into the saddle, pulled down his hat yet another time, which meant he was either rattled or annoyed or both, and ducked to ride through the doorway into the bright October sunshine.

"What would you say if I told you I'd been thinking about retiring from the rodeo and settling down for good?" he asked, when they were both outside.

"I guess it would depend on where you planned on settling down," Conner said.

"Where else but right here?" Brody asked, with a gesture that took in the thousands of acres surrounding them. The Creed land stretched all the way to the side of the river directly opposite Tricia McCall's campground. "I respect Steven's decision to buy a place with no history to it, make his own mark in the world instead of sharing this spread with us, but I'm nowhere near as noble as our cousin from Boston, as you already know."

Conner made a low, contemptuous sound in his throat and nudged his horse into motion, riding toward the open gate leading into the first pasture. The range lay beyond, beckoning, making him want to lean over that gelding's neck and race the wind, but he didn't indulge the notion.

He didn't want Brody thinking he'd gotten his "little brother" on the run, literally or figuratively. "You're right about this much, anyway," he said, his voice stony-quiet. "You're nothing like Steven."

Brody eased his gelding into a gallop just then, but he didn't speak again. He just smiled to himself, like he was privy to some joke Conner didn't have the mental wherewithal to comprehend, and kept going.

The smug look on Brody's face pissed Conner off like few other things could have, but he wouldn't allow himself to be provoked. He just rode, tight-jawed, and so did Brody, both of them thinking their own thoughts.

About the only thing he and Brody agreed on, Conner reflected glumly, was that Steven, as much a Creed as either of them, should have had a third of the ranch and the considerable financial assets that came along with it. Steven had refused—hardheaded pride ran in the family, after all—and set up an outfit of his own outside Stone Creek.

He'd met and married Melissa O'Ballivan there, Steven had, and he seemed happy, so Conner figured things had worked out in the long run. Still, he could have used his cousin's company *and* his help on the ranch, since Brody was about three degrees past any damn use at all.

It might have been different if Steven had ever wanted for money, but his mother's people were well-fixed, high-priced Eastern lawyers, all of them. Steven, whom Brody invariably called "Boston," had grown up in a Back Bay mansion, with servants and a trust fund and all the rest of it. Summers, though, Steven had come west, to stay on the ranch, as his parents had agreed. And he'd been cowboy enough to win everybody's respect.

Even though he could have had an equal share of the Colorado holdings, which included the ranch itself, some ten thousand acres, a sizable herd of cattle, and a copper-mining fortune handed down through three generations, multiplying even during hard times, Steven had wanted two things: a family and to build an enterprise that was his alone.

And he was succeeding at both those objectives.

Conner, by comparison, was just walking in place, biding his time, watching life go right on past him without so much as a nod in his direction.

Brody had accused him of jealousy, back there at the barn, claiming that Conner had played the stay-at-home son to Brody's prodigal, and was resentful of his return. The implications burned their way through Conner's veins all over again, like a jolt of snake venom.

Conner had to give Brody this much: it was true enough that he'd gotten over Joleen with no trouble at all. What he *hadn't* gotten over, what he couldn't shake, no matter how he tried to reason with himself, was being betrayed by the person he'd been closest to, from conception on.

The idea that Brody, so much a part of him that they were like one person, the one he'd been so sure always had his back, would sell him out like that, with no particular concern about the consequences and no apology, either, well, *that* stuck in Conner's gut like a wad of thorns and nettles and rusted barbed wire. It chewed at him, on an unconscious level most of the time, but on occasion woke him out of a sound sleep, or sneaked up from behind and tapped him on the shoulder.

Brody's presence wasn't just a frustration to Conner— it was a bruise to the soul.

Reaching the herd, the brothers kept to opposite sides, helping the four ranch hands Conner and Davis employed year-round—there had been three times that many at roundup—drive nearly three hundred bawling, balking, rolling-eyed cattle across the ford in the river.

The work itself was bone-jarringly hard, not to mention dusty and hot, even though summer had passed. It took all morning to get it done, because cattle, which, unlike dogs and horses, are not particularly intelligent, can scatter in all directions like the down from a dandelion gone to seed. They get stuck in the mud and sometimes trample each other, and many a seasoned cowboy has fallen beneath their hooves, thrown from the saddle. Once in a while, the man's horse fared even worse, breaking a leg or being gored by a horn.

Brody proved to be as good a hand as ever, considering that he probably did most of his riding for show now that he was a big rodeo star, but what did that prove? Good horsemen weren't hard to come by in that part of the country—lots of people were practically born in the saddle.

Good brothers, though? Now, there was a rare commodity.

Once all the cattle were finally across the river, enjoying fresh acres of untrampled grass, their bawls of complaint settling down to a dull roar, Conner spoke briefly with the foreman of the crew and then reined his horse toward home. He wanted a shower, clothes he hadn't sweated through and a sandwich thick enough to cut with a chain saw. For all his lonesomeness, an emotion endemic to bachelor ranchers, he wanted some time alone, too, so he could sort through his thoughts at his own pace, make what sense he could of recent developments.

No such luck.

Brody caught up to him as he was crossing the river, their horses side by side, drops of water splashing up to soak the legs of their jeans.

It felt good to cool off, Conner thought. At least, on the outside. On the inside, he was still smoldering.

"That old house sure has seen a lot of livin'," Brody remarked, once they'd ridden up the opposite bank onto dry land, standing in his stirrups for a moment to stretch his legs. The ranch house, though still a good quarter of a mile away, was clearly visible, a two-story structure, white with dark green shutters and a wraparound porch, looked out of place on that land, venerable as it was. A saltbox, more at home in some seaside town in New England than in the high country of Colorado, it was genteel instead of rustic, as it might have been expected to be.

In the beginning, it had been nothing but a cabin—that part of the house was a storage room now, with the original log walls still in place—but as the years passed, a succession of Creed brides had persuaded their husbands to add on a kitchen here and a parlor there and more and more bedrooms right along, to accommodate the ever-increasing broods of children. Now, the place amounted to some seven thousand square feet, could sleep at least twelve people comfortably and was filled with antique furniture.

Conner, spending a lot of time there by himself, would have sworn it was haunted, that he heard, if not actual voices, the echoed *vibrations* of human conversation, or of children's laughter or, very rarely, the faint plucking of one of the strings on his great-great-grandmother Alice's gold-gilt harp.

Spacious and sturdily built, the roof solid and the walls strong enough to keep out blizzard winds in the winter, the house didn't feel right without a woman in it. Not that Conner would have said so out loud. Especially not to Brody.

"I guess the old place has seen some living, all right," he allowed, after letting Brody's comment hang unanswered for a good while.

"Don't you get lonely in that big old house, now that Kim and Davis are living in the new one?"

Conner didn't want to chat, so he gave an abrupt reply to let Brody know that. "No," he lied, urging his tired horse to walk a little faster.

"You remember how we used to scare the hell out of each other with stories about the ghosts of dead Creeds?" Brody asked, a musing grin visible in spite of the shadow cast over his face by the brim of his hat.

"I remember," Conner answered.

They were nearing the barn by then. It was considerably newer than the house, built by the grandfather they'd never known, after he came home from the Vietnam War, full of shrapnel and silence.

He'd died young, Davis and Blue's father, and their mother hadn't lasted long after his passing. Now and then, in an unguarded moment, Conner caught himself wondering if he'd stayed single because so many members of the family had gone on before their time.

"You ever smile anymore?" Brody asked casually, as they dismounted in front of the barn. "Or say more than one or two words at a time?"

"I was thinking, that's all," Conner said.

"All the way up to *five* words," Brody grinned. "I'm impressed, little brother. At this rate, you're apt to talk a leg right off somebody."

Conner led his horse inside, into a stall. There, he removed the gear and proceeded to rub the animal down with one of many old towels kept on hand for that purpose. "I don't run on just to hear my head rattle," he said, knowing Brody was in the stall across the aisle, tending to his own horse. "Unlike some people I could name."

Brody laughed at that, a scraped-raw sound that caused the horse he was tending to startle briefly and toss its head. "You need a woman," he proclaimed, as if a man could just order one online and have her delivered by UPS. "You're turning into one of those salty old loners who talk to themselves, paper the cabin walls with pages ripped from some catalog, grow out their beards for the mice to nest in and use the same calendar over and over, figuring it's never more than seven or eight days off."

A grin twitched at Conner's mouth at the images that came to mind—there were a few such hermits around Lonesome Bend—but he quelled it on general principle.

"That was colorful," he said, putting aside the towel and picking up a brush.

When Conner looked away from the horse he was grooming, he was a little startled to find Brody standing just on the other side of the stall door, watching him like he had a million things to say and couldn't figure out how to phrase one of them.

Sadness shifted against Conner's heart, but he was quick to dispense with that emotion, just as he had the grin.

"Sooner or later," Brody said, sounding not just solemn, but almost mournful, "we've got to talk about what happened."

"I vote 'later,'" Conner replied, looking away.

"I'm not going anywhere, little brother," Brody pressed quietly. "Not for any length of time, anyway. And that means you're going to have to deal with me."

"Here's an idea," Conner retorted briskly. "*You* stay here and manage the ranch for a decade, as I did, and *I'll* follow the rodeo circuit and bed down with a different woman every night."

Brody laughed, but it was a hoarse sound, a little raspy around the edges. "I hate to tell you this, cowboy, but you're too damn *old* for the rodeo. *That* stagecoach already pulled out, sorry to say."

The brothers were only thirty-three, but there was some truth in what Brody said. With the possible exceptions of team and calf roping, rodeo was a young man's game. A *very* young man's game, best given up, as Davis often said, before the bones got too brittle to mend after a spill.

Again, Conner felt that faint and familiar twinge of sorrow. He was careful not to glance in Brody's direction as he made a pretense of checking the automatic waterer in that stall. The devices often got clogged with bits of grass, hay or even manure, and making sure they were clear was second nature.

"What now, Brody?" he asked, when a few beats had passed.

"I told you," Brody answered, evidently in no hurry to move his carcass from in front of the stall door so Conner could get past him and go on into the house for that shower, the triple-decker sandwich and some beer. "I'm fixing to settle down right here on the ranch. Maybe build a house and a barn somewhere along the river one of these days."

"There's a big difference," Conner said, facing Brody at long last, over that stall door, "between what you say you're going to do and what you follow through on—*big brother*. So if it's all the same to you, I won't hold my breath while I'm waiting."

Brody finally stepped back so Conner could get by him, and they both fell into the old routine of doing the usual barn chores, feeding the horses, switching some of the animals to other stalls so the empty ones could be mucked out.

"I meant it, Conner," Brody said gruffly, and after a long time. "This place is home, and it's time for me to buckle down and make something of the rest of my life."

Surprised by the sincerity in his brother's voice, Conner, in the process of pushing a wheelbarrow full of horse manure out to the pile in back of the barn, a fact that would strike him as ironic in a few moments, stopped and looked at the other man with narrowed eyes.

Brody's gaze was clear, and he wasn't smirking.

Conner almost got suckered in.

But then he reminded himself that this was *Brody* he was dealing with, a man who'd rather climb a tall tree to tell a lie than stand flat-footed on the ground and tell the truth.

"Brody?" he said.

"What?" Brody asked, a wary note in his voice.

"Go to hell," Conner answered, wheeling away with the load of manure.

"YES!" SASHA CRIED, glowing and fairly jamming Tricia's cell phone under her nose as she searched the commercial real-estate listings on the internet in her kitchen, hoping to discover that places like River's Bend and the derelict drive-in theater were finally starting to sell again. "Mom and Dad landed in Paris without a problem, and they think it would be *wonderful* if you and I went horseback riding on the Creed ranch next Sunday!"

Discouraged—there *were* no properties like hers for sale online, it seemed—Tricia smiled nonetheless. Above their heads, a light rain began to patter softly against the roof, and twilight, it seemed to Tricia, was falling a little ahead of schedule. Valentino and Winston were curled up together on Valentino's dog bed over in the corner, like the best of friends, snoozing away.

"Yep," Tricia said, accepting the phone and reading the text message for herself. "That's what it says, all right." She felt resignation—she'd been hoping Diana would refuse to grant Sasha permission to ride strange horses—but there was also a little thrill of illicit anticipation at the prospect of spending time with Conner Creed.

Of course, it would have helped if she'd known the first thing about horses, and if the very thought of perching high off the rocky ground in some hard saddle didn't scare her half to death. Sasha, perceptive beyond her tender years, rested a hand on Tricia's arm and looked at her with knowing compassion. "You can *do* this, Aunt Tricia," she said earnestly. "And I'll be right there to take care of you, the whole time."

Tricia's heart turned over. The child was only ten, but she meant what she said—she'd do her best to keep Tricia safe. And that was way too much responsibility for one little girl to carry.

"I'll be just fine," Tricia assured Sasha, giving her a quick, one-armed hug.

Sasha's attention had shifted to the computer monitor. "How are things in the real-estate business?" she asked, again sounding much older than she was.

Tricia sighed. "Not terrific, I'm afraid," she replied.

"Dad says the economy is coming back, no thanks to the politicians," Sasha told her. "He says he's nonpartisan, but *Mom* says he doesn't trust *any* elected official."

Tricia smiled and pushed back her chair, being careful not to bump Sasha. Ten years old, and the kid was using words liked *nonpartisan*. There was no question that homeschooling worked in her case, but was she growing up too fast? Childhood was fleeting and, sure, knowledge was power and all that, but Tricia couldn't help considering the possible trade-offs.

None of your business, she reminded herself silently, and turned up the wattage on her smile a little as she touched Sasha's nose. "Let's walk Valentino once more and then start supper."

Sasha glanced at the window and gave a little shiver. "But it's starting to rain," she protested, not quite whining, but close.

"You're from Seattle," Tricia pointed out. "You won't melt in a little rain."

"But Valentino is *sleeping*," Sasha reasoned, widening her eyes. "Maybe we shouldn't disturb him. And if we go out, Winston will be all alone in the apartment."

Tricia crossed to the kitchen door, took her jacket off one of the pegs and held Sasha's out to her. "Winston," she said, "will find ways to amuse himself while we're gone." Valentino awakened, apparently sensing that there was a walk in the offing, and stretched luxuriously. He went to Tricia, waited patiently for her to fasten the leash to his collar.

Sasha resigned herself to the task ahead and pulled on her coat. Her mind was like quicksilver, and she immediately backtracked to the Seattle reference Tricia had made earlier. "You're from Seattle, too," she said. "Are you *ever* coming back?"

"Yes," Tricia answered, though there were times when she wondered if she'd ever get out of Lonesome Bend. It wasn't just the properties her dad had left her—she'd made a lot of friends in town and, besides, the thought of leaving Natty alone in that big house bothered her.

They stepped out onto the landing and found themselves in a misty drizzle and a crisp breeze. It wasn't quite dark, but the streetlights had already come on, and a car splashed by, the driver tooting the horn in jaunty greeting.

Busy descending the outside stairs, Tricia and Sasha both took a moment to wave in response.

"Who was that?" Sasha inquired, taking Valentino's leash from Tricia when they reached the bottom.

Tricia laughed. "I have no idea."

"When, though?" Sasha asked.

Tricia blinked. The child did not do segues. "Huh?"

"*When* are you moving back to Seattle?" Sasha sounded mildly impatient now, as they crossed the lawn to step onto the sidewalk.

"When I sell the campground and the drive-in theater," Tricia answered, putting herself between the little girl and the dog and the rain-washed street. "And, of course, I'll have to make sure my great-grandmother will be looked after."

"Oh," Sasha said, her expression serious as she weighed Tricia's reply. "Then are you going to marry Hunter?"

Tricia sighed. For all their "carrying on," as Natty referred to it, she and Hunter had never actually talked about marriage. "Do you want me to?" she asked, stalling.

To her surprise, Sasha made a face. "No. I just want you to live close to us again, so we can do things together, the way we used to."

Tricia didn't pursue her goddaughter's obvious distaste for Hunter, though she felt a slight sting of resentment toward Diana for passing her unfair antipathy toward him on to the child. "You're going to be living in Paris for a few years, remember? So we won't be seeing each other as often anyway."

Sasha looked up at her with big, worried eyes. "I miss you when we're not together, Aunt Tricia," she said. "You *are* coming to visit us in Paris, aren't you?

We could go to the top of the Eiffel Tower and visit the Louvre—"

"I'll do my best," Tricia promised quietly, hoping Sasha would cheer up a little. "France is a long way from here, though, and the airline ticket would cost a lot of money."

"I'll bet you could get a ticket with Dad's frequent-flier miles. He's got a million of them."

"We'll see," Tricia hedged, as they all stopped to wait for Valentino to sniff the base of a streetlight.

Sasha changed the subject again, this time to the horseback ride on the Creed ranch, scheduled for the following Sunday afternoon. She was practically skipping along the sidewalk, she was so excited.

Tricia listened and smiled, gently taking Valentino's leash from Sasha, but behind that smile, she was wishing for a gracious way to get out of the whole thing.

With Natty away, she really should help run the rummage sale and chili feed, and she'd already be super busy at the campground and RV park, with so many customers reserving spots. The biggest job—cleaning up—would come after everyone had gone home, but Murphy's Law would be in full operation throughout the weekend, too. Things invariably went wrong with this electrical hookup or that part of the antiquated plumbing. Such situations made for unhappy campers, and Tricia had to be on call to make sure the repairs were done promptly.

Where, she wondered now, had she thought she would get the *time* to go riding on the Creed ranch? And what if she got hurt?

Valentino made good use of his walk, and Tricia, carrying her trusty plastic bag, picked up after him.

Back at the apartment, Valentino and Winston greeted each other as joyfully as if they'd expected to be apart forever, touching their noses and then retiring to the dog bed again.

Tricia washed up and started supper—a simple meat loaf made from canned soup—and Sasha, having been granted permission, sat down in front of the computer and went online to check her email.

It seemed to Tricia that kids today came into the world already hard-wired for all forms of technology. When *she* was Sasha's age, she reflected, personal computers were just coming into common use, and things like digital cameras and MP3 players hadn't even been *invented* yet. She'd listened to CDs and watched movies on VHS and wondered how her parents, not to mention her great-grandmother, had gotten by with vinyl records and analog TV.

She was considering all this, and keeping one eye on Sasha and the display on the computer monitor, *plus* chopping vegetables for a salad to go with the already-baking meat loaf, when the wall phone jangled.

"Hello?"

"It's you, dear," Natty's quavery voice responded, with relief. Whom, Tricia wondered, had her great-grandmother *expected* to answer?

Natty promptly answered that unspoken question, as it happened. "I meant to call Conner Creed," she said. "I must have dialed your number out of habit. How are you, dear? How is Winston?"

Tricia barely registered the words that came after *I meant to call Conner Creed,* but she managed to get the gist of them. "Winston and I are both doing fine. How are you?"

Natty sighed. "I'm afraid I've developed a little hitch in my get-along," she said. Then, almost too quickly, she added, "Not that it's anything serious, of course. I planned to be back in Lonesome Bend before the weekend, so I could oversee the chilimaking, but it seems my heartbeat is a tiny bit irregular and the doctors don't want me traveling just yet."

Tricia was so alarmed that she forgot to ask why Natty wanted to call Conner. "Your heartbeat is irregular? I don't like the sound of that—"

"I'll be fine," Natty broke in, chirpy as a bird. "Don't you dare waste a moment worrying about me."

Tricia closed her eyes, opened them again. Forced a smile that she hoped would be audible in her voice. "I have a visitor," she said, and proceeded to tell her great-grandmother all about Sasha and the move to Paris. "Oh," honor compelled her to add, at the tail end of the conversation, "and I'm fostering a dog. I hope you don't mind. He's really very well behaved and Winston seems to like him a lot."

"I didn't object to Rusty," Natty said, sounding less shaky-voiced than before and thereby lifting Tricia's spirits, "and I certainly won't object to this one. You're alone too much. A dog is at least *some* company."

Sasha, eavesdropping shamelessly, frowned.

When Natty and Tricia finally said goodbye, Sasha planked herself in front of Tricia, hands on her hips. "You're just *fostering* Valentino?" Sasha demanded. "He doesn't get to stay with you?"

CHAPTER SEVEN

CONNER, WHO HAD TAKEN his sandwich and his can of beer out onto the porch so he could watch the rain fall while he ate—and, in the process, ignore Brody—fumbled for his ringing cell phone, juggled it and finally rasped a gruff "Hello?" into the speaker.

His favorite elderly lady announced herself in a perky tone. "Natty McCall here," she said brightly. "I *am* speaking to Conner, aren't I?"

He chuckled. "You are," he said. Seated in the wooden swing some ancestor had added, Conner shifted to set the beer and his sandwich plate aside on a small wicker table. "Are you back in town, Natty, or do we have to get by without you for a little while longer?"

"You always were a charmer," Natty said, all aflutter. "Alas, I've been detained in Denver for a little longer, and I have a favor to ask."

Conner smiled at her terminology—the word *detained* made it sound as if she'd been arrested. "Have you been carousing around the Mile High City again, Natty?" he teased. "Riding mechanical bulls in honky-tonks and the like?"

She tittered at that, well aware that he was joking, but probably a little bit flattered to be thought *capable* of walking on the wild side, too. "I do declare," she said, and he could actually hear a blush in her voice.

That was when the screen door creaked on its hinges, and out of the corner of his eye, he saw Brody step out onto the porch. "You know you're my best girl," he told her. "What's the favor?"

Natty was warming to her subject; there was a sense of revving up in the way she spoke—it reminded him of the toy cars and trucks he and Brody had as kids, the kind a kid winds up by rolling them fast and hard on the floor before letting them speed away. "Nothing big," she said. "I'd like you to check on my house now and then, that's all. Just to make sure everything's all right with—well—with the *plumbing* and things of that sort."

Conner raised his brows slightly, avoiding Brody's gaze, though he could see out of the corner of his eye that his brother was leaning idly against the porch rail, rain dripping from the eaves in a gray curtain behind him, his arms loosely folded. He wasn't even trying to pretend he wasn't listening in.

"The plumbing?" Conner echoed, searching his memory for any occasion when Natty had expressed concern about the pipes in her house, to him, anyway.

It crossed his mind that the old woman might be up to some matchmaking between him and Tricia, but he quickly dismissed the thought as unworthy of Natty.

"Pipes can freeze, you know," Natty fretted, her voice still picking up speed. "And I would hate to come home and find that there had been a flood in my kitchen or something like that. Those floors are original to the house, and it would be a pity if they were ruined, being irreplaceable and all—"

"Natty," Conner interrupted gently.

She paused, drew an audible breath and let it out again. "What?"

"I'll be happy to check on the plumbing at your place," he said.

Brody grinned at that. Shook his head slightly, as if he was at once bemused and disgusted.

"It's mainly the pipes under the house that I'm concerned about," Natty went on. "I couldn't ask Tricia to crawl around under the house. There might be spiders."

"I'm on it," Conner reiterated, "but I do have one question." He'd never known Natty to miss the annual rummage sale/chili feed. She was, after all, the Keeper of the Secret Recipe. "Are you all right?"

"I'm fine," Natty said briskly.

He suspected that she was fibbing, but challenging an old lady's statement hadn't been part of his upbringing. Elders, be they friends, like Natty, acquaintances or total strangers, were to be treated with respect—particularly if they happened to be female.

"You're sure?" he ventured just the same, slanting a glare at Brody then. *Go away.*

Brody, being Brody, didn't budge an inch. He just broadened his grin by a notch.

"I'm *absolutely* sure, Conner," Natty replied. Then she gave a trilling little laugh that sounded almost bell-like. Years fell away, and Conner could easily picture her as a young woman, and a pretty one, not unlike her great-granddaughter. "I'm perfectly fine. Fit as a fiddle."

"It's just that the rummage sale is coming up," Conner pressed, still concerned.

Brody frowned comically at this.

"I've stepped down from chairing the committee," Natty told him. "I am getting on a little, you know."

She'd been ninety-one on her last birthday, Conner knew, though he'd missed the party because he was down in Stone Creek at the time, helping Steven paint the nursery before the twins were delivered.

"You're younger than springtime," Conner said, recalling the line from one of the old songs Natty liked to play on her stereo.

"And you're full of beans," Natty shot back, always ready with another cliché. She was getting tired, though; he could hear that in her voice.

The chat ended soon after that and, for all Natty's insistence that she was "just fine," Conner was still worried. He sat there frowning for a few moments, then decided he'd head for Natty's house as soon as the chores were done the next morning. Take along some insulation and some duct tape to wrap around the pipes under the house.

Tricia probably wouldn't be around, of course. She'd be over at the campground, working, or maybe at the drive-in theater—a spooky place, closed down long before the multiplex movie houses in Denver came along—doing whatever might need doing.

He'd track her down, ask her if she'd spoken to Natty recently.

Brody, still lounging against the porch railing, shifted his weight from one side to the other, distracting Conner from his thoughts. "For a minute there," Brody said, in a low drawl, "I had high hopes that you were lining up a hot date."

Conner realized that he was still holding his phone and dropped it back into the pocket of the clean but worn flannel shirt he'd put on, along with a pair of jeans, after his shower. Then he reached for his beer and took a long draw of the stuff before answering, "There are other things in life besides getting laid, you know." The statement sounded prissy-assed even to him, and Conner immediately wished he could take it back.

"Like what?" Brody joked.

Conner didn't reply, but simply sat there, holding his beer and wishing Brody would go away. To another state, say. If not another planet.

"Once upon a time," Brody said easily, determined to push, "you had a sense of humor."

"I still do," Conner said, staring past Brody, into the gray drizzle. "When something's funny, I laugh."

Brody heaved a sigh. Pushed away from the porch rail, finally, to stand up straight. His arms fell to his sides. "It's hard to imagine that," he said, very quietly, and then he went back inside the house. The screen door shut behind him with barely a sound.

And Conner felt guilty. How crazy was that? If Brody had expected to just pick up where they'd left off— before their knock-down-drag-out over Joleen—he'd been kidding himself. Conner swore under his breath and used the heels of his boots to thrust the ancient porch swing into slow, squeaky motion.

Brody wouldn't stay long, he thought, trying to console himself. His brother was bound to get bored with Lonesome Bend and the ranch, sooner rather than later, and hit the road again, following the rodeo. Or some woman.

The rain picked up, and the wind blew it in under the roof of the porch, and Conner finally had to give up and go inside. He climbed the front staircase, noticing that the crystal chandelier was dusty, and headed for the master bedroom. The suite had belonged to Kim and Davis before they moved into the new house, and it didn't lack for comfort. There was a big-screen TV on one wall, and the private bath was the size of an NFL locker room, with slate-tile floors, a big shower with multiple sprayers and a tub made for soaking the ache out of sore muscles.

While all that space might have made sense for his aunt and uncle, it felt cavernous to Conner. He probably would have moved back into the room at the other end of the corridor—the one he'd shared with Brody and, in the summertime, Steven, too, when they were all growing up—but he knew Brody had stowed his gear in there.

Conner switched on the TV, then switched it off again, in the next moment. In his opinion, TV sucked, for the most part. He did enjoy watching athletic women in bikinis "surviving" in some hostile environment, but that was about all.

He hauled his shirt off over his head, to save himself the trouble of unbuttoning it, and tossed the garment to one side. Then he sat down on the edge of the bed, which was way too big for one person, and got out of his boots and socks. Standing up again, he dispensed with his jeans, too, and stood there, in the altogether, thinking Brody wasn't so far wrong, implying that he didn't have a life.

In the end, he tossed back the covers, crawled between them and reached for the thick biography of Thomas Jefferson sitting on the nightstand. He sighed. Another night with nobody but a dead president for company.

Yee-freakin'-haw.

TRICIA OPENED ONE EYE—how could it possibly be morning already?—and slowly tuned in to her surroundings, glimmer by glimmer, sound by sound, scent by scent.

The sun was shining. Rain dripped from the eaves, but no longer pelted the roof. The timer on the coffeepot beeped, and the tantalizing aroma of fresh brew teased her nose.

Valentino approached, laid his muzzle on her pillow, inches from her face, and whined almost inaudibly.

Something, somewhere, was clanging.

Tricia sat up, glanced at her alarm clock, which she'd forgotten to set the night before, and sucked in a breath. She'd overslept. And that wasn't like her at all.

Clang, clang, clang.

Since she was wearing a sweatsuit, and she figured that was the next best thing to being fully dressed, Tricia didn't bother with a robe. Nor did she pause to put on the ugly pink slippers. Sasha, still clad in pink pajamas, joined her in the kitchen.

The child's eyes were big. "What *is* that?" she asked, nearly in a whisper.

"I'll find out," Tricia said, annoyed but not alarmed. She went to the sink and, wadding up a dish towel, wiped a circle into the steam covering the window so she could peer out at the backyard.

The driveway was empty.

"Is something going to blow up?" Sasha fretted, probably imagining an antiquated furnace, or even a steam boiler with a pressure gauge, chugging cartoonishly away in Natty's basement, building up to a roof-raising blast.

"No, sweetie," Tricia said, offering what she hoped

was a reassuring smile. "I'm sure nothing is going to explode. This is an old house, and sometimes the pipes make odd noises. So do the floorboards."

"Oh," Sasha said, clearly unconvinced.

Valentino, meanwhile, was standing very close to Sasha, actually leaning into her side. Clearly, he was no guard dog.

"Wait here, while I go downstairs and have a look around," Tricia told them both.

Sasha swallowed visibly, looking small and vulnerable, and then nodded.

The clanging resumed, intermittent and muffled.

Tricia descended the inside stairway and followed the sound through Natty's chilly rooms to the kitchen.

Silence.

Then the clang came again, this time from directly under her feet.

Tricia started slightly, then after gathering her resolve, marched over to Natty's basement door. She barely registered the rapid rush of footsteps on the wooden stairs beyond—she hadn't had coffee yet—and she'd turned the knob and pulled before it occurred to her that the idea might not have been a good one.

A squeak scratched its way up her windpipe and past her vocal cords when she found herself staring directly into Conner Creed's smiling face. Because he was still on the basement stairs, they were at eye level.

And that alone was disconcerting.

"Sorry," he said, clearly delighted by her expression. "I didn't mean to scare you."

"What are you doing here?" The squeak had turned to a squawk, but at least she could speak coherently now.

Tricia's heart seemed to be trying to crash through her rib cage.

Conner held up a roll of gray duct tape in one hand and a wrench—no doubt the source of the clanging sounds—in the other. "Plumbing?" he asked, as though he wasn't entirely sure what he'd been doing and wanted Tricia to affirm it for him.

She folded her arms, foolishly barring his way into the kitchen. "You could have knocked," she said.

Conner lifted one shoulder, lowered it again. His grin didn't falter. "Natty called me last night and asked me to wrap the pipes. I crawled around under the house with a flashlight for a while, making sure there weren't any obvious leaks, and then I checked the situation in the basement." He paused, ran his eyes lightly over Tricia's rumpled hair, coming loose from its braid, before letting his gaze rest on her lips for one tingly moment. "The padlock on the cellar door probably rusted through years ago. I didn't need the key Natty told me about."

At last, Tricia found the presence of mind to back up so Conner could step into the kitchen. Now he stood a head taller.

"I'll be happy to replace it," he added. His eyes narrowed a little as he watched her, as if he'd suddenly noticed something new and disturbing about her.

"Replace what?" she asked.

The grin returned, faintly insolent and, at the same time, affable. Even friendly.

"The padlock?" he prompted, in the same guessing-game tone he'd used moments before.

It was the most ordinary conversation—about padlocks and plumbing, for Pete's sake. So why did she feel like a shy debutante about to step onto the dance floor at her coming-out ball?

"Oh," she finally managed. "Right. The padlock."

Natty's kitchen was frigidly cold, and yet, because they were standing within a few feet of each other, the hard heat coming off Conner's body made Tricia feel as though she were standing in front of a blazing bonfire.

Or was *she* the source of it?

Conner set the duct tape and the wrench aside on a countertop, rested his hands on his hips. "Will you be joining us for the trail ride on Sunday?" he asked.

Not for the first time, Tricia had a strange sense of needing to translate the things this man said from some other language before she could grasp their meaning. "I—guess," she said, recalling in the next instant that she'd promised Sasha the outing, and backing out wasn't an option.

"But—?" he asked, watching her.

She finally rustled up a smile, but it felt flimsy on her mouth and wouldn't stick. "It's just that I've never been on a horse before," she admitted.

His eyes lit at that, blue fire framed by a narrow rim of steely gray, and his mouth crooked up in that way Tricia couldn't seem to get used to. "No problem," he told her, his tone faintly gruff.

No problem.

Easy enough for *him* to say, she thought, just as Valentino and Sasha clomped down the stairs from her apartment. Conner Creed had probably been born in the saddle, growing up on a ranch the way he had. She, on the other hand, had never ridden anything more dangerous than a carousel.

"We'll put you on one of the mares," Conner went on, when she didn't speak. "Sunflower would be a good choice—she's three years older than dirt and you'd be more likely to get hurt riding a stick horse."

Tricia was relieved and, at the same time, a little indignant. Before she could come up with a fitting response, however, Sasha and Valentino made their appearance.

Seeing Conner, Sasha beamed. "Hello, Mr. Creed," she said.

He nodded to the child, smiled back. "It's okay to call me Conner," he told her.

Pleased, Sasha barely glanced at Tricia, stroking Valentino's head as the two of them stood just inside the kitchen doorway. "I'm Sasha," she announced.

"I remember," Conner said easily. "My nephew, Matt, introduced us at the barbecue last weekend, didn't he?"

Sasha nodded eagerly. "He's pretty nice, for a little kid," she said.

Conner chuckled and looked briefly in Tricia's direction—just in time to catch her sneaking a step back. She felt magnetized, like a passing asteroid being pulled into the orbit of some enormous planet.

He smiled, dashing all hope that he hadn't noticed.

Tricia's cheeks flamed. She'd worked hard, ever since high school, to overcome her natural shyness, but when it came to this man, all that effort seemed to be for nothing. A look from him, a word, and every cell in her body suddenly leaped to electrified attention.

It was ridiculous.

"Do you think Natty's all right?" he asked, his expression serious now. His face could change in an instant, it seemed, and that made him hard to read.

Tricia didn't like it when people were hard to read.

"Why do you ask?" she inquired, a little jolt of alarm trembling in the pit of her stomach.

Conner wasn't wearing a hat, being indoors, though she could tell that he'd had one on earlier. He ran the fingers of his left hand through his hair, watched with a smile in his eyes as Sasha excused herself and left the room, Valentino trotting alongside.

"I guess it bothers me a little that she's staying on in Denver," Conner sighed, when he and Tricia were alone in the big kitchen again. "It's not like your great-grandmother to miss out on the big weekend, even if she has stepped down as head chili commando."

Though quiet, his tone was so genuine that it touched something deep and private inside Tricia, stirred a soft but still-bruising sweetness where he shouldn't have been able to reach. They were basically strangers, she and Conner—they certainly hadn't been more than summer acquaintances growing up—and yet it was as if they'd known each other well, once upon a time and somewhere far, far away.

When she thought she could trust herself to speak, Tricia found another smile, and managed to hold on to it a little longer this time. In truth, she was worried, too. Should she mention that Natty was staying in Denver at the suggestion of her doctor?

No, she decided, in the next second. If Natty had wanted Conner to know why she'd postponed her return to Lonesome Bend, she would have told him herself.

"I'm sure she's fine," she said at last, though of course

she wasn't sure at all. Natty *had* said her heart had been racing.

Conner studied her for a few moments, looking like he wanted to say something but wouldn't, and then he flashed that dazzling grin at her again. It was like stepping into the glare of a searchlight on a moonless night, and Tricia blinked once.

"You might want to keep it a little warmer in here," he said, in another of those hairpin conversational turns of his. "Even wrapped, some of the pipes might freeze if you don't turn on the heat."

Tricia nodded, feeling stupid because no response came to mind.

Conner grinned, gave his head an almost imperceptible shake. "Sorry if I scared you a little while ago, banging on the plumbing with my wrench. I got here a little earlier than I expected and, though it seems ironic now, I was pretty sure you'd already gone out."

Again she felt that sugary sting, inexplicably pleasant, but highly discomforting, too. "Natty asked you to come over," she said, with a verbal shrug, "and I'm sure she appreciates your help."

His grin was rueful now, but it tugged at her, nonetheless. "I'd do just about anything for Natty," he said, moving to retrieve the duct tape and the wrench from the nearby counter and then stopping to look back over one shoulder. "Turn up the heat," he added.

Tricia almost said, "I beg your pardon?" but she stopped herself in time. Nodded again.

"Sixty-eight degrees ought to do it," Conner said. He took another long, slow look at her. "See you around," he told her, heading for the back door.

See you around.

That was all he'd said. And it was a perfectly normal remark, too.

Just the same, Tricia stood as still as if her feet were glued to the floor until several seconds after he'd closed the door behind him.

The first thing she did, once she could move again, was turn the lock. The second was to find and adjust the downstairs thermostat.

Now, she thought, making the climb back up to her own space, if she could just turn down the heat inside *herself.*

Upstairs, she found Sasha eating cold cereal at the table, while Winston and Valentino enjoyed their separate bowls of dry food.

After pouring a cup of much-needed coffee, Tricia booted up her computer. The screen saver loomed up automatically, filling the monitor and taking Tricia a little aback, even though she'd seen that picture of herself and Hunter, in front of the ski lodge, at least a jillion times.

"Mom says you can do a lot better than Hunter," Sasha remarked casually, no doubt prompted by the photograph.

A little of Tricia's coffee splashed over the rim of her cup and burned her fingers, but beyond that, she showed no outward reaction. "Does she, now?" she asked, amused but mildly resentful toward Diana, too. Surely her very best friend in the world hadn't meant to make such an observation within her daughter's earshot.

"That's what she told my dad," Sasha said, and resumed her cereal crunching.

Tricia kept her back to the little girl, focusing on the

computer's keyboard instead, going online and clicking on the mailbox icon at the top of the screen.

Normally, she would have felt a little thrill to find no less than three messages from Hunter in among the usual sales pitches for miracle vitamins, quick riches and sexual-enhancement products. This morning, in the wake of another encounter with Conner Creed, all Tricia could work up was a dull sense of futility. Seattle seemed very far away, and so did Hunter.

Sasha, apparently, was determined to keep the verbal ball rolling. "I think Conner is *really* handsome," she observed.

"Hmm," Tricia responded noncommittally, without turning around. She'd opened the first of Hunter's emails.

Hi, babe, he'd written.

Much to her own surprise, Tricia bristled a little. *Babe?* Mexican cruise or not, where did Hunter get off calling her *babe?* After all, the man virtually ignored her for weeks—if not *months*—at a time. Wasn't that term a touch on the intimate side, considering how they'd drifted apart?

Tricia felt a twinge then; when her conscience spoke, it was usually in Diana's voice. *You* did *accept the invitation, Miss Hot-to-trot,* came the brisk and typically no-nonsense reminder. *Did you think Hunter was suggesting a platonic getaway?*

Tricia's spine straightened. Why—oh, *why*—had she blithely side-stepped what should have been obvious to anyone?—*that she and Hunter would be sharing a cabin on the ship. And that meant sex.*

"Oh, Lord," she said aloud.

"Huh?" Sasha asked, from the table.

"Never mind," Tricia said, focusing in on the rest of Hunter's email.

It amounted to online foreplay, essentially, and she closed it with a self-conscious click of the mouse. Then she deleted it entirely. And felt even more foolish than before.

In that moment, she would have given just about anything to exchange some girl talk with Diana, despite the sure and certain knowledge that her best friend would tell her to kick Hunter to the curb and get on with her life.

With her friend in another time zone, though, and Sasha right there in the same room, a chat simply wasn't feasible.

"Don't you have to work today?" Sasha asked. Tricia hadn't heard her push back her chair to rise, but the little girl was standing at her elbow now, studying her thoughtfully.

Tricia couldn't find a smile. Maybe, she thought, with rueful whimsy, she could pick one up at the rummage sale.

"There isn't much to do, with the camping season coming to an end," she said. "We're all ready for the weekend, so I thought we'd go over to the community center and help set up for the rummage sale."

Sasha, who had probably never rummaged for anything in her admittedly short life, lit up at the prospect. "Awesome!" she enthused. "Can Valentino come, too?"

"I don't think he'd enjoy that," Tricia answered diplomatically. "What do you say we get ourselves dressed and take a certain dog out for a quick walk?"

CHAPTER EIGHT

BRODY WAS DEFINITELY up to something, though damned if Conner could figure out what it was. He'd helped himself to a pair of Conner's own jeans, Brody had, and one of his best shirts, too, and he'd shaved for the first time since his return to Lonesome Bend. If his hair hadn't been longer than Conner's, and way shaggier, they'd have been mirror images of each other.

And if all that wasn't bothersome enough, Brody not only had the coffee on by the time Conner wandered into the kitchen, after making the run into town to check on Natty McCall's pipes, he was cooking up some bacon and eggs at the old wood-burning stove.

Conner meandered over to the counter, took the carafe from its burner and poured himself a dose of java. He'd been thinking about Tricia ever since he'd scared the hell out of her at the top of Natty's basement steps that morning, and irritation with his brother provided some relief.

"Mornin'," Brody sang out, as if he were just noticing Conner's presence.

Conner squinted, studying his brother suspiciously. He'd gotten used to living his life as a separate individual since Brody left home, and it was a jolt to look up and see *himself* standing on the other side of the room.

Gave him a familiar but still weird sense of being in two places at once.

"Since when do you cook?" he asked, after shaking off the sensation and taking a sip from his mug. Only then did he take off his coat and hang it from its peg by the back door.

Brody laughed at that. "I picked up the habit after I left home," he replied easily. "Believe it or not, I find myself between women now and then."

Conner rolled his eyes. "So then you just knock some hapless female over the head with a club and drag her back to your cave by the hair? Tell her to put a pot of beans on the fire?"

Brody slanted a look at him, and there was a certain sadness in his expression, Conner thought, unsettled. "I didn't mean it like that," Brody said, his voice quiet.

"Right," Conner said, his voice gone gruff, all of a sudden, with an emotion he couldn't name. He looked his brother up and down. "So what's up with the clothes?"

Again, the grin flashed, quick and cocky. Brody speared a slice of bacon with a fork and turned it over in the skillet before looking down at Conner's duds. "All my stuff is in the laundry," he said. "Hope you don't mind."

Conner scowled and swung a leg over the long bench lining one side of the kitchen table, taking more coffee on board and trying to figure out what the hell was going on.

"Would you give a damn if I *did* mind?"

Brody didn't say anything; he just went right on rustling up grub at the stove, though he did pause once to refill his own coffee cup, whistling low through his teeth as he concentrated on the task at hand. That tuneless drone had always bugged Conner, but now it *really* got on his last nerve.

"If you insist on staying," he told Brody's back, "why don't you bunk in over at Kim and Davis's place?"

Brody took his sweet time answering, scraping eggs onto a waiting platter and piling about a dozen strips of limp bacon into a crooked heap on top.

"I might have done just that," Brody finally replied, crossing to set the platter down on the table with a thump before going back to the cupboard for plates and flatware, "except that they've already got a housesitter, and she happens not to be one of my biggest fans."

Conner stifled an unexpected chuckle, made his face steely when Brody headed back toward the table and took one of the chairs opposite. They ate in silence for a while.

Kim *had* mentioned hiring somebody to stay in their house while she and Davis were on the road, Conner recalled. Most likely, it was Carolyn Simmons; she was always housesitting for one person or another.

"Carolyn," Conner said, out loud.

Across the table, Brody looked up from his food and grinned. "What about her?"

Conner felt his neck heat up a little, realizing that there had been a considerable gap between Brody's remark and his response. "I was just wondering how you managed to make her hate you already," he said, somewhat defensively, stabbing at the last bite of his fried eggs with his fork.

"I didn't say Carolyn hated me," Brody explained, the grin lingering in his eyes, though there was no vestige of it on his mouth. "I said she isn't one of my biggest fans."

He paused, finished off a slice of bacon, and finally went on. "We have a—history, Carolyn and I."

To Conner's knowledge, Brody hadn't been anywhere near Lonesome Bend in better than a decade, and Carolyn hadn't moved to town until a few years ago. Which begged the question, "What kind of history?"

Brody sighed deeply, crossed his fork and knife in the middle of his plate and propped his elbows on the table's edge, his expression thoughtful. Maybe even a little grim. His gaze was fixed on something in the next county.

"The usual kind," he said, at some length.

"How do you know her?"

Why, Conner wondered, did he want to know? He liked Carolyn, but things had never gone beyond that, attraction-wise.

Brody met his eyes with a directness that took Conner by surprise. "It's a small world," he said. After a beat, he added, "You interested in her? Carolyn, I mean?"

Conner made a snortlike sound, pushed his own plate away. "No," he said.

"Then why all the questions?"

"What questions?"

"'What kind of history?'" Brody repeated, with exaggerated patience. "'How do you know her?' *Those* questions."

"Maybe I was just trying to make conversation," Conner hedged. "Did you ever think of that?"

"Like hell you were," Brody scoffed, with a false chuckle. "You can't wait to see the back of me and we both know it. But here's the problem, little brother—I'm not going anywhere."

Something tightened in Conner's throat. He might have said he was sorry to hear that Brody was staying, but he couldn't get the words out.

Brody shoved back his chair and stood, picking up his empty plate to put it in the sink, the way Kim had trained all three of "her boys" to do after a meal, from the time they could reach that high. "I could tell you a few things, Conner," he said hoarsely, "if I thought there was a snowball's chance in hell that you'd listen."

With that, Brody turned and walked away.

He set his plate in the sink and banked the fire in the cookstove and slammed out the back door—after shrugging into Conner's flannel-lined denim jacket.

FOLKS WERE LINED UP all the way to the corner that next Saturday morning when Tricia and Sasha drove past the community center and circled around back to park in one of a half-dozen spots reserved for volunteers. They'd already stopped by River's Bend, where every camping spot and RV hookup was in profitable use by the annual influx of visitors, just to make sure everything was in order.

Although they'd spent much of the previous day helping to set up for the big sale, and were therefore in the much-envied position of having seen the plethora of merchandise ahead of time, Sasha was impressed by the size of the crowd.

"There must be a lot of hoarders in this town," she said. "Why do they want to buy the stuff other people gave away?"

Tricia chuckled, then squeezed the Pathfinder into

the last parking space and checked her watch. "It must be the thrill of the hunt," she answered. "Or it could be the chili. Natty's been offered a small fortune for the recipe."

Sasha considered the reply, still fastened into her booster seat, then observed, "It was funny, how you made all those other ladies turn their backs while you put in the secret ingredients."

After consulting Natty by telephone the day before, Tricia had run the family chili recipe to ground and memorized the unique combination of spices some ancestor had dreamed up. She had indeed insisted that all present look away while she extracted various metal boxes and sprinkle jars from a plain paper bag and added them to the massive kettles of beans already simmering on the burners of the community center's commercial-size stove.

Her great-grandmother's cronies, tight-lipped at all the "folderol" involved in keeping the formula a secret, had agreed only because the event just wouldn't be the same without Natty's chili. Indeed, Minerva Snyder had allowed, there might even be a riot if they failed to deliver.

Chuckling at the memory, Tricia got out of the rig and went to help Sasha release the snaps and buckles holding her in the booster seat.

Sasha's eyes twinkled with excitement. She'd sneaked a peek at the mysterious items while Tricia was doctoring the chili the day before and, given the child's IQ, Tricia had no doubt that she could have recited the recipe from memory. "Remember," Tricia said, putting a finger to her lips, "Natty doesn't want anybody to know what's in that chili."

After jumping to the ground, Sasha nodded importantly. "Well, there are beans and some hamburger. Everybody knows that part."

"Yes," Tricia agreed, going around behind the Pathfinder to raise the hatch. "Everybody knows that part." They'd left Valentino at home, contentedly sharing his dog bed with Winston while they both snoozed, but Tricia, feeling inspired, had scrounged up a few more donations the night before, including the pink furry slippers Diana had given her, tossing them into a cardboard box with some other stuff. She'd put the slippers at the bottom, hoping Sasha wouldn't spot them and report the incident to her mother the next time they talked or texted.

Just as Tricia turned around, having hoisted the somewhat unwieldy box into both arms, juggling it awkwardly while she shut the hatch again, Conner Creed walked up to her. Her breath caught, and the box wobbled in her arms.

Conner took it from her just before she would have spilled its contents into the dusty gravel of the parking lot.

How did he manage to startle her the way he did? Tricia wondered, bedazzled, as always, by his ready grin. It was an unfair advantage, that grin.

"Hello," she said stupidly.

"Howdy," he replied, holding the cumbersome box easily in his two muscular arms. He looked down at Sasha and winked. "Hey," he greeted the enthralled little girl. "Are we still on for the trail ride tomorrow afternoon?"

Sasha nodded eagerly and then blurted out a happy "Yes!" for good measure.

"Good," Conner said, heading toward the back door of the community center, which was propped open with a big chunk of wood that had probably served as somebody's chopping block, sometime way back. People in Lonesome Bend liked to put things to use, no matter how ordinary.

Tricia locked the Pathfinder with the button on her key fob and followed Conner and Sasha, who was practically skipping alongside the man, toward the rear entrance.

"More stuff?" one of the women in the kitchen chimed. Several volunteers had stayed through the night, keeping an eye on the simmering pots of chili. "That Kim. She always donates twice as much rummage as anybody else in town!"

Conner, his back still turned to Tricia, chuckled at that. "True," he said. "But Tricia brought these things."

Tricia peeked around him, waggled her fingers in greeting. Some of Natty's friends, like a flock of old hens, still had ruffled feathers from yesterday's intrigue involving the spices for the chili.

One or two straightened their apron strings, and another harrumphed, but these were small-town women, basically sociable, and they wouldn't hold a grudge—not against Natty McCall's great-granddaughter, anyway.

Conner seemed to know where to set the box down— there were plenty of last-minute donations, it appeared, even though the door was about to open to the anxious public.

"Thanks," Tricia said, as Conner passed her, doubling back toward the kitchen.

"You're welcome," he told her, with a nod of farewell.

She hadn't really expected Conner to hang around the rummage sale all day—it was a rare man who did—but Tricia felt oddly bereft when he'd left, and when Sasha tugged at her hand to get her attention, she realized she'd been staring after the man like some moonstruck teenager.

Carolyn Simmons turned up just then, greeting Tricia with a smile and a gesture toward the front of the building, where the waiting customers were already pressing their faces to the windows, ogling the chicken-shaped egg timer, the row of ratty prom dresses, the chipped teapots, and the dusty books and the jumbles of old shoes piled on the table marked, "Everything 50 Cents!"

"Looks like we're in for another big year!" Carolyn said. Her attractively highlighted blond hair was pulled up into a ponytail and, like Tricia, she wore jeans, a long-sleeved T-shirt and sneakers.

"Looks that way," Tricia agreed, while Sasha sat down on the lid of a donated cedar chest, which had been découpaged at some point in the distant past with what looked like pages torn from vintage movie magazines, and folded her hands to wait for the onslaught.

The whole thing probably seemed pretty exotic to a little girl raised in Seattle, Tricia thought, with that familiar rush of tenderness. What a gift it was, this visit from Sasha, and how quickly it would be over.

Evelyn Moore, one of the women from the kitchen, bustled to the foreground, holding a stopwatch in her plump hand, and a great production was made of the countdown.

"Three—two—one—"

New Year's Eve in Times Square had nothing on Lonesome Bend, Colorado, Tricia thought, amused, when it came to ratcheting up the suspense.

At precisely nine o'clock, Evelyn turned the lock and took some quick steps backwards, in order to avoid being trampled by eager shoppers.

The next hour, naturally, was hectic indeed—at one point, when two women wanted the same wafflemaker and seemed about to come to blows, Tricia and Carolyn had to intervene.

"It probably doesn't even work anymore" Sasha observed, with a nod at the small appliance. She'd been helping to bag people's purchases, and when Tricia's pink slippers went for a nickel, she hadn't so much as batted an eye. "And, besides, the cord is frayed."

"The hunter/gatherer phenomenon," Carolyn explained, though she looked as mystified as Sasha did.

Tricia gave one of Sasha's pigtails a gentle tug. "Let me know when you're ready to try the chili," she said.

"We just had *breakfast,*" Sasha reminded her, casually horrified.

Tricia laughed and then there was a rush on the prom dresses and they both went back to work.

"Look," Sasha said, when the rush had subsided a little, sometime later, "Conner's back." Her forehead creased into a frown. "Who is that woman with him?"

Tricia, feeling that annoying tension Conner Creed always aroused in her, turned to see a couple just coming through the main door. She blinked. The tension ebbed away.

The man smiling down at the beautiful red-haired woman, his hand pressed solicitously to the small of her back, *wasn't* Conner. It was Brody.

Tricia couldn't have said how she knew that, because the resemblance was stunning; Brody was a perfect reflection of Conner, right down to his clothes and a very recent haircut.

Back in the day, the Creed brothers had been infamous for impersonating each other and, not knowing them well, Tricia had been fooled, like almost everyone else.

Now, he approached her, the lovely Joleen Williams trailing behind him, bestowing her breathtaking smile on all and sundry. "Tricia," he said, with a little nod.

Her hand tightening slightly on Sasha's shoulder, to keep the child from blurting out something *Tricia* would regret, she replied, "Hello, Brody." She looked past him, nodded. "Hi, Joleen. It's been a long time."

"Yes," Joleen said thoughtfully, sizing Tricia up with a slow sweep of her emerald-green eyes. "So long that I can't remember, for the life of me, who you are."

"Tricia McCall," Tricia offered, amused. Of course, being one of the most popular girls in town, Joleen wouldn't remember her, the summer visitor who rarely said more than two words running.

Brody gave Joleen a mildly exasperated glance.

"You're Conner's *twin*," Sasha said, with the air of one having a revelation. "You were at the barbecue by the river."

"Yep," Brody said.

"You didn't look so much like him then," Sasha went on, nonplussed. "Your hair was longer and your clothes were different. Now, you look *exactly* like Conner. I thought you *were* Conner."

"Sasha," Tricia said, squeezing again.

Joleen, evidently bored, wandered off.

"How are people supposed to tell you apart?" Sasha demanded, as though confronting an imposter.

Brody chuckled. "I'm the good-looking one," he said.

Sasha wasn't amused, though Tricia, knowing her well, saw that she was softening a little.

"Most kids like me," Brody said, with a twinkle in his eyes, as his gaze connected with Tricia's again. "But I seem to be zero-for-zero with this one."

Sasha, Tricia noticed, was watching Joleen. "Is she your girlfriend?"

"Sasha!" Tricia said.

But Brody didn't seem to be bothered by the question. He crouched, so he could look directly into Sasha's face. "Nope," he said seriously. "Is that a good thing or a bad one?"

"Depends," Sasha answered, sliding another glance in Joleen's direction and neatly slipping out of shoulder-squeezing distance from Tricia. "Does Conner like her?"

Tricia's mouth fell open.

Brody chuckled, shook his head. "I don't think so," he said. As he straightened up again, he was looking at Tricia's overheated face. Something shifted in his eyes, with a distinct but soundless click. "Guess I'd better get in line if I want any of that famous chili," he finished, before walking away.

Tricia looked around for Sasha, found her behind the book table, looking very busy as she restacked the volumes into tidy piles. If Carolyn hadn't been standing right next to Sasha, Tricia probably wouldn't have noticed the way the other woman followed Brody's progress through the crowd.

She recalled something Carolyn had said the week before, when they were cleaning up after the barbecue at River's Bend. *What a fool I was, way back when.*

As though she'd felt Tricia watching her, Carolyn swung her gaze away from Brody and back to her friend's face. She made a funny little grimace and shrugged.

Tricia's curiosity was piqued, but she was a great believer in her late father's folksy philosophy: everybody's business was *nobody's* business. She didn't know Carolyn well enough to grill her about her fascination with Brody, though a part of her wished she did. Because then she would have had someone to confide in about *Conner.*

It was all so confusing, and Diana was so far away.

You, Tricia McCall, she thought glumly, *are flirting with slut-dom. You're going on a romantic cruise with one man, and getting all hot and bothered over another. Not becoming. Not becoming at all.*

Fortunately, there was a new run on the community center when the chili was finally served, and Tricia was so busy helping to ring up the sales—if making change from a cigar box could be called "ringing up"—that she didn't have a chance to think about Brody *or* Conner again until early afternoon.

There was a lull, so she and Sasha grabbed the opportunity to go home, take Valentino out for a walk and measure more of the top-secret spices into plastic bags, to be added to tomorrow's batch of chili as soon as the door closed on the last of the rummagers at six that evening.

They were about to head back, in fact, when a hired sedan drew up at the curb in front of the house and who should get out of the back, with the driver's careful assistance, but Natty McCall herself.

Tiny, with a cloud of silver hair pinned into a billowing Gibson-girl style, Natty reminded Tricia of the late stage actress Helen Hayes. She had beautiful skin, virtually wrinkle-free and glowing with good health, and blue eyes that snapped with intelligence, energy and, occasionally, mischief.

"Natty!" Tricia cried, descending on her great-grandmother with open arms. "You're home!"

"I couldn't stand being away any longer," Natty admitted, fanning herself with one hand. "Worrying about the chili recipe, I mean. Surely *that* wasn't good for my heart or my blood pressure."

Smiling, the balding, middle-aged driver left Natty in Tricia's care and went to collect her suitcases from the trunk of the Town Car.

"And who is this lovely person?" Natty asked, her gaze falling, benevolent but unusually weary, on Sasha.

Tricia made the introductions.

"And this is Valentino," Sasha chirped, indicating the dog, who seemed on the verge of genuflecting to Natty. She had that effect on people, as well as animals, with her queenly countenance. "He lives with Aunt Tricia, but she says she's not going to keep him."

"Famous last words," Natty commented wryly, allowing Tricia to take her arm and escort her toward the front steps, while Sasha and Valentino and the driver followed. "I *have* missed Winston sorely," the older woman confided, handing the key to Tricia, who unlocked the front door.

Winston was right there, waiting to greet his elderly

mistress with a plaintive meow that might have translated as, *Thank heaven you're home. Another day, and I would have starved.*

Delighted, Natty scooped the cat up into her arms and held him while Tricia squired her to her customary chair in the old-fashioned parlor.

"You should have called," Tricia fretted, glad Conner had persuaded her to turn up the heat that morning, when he stopped by to bang on the pipes with a wrench. "I would have had a nice fire going, and prepared a meal—"

"Don't be silly, dear," Natty scolded, in her sweet way, once she was settled in her chair, Winston purring and turning happy circles in her lap. She handed her small, beaded purse to Tricia. "Pay the nice man, won't you?" she asked, indicating the driver.

Tricia settled up with the fellow from the car service, and he left. Natty's baggage stood in the entryway.

Both Sasha and Valentino seemed fascinated by the old woman. They stared at her, as though spellbound by her many charms.

"Would you mind building a fire now, sweetheart, and putting on a pot of tea?" Natty asked Tricia, stroking Winston with a motion of one delicate hand. The cat purred like an outboard motor.

"Of course I wouldn't mind," Tricia said, grateful, now, that Conner had laid a fire on the hearth and all she had to do was open the damper and light a match to the crumpled newspaper balled up under the kindling.

Soon, cheery flames danced on the hearth.

Tricia tucked a knitted shawl around Natty's shoulders before hurrying into the kitchen. While she was making the requested tea, she listened to the rise and fall of voices as her great-grandmother and her goddaughter chatted companionably, getting to know each other.

"And I think Aunt Tricia really *likes* Conner," Sasha was saying, as Tricia entered the parlor carrying a tea tray. "He likes her, too. You can tell by the way he looks at her. It's the same way my dad looks at a cheeseburger."

Natty smiled at that, and her wise, china-blue eyes shifted to Tricia with a knowing expression. "How is the rummage sale going?" she asked.

Tricia set the tray down, poured hot, fresh tea into a delicate china cup for her favorite elderly lady. "It's an enormous success, as always," she answered.

"You'd better get back there," Natty said, after taking a sip of tea. "I wouldn't put it past Evelyn to sneak a sample of that chili out of the community center and have it analyzed by some lab, just so she could find out what makes it so special."

Tricia smiled, sat down on the chair nearest Natty's. There were blue shadows under the old woman's lively eyes, and she looked thinner than she had before she left for Denver. "I'll guard that recipe with my life," she vowed, making the cross-my-heart-and-hope-to-die sign. "But right now, I'm more concerned about you."

Sasha, by that time, was busy entertaining Valentino on the rug in front of the fire, so Tricia felt free to express her concern.

"I'll be perfectly all right," Natty said, looking down at Winston with a fond expression and continuing to stroke his sleek back. "Now that I'm home, where I belong."

"Just the same—"

Natty yawned and patted her mouth. "Winston and I,"

she said, "would love a nap." She sighed, a gentle, joyous sound, full of homecoming. "Right here, in our very own chair. Do hand me the lap robe, Tricia dear."

Tricia obeyed.

"I could stay here and look after Natty," Sasha said, in a loud whisper, when Natty had closed her eyes and, apparently, nodded off. "Valentino, too."

Tricia was reluctant to agree. After all, Sasha was only ten.

"Please?" Sasha prompted. "It's so nice here, with the fire and everything."

"You know my cell number," Tricia said, relenting. She nodded to indicate Natty's old-fashioned rotary phone, in its customary place on the secretary, over by the bay windows.

Sasha seemed to read her mind. "I know how to use one of those, Aunt Tricia," she said patiently. "Dad bought one on eBay last year, and he showed me how it works."

Tricia chuckled. "Okay," she said, with a fond glance at Natty, who was snoring delicately now, obviously happy to be home. In a day or two, she'd probably be her old self again. "I won't be long, in any case. I just have to make sure tomorrow's chili is underway."

"Valentino and I will take care of Natty," Sasha promised solemnly.

Overcoming her paranoia, Tricia went into Natty's kitchen, measured out the spices and peeked into the parlor once more as she passed.

Natty was unquestionably sound asleep. So was Valentino.

But Sasha sat on the ottoman at Natty's feet, watching

her intently, as though poised to leap into action at the first sign of any emergency.

Touched, Tricia left the house again, with the chili ingredients safely stashed in her purse.

The rummage sale/chili feed was going at full tilt when Tricia arrived back at the community center, so she pushed up her sleeves and got busy helping, careful to keep her cell phone in the pocket of her jeans in case Sasha called.

After an hour, Tricia took a break and dialed Natty's number, just in case.

Natty answered, sounding quite chipper. Evidently, the nap had restored her considerably. "We're doing just fine, dear," the old woman said, in reply to Tricia's inquiry. "Sasha and I are about to play Chinese checkers, right here by the fire, where it's cozy." A girlish giggle followed. "The child swears by all that's holy that she's never played this game before, but I suspect she'll trounce me thoroughly at it, just the same."

Tricia smiled, impatient to join Natty and Sasha at home. She'd missed her great-grandmother sorely while she was away and, with the move to Paris looming, she wanted to spend as much time with Sasha as she could.

"No one ever beats you at Chinese checkers," Tricia said.

Again, Natty giggled. "I used to be pretty wicked at Ping-Pong, too, if you'll recall," she replied sweetly. "But I'm not as quick with a paddle as I used to be."

Tricia smiled again, recalling some lively Ping-Pong tournaments she and her dad and Natty had competed in, after stringing a net across the middle of the formal table in Natty's dining room.

Her great-grandmother had indeed been formidable in those days. Neither Tricia nor Joe had been able to beat her, except when she decided to throw a game so they wouldn't lose interest and stop playing.

"Shall I bring some chili home for supper?" Tricia asked, feeling an achy warmth in her heart that was partly love for the spirited old woman and partly nostalgia for those long-ago summers, when her dad was still around. "I'm sure there are some plastic containers I could borrow."

"Yes," Natty decided immediately. "And bring home some of Evelyn's cornbread, too, if the supply hasn't been exhausted already."

Tricia promised to head home with supper as soon as possible.

Along with Carolyn and several other volunteers, she waited on the steady stream of customers—it never ceased to amaze her how many people showed up for the event. Many of them, of course, were out-of-towners, staying at River's Bend, but the locals came in waves, often for both lunch *and* supper.

At six the last few stragglers wandered out, and Evelyn promptly locked up behind them.

By then, the huge kettles had been emptied, scrubbed and filled with fresh salted water and bags full of dried beans, and while the others sat at the public tables in the front of the community center, relaxing and enjoying a well-earned meal of their own, Tricia stirred spices into the cooking pots.

A few minutes later, Tricia left by the back door, carrying two bulky plastic-lidded bowls full of food, and spotted Carolyn, just getting into her aging compact car.

She made an oddly lonely figure, in the twilight-shadowed parking lot and, on impulse, Tricia called out to her. There was a kind of brave sadness about Carolyn that she hadn't noticed before.

Smiling, Carolyn turned from her open car door. "I should have thought of that," she said, with a nod to Tricia's takeout.

"There's plenty," Tricia said. "Why don't you join Natty and Sasha and me for supper?"

Carolyn hesitated—she looked tired—but then she gave a little nod. "I'd like that," she said.

"Good," Tricia said. "Follow me."

CHAPTER NINE

THE FOUR OF THEM—Natty, Sasha, Carolyn and Tricia—
had enjoyed a lively supper of chili and cornbread, seasoned with plenty of laughter, sitting around Natty's
kitchen table, and Carolyn had stayed to help clear away
after the meal.

Natty, explaining that the effects of her afternoon
nap had worn off, excused herself from the kitchen and
made her way to her bedroom, Winston soft-footing it
along behind her, his tail curved like a question mark.
Valentino looked almost sad as he watched his feline
friend disappear into the hallway without so much as a
backward glance.

Sasha, alternately giggling and yawning, asked if she
could use the computer upstairs; her parents had taken
their laptop to France with them, and though they'd
had some problems accessing wireless services in their
hotel room, the little girl was certain they must have
resolved the trouble by now. She was eager to send an
instant message and, hopefully, receive an immediate
response, and Tricia didn't have the heart to point out
that since it was after 2:00 a.m. in Paris, Paul and Diana
were probably sleeping.

Although she did fine in the daytime, when there was
plenty going on to engage her interest, Sasha missed her
mom and dad more poignantly after sunset. Tricia well

remembered being her goddaughter's age, how she'd felt for several weeks every September, when she was back in Seattle to start the new school year. With her mother working nights at the hospital, and Mrs. Crosby from downstairs as a babysitter, Tricia had lain in her childhood bed and silently *ached* for her life in Lonesome Bend, for her dad's easy companionship, and for Natty's, and for the fleeting magic of little-girl summers in a small town.

"This is a terrific old house," Carolyn commented, effectively bringing Tricia back from her mental meanderings. "It has so much character." She spoke with sincere appreciation, her blue eyes taking in the bay windows, with their lace curtains, the lovely hand-pegged floors, the fine cabinetry, the antique breakfront full of translucent china, every piece an heirloom.

"On Natty's behalf," Tricia smiled, "thank you. The house was one of the first to be built, when the town was just getting settled." Tricia pulled on her jacket, which she'd left draped over the back of her chair earlier, when she and Carolyn had first arrived with their rummage-sale supper, and took Valentino's leash from the pocket.

The dog's ears perked up at the sight of it, and he came to Tricia, waiting patiently while she fastened the hook to the loop on his collar.

"I wonder what it would be like," Carolyn mused, "to have such deep roots in a community." She spoke in a light tone, but there was some other quality in her voice, something forlorn that made Tricia think of the way Valentino had watched Winston follow Natty out of the room—as if he'd lost his last friend in the world.

What could she say to that? Tricia liked Carolyn

tremendously, but even after working with her at the community center all day and then sharing a meal, they were still essentially strangers.

Tricia was quite shy, though she'd made a real effort to overcome the tendency, especially since she'd returned to Lonesome Bend to sell off her dad's properties and make sure Natty really *would* be okay on her own, as she claimed. Carolyn, on the other hand, didn't seem shy at all, but merely—well—*private*. She was a person with secrets, Tricia was sure, though not necessarily dark ones.

Valentino was anxious to get outside, so Tricia opened the back door, instead of heading for the front, and Carolyn followed. Both women were silent as they walked around the side of the hulking old house, Tricia juggling the leash, Carolyn with her hands thrust into the pockets of her blue nylon jacket.

Carolyn's car was parked out front, in a pool of light from a streetlamp, and her keys made a jingling sound as she took them from her pocket. "Thanks for inviting me over tonight," she told Tricia, who was gently restraining Valentino. He wanted to head off down the sidewalk, make the most of his final walk of the day.

"I enjoyed having you here," Tricia said truthfully. "So did Sasha and Natty."

Carolyn flashed her warm, wide smile. "I was too tired to stay and eat with the other volunteers after the sale closed for the day, but the prospect of dining alone wasn't doing much for me, either."

Valentino began to tug harder at the leash. He needed a little training, Tricia thought. Maybe, when she found a permanent home for him, he could learn to heel instead of crisscrossing in front of her, nearly making her trip.

Tricia chuckled ruefully and shook her head, and Carolyn gave a little laugh, too. "I'll see you at the community center tomorrow?" Carolyn asked, stepping off the sidewalk and going around to open the driver's-side door of her car.

"Yes," Tricia said, as Valentino yanked her into motion. "See you there."

"And you'll be going on the trail ride, too?" Carolyn persisted. "The one at the Creeds'?"

Looking back over a shoulder, Tricia nodded. Carolyn had seemed uncomfortable around Brody Creed earlier, but evidently she was over that now. Possibly, she didn't expect to see him on the ranch the next day.

"I'm afraid I can't get out of that," Tricia responded. "Sasha's counting on some time in the saddle."

Carolyn's face, like her hair, was lit with moonlight. She had, Tricia noticed, the bone structure of a model; she was one of those women who, like Natty, remained beautiful as they aged.

"It'll be *fun*," Carolyn insisted. "You'll see."

With that, she got into her car, shut the door and started the engine. The headlights were bright enough to make Tricia blink as the rig drew up alongside her and Valentino. Carolyn gave the horn a little toot and drove away.

It'll be fun. You'll see.

Tricia still wasn't entirely convinced of that. Horses were foreign creatures to her, huge and disturbingly unpredictable, and not only did they shed, they'd been known to bite. *Plus,* it was a very long fall from their backs to the hard ground and what if she—or worse,

Sasha—was not only thrown, but stepped on? Or what if something spooked the horses, and they ran away? She'd seen it happen a hundred times in the vintage Western movies her dad had loved.

Conner Creed's face rose in her mind in that moment and, somehow, Tricia knew—*just knew*—that he wouldn't let anything happen to Sasha, or to her, or to anyone else who might be joining them on the trail ride the next day. She knew less than nothing about horses, it was true, but *Conner* was an expert. For that matter, so was Sasha, though, of course, she wasn't as experienced as he was, being only a child.

It didn't take long to traverse Lonesome Bend from one end to the other, even on foot, and Tricia and Valentino got all the way to the old drive-in theater before Tricia decided they'd walked far enough. Farther on, the road curved dark along the edge of the river, and there was only the glow of the moon to light the way.

While Valentino was occupied in the high grass alongside the collapsing fence, Tricia looked up at the big, ghostly remnant of the outdoor movie screen. It was faced with corrugated metal, the white paint chipping and peeling, and time had bent one rusted corner inward, like a page marked in a book.

The projection house/concession stand was dark, naturally, and the rows of steel poles supporting the individual speakers tilted this way and that, resembling pickets in a broken fence. Or tombstones in a forgotten graveyard.

A shiver went up Tricia's back, then tripped back down. A *graveyard?* That, she decided, was an unfair analogy—the Bluebird Drive-in Movie-o-rama had been a happening place in its heyday. The sad old screen had been lit up with light and color and pure Hollywood glamour five nights a week in summer. Her dad must have told her a dozen stories about how thrilling it was to sprawl on the roof or the hood of somebody's car, or in the bed of a truck, the sky a dark canopy overhead, liberally dappled with stars, while John Wayne headed up a cattle drive, or the Empire struck back, or Rock Hudson and Doris Day fell in love, or James Dean rebelled without a cause—

A lump formed in Tricia's throat. Her own memories of the drive-in were scented with buttery popcorn from the big machine on the concession counter; she recalled the scratchy sounds of music and dialogue crackling from the cumbersome speakers, designed to hook onto the car windows, and the delicious frustration of waiting for darkness to fall, so the movie could be shown to advantage.

Still, business had already dropped off dramatically by the time Tricia began tagging along to the theater with her dad on those sultry, star-spattered summer nights, and the films were the sort that go straight to DVD or cable now, without ever hitting the big screen in the first place.

"It's the end of an era," she remembered Joe McCall saying sadly, one late-August night, when the credits were rolling on the last offering of what would turn out to be the Bluebird's final season, though Tricia hadn't known that then. She'd been twelve at the time, not even a teenager, and scheduled to board a flight from Denver to Seattle first thing the next morning.

"The end of an era," Tricia repeated softly.

Now Valentino was on the move again, making for

the bright lights of town, and he pulled her right along with him.

Tricia's eyes burned, and she had to wipe her cheek once, with the back of one hand. Later, when she was older, and she had her dog, Rusty, and the drive-in was starting to look downright decrepit, she'd been a little ashamed of the place. "Why don't you sell it?" she'd asked her dad once, when they'd spent a hot afternoon picking up litter, the drive-in being a popular spot for illicit parties, and mowing the grass.

He'd laughed and said times were hard because the Republicans—or had it been the Democrats?—were in office, so nobody was spending much money, particularly when it came to commercial real estate. Then, more seriously, that sadness back in his eyes, Joe had said, "Someday, it'll be yours—the drive-in, the campground and the rest of it. This is all riverfront property, Tricia—that's Creed ranch land over on the other side—and when the time is right, you'll sell it for a good price, and you'll be glad I held on to it for you."

Hauled along by Valentino, now determined to go home, it would seem, Tricia glanced back over one shoulder, took in the shadowy form of the big For Sale sign nailed to the front gate next to the rickety ticket booth—the whole scene awash in the orangish shimmer of a harvest moon, partially obscured by clouds now—and sighed. Her dad had been so certain that he was leaving her something of value. If Joe had lived, though, he'd have been very disappointed in the state of his legacy, and maybe in her, too.

Another tug from Valentino's end of the leash alerted Tricia to the fact that she'd stopped walking again—it was as though the past had somehow reached out, with invisible hands, and held her in place.

"Sorry," she told the dog, getting into step.

When they got back to the house, the downstairs lights were off, except for the one on the porch, and, Valentino at her side, Tricia climbed the front steps instead of taking the outside stairway, as she would normally have done. She wasn't sure the door was properly locked; Natty had been overtired and she'd most likely forgotten, and Tricia and Carolyn had left the house by the back way.

Sure enough, the knob turned easily.

Suppressing a sigh, Tricia stepped over the threshold, as did Valentino. She took off his leash, wound it into a loose coil and stuffed it back into her jacket pocket. Valentino looked up at her questioningly and she smiled, turning to engage the lock on the front door.

She flipped a nearby switch and the chandelier came on, spilling crystalline light into the entryway. Tricia proceeded toward the kitchen, intending to secure the back door, which she'd left unlocked on her way out, but Valentino took a detour as they passed the stairs and trotted up to the apartment, perhaps looking for Sasha, though he might just as well have been hoping for Winston's return. He'd become attached to that cat.

Natty was sitting at the round table when Tricia reached the kitchen, sipping herbal tea from one of her prized china cups. She wore a cozy blue chenille bathrobe, the front zipped to her chin, and her lovely silver hair, held back at the sides by graceful little combs, trimmed in mother-of-pearl, fell nearly to her waist, still curly and thick even after nine decades of life.

Seeing Tricia, the old woman smiled sweetly, and

her cup made a delicate clinking sound as she set it in the matching saucer.

"I think Carolyn needs a friend," Natty said, with a gentle smile.

I know I *could use one,* Tricia thought wearily. Diana was and would always be her closest confidante, but they lived in separate states as it was, and soon they'd be on separate *continents*.

"I agree," Tricia replied, after securing the lock on the back door. She glanced toward the ceiling, and Natty read the gesture with an astuteness that was typical of her.

"Sasha is just fine," she said. "She got through to her parents, via the computer, and she was so excited that she came downstairs to tell me all about it."

"And that's why you're still awake?" Tricia asked, with an effort at a smile. She'd put in a long day at the community center, and she couldn't wait to soak in a hot bath and tumble into bed for eight hours of semi-comatose slumber.

"Heavens, no," Natty replied. "I watched some television in my room—you know, to unwind a little—and I do like a cup of raspberry tea before I turn in."

"You'd tell me," Tricia said, "if you didn't feel well?"

"I'd tell you," Natty said, eyes twinkling. "You worry too much, young lady."

Still wearing her jacket, Tricia went to stand beside her great-grandmother's chair, and laid a gentle hand on one of the woman's fragile shoulders. "Of course I worry," she responded. "I love you."

Natty reached to pat Tricia's hand lightly. "And I love you, dear," she said. Then she gave a small, philosophical kind of sigh. Her cornflower-blue eyes caught Tricia's gaze and held it. "If anything *did* happen to me, you'd make sure Winston was looked after, wouldn't you?"

Tricia crouched next to the old woman's chair, her vision blurred by hot, sudden tears. Despite Natty's advanced age, and her recent health issues, the thought of her passing away was almost inconceivable. "No matter what," Tricia said, her throat thick with the same tears that were stinging in her eyes, "Winston will be fine. I promise you that."

Natty rested one cool, papery palm against Tricia's cheek. "I believe you," she said tenderly. "But can you promise me that *you* will be fine as well? I'd feel so much better if you were married—"

Tricia gave a small, strangled giggle as she stood up straight again. She felt torn between going upstairs to Sasha—it was past the girl's bedtime—and keeping Natty company in the dearly familiar kitchen. "I can take care of myself," she reminded her beloved great-grandmother softly. "Isn't that better than being married just for the sake of—well—*being married?*"

Natty chuckled fondly. Shook her head once. "I know you think I'm old-fashioned," she said, "and you're at least partially right. But it's a *natural thing,* Tricia, for a man and a woman to love and depend on each other. Certain members of your mother's generation—and yours, too—seem to see men as—what's the word I want?—*dispensable.* I think that's sad." As tired as Natty looked, the twinkle was back in her eyes. "There's nothing worse than a bad man, I'll grant you that," she summed up, waggling an index finger at Tricia, "but there is also nothing *better* than a *good* one."

Tricia laughed. "Duly noted," she said. "Shall I help you back to bed?"

"I can get *myself* back to bed," Natty informed her. "Besides, I haven't finished my tea. I may even have a second cup."

Tricia was moving away by then, though her pace was reluctant, shrugging out of her coat as she started for the hallway and the staircase beyond, "If you need anything—"

"I'll be fine," Natty said, making a shooing motion with one hand. "You just think about what I said, Tricia McCall. Fact is, I'm not sure you'd know a good man if he was standing right in front of you."

Tricia stopped, turned around in the doorway to the hall, narrowing her eyes a little. Like Diana, Natty wasn't keen on Hunter. *Un*like Diana, she'd never met him.

"If that was a reference to—"

"It was a reference," Natty interrupted succinctly, "to Conner Creed."

"I barely know the man," Tricia pointed out, lingering when she knew it would be better—and wiser—to go upstairs.

"Well," Natty said, rising from her chair and picking up her saucer and empty cup, apparently having decided against a second helping of tea, "perhaps you ought to make an effort, dear. To get to know him, I mean. He comes from very sturdy stock, you know. Granted, Conner's dad was something of a renegade, and it looks as though Brody takes after Blue, but Conner's more like Davis, and a finer man never drew breath. Unless it was my Henry, of course."

The corner of Tricia's mouth twitched. "Of course," she said.

Her great-grandfather, Henry McCall, had been dead for decades, but thanks to Natty, his legend as a man and as a husband lived on. Their only child, Walter, Tricia's grandfather, had died in a car accident, along with his wife, when Joe was still in high school.

Tricia's dad had gone away to college the following year, then served a stint in the Army. Having met and married Tricia's mother soon after his discharge, he'd gone to Seattle and tried hard to make a life there, while a still-spry Natty ran the drive-in and the campground for him. After the divorce, Joe had returned to his home-town and, at his grandmother's urging, converted the second story of the old house into an apartment. He'd lived there until his own death, from a heart ailment, only two years before.

"Good night, Tricia," Natty said, setting the cup and saucer carefully on the countertop, next to the sink. "Sleep tight."

"Good night," Tricia said, feeling as though she and her great-grandmother had just engaged in some sort of gentle contest, and Natty had come out the winner.

Which was just silly.

THE ATMOSPHERE IN THE community center's kitchen was redolent with the delicious aromas of spicy chili and fresh coffee the next morning, when Tricia, Sasha and special guest star Natty McCall entered through the propped-open back door.

The night shift—three women who had remained at the center to oversee the kettles of fresh chili sim-mering on the stove—reacted with delight when they spotted Natty. She didn't even get a chance to take off her tailored black coat before they were hugging her and telling her how much they'd missed her, all of them talking at once. So far, one of the women reported, the profits from the event were even higher than last year's had been. People had come from miles around to sample Natty's famous chili, and sales of the donated goods were up, too. Those fancy new uniforms for the high school marching band were as good as ordered.

"See?" Natty told her friends, her cheeks flushed, her eyes bright, as Tricia helped her out of her coat. "I *told* you the sky wouldn't fall if I retired as head of the committee, didn't I?"

Sasha took Natty's coat from Tricia and went to hang it up on the portable closet in the storage room. "There must be fifty million people lined up out front," she said, when she returned. "*Again.* I can't figure out where they're all coming from."

"Everywhere," Natty told the child, after winking at Tricia. "Henry McCall's secret chili recipe attracts foodies from all over the United States and Canada."

That, Tricia thought wryly, might have been something of an exaggeration, but it *was* true that Natty had had several opportunities to sell the recipe over the years, not only to two different manufacturing firms, but to a well-known chain of restaurants, too. Tricia had seen the letters herself.

Someone brought Natty a cup of coffee, once she was settled at the long table in the kitchen. Evelyn barely opened the door separating them from the main part of the building and peered through the crack, clucking her tongue at the size of the crowd waiting on the sidewalk out front.

"Just imagine how many there would be if *church* services weren't in session all over town," she said. "We'd need the riot squad, or even the National Guard."

Natty and her friends chortled merrily at that. All of them were faithful members of their various churches, but every year when the rummage sale/chili feed weekend rolled around, they threw themselves upon God's patient understanding and skipped a week.

"I say it's a good thing today's a half day," one of the other women remarked, after stifling a yawn with one hand. "We're not getting any younger, ladies."

Carolyn hurried in through the back door just then, pulling off her jacket as she walked. "*Who's* not getting any younger?" she teased happily.

"Well," Evelyn conceded, smiling, "you and Tricia *might* be. Maybe it's time for you to take over the biggest event of the year so all us old ladies can follow Natty's lead and put our feet up."

"You'd miss it too much," Carolyn replied.

Natty checked the wall clock above the giant coffee percolator on the nearby counter. "It's almost time to admit the eager hordes," she said.

Evelyn huffed at that. "It won't kill those people to wait a few more minutes, Natty. They bought everything they really wanted yesterday, you can bet on that, and today they're just here to inhale every last chili bean and buy back the stuff they wish they hadn't given up when we held our big donation drive back in August."

Tricia and Carolyn exchanged amused glances.

Sasha, standing close to Natty's chair, rubbed her small hands together. "I wouldn't mind opening the door," she allowed diplomatically, "if no one else wants to do it."

Evelyn chuckled and handed over the keys. "Wait five more minutes," she told a beaming Sasha. "Our kitchen reinforcements haven't arrived, and Carolyn and Tricia can't be expected to wrangle that mob without help, either."

Sasha's eyes were wide with solemn excitement. "But *I'd* be there to help them," she said.

Evelyn patted the girl's head. "Of course you would," she agreed. "Mind, you stay behind the door when you open it. Junk collectors are a dangerous breed—they might just run right over a little bitty thing like you."

About that time, the day crew arrived to monitor the sales of chili and hot coffee, and Evelyn and her bunch put on their coats, picked up their large patent-leather purses, said goodbye and left.

Two other women turned up to help Carolyn and Tricia out front, and Sasha raced to unlock the door.

Time, as Natty had always maintained, had wings. The morning flew by, the chili was consumed, along with two giant urns of coffee and all the canned soda that was left from the day before, and the last of the rummage was boxed up for charity.

"Now we can go riding!" Sasha cried, all but jumping up and down in the kitchen.

Tricia had taken Natty home some time before and the day crew was busy scrubbing out the huge soup kettles, sweeping up and putting the third load of dirty coffee cups into the dishwasher.

"Yippee," Tricia said mildly, putting on her jacket.

Since they'd dressed casually for rummage sale duty, and she'd taken Valentino out for a quick walk when she drove Natty back to the house earlier, there was no reason go home.

Tricia and Carolyn left the center together, Sasha skipping along behind them, unable to contain her joy. "It's still an hour before the trail ride starts," Carolyn said, after looking at her watch. "Why don't you and Sasha follow me back to Kim and Davis's place, and we'll head over to the main house when the time comes?"

Tricia recalled that Carolyn was housesitting for Davis and Kim, who were away on one of their frequent road trips. She considered both of them friends, but she'd never actually visited their home, and she was a little curious, so she agreed.

Once Sasha was safely ensconced in her booster seat, Tricia got behind the wheel of the Pathfinder and followed Carolyn out of the parking lot, into the alley behind the community center and then onto a paved street.

The drive out into the countryside was spectacular, the hillsides practically on fire with changing leaves in every shade of orange and crimson, yellow and rust, the sky so blue that just looking at it made Tricia's throat constrict a little.

Carolyn led them past the colonial-style ranch house that had stood even longer than Natty's house in town. Like Natty's property, it was well-maintained, with grass and a picket fence and venerable old rosebushes everywhere. The barn, though it looked sturdy enough to last another century, showed its age. The reddish paint, fading and peeling away in places, lent it a distinctly rural charm.

The rambling one-story log house Kim and Davis Creed called home stood high on a ridge, overlooking much of the ranch, and was considerably newer than its counterpart, though it had a rustic appeal all its own. The driveway was paved, and there was a huge metal outbuilding, which most likely housed the couple's RV.

The Creeds had a barn, too, smaller than the one down the hill, but surrounded by a large, fenced-in pasture. Three horses grazed the plentiful remains of that year's grass crop.

"Are they the ones we're going to ride?" Sasha piped up, before she was even out of the booster seat. She was pointing toward the buckskin, Appaloosa and bay in the field.

Carolyn, having parked her car and waited for Tricia and Sasha to get out of the Pathfinder, smiled and shook her head. She looked every inch the country woman, Tricia thought, standing there in her jeans and boots and Western-cut blouse, with her hands in the pockets of her coat.

"Nope," Carolyn answered. "These guys are all retired. They're basically pets. The horses we'll be riding are down at the other place."

Sasha frowned. "I didn't see any horses there," she said.

Carolyn chuckled. "Trust me, they're around," she promised. "Let's go inside."

They entered through a side door, stepping into a spacious modern kitchen. Everything gleamed—the windows, the floors, the appliances and the countertops.

"Kim's a housekeeping demon," Carolyn explained, evidently reading Tricia's mind. "It's intimidating, isn't it?"

Tricia laughed. "I'd be dusting twice a day."

Carolyn nodded, hanging her shoulder bag from a peg on the wall next to the door and then placing her jacket on top of it. "If Kim wasn't such a nice person," she agreed, "I'd probably be so paranoid about messing something up that I couldn't housesit."

Sasha, a city child, was taking in the wide-open spaces of a Colorado ranch house. "Is it scary, staying here all alone?" she asked.

"No," Carolyn answered, with a smile. "I like it a lot."

"Can we look around?" Sasha asked, barely noticing as Tricia helped her extract herself from her coat.

"Sure," Carolyn said. "Let's take the tour."

The living room and dining area were one huge room, and the table, surrounded by more than a dozen charmingly mismatched chairs, must have been twenty feet long. The natural-rock fireplace was so big that Sasha could have stood upright in the cavity, and there were floor-to-ceiling windows on all sides.

The view was quite literally stunning.

"Wow," Tricia said.

"Yeah," Carolyn agreed wryly. "*Wow* is definitely the word."

By tacit agreement, they didn't go into the master suite, but the other bedrooms, one of which Carolyn was using, were all impressive. Each boasted its own bath and, like the ones in the living/dining room, the windows offered a grand tableau of the mountains and the vast expanse of rangeland.

A well-stocked library with a baby grand piano and a spacious, leather-scented studio, where Davis did his saddle making, completed the house.

"Where do you live when you're not here?" Sasha asked Carolyn, when they were back in the kitchen.

Something flickered in Carolyn's eyes—the briefest flash of sorrow, Tricia thought—but her smile didn't waver.

"All over," Carolyn answered. "That's my job. I take care of people's houses for them when they're away."

"But where's *your* house?" Sasha persisted.

"Sasha," Tricia protested quietly.

Carolyn swallowed, went to shove her hands into her jacket pockets before remembering that she wasn't wearing the garment. Still, her smile held. "I don't really need a house," she told the child, after tossing an *It's okay* sort of glance at Tricia.

"*Everybody* needs a house," Sasha maintained. She could be stubborn, when she took a notion.

"Sasha," Tricia repeated, this time more forcefully. "That's enough, honey."

Sasha looked up at her then, and Tricia was startled to see tears shining in the little girl's eyes. "But what if people stop going on trips?" she fretted. "If everybody stays home, all at once, Carolyn will be *homeless*."

Tricia felt that familiar pang of love for this amazing child, but she was a little embarrassed by the outburst, too. "I'm sure Carolyn earns a very good living," she said, in an awkward rush. The words were out of her mouth before she realized how lame they sounded.

Carolyn smiled and gave Sasha a sideways hug. "As the cowboys say, don't you worry your pretty little head, missy. I enjoy being a gypsy."

Sasha looked only partly mollified by the claim. In her world, people without homes slept on sidewalks and panhandled for change in downtown Seattle. "But, you don't *look* like a gypsy—"

"Figure of speech, kiddo," Carolyn said, the soul of kindness. Then she held up one arm and tapped at the face of her watch. "Look at the time," she went on, her smile mega-bright. "We'd better get ourselves down to the main barn if we want first pick of the horses."

That was all it took to distract Sasha from the plight of the homeless. For the moment, at least.

The ten-year-old let out a whoop of sheer pleasure and dashed for the door, grabbing her coat from the peg where Tricia had hung it earlier, along with her own.

Within moments, they were back in their vehicles, on their way to one of the last places Tricia wanted to go. And it wasn't just because she was timid around horses.

Tricia would have liked more time to brace herself for another encounter with Conner Creed, but, alas, it wasn't to be. He was standing in front of the barn when they pulled in, and he looked wicked good.

CHAPTER TEN

IF BRODY CREED WAS AROUND, there was no sign of him, which probably accounted, at least in part, for Carolyn's good spirits. Not that Tricia was really paying that much attention; even before she'd parked the Pathfinder beside her friend's car and turned off the ignition, she was feeling it again, that sense of being *magnetized* to Conner.

The vulnerability of that made her want to drive right on past, back to town. Forget the whole crazy idea of going on a trail ride, of all things, with a guy who affected her like a turn on a runaway roller coaster.

As if escape were even possible, with Sasha along and excited enough to jump out of her skin.

Although she didn't notice until after the fact, there *were* other people around, and other vehicles, mostly trucks and large SUVs, with horse trailers hitched behind them. Friends and neighbors began unloading various mounts and saddling up.

"This is Buttercup," Conner said, as Sasha hurried up to him, Tricia lagging a pace or two behind the child.

Tricia blinked. The docile-looking mare might have materialized beside Conner by magic, so thoroughly had the creature evaded her notice.

Conner's smile was slow and easy, and fetchingly crooked in that way that made Tricia's nerves skitter wildly out of control. Holding Buttercup's reins loosely in his left hand, he stroked the horse's neck with the other.

"Is that the horse I get to ride?" Sasha asked, almost breathless.

"Nope," Conner replied, never looking away from Tricia's face. "Buttercup is more suited to a greenhorn." At last, his gaze slanted to Sasha. "You'll be on the one we call Show Pony. She's gentle, too, but old Buttercup, here, she's practically a rocking horse."

Tricia tensed ever so slightly, her pride nettled by the term *greenhorn*. Okay, so she wasn't an experienced rider. She wasn't a coward, either. She was *there*, wasn't she, in spite of all her very sensible trepidation, willing to try something new?

A blue spark ignited in Conner's eyes, there for an instant and then gone again, and Tricia knew he'd been joshing her a little. "Ready?" he asked, watching her in a way that made her feel electrified.

Everyone except for the two of them and Buttercup seemed to have slipped into some kind of dimly visible parallel universe. There was an indefinable charge, a silent buzz, in the crisply cool air, too, and Tricia was startled to recognize it as anticipation, not fear.

"Ready," she confirmed.

Carolyn came out of the barn, leading a pinto mare she must have saddled herself, and a smaller horse that was probably Show Pony. Sasha needed no urging at all to scramble up into the waiting saddle.

Tricia, meanwhile, tried to follow Conner's quiet instructions. Approaching Buttercup's side, she put her left foot into the stirrup, as he told her to do, and reached up to clasp the saddle horn in both hands, praying she could make it without needing a boost.

And then she was up, sitting astride Buttercup's narrow back, and she'd gotten there under her own power, too, without the humiliation of being goosed in the backside. Exhilaration filled Tricia, straightening her spine, raising her chin a notch or two. Buttercup stood still as stone, bless her equine heart.

Conner smiled. "You're doing fine," he said. Then, with a twinkle in his eyes, he added, "It's okay to let go of the saddle horn now." He reached up, placing the reins in Tricia's hands. Although their fingers barely brushed against each other, the contact sent a hot jolt racing through Tricia's entire body. "That's it," he said. "Just let the reins rest easy in your grasp, and whatever you do, don't wrap them around your hands."

Tricia nodded, one step from terror and, at the same time, thrilled through and through.

She was on a real horse.

Of course, it wasn't *moving* yet, but so far, so good.

Sasha rode up, buckling on the riding helmet Carolyn must have brought from the barn. The little girl's smile stretched from ear to ear.

"You're a natural!" Sasha said, beaming at Tricia.

Carolyn, riding up beside Sasha, held out a second helmet to Tricia. "Put this on," she said, with an encouraging smile. Tricia knew, even without looking around, that she and Sasha were the only riders present who'd be wearing headgear, but she didn't care. She *did* have a moment of panic, however, when she looked around for Conner and realized that he was gone.

Buttercup didn't so much as flick her tail, but Carolyn leaned from the saddle to take a light but firm grip on the mare's bridle strap, probably so the animal wouldn't spook while Tricia was putting on the helmet.

Conner reappeared a moment later, ducking with magnificent grace as he rode out through the wide doorway of the barn, mounted on a black gelding with three white boots and a matching blaze on its face.

The sight of him, so at ease riding that powerful horse, literally took Tricia's breath away. Her heart started to pound as Conner adjusted his hat with a second-nature motion of one hand, grinning at the other riders as he passed through their midst to rein in beside Tricia.

Even then, Buttercup didn't move a single muscle. She might have been stuffed, that mare, for all the animation she seemed to possess. And that was just fine with Tricia.

The problem was that everybody else was on the move—even Sasha and Carolyn were riding away, like all the others, toward the gate opening onto the rangeland beyond the corral and the pasture.

Conner waited, shifting in his saddle once, adjusting his hat in what must have been an attempt—a vain one—to hide his grin in the shadow of the brim.

Buttercup stood still as a statue.

"Should I—well—nudge her with my heels or something?" Tricia asked.

A few of the other riders were looking back at her and Conner, and some of them were smiling. Exchanging little comments Tricia was glad she couldn't hear.

"You could do that," Conner answered affably, and in his own good time. "But Buttercup won't go anywhere until Lakota heads out."

Lakota, Tricia deduced, was the gelding Conner rode.

"Oh," she said, at something of a loss. Now what?

This time, Conner made no attempt to hide his

amusement. Tricia could have hit him if she weren't afraid to let go of the reins. She felt silly, sitting there like a child waiting for the carousel to start turning, the only grown-up wearing a helmet.

"Buttercup is Lakota's mama," Conner explained, in that same slow drawl he'd used before. "She likes to keep him in sight when they're out of the corral."

"I see," Tricia said, though she *didn't,* actually. All she could think of was a special she'd seen on TV once, and it had been about elephants, not horses. It seemed that baby elephants would follow their mother for their entire lives, unless, of course, they were separated.

"If you're ready," Conner went on, "we'll start."

Tricia swallowed hard. Sasha and Carolyn and the other participants in the trail ride—over a dozen of them—were way ahead. A few of the more experienced people were even racing each other.

"I'm ready," Tricia lied.

Conner nodded, clicked his tongue once, and Lakota started to walk away.

Buttercup didn't actually bolt, but she moved forward so quickly that Tricia was nearly unseated.

"You're doing fine," Conner told Tricia, riding along-side and obviously controlling the gelding, which wanted to run. Tricia could tell that by the way the muscles bunched in its haunches.

And then, they were trotting. Tricia bounced un-ceremoniously in the saddle. Conner and the others, by contrast, Sasha included, moved *with* their horses, almost as though they were part of them.

"It takes practice," Conner said.

Tricia didn't dare answer, bouncing like that. She'd sound like someone driving a springless wagon over a washboard trail, and maybe even bite her tongue in the process.

Practice? she thought, skeptical. She would probably have bruises after this, along with back spasms and, as for her thigh muscles, forget about it. She was doomed.

Conner's mouth kicked up at one corner again as he slowed Lakota to a walk, which prompted Buttercup to stop trotting, too, of course. Once again, he resettled his hat, the gesture so innately masculine that, for a moment, Tricia's immediate predicament went right out of her head. She even allowed herself to imagine—very briefly—what it would be like to make love with Conner Creed.

Her cheeks burned as if the scene had been flashed onto the screen at the Bluebird, on a very dark night, instead of on the back of her forehead.

"You must want to ride with the others," she said, in a tone of bright misery, nodding across the widening breach between her and Conner and the rest of the party. "We haven't gone far. I could walk back."

Conner tilted his head to one side, looked at her from under the brim of his hat. It was an ordinary thing to do, especially for a cowboy on horseback, but it had the same impact as before, practically knocking the breath out of her. Like a hard fall.

"You'd probably never live that down," he teased. "Walking back to the house, I mean."

Never mind living anything down, Tricia thought, with bleak resignation. She had to keep Sasha in sight, the way Buttercup did Lakota. Even though the child was perfectly safe riding with Carolyn.

"Probably not," she replied, just so Conner wouldn't think she'd been struck dumb in the interval.

"As I said, learning to ride takes time and some practice, same as anything else," Conner told her.

"That's easy for you to say," Tricia responded, though she was smiling. Even starting to relax a little. "You've probably been riding horses since you were a baby."

He chuckled. Made that hat move again. "Before that," he said. "According to Davis, Brody's and my mother was a champion barrel racer. She competed until about a month before we were born, and wouldn't have quit then if the rodeo people hadn't banned her from the event."

While it wasn't a particularly intimate thing to talk about, Tricia still felt moved, as though she'd received some kind of rare gift. She didn't know a lot about Conner Creed, beyond the fact that he was dangerously attractive, but she *was* aware that he was the quiet type, not exactly an introvert, but not an extrovert, like Brody, either.

"I don't think I ever met your mother," she said, mostly to be saying something. Otherwise, his words might have just hung there, between them, fragile as icicles in a spring thaw.

Conner wasn't looking at her now, but straight ahead, at the other riders. "Nobody around here ever did," he said quietly, and after some time had gone by. "She wasn't a very big woman, and carrying twins was hard on her. She fell sick right after Brody and I were born, and never got better. After the funeral, our dad brought us home to the ranch, and we were still pretty little when he died, too."

Tricia's heart found its way into her voice. "I'm sorry," she said.

Conner's smile came as a surprise, given the psychological weight of what he'd just told her. "We were lucky," he said. "Davis and Kim raised us like we were their own. Gave us a good life."

A rush of emotion, partly admiration for Conner's uncle and aunt and partly something considerably harder to identify, surged through Tricia like the first hopeful breeze of a hard-won spring. Conner was stubborn, and he could be taciturn, she knew, but he was also rock-solid, to the very core—a grown *man,* not a boy, like so many other guys his age.

The realization shook Tricia up, and left her with a lot to think about.

The ride went on, Buttercup and Lakota moving at a snail's pace. That didn't seem to bother Conner, though Tricia could tell that he was keeping a close eye on the goings-on up ahead.

This was his ranch, and because of that, he probably felt a responsibility for every person and every animal on that trail ride.

"Your turn," he said presently, and it took Tricia a moment or two to pick up on his meaning. "I knew your dad—he and Davis were good friends—but nobody ever said much about your mother, Natty included."

Tricia was getting used to the slow rhythm of Buttercup's plodding stride. She was still going to be sore, she knew that for certain, but at least she had some inkling of why people liked to ride horses. There was a sort of freedom in it, a kind of quiet power, and she could see a long way into the distance.

"Mom's a trauma nurse," Tricia said. "She and Dad

were divorced when I was seven, which is why I split my time between Seattle and Lonesome Bend while I was growing up. She's out of the country now, working for one of the emergency relief agencies."

"It was like that for Steven," he said. "The going back and forth between his folks, I mean. His mom and Davis were married for about five minutes before they realized they'd made a terrible mistake—they might as well have come from different universes—and went their separate ways. Davis wanted to be part of his son's life, though— he insisted Steven had to grow up as a Creed, and spend his summers here in Colorado until he was old enough to decide things for himself, and he paid child support right along, even when Steven's mother said it wasn't necessary because she didn't need his money."

There it was, Tricia thought. That quiet integrity, that steadiness she'd recognized in Conner a few minutes before. Maybe he'd inherited the trait, though not from his dad, to hear Natty tell it. Just the night before, she'd described Blue Creed as a "renegade," said Brody took after him, but not Conner.

In this case, Tricia figured it was more a case of nurture than nature. Conner was the way he was because, despite losing both parents, he'd been raised in a loving household. It had mattered to Davis and Kim Creed how their infant nephews turned out.

Brody's famous wild streak, on the other hand, was harder to figure out. Maybe, in his case, the reverse had been true, and nature had prevailed over nurture. The whole thing was beginning to tangle Tricia's brain.

The two of them rode in companionable silence for a while and, eventually, the riders up ahead stopped along a quiet inlet in the river, to dismount and stretch their two legs, and let their four-legged companions drink.

Even from so far back, Tricia could see that Sasha was having a good time—maybe the best since she'd arrived in Lonesome Bend for a visit that was already halfway over—and that touched her heart.

Her feelings must have shown in her face, because Conner commented, "That little girl means a lot to you."

"Yes," Tricia agreed, after swallowing. "Sasha's mother, Diana, and I are close friends." She sighed, and then added, without meaning to at all, "Seattle won't be the same without them." A pause. "They're moving to France, because of Paul's job. That's Sasha's dad."

Conner absorbed that. Nodded. "You're planning on going back there?" he asked presently. "To Seattle?" His voice was quiet, and if he cared about the answer, one way or the other, there was nothing in his tone to indicate it.

"If I ever manage to sell the drive-in and River's Bend," she said, "I'll definitely go back. I loved living there."

"Why?" Conner asked.

The simplicity and directness of that question caught Tricia off guard. "I guess I'm a city girl at heart," she finally replied. "And Seattle is a great town."

"I hear it rains a lot." His tone was noncommittal and a little flat.

Tricia grinned. "Not as much as the hype would lead a person to believe," she replied. "When the weather is good, Seattle is unbelievably beautiful. It's so green, and the Olympic Mountains are white with snow year-round.

The seafood is excellent, and you can buy the loveliest fresh flowers at the Pike Place Market—"

Conner didn't comment.

Tricia watched him out of the corner of her eye for a few moments, then went on talking. She wasn't one of those women who couldn't stand silence, but today, for some reason, it made her uncomfortable. "I guess it's all a matter of perspective," she said tentatively, standing up in the stirrups because her thighs ached.

After this, she was going to be bow-legged.

"I guess so," Conner agreed. "I can't imagine living anyplace but here."

They'd almost reached the river's edge by then, where the other riders and their horses were taking a break, and she could see the campground on the opposite side of the water, and beyond that, a glimpse of the top of the peeling screen at the Bluebird Drive-in, since the two properties adjoined each other.

Over the years, Diana had accused Tricia of not knowing when to cut her losses and run—referring to Hunter, in most instances—and this was evidently one of those times. She knew she should shut up, but the words just kept spilling out of her. "You've never even thought about living anywhere but Lonesome Bend?" she asked, finding that hard to believe.

"I went to college in Denver," Conner said, tugging his hat brim down lower over his eyes and keeping his face in profile. "Couldn't wait to graduate and get back here."

To Joleen, Tricia thought, with a bruising sting in the center of her heart, and then wondered where in the heck *that* had come from.

"What about Brody?"

Conner spared her a sidelong glance, but it didn't last more than a moment. "What about him?" he asked, and there was a tautness in his voice now. The Conner who'd told her about his mother, the pregnant barrel racer, was gone.

Tricia closed her eyes for a moment, realized how tightly she was gripping the reins and eased up a little. "I just meant—well—he left Lonesome Bend—"

"That he did," Conner bit out.

Tricia sighed, watching him out of the corner of her eye. *Shut up, shut up,* said the voice of common sense.

"And now he's back," she went on, against her own advice.

"Yeah," Conner said. "Until he starts itching to follow the rodeo again, anyhow." His tone was entirely civil, but it was also cold. Even dismissive. He was telling her, as surely as if he'd said it in so many words, that he didn't want to talk anymore.

Not to her. And not about Brody.

Before, they'd been enjoying an easy, open exchange, a friendly chat. When, Tricia wondered, saddened, had things taken this unhappy turn? When she'd told him that she planned on leaving Lonesome Bend, once she'd sold her land, she thought. But, no, that couldn't be it. Why would Conner Creed care whether she stayed or moved away?

By then, they'd caught up with the others, and Sasha rushed over on foot, bright-eyed from the fresh air and an afternoon spent doing something she clearly loved. She gripped Buttercup's bridle expertly and smiled up at Tricia.

"Get down and walk around," the little girl said. "That way, you won't be as sore later on."

Conner swung down off Lakota's back and left the horse to graze. He waited, probably intending to help Tricia down from the saddle, but she, smarting at the way he'd suddenly shut down, had something to prove.

And that something was that she didn't need Conner Creed's help to get down off a horse.

She dismounted, glad her back was turned to him when her feet struck the ground, because pain raced up her legs on impact, so intense that she caught her breath and squeezed her eyes shut for a few seconds.

"You shouldn't jump down like that," Sasha counseled solemnly, and very much after the fact. "It usually hurts a lot, landing on the balls of your feet. Has to do with the circulation."

Tricia lifted her chin. Then turned, smiling, from Buttercup's side.

"No worries," she said, too quickly to be really credible, even to a child.

Conner sliced one unreadable look at her and then walked away, engaging Carolyn and some of the other riders in conversation. In its own way, that hurt as much as making contact with the ground had.

"You're doing really well," one of the rancher's wives told Tricia. Her name, Tricia recalled, was Marissa Rogers. In the old days, she'd been part of Joleen Williams's crowd, with no time for the likes of Tricia.

Now, though, the look in Marissa's clear eyes was kind and friendly.

"Thanks," Tricia said, managing a little smile. It wasn't as though Marissa had shunned her when they were kids, or bullied her in any way. She'd simply ignored her, and it had all happened a long, long time ago.

"I hear Natty's back from Denver," Marissa went on. "I'd love to stop by the house and say hello, but I don't want to intrude if she's not feeling well."

"Natty's a little tired," Tricia replied carefully. Her great-grandmother was a sociable person, and she enjoyed company, but she wasn't a hundred percent by any means. "I'm sure she'd be glad to see you, though."

"I'll give it a few days," Marissa said, with a smile. But then she was looking past Tricia, her eyes narrowing a little. "Uh-oh," she murmured, so quietly that Tricia nearly didn't hear her. Automatically, Tricia turned to follow Marissa's gaze.

Brody and Joleen were riding toward them, at top speed, both of them laughing, though the sound didn't carry above the sound of their horses' hooves. They were racing, and it was neck-and-neck, a dead heat.

Tricia looked around for Conner, and this was an automatic response, too, but her glance snagged on Carolyn first. Her friend's face was full of pain.

Tricia started toward her, but before she could make her way to Carolyn's side, the other woman was back on her horse and riding along the riverbank, her head held high, her spine rigid.

"Poor Carolyn," Marissa said, in a tone of genuine sympathy, standing at Tricia's elbow.

Tricia didn't ask what Marissa had meant by that, though she wanted to. To do so would have been a little too much like gossiping behind Carolyn's back.

Sasha had Show Pony by the reins again, and she looked as though she might mount up and chase after Carolyn herself.

"Let her go," Tricia said, very gently, putting a hand on Sasha's shoulder.

After that, though it was a while before everybody headed back, the party was essentially over. If Brody and Joleen cared, they gave no sign of it; they didn't even slow their horses as they shot past, both of them leaning low over the animals' necks and shedding happy laughter behind them like a dog shaking off water.

When the time came to get back in the saddle, Tricia hauled herself up onto Buttercup with a difficulty she hoped no one else noticed. Conner had left Lakota standing nearby, and he mounted up with barely a glance at Tricia.

He stayed close beside her all the way back to the barn, dutiful but silent, the small muscles along his jaw-line bunched tight. And for all that Tricia could have reached over and touched him, she knew by the set of his shoulders and the way he held his head that his thoughts were far away.

ON THE WAY HOME, Conner was careful to hold Lakota in check—the horse wanted with everything in him to bolt for home at a dead run, and it wasn't going to happen. Buttercup, despite her age, would go from zero-to-sixty in hardly more than a heartbeat, causing Tricia to either fall off or be scared half to death.

You're a damn fool, Conner Creed, he told himself grimly. By his reckoning, any half-wit should have known a woman like Tricia wouldn't be content to spend the rest of her life in a backwater place like Lonesome Bend. Why, she'd fairly shimmered before, telling him about Seattle, with its seafood and its cut flowers and its snow-covered mountains.

Hell. *Colorado* had snow-covered mountains aplenty, and fields *full* of wildflowers three seasons of the year. As for seafood—who needed it, when the river and the creeks and a dozen lakes were all right there, handy and practically brimming with fish?

Conscious of Tricia beside him, Conner went right on ignoring her. He knew she wasn't going back to Seattle at the first opportunity because of that city's many charms. The real draw was the guy he'd glimpsed on her computer monitor that first morning, when he'd dropped by with Natty's firewood.

Conner unclamped his back molars, to ease the growing ache in the hinges of his jaws. He supposed the yahoo in that screen-saver picture was good-looking enough to suit most women, but Conner figured him for an idiot, if only because he'd let Tricia McCall out of his sight for what—a year and a half? In the other guy's place, he would have visited often, at the very least, and probably made sure there was an engagement ring on her finger, too. One with plenty of sparkle, so any man with eyeballs would know she was spoken for.

He was thinking like a cave dweller, thinking like *Brody*—Conner knew that. But he couldn't seem to get a handle on his attitude. Being around Tricia made him feel as though all the known laws of physics had been suspended—up was sideways and down was someplace beyond the clouds.

Conner swept off his hat with one hand, ran the other through his hair and sighed. And if all that wasn't enough to chap his hide, there was that little show Brody and Joleen had put on, out there on the range.

What the hell was *that* about?

And why had Brody helped himself to Conner's

clothes and gotten his hair cut shorter? It gave Conner a schizophrenic start just to look at his twin, since he'd gone to the barbershop the other day as Brody and come out as a more-than-reasonable facsimile of Conner.

Yep, Brody was definitely up to something. But what?

"Conner?" Tricia said, out of the blue.

They'd almost reached the far side of the inner pasture by then, moving, as they were, at the breathtaking speed of rocks trying to roll uphill, and the rest of the trail riding party was already at the barn. Folks were unsaddling their horses, leading them into their trailers. Hell, some of them were already on the road home.

"What?" he asked, sounding more abrupt that he'd intended. Out of the corner of his eye, he saw her bite her lower lip.

When she'd formulated her reply, she said, "Thank you."

He turned his head to look straight at her then. "For—?"

She blushed. Her eyes dodged his, widened when she forced herself to face him again. "Inviting Sasha and me on the trail ride," she told him shyly.

He felt like a jerk. "You're welcome," he bit out.

CHAPTER ELEVEN

"DON'T ASK ABOUT the trail ride," Tricia told Natty early the next morning, when she and Valentino got back from their walk. "It was an absolute disaster."

Still in her robe and slippers, though she had pinned her silver-white hair up into its customary Gibson-girl style, Natty sat at her kitchen table, Winston perched on the chair next to hers while she fed him little morsels of sardine.

"Did I ask about the trail ride?" Natty inquired sweetly.

Sasha was out of bed, Tricia thought, with a glance up at the ceiling. She could hear the shower running upstairs.

"You were *about* to ask," she said, unfastening Valentino's leash so he could walk over and rub noses with Winston.

Natty waited a beat. "Why was the trail ride a disaster, dear?"

Tricia sighed, shoved the leash into the pocket of her jacket, and helped herself to a cup from Natty's cupboard and coffee from her old-fashioned plug-in percolator. "Let me count the ways," she said, after a few sips.

Valentino lost interest in Winston and focused on the little plate of sardines instead. Natty fed him the last smidgen, much to her cat's consternation, and rose to set the dish in the sink and wash her hands.

"Sasha had a *marvelous* time," Natty observed, drying her fingers on a small embroidered towel with a fussy crocheted edge and returning to her seat at the table.

Winston, disgruntled, leaped down from his chair and pranced into the hallway. Valentino was right behind him.

"Sasha," Tricia said patiently, "knows how to ride a horse. She didn't need babysitting the whole time, the way I did."

Natty arched one snowy eyebrow. "'Babysitting'?" she repeated. Her tone was innocent, but her eyes danced with amused interest.

"Conner gave me a horse reserved for greenhorns, and rode beside me the entire time," Tricia said.

"Why, that awful man," Natty teased.

Tricia frowned. When it came to the list of things she wanted to talk about, Conner Creed ranked dead last. "It was embarrassing," she said, somewhat lamely.

Natty sighed deeply. "How I miss that particular brand of embarrassment," she said. "In my day, we women *liked* being protected by a handsome cowboy."

Tricia huffed out a breath.

And Natty chuckled. "From what you've told me so far," she said cheerfully, "I'd hesitate to describe the experience as a 'disaster.' But that's just me."

Tricia thought of Carolyn then, and the way she'd vanished after Brody and Joleen showed up out there on the range, racing their horses and laughing into the wind. She'd looked for her friend after she and Conner got back to the barn area, but Carolyn had already put her horse away, gotten into her car and left.

"All right," she conceded, "maybe *disaster* is too strong a word."

Just then, there was an exuberant clatter of small feet on the inside stairway and, moments later, Sasha burst into Natty's kitchen, fully dressed, her hair still damp from the shower. "Mom and Dad sent me an email!" she announced. "They're coming back early!"

While this was obviously good news to Sasha, who had missed her parents a lot, it further dampened Tricia's already low spirits. "Oh," she said, aware of the understanding glance Natty sent her way.

"They found the *perfect* house for us to live in," Sasha said, bubbling with enthusiasm, "and they're lonesome for me, so they're catching an earlier flight. Mom said she'll call you later today, on your cell phone, so the two of you can decide what to do next."

Tricia managed a smile—if Sasha was happy, *she* was happy—and went to hug the child. "I'm going to miss you something fierce," she said.

"You could live in Paris, too," Sasha suggested. "Then we could all be together, you and me and Mom and Dad, whenever we wanted."

Tricia held on to her smile, though it felt shaky on her mouth, as if it might fall away at any moment. "I'll visit if I can," she said, very quietly. "In the meantime, let's make the most of our together-time. I'll fix us all some breakfast, and then, while Natty's resting, you and I will go over to the campground and make sure it's still standing."

Sasha nodded, pleased by the simple prospect of food and an outing. Of course, her excitement might wane a little when she realized they were going to pick up litter and sweep ashes out of the fire pits.

Breakfast was a speedy matter of cold cereal, sliced bananas and milk, as it happened. Natty declined the meal and went into the "parlor" to watch her favorite morning news show on television. She was a big fan of Robin Roberts.

By the time Tricia, Sasha and Valentino reached River's Bend in the Pathfinder, the campers were all gone, though it looked as if they'd left the place in unusually tidy condition. Without the tents and the RVs, not to mention the people, the campground had the lonely feel of a ghost town, not only deserted, but forgotten as well.

"Why are you so sad?" Sasha asked, tugging at the sleeve of Tricia's jacket to get her attention. Her eyes were huge and somber in little face.

Tricia swallowed. "I'm not sad," she said, and her voice came out sounding hoarse. "I'm just feeling a little nostalgic at the moment, that's all."

"Isn't nostalgia the same thing as sadness?"

Tricia smiled and tugged lightly at one of Sasha's pigtails. "A perceptive question if I've ever heard one," she replied. "But there is a subtle difference. Nostalgia is a way of remembering people and places and things, and wishing things hadn't changed. It has a sweetness to it. Sadness is just—well—*being sad*."

"Okay," Sasha said, drawing the word out and looking benignly skeptical.

Tricia laughed, though her eyes were stinging.

"I'm glad I came to Lonesome Bend," Sasha said, when they'd both been quiet for a while. Valentino had wandered down to the swimming beach, and he was sniffing at some invisible trail running along the edge of the river. "Now, when I think about you, I'll be able to put houses and people around you in my head."

Tricia bent, kissed her goddaughter on top of the head. "I'm glad you came to Lonesome Bend, too," she said. "Let's go inside and get a fire started. I have some paperwork to do, and I want to check the voice mail one last time before I shut this place down for the winter."

Sasha nodded, but her arm was still around Tricia's waist, and her face was pressed into her side. It took Tricia a moment to realize that the little girl was crying.

"What is it, honey?" she asked, leading Sasha to the nearest picnic table, so they could sit down side by side on the bench.

Sasha sniffled and rested her head against Tricia's upper arm. "I know you love your great-grandma Natty and Valentino," she replied, "but it makes me have nostalgia when I think about you being here and Mom and Dad and me being all the way over a whole ocean, in Paris, France."

Touched, Tricia held the child close for a long moment. "You're going to have a wonderful time in Paris," she said, when she could trust herself to speak. "But you won't be in Europe forever. Your mom is pretty sure your dad will be transferred back to Seattle in a couple of years, and I'll be right there waiting for you when you get home."

"But I'll be a different me then," Sasha protested, "and you'll be a different *you*."

"And we'll still be the very best of friends," Tricia promised gently. Then she gave a little shiver—the wind blowing in off the river had a bite.

Valentino came when Tricia summoned him, and settled himself in front of the fire inside the office as soon as she'd gotten it going.

Sasha, though still a bit subdued, explored the tiny lodge while Tricia booted up her computer to enter the weekend's receipts from River's Bend into her accounting program. Joe had taken a number of black-and-white photographs of the place over the years, and he'd framed a lot of them.

"Is that you, with the fishing pole?" Sasha asked once.

"Um-hmm," Tricia replied, concentrating on debits and credits. Once she'd made her entries, she would write up a bank deposit slip.

"That must be your dad," Sasha said, a little later. "The guy standing on the swimming dock with the kayak?"

"Yup," Tricia said. "That's him."

Soon, the little girl got bored, since there was only so much to see in a place that small. She curled up on the rug next to Valentino, wrapping both arms around him, and drifted off to sleep.

The sight brought tears to Tricia's eyes again, but she blinked them away. Parting would be difficult, but that was life for you. There was always someone to say goodbye to, always someone to miss when they were gone.

Determined to keep it together, Tricia added up checks, cash and credit card slips from the weekend just past, and filled out the deposit slip.

Then, reluctant to disturb Sasha and Valentino—why trifle with a perfect moment before it was absolutely necessary?—she dialed the number and access code

for her voice mail. She was pretty much going through
the motions, given that the season was over and people
wouldn't be asking for reservations at the campground
or looking for a place to park travel trailers and RVs
until early spring, at least.

Tricia wondered if she'd still be in Lonesome Bend
then, marking time, waiting for somebody to buy River's
Bend and the Bluebird Drive-in and getting older by the
minute. It was a dismal thought.

"You have two messages," a robotic female voice
reported from inside the ancient telephone receiver.

Tricia frowned slightly and settled back in her uncomfortable desk chair to wait.

"This is Carla, with Lonesome Bend Real Estate,"
said another voice, this one fully human. "It's Monday
morning, early. Call me. I have big news."

Tricia's heart shinnied up into the back of her
throat.

The second message came on. "It's Carla again. I
forgot to leave my cell number, and since you might not
have it handy—" A pause, during which Carla drew in
an audible breath. "It's 555-7242. *Call me.*"

Tricia hung up the handset, picked it up again and
worked the rotary dial with an unsteady index finger.

Carla didn't even say hello when she answered her
cell, she simply blurted out, "Two offers! Tricia, we have
two offers on your properties, and they're good ones!"

Tricia put a hand to her heart, temporarily speechless.
Nearly two years without a single showing, and now, all
of a sudden, they had *offers?*

"One came in this morning, and one was waiting
in my fax machine when I got home last night," Carla
rushed on. "It was late, or I would have called you then.

I was so excited, I didn't even *think* about leaving a message on your cell."

"But how, who—?"

Carla laughed. "Well, that's the mystery," she said merrily.

"The mystery?"

"It's corporate," Carla said, almost whispering, like she was confiding a secret. "That's how these big companies operate. They buy real estate through their attorneys—most often as tax write-offs, but sometimes as investments."

Tricia wondered why she wasn't happier. After all, she'd been waiting for this news. Hoping for it. Constructing her whole future around it.

Now here it was—her problems, the financial ones, at least—were over. And she felt hollow, rather than jubilant.

"Okay," she managed. "What happens now?"

"Well," Carla nearly sang, "we're in the enviable position of choosing between two excellent offers. They're very similar, both a little over the asking price, if you can believe it, and all cash." She paused, clearly savoring what she was going to say next. "There might even be a bidding war, Tricia."

Tricia's head was spinning by then, and Valentino and Sasha were both awake, and watching her. *A bidding war?* Was this really happening? It was all too much to take in.

"Tricia?" A giggle from Carla. "Are you still there? You didn't faint, did you?"

"I'm here," Tricia said woodenly. "These corporations—which ones are they?"

"Why should we care?" Carla reasoned. "We're going

to be laughing all the way to the bank, as the old saying goes." She was quiet for a moment. "Tricia, this *is* what you want, isn't it?"

Tricia imagined leaving Lonesome Bend. Leaving Natty. Leaving her apartment. Maybe never seeing Conner again.

"I—yes—yes, *of course* this is what I want."

She'd set the asking price high, in the beginning, to leave room for negotiation. Even after settling debts and paying taxes, *and* opening her own art gallery in Seattle, she would be very well off indeed. In fact, working would be optional—so maybe she'd take that trip to France after all. She'd set herself up in a modest hotel, refusing to impose on Diana and Paul, and get to know Paris. She might even purchase a train pass and explore the Continent—

But what about Natty?

Her great-grandmother might be seriously ill—after all, she was over ninety—and Tricia had made certain promises. Just that morning, in fact, she'd assured Natty that Winston would be looked after, no matter what.

And then there was Valentino. She couldn't—*wouldn't*—abandon him just because she suddenly had the means to live anywhere she chose. No, she would have to find the dog a home—and just the right one, too—before she could even consider leaving town for good.

"Tricia?" Carla prompted again.

"Still here," Tricia said weakly.

"Forgive me," Carla said, gentle now. "I guess I got a little carried away for a minute there. I know River's Bend and the Bluebird have been in your family for a long time, and you *must* have a sentimental attachment to them. Letting go won't be easy, and we don't have to decide this second."

Realistically, Tricia couldn't afford to miss out on this opportunity, and she knew it. What if both buyers changed their minds, and she never got another chance to sell the businesses? River's Bend barely brought in enough to cover local taxes and a very modest living allowance for her. The Bluebird, going unused, was probably *costing* her money.

"Get the best deal you can," she told Carla.

"Leave it to me," Carla said. Very briefly, she outlined her plan to contact both buyers' representatives and explain the situation. "I'll get back to you as soon as I know anything more."

When the conversation was over, Tricia was slow to hang up.

"I guess that wasn't my mom calling," Sasha said, approaching Tricia to perch on the arm of her chair and slip an arm around her shoulders.

"No," Tricia said. "It wasn't your mom."

"Is something wrong?" Sasha asked, in a small voice, looking worried. "You'd tell me if something happened to my mom and dad, wouldn't you? If their plane went down or they got into a really bad car crash, like Princess Diana did?"

"They're *fine*," Tricia told the child, pulling her onto her lap and hugging her tightly. "That call was from my real-estate agent, Carla Perkins. The news is good, kiddo. Somebody—*two somebodies*, actually—wants to buy the properties my dad left me."

"Then how come you look like you're going to cry?" Sasha asked. "Are you nostalgic, or sad?"

Tricia smiled, kissed the little girl's forehead. "Nostalgic," she said.

"Good," Sasha said.

"Tell you what," Tricia began. "We'll run by the bank, you and me and Valentino, so I can make a deposit to my account, and then we'll go home and make lunch. By then, I'll bet we'll have heard from your mom."

Sasha smiled, slid off Tricia's lap. "Grilled cheese sandwiches?" she asked. "They're my favorite thing to have for lunch, and Natty likes them, too. She told me so."

"Well, that settles it, then," Tricia said. "Grilled cheese it is."

CONNER HELD THE CORDLESS PHONE away from his head for a moment, glared at it, and then pressed it to his ear again. "What do you mean, there's another offer? Those properties have been for sale since Joe McCall died and now, all of a sudden, there's a land rush?"

Conner's lawyer, Mike Summerville, chuckled. "Somebody else wants the Bluebird Drive-in Movie-o-rama and that sorry, run-down excuse for a campground. Go figure."

"Who?" Conner demanded.

"How should I know?" Mike retorted good-naturedly. "According to Ms. McCall's real-estate agent, the other offer is solid, all cash, ready to go into escrow."

Brody ambled into the kitchen, having slept in late enough to miss helping out with the chores. Some things just never changed.

Conner glared at his shirtless brother, who yawned, took a mug from a shelf and headed for the coffeemaker, paying him no mind at all.

Mike waited.

Conner glowered at Brody.

Brody grinned and raised his coffee mug in a smart-ass toast. "Cheers," he said.

Mike cleared his throat. "Business is business, Conner," he said. "Do you want to raise the offer you made, or let it ride?"

"I want you to find out who the competition is and what they plan on doing with that land, Mike," Conner responded.

"What are *you* planning to do with it?" Mike countered. He was a friend of the family, having gone through law school with Steven, so he could ask questions like that and get away with it.

"Add it to the ranch, I guess," Conner said. He'd made the offer for one reason and one reason only—so Tricia could leave town, if that was what she wanted, and go back to Seattle and the guy in the ski gear.

"For as long as I can remember," Mike said, "the party line has been that the ranch is big enough already. Why make it bigger?"

"I just want to, that's all," Conner replied, still peevish.

Brody snickered, shook his head once, and took a slurp from his coffee mug. It would be nice if he'd at least *pretend* he wasn't eavesdropping, Conner thought, but that was probably too much to ask.

"All right, all right," Mike sighed. "I'll try to find out who else is interested, and get back to you."

"Fine," Conner said. Then he bit out a testy "Goodbye" and hung up.

"Still mad because Joleen and I crashed the trail ride

yesterday?" Brody asked, with that damnable tilted grin of his.

"I never gave a rat's ass in the first place," Conner replied. "I believe I've already told you that."

"Right," Brody drawled.

"If you want to get under my hide, brother," Conner challenged grimly, "you're going to have to do a little better than that."

Brody laughed. Nodded in the general direction of the phone. "You in the market for some real estate?" he asked, with a casualness that should have alerted Conner to what was coming, but didn't.

"Maybe," Conner said.

"I'll outbid you," Brody told him.

Conner, about to open the fridge and see if there was anything in there that could possibly be construed as lunch, froze in his tracks.

"What?" he asked.

"I want that land," Brody said easily. "And I'm willing to pay for it."

Conner narrowed his eyes. He could barely believe what he was hearing. "*You're* the competition?"

Brody raised one hand to shoulder level, like he was swearing an oath. "That's me," he said.

"Now why the *hell* would a saddle bum like you want that land?"

Brody made a shruglike movement, all but imperceptible. "Maybe I'm tired of being a saddle bum," he said. He was using that quiet voice again, the one that didn't sound like it was really him talking. "I mean to bulldoze the whole thing—except for the trees, of course—and build myself a house overlooking the river. A barn, too."

Conner gave a raspy laugh, without a trace of amusement in it. "Half of this place is legally yours," he reminded his twin. "Remember?"

"And I feel about as welcome here as a case of whooping cough on a transatlantic flight," Brody replied. He set his coffee aside and leaned back against the counter, folding his arms. "We'll share the rangeland—if I'm going to run cattle, I'll have to put them someplace. Otherwise, you can keep to your side of the river and I'll keep to mine and that'll be that."

Conner opened his mouth. Closed it again. Shoved a hand through his hair. "You're crazy," he said, at length.

Again, Brody chuckled. "So I'm told," he said. "But the prodigal son is home for good, little brother, and you'd better start getting used to the idea."

"I'll believe it when I see it," Conner snapped. He didn't dare hope Brody meant to stay—it would hurt too damn bad when he changed his mind and took off again.

"Start believing," Brody said. "Unless you slow things down by making a pissing match out of this, I'm going to buy that land, Conner. I'll live in that chicken coop Joe McCall called a lodge until spring, and then I'll start on the house and barn. I want something to leave to my kids when I die. A legacy, you might say."

For a long moment, Conner just stared at his brother, at this confounding version of himself, and then he said, "*You* have kids?"

Brody laughed. "Not that I know of," he replied. "But I'm capable of making some, when the time and the woman are right."

"With Joleen?" Conner asked. In the next instant, he wished he'd bitten off his tongue first.

"I've already told you," Brody said, serious again. "Joleen is just a friend. And frankly, I'm a little surprised at the way you keep bringing up her name. I would have sworn you were taken with Tricia McCall."

Conner swallowed hard. Felt his neck go red and the blood pound under his cheekbones. "If that's what you think," he seethed, "why haven't you made a move on her?"

Brody sighed. It was a heavy sound, and bleak.

Conner was almost convinced.

"You think I'd do a thing like that?" Brody asked.

"I *know* you would," Conner shot back, grabbing his jacket off the hook beside the back door. "From experience."

"Conner—"

"Buy the land," Conner broke in furiously. "Build your house and your barn and run all the cattle you want to, but, for once in your life, Brody, keep your word. Stay on your own side of the river."

Brody raised both hands, palms out. The look in his eyes might have been pain. More likely, it was just good acting.

"Have it your way," he said.

And Conner slammed out, got into his truck. His stomach rumbled, almost as loudly as the motor.

He'd get lunch in town, he decided.

"DIANA?" TRICIA SAID, smiling into the mouthpiece of her cell phone. She was standing in front of her kitchen stove in the apartment, making grilled cheese sandwiches for Sasha, Natty and herself.

"Hello!" Diana chimed. "How is my lovely child?"

"Lovely," Tricia answered, with a fond glance at Sasha. She and Valentino were playing nearby, with the blue chicken Tricia had bought for the dog just after she got him.

"Did she tell you we found the perfect house—not a flat, mind you, but a *house?* It's a five-minute walk from the nearest Metro stop, and the neighborhood is simply wonderful. There's even a park across the street."

"It sounds great," Tricia said.

Diana was quiet for a few moments. "So much for wild enthusiasm on your part," she said, sadly but gently.

"I'm going to miss all of you," Tricia said. "But I'm happy for you. I truly am."

"I know," Diana responded. Then her voice brightened. "Listen, here's the plan. Paul and I arrive in Seattle on Wednesday. You and Sasha can meet us there, and we'll all have a grand old time together."

"I have a dog now," Tricia said, and then marveled at her own inanity. She'd been off-kilter ever since she'd found out about the offers for River's Bend and the drive-in.

"Bring the dog, then," Diana said.

"And a great-grandmother," Tricia added.

Diana laughed. "Bring her, too."

Tricia sighed. Dragging her great-grandmother onto an airplane was out of the question, and so was making Valentino ride in the cargo hold.

Her mind raced. Carolyn already had a housesitting job, but maybe she knew somebody who could come and stay in the apartment for a week or so, taking care of Valentino and keeping an eye on Natty at the same time.

After all, the properties were as good as sold. There would be money soon, and plenty of it.

Shouldn't she be looking at condos in Seattle? Checking out possible sites for her art gallery?

And, oh, yeah, maybe *seeing Hunter?*

Strangely, the man had slipped her mind entirely.

"Tricia?" Diana asked.

"If I can find someone to take care of Valentino and look out for Natty while I'm away, I'll come," Tricia decided aloud. "If not, I suppose Sasha would be all right flying alone, the way she did on the way out here. Or I could accompany her to Seattle and then turn right around and come back home—"

"I thought *Seattle* was home," Diana said.

Tricia bit her lip. "It is," she said, but not right away.

Diana caught the hesitation, but she refrained from comment. "Text me if you can get a dog-and-grandmother sitter," she said. "If necessary, either Paul or I will make a stop in Denver to connect with Sasha. We didn't think we'd worry, letting her fly by herself, but we did."

Tricia closed her eyes for a moment, realized the grilled cheese sandwiches were scorching, grabbed a pot holder and pushed the skillet off the burner. "I'll text you as soon as I can," she told her friend.

Sasha, having abandoned Valentino and the blue chicken, was already at her side. Her eyes glowed, and she was all but jumping up and down.

"Here's your daughter," Tricia said to Diana, and then she handed over the phone.

CONNER DROVE PAST Natty McCall's house three times, thinking up a new excuse for dropping in on every pass. He didn't have wood to deliver, and Natty hadn't called to say she was afraid the pipes might freeze.

Bottom line: He just wanted to see Tricia again.

Figure out some way to make up for the way he'd treated her the day before, on the trail ride. At least, that way, they could part friends.

Going around the block for the fourth time, he came up with an excuse, if not an explanation for behaving like a jerk out there on the range. Tricia had mentioned wanting to find a home for the dog, what's-his-name. He'd had it up to here with living alone. If she hadn't changed her mind in the meantime, he'd offer to take the critter in.

He parked the truck in front of Natty's place, instead of pulling into the driveway as he usually did, and sat there for a minute, just to give himself a chance to think better of the idea and drive away. Silently, he rehearsed his speech about the dog.

Damn if he could think of any reason for yester-day's rudeness, though. The truth—that he was attracted to Tricia and wanted a chance to see if that would go anywhere—was flat-out unsayable. And anything else would be a lie.

Finally, Conner shut off the truck, shoved open the door and got out. He'd bought himself a hamburger at the drive-through, and it felt like a fieldstone in his stomach. He tugged at one jacket cuff and then the other. Squared his shoulders and pointed himself toward the outside staircase. He made the climb fast, because with every step he wanted to turn around and flee before anybody saw him playing the fool in Natty McCall's front yard.

He knocked at the glass in Tricia's door. Saw her and the little girl through the oval window; they were a pair of murky shapes, like they were underwater.

Tricia opened the door.

The smell of burned food roiled out and surrounded him.

"Conner," she said, like he was the last person she'd expected—or *wanted*—to see. The dog appeared at her side, giving an uncertain woof and then sniffing at the leg of his jeans.

The animal's name came back to him in that oddly disjointed moment. *Valentino.* That was way too fruity a handle for a cowboy's dog. Maybe he'd call him Bill.

Slowly, Tricia stepped back out of the doorway, so Conner could come in.

"Hi, Conner," Sasha chirped, from the table. "We were supposed to have grilled cheese for lunch, but Tricia wrecked the first batch, so we're eating peanut butter and jelly instead. Want some?"

"Sasha," Tricia scolded softly.

"It's all right," Conner said, finding his voice at last. It was a discovery he'd soon regret. "I just stopped by to see if you still planned on giving away this dog."

All the eager welcome drained out of Sasha's face in a single moment, and Conner was terrified that she was fixing to cry. There was only one thing worse than a woman shedding tears, in his estimation, and that was a *child* shedding tears. Particularly a *girl* child.

By contrast to the little kid, Tricia looked as though she might cuss him out, breathe fire on him, or maybe brain him with the skillet that was still smoking a little, there in the sink.

She must have decided that none of those options were viable, with Sasha around anyway, because she just stood there, glaring at him, and didn't move or speak at all.

He dug up a grin. Finally remembered to take off his hat.

"I guess that was a little blunt," he allowed.

Tricia's cheeks were bright pink, and her blue eyes flashed. "Ya think?" she said.

CHAPTER TWELVE

TRICIA REMINDED HERSELF that Conner Creed was a guest in her home, albeit an uninvited one, and hadn't she just told Diana over the telephone that she would fly over to Seattle on Wednesday if she could be sure both Valentino and Natty would be all right during her absence?

Her great-grandmother's care remained a problem, but Tricia knew in her very bones that Valentino would be fine in Conner's care. Half the dilemma solved.

"Sit down," she told him, her tone clipped. Then, addressing Sasha, Tricia forced a wobbly smile and said, "Do you suppose Natty is ready to have some lunch now? Would you mind checking with her, please?"

Sasha was flushed, and there was a rebellion brewing in her normally clear eyes.

Valentino, having skulked under the table by then, let out a worried little whimper.

Conner sat down, after shooting an unreadable glance at Tricia, and bent to peer under the tabletop and speak quietly to the dog. "There, now, buddy," he said. "Don't be scared. Nobody's gonna hurt anybody."

As tough and masculine as he was, Conner's voice sounded almost fatherly, comforting Valentino like that.

"*Go,*" Tricia told Sasha.

Sasha got to her feet, but she was none too happy about obeying, that much was plain to see. "Mom *said* you could bring Valentino to Seattle!" she reminded Tricia, but she was on her way toward the inside stairs.

"Seattle is a city," Tricia told the little girl quietly, and very gently. This outburst, she knew, wasn't entirely about the dog. Sasha was realizing a lot of things, like how far away Paris actually was, and how different her life would be there. The move, probably just an abstraction to her before, was taking on substance now. "Valentino will be happier on a ranch."

"No, he *won't!*" Sasha cried. "He'll know you went off and *left him!*" With that, she bolted, clattering down the inside staircase.

Tricia closed her eyes, praying the child wouldn't fall and hurt herself.

"Well," Conner said, after clearing his throat, "now I wish I'd kept my mouth shut about the dog."

"Me, too," Tricia said, with icy sweetness. A part of her still wanted to wring the man's neck but, fortunately, good sense and civility prevailed. "Valentino needs another place to live," she said carefully, moving to stand behind the chair opposite Conner's and gripping its back so hard that her knuckles ached. "If you promise he'll be *loved,* not just tolerated—that you won't make him live outside or in the barn or anything like that—he's yours."

Tricia had to turn her head then, since she felt as though the words had been coated with hot wax, pressed into her flesh and then ripped away. Merely *saying* them had left a raw sting in her throat.

She heard Conner's chair slide back and then he was

in front of her, taking a firm but gentle hold on her shoulders, the blue of his eyes practically burning into her face.

"Dammit," he rasped, on a single hoarse breath. And then, just like that, Conner *kissed* Tricia—hard and deep and with a thoroughness that left her gasping when he drew back.

Even after the fact, lightning continued to bolt through Tricia, fairly fusing her feet to the floor. She stared at him, amazed by what he made her feel. By what he made her *want*.

"No," she heard herself say. And she had no earthly idea what she was talking about, or who she was talking *to,* exactly. It might have been Conner, it might have been herself, it might have been the universe as a whole. *"No."*

Conner's gaze softened unexpectedly and a smile kicked up at the corner of his mouth as he brushed her cheek with a touch so light and so fleeting that it might have been a soft summer breeze instead of a caress.

He was smiling. He'd just rocked her world, and he was *smiling*.

A passionate rage rose up inside Tricia, fierce and delicious, and there was no telling what she might have said to that man if Natty hadn't appeared at the top of the stairs at that exact moment, her breathing rapid and a little shallow, one be-ringed hand pressed to her chest.

"Good heavens," Natty said, when she could speak. "What's the matter with Sasha? Why, the child is practically hysterical!"

Stricken with alarm, Tricia started toward Natty, meaning to take her arm and help her to a chair, but

Conner got there first. He sat the old woman down and went straight to the sink to run a glass of water for her.

Even in that fractured moment, Tricia had to admire his presence of mind. He was so *calm.*

Natty sat fluttering one hand in front of her face. "I'm *fine,*" she insisted. "It's *Sasha* who needs tending."

Tricia's gaze collided with Conner's, over Natty's head, then ricocheted away, like a bullet.

"I'll see to Sasha," she said quietly.

Conner gave a nod, his face grim, and brought Natty the glass of water.

Tricia found her goddaughter in Natty's pantry, sitting on the floor between the built-in flour bin and a ten-pound sack of potatoes, her face buried in her hands.

"Sweetheart," Tricia said softly, crouching. Reaching out to touch the child.

But Sasha must have been peeking between her fingers, because she knew the touch was coming and jerked away to avoid contact. Sobs racked the little girl, causing her shoulders to shake, and she was making an awful wailing sound, woven through with threads of pure, childlike despair.

"Go away!" she almost shrieked.

Tricia shifted to her knees, facing her best friend's daughter. "Sasha, honey—please listen to me—"

"No! I don't *want* to listen, I want to *cry! Leave me alone!*"

Tricia wasn't going anywhere. The hard floor made her knees ache, so she sat cross-legged on the pantry floor, facing Sasha, prepared to wait the child out, no matter how long that might take.

Having already expended considerable energy, Sasha

soon began to wind down. The sobs became sniffles, and then hiccups, and finally, after what seemed like a very long time, she lowered her hands and looked at Tricia with red-rimmed, swollen eyes.

"Everything is changing," Sasha said, her voice so small that Tricia barely heard her, even in that small space. "I'm *tired* of things changing!"

Tricia spotted a roll of paper towels within easy reach on a low shelf and picked it up. Tore away the plastic wrapper and handed Sasha a sheet.

"I know," she said tenderly. "Same here. Blow."

Sasha wadded up the paper towel and blew her nose into it.

"Sometimes it's really hard when things change," Tricia said. She drew a deep breath, let it out. "You're going to love Paris, Sasha," she went on. "You'll make new friends and see wonderful things and learn more than you can even imagine right now. Best of all, your mom and dad will be right there with you, the whole time, loving you and keeping you safe."

Sasha pondered all that. Crumpled the used paper towel in one hand. At considerable length, she asked, "What if Valentino doesn't *like* being a ranch dog?"

Tricia moved to sit beside her. Slipped an arm around the child, but loosely, because the moment was fragile and so was this beloved child. "He will," she said. "Valentino's going to be a very big dog one of these days, Sasha. And big dogs need space to run. Plus, he'll enjoy riding around in Conner's truck and all the rest of it."

"There are dog parks in Seattle," Sasha wasted no time in reminding her. "And lots of people have big dogs. It's not as if they're *illegal* or anything."

"Valentino would be alone in some condo all day,

honey, while I worked. He'd be lonesome and bored and he wouldn't get enough exercise." Tricia paused, surprised at how attached she'd become to that silly dog in such a short time. "Trust me, if I could offer him a choice, he'd take the ranch life, any day."

Sasha drew up her knees and rested her forearms on them. "Don't you want to keep him, even the littlest bit?"

"I'd *love* to keep Valentino," Tricia replied. "But we're not talking about what I want, here, Sasha. We're talking about what's best for a growing dog."

Sasha turned to her, looked up at her with tired eyes, and dropped a bombshell. "You could marry Conner, and then you and Valentino would *both* live on the Creed ranch. That would be the perfect solution."

Tricia laughed, hugged Sasha close and rested her chin on top of the little girl's head. "It's not that simple, honey," she said, but just the same, she couldn't help imagining what it would be like to live under the same roof with Conner. Her body did a déjà vu thing, reliving that kiss they'd shared earlier.

Sasha gave a big sigh. "I'm sorry, Aunt Tricia. For acting like a baby and everything."

Tricia squeezed her again. "Don't worry about it," she said. "You're allowed to have feelings, you know."

"I'm going to miss Valentino," Sasha admitted.

By some unspoken agreement, they both stood up.

"So will I," Tricia said.

"And I'll miss *you*," the child replied. "I thought I'd gotten used to it, you've been away from Seattle for so long, but being here with you, and doing fun stuff—" Sasha fell silent, and Tricia was afraid she'd start to cry again. Afraid both of them would.

So Tricia paused, when they were out of the pantry and standing in Natty's quiet, fragrant kitchen. She cupped a hand under Sasha's chin, and gently lifted. "I'll miss you, too. But we can email, write each other letters, talk on the phone once in a while, and maybe—" she tried to look stern, but a smile broke through "—*just maybe*—no promises, now—I'll come to visit."

Sasha threw both her arms around Tricia's waist and hugged her hard, clinging a little.

A bittersweet ache filled Tricia, made up of love for this child, for Natty and her lost father and her dog, Rusty. Love for Seattle *and* for Lonesome Bend, for life itself, so fleeting and so very precious.

Love hurts, she thought, as the wispy strains of an old song drifted up from her memory. That was the paradox—love *did* hurt, though not always, of course. Yet, just as the poet said, it was surely better to have loved and lost than never to have loved at all.

"Let's go upstairs and see how Natty's doing," Tricia said. "She needs to know you're all right, for one thing."

Sasha nodded and led the way, her small hand clasping Tricia's. They arrived to find Natty looking much restored, her color good and her eyes shining, chatting happily away while Conner stood at the stove, listening and tending a whole new batch of grilled cheese sandwiches.

Sasha went straight to Natty, and the old woman gathered the child into an embrace. Tricia had to look away—if she hadn't, she would have burst out crying for sure—but as luck or fate would have it, her gaze landed on Conner's face and stuck there.

Something silent and powerful passed between them;

for Tricia, it was as if their two souls had met and joined, in a way their bodies never had, sealing some sacred bargain. Or *renewing* one that was older than the stars.

Tricia might have thought she was going crazy if she hadn't seen a flicker of confounded shock ignite in Conner's eyes. Within half a heartbeat, the look was gone, but it had been there, all right—proof that he'd felt something, too.

Deftly, Conner picked up a spatula and scooped one of the golden-crisp sandwiches he'd made onto a plate, and then carried it over to Natty.

Natty looked up at Tricia, who was still trying to recover her inner equilibrium, and winked. "He even cooks," she said, as though Conner wasn't standing right there, hearing every word. "If I were sixty years younger, Tricia McCall, I'd give you a run for your money."

Tricia's cheeks blazed.

Conner gave her one of those tilted grins, probably to let her know he was enjoying her obvious discomfort, and Sasha sank into the chair nearest Natty's and chimed, "That sandwich smells a lot better than the ones *Tricia* made. Hers were burnt offerings."

Conner laughed at that, breaking the spell he'd cast over Tricia. "Want one, shortstop?" he asked the child.

"Yes, please," Sasha said. Like Natty, she appeared to have recovered completely—Tricia was the only one still traumatized.

Conner's glance slanted to Tricia. "Hungry?" he asked. He had a puzzled expression in his eyes now, and his voice was husky.

Oh, she was *hungry,* all right—but not for grilled cheese sandwiches.

The air seemed to collapse and then withdraw, leaving a vacuum behind.

"N-No, thanks," she said.

He dished up a second sandwich and set it before Sasha, who would have dug in immediately if Tricia hadn't warned, "Wash your hands."

Sasha sighed dramatically and headed for the bathroom.

"Yes, indeed," Natty went on, as though there had been no interruption in her observations, "a man who cooks is a rare commodity."

"Oh, for Pete's sake," Tricia muttered, mortified all over again.

"You can't blame a girl for trying," Natty remarked, singsong.

Tricia set her hands on her hips, wondering which 'girl' Natty was referring to—herself or her great-granddaughter. "Oh, yes, you can," she replied.

Conner interceded skillfully, retrieving his jacket from the back of the chair, shrugging it on with a gesture that could only be described as masculine grace. "I'll come back for Valentino another time," he told Tricia, just as Sasha bounded back into the room.

"Good idea," Tricia said, her voice taut. She was careful not to look directly at Conner.

He *still* didn't leave. *When* was the man planning to *leave?*

All his attention was on Sasha now, and she was about to inhale her grilled cheese. Apparently, the major emotional storm over Valentino's impending change of address hadn't done her appetite any harm.

"If I don't see you again for a while," Conner told

the little girl, "it's been good to have you around. You be sure to come back and see us as soon as you can."

To Tricia's surprise, Sasha suddenly sprang out of her chair, the much-anticipated sandwich temporarily forgotten, it would seem, and propelled herself across the room and into Conner's arms.

He picked her up, hugged her once and set her down again.

"Goodbye, Conner," Sasha said solemnly, sounding very grown-up.

He tugged lightly at one of her pigtails. "See you around, kid," he said.

Sasha went back to her chair and her sandwich.

Natty waggled her fingers at Conner in farewell, a little smile lurking around her mouth but not quite coming in for a landing.

Conner headed for the door and, interestingly, Valentino followed him that far. Conner leaned down to pat the dog's head once, and say something Tricia didn't hear, and then he was gone.

"You should marry him, Aunt Tricia," Sasha announced, talking with her mouth full.

Tricia didn't reprimand her, either for the breach in table manners or the outrageous statement she'd just made.

"Amen," Natty agreed. She'd finished her sandwich by then—eaten everything but the crusts, in fact—and now she waved one hand in front of her face as though she were overheated. "Phew," she said. "It's *tense* in here."

"Thanks to you," Tricia said dryly, but with a little smile, as she started water running in the sink.

"Oh, quit puttering and sit down," Natty commanded,

when Tricia began washing cereal bowls left over from breakfast. By then, Sasha had finished eating and she and Valentino were in the living room, playing the kinds of games kids and dogs play when they're indoors.

Tricia sighed, rinsed the suds off her hands, and dried them on a towel. With the big rummage sale over and River's Bend not only closed for the season, but almost certainly sold, she didn't exactly have a full agenda for the day. So she sat.

"I've been thinking," Natty began, with soft portent, and she wasn't smiling now.

Instinctively alarmed, Tricia leaned forward in her chair. Waited.

Few things the old woman could have said would have caught Tricia so off guard as what came out next.

"This drafty old house is getting to be too much for me," Natty told her, her expression solemn, regarding her levelly. "And I've come to the conclusion that Winston and I might be better off in Denver, living with Doris. My sister is getting on in years, you know, and she has only those two little toothless Pomeranians for company."

Doris was indeed "getting on," though she was younger than Natty, but Tricia didn't remark on that, because she was too stunned by her great-grandmother's calm decision to skip town. For good.

Natty had lived in that house literally all her life. She'd been born in the upstairs bedroom that was now Tricia's, and, when she married Henry, the two of them had taken up residence there immediately after the honeymoon. Both Natty's mother and grandmother were still living then, and she'd looked after them until they died.

If she'd said she planned on dying in the same place

she was born one time, she'd said it a *hundred* times. Now, suddenly, she'd decided to take Winston and move to Denver?

Tricia supposed she should have been relieved— just as she should have been happy to sell the Bluebird and River's Bend. After all, with Valentino slated to be Conner's dog, and Natty safe and sound in Denver, with her beloved sister, she herself was free to leave Lonesome Bend and resume her old life in Seattle.

Instead, the whole thing gave her a sinking feeling, as though she couldn't trust her own footing, needed to reach out and grab hold of something to stay upright.

When Tricia didn't speak right away—she was too busy blinking and swallowing—Natty took her hand, gave it a gentle squeeze. "I was happy in Denver," she confided quietly. "Doris and I get along very well. We like the same books and the same television programs and, more importantly, we have the same *memories*." As Natty went on, her voice grew even quieter, and yet there was conviction in it. "No one else remembers my Henry as well as Doris does, or your grandfather, my son, Walter, or the kind of boy your dad was. When we talk about old times, Tricia, it's as though we're back there for a little while, with all our loved ones still around us."

Tricia's throat ached. She turned her hand over in Natty's and held on.

Sasha was right, she thought. Too many things were changing.

"I understand," she managed, after a hard swallow. She didn't try to hide the tears standing in her eyes. Natty wouldn't have missed them, or even have pretended she did. "It's just—I mean—I didn't see this coming, that's all."

"As you know," Natty continued, tossing one hasty glance over her shoulder to make sure Sasha was still busy in the living room with Valentino, "Doris and her Albert never had any children. She's leaving her estate to various charities. But my sister and I both agree that you ought to have the chili recipe, along with this house and my savings, such as they are."

Tricia didn't say anything. She *couldn't*.

Natty, it seemed, had no such problem. She picked up conversational speed, wanting, apparently, to get everything said as quickly as possible. "This house and the chili recipe," she confided, "are *family* holdings. That's why they're going to you."

Tricia could only nod. The thought of Natty leaving this house forever, whether for Denver or for the Great Beyond, was painful even to contemplate.

Natty patted Tricia's hand. "Now, I know you planned on going back to Seattle once you'd sold your father's businesses, and I wouldn't *think* of persuading you otherwise, but I do hope you'll keep the house until precisely the right buyers come along."

"H-How will I know?" Tricia choked out, lest Natty start worrying that she'd lost her voice forever. "That the buyers are the right ones, I mean?"

Natty smiled fondly. Looked around her, seeing memories everywhere, it seemed. Good ones. "You'll know," she promised. "You'll just know."

For a long time, the two kinswomen sat in silence, Natty's thoughtful and reflective, Tricia's stricken and forlorn.

Sasha and Valentino popped into the kitchen.

"It's snowing!" Sasha announced. "It's actually *snowing!*"

CONNER SHIVERED ONCE as the first flakes of snow drifted past the windshield of his truck. Winter was a challenge in the high country, where blizzards had been known to bury entire stretches of rangeland, along with houses and barns and whole herds of cattle. Since he'd never taken much interest in skiing or racing around on snowmobiles, Conner hated to see cold weather coming on.

It made every aspect of ranch life just that much harder.

Generators failed. Truck and car motors wouldn't even turn over, let alone start, well pumps froze and roofs gave way. Even with county snowplows working around the clock, the roads were sometimes impassable for days at a time.

Two years back, Conner had been stuck in a dark, cold house for a full week, while a record-setting storm raged all over that part of Colorado. Fortunately, the tractor still ran, and he'd scraped out a path between the house and the barn, and managed to keep it plowed so he could feed the horses. During that ordeal, Kim and Davis had been coping at their place in pretty much the same way.

The Creeds had sacrificed some twenty head of cattle to that one storm, and they'd have lost more if the Bureau of Land Management hadn't sent up helicopters to drop bales of hay over a few hundred square miles, so the livestock and the wildlife wouldn't starve.

Even with all that, though, it wasn't the cold or the

snow that worried Conner most. It was the loneliness, the shrill ache of enforced solitude so deep and so lasting that there were times when a man needed the sound of another human voice almost as desperately as he needed his next breath. It wasn't the kind of thing people talked about, of course. Not men, anyhow.

Davis and Kim had each other, and most of the folks on surrounding farms and ranches were married, with kids. The year of the big snow, Conner would have been glad even to have *Brody* around, and that was no small thing.

They'd have argued, for sure, especially shut in by a blizzard, but even butting heads would have been better than that snow-muffled silence.

The flurries increased as he drove out of Lonesome Bend proper and into the countryside. The heater was going, and so was his CD player, but Conner couldn't seem to shake the blue chill that had settled on him after he left Tricia's apartment.

He doubled up one fist and struck the steering wheel with the fleshy side, just hard enough for emphasis.

Tricia.

If only he hadn't kissed her, things might not seem so bleak and hopeless now. But he *had* kissed her and in the process, he'd stumbled and then fallen headlong, right down the proverbial rabbit hole.

And he was still falling.

It was an internal thing, of course, but Conner had no more control over it than he would have if he plunged into a mile-deep mine shaft. End over end, in slow motion, he fell and fell and fell.

When he reached the ranch road, he was irritated to find the gate standing wide open and dust billowing from under the rear tires of a double-decker semi loaded with impatient cattle. Brody's old pickup was parked in front of the barn, and he'd saddled a horse and left it to graze on snow-dappled grass, but he was nowhere in sight.

Conner stopped his own truck, got out and shut the gate, swearing under his breath and secretly glad to have something to be pissed off about, because that gave him a respite, however brief, from thinking about winter coming on and Tricia leaving Lonesome Bend forever.

When he noticed that two *other* semis had arrived ahead of the first one, Conner swore and scrambled behind the wheel again, laid rubber on that dirt driveway getting where he wanted to go.

Brody and the few cowboys who'd be wintering over on the ranch in distant house trailers were herding horses, a great many cows and several Brahma bulls through the gate opening between the corral and the open range.

"What the hell—?" Conner snarled, to nobody in particular, as he sprang out of his truck again and strode toward his brother.

Brody looked a sight, standing there in the swirling snow, covered from his hat brim to his boot soles in good Colorado dirt, and grinning like a fool.

"I told you I was serious!" he called, over the bawling of the cows, the snorting of the bulls and the whinnying of the horses.

Conner strode over to him, full of a strange and hopeful fury.

Critters streamed past, raising more dust and carrying on like the devil was chasing them with a whip. Only

Brody would have unloaded broncos and bulls in the same place at the same time. The man had no patience, no apparent need to do things *right,* dammit.

In the midst of all that ruckus, Conner didn't fail to notice that the horses, like the bulls, were big and sturdy and just plain wild. He dragged off his hat, slapped it against his right thigh in a burst of frustration, and then jammed it back onto his head.

"This is a historic moment, little brother," Brody shouted affably, above the unholy din. "You are witnessing the birth of the Creed Stock Company!"

Conner was torn between chewing the bark off the nearest tree and grabbing Brody by the shirt and slamming him against the nearest hard surface. Since there were no trees handy, he went for the latter choice.

Brody flew back against the weathered gatepost, while his hat went rolling into the path of the controlled stampede. He looked surprised at first, but when he came off that post again, he'd made the switch to pissed off.

He threw a punch at Conner, who ducked it and offered an uppercut as a response. Before it could make contact, though, two of the ranch hands stepped in to drag the brothers apart.

"Now you know that won't do either one of you any good," drawled old Clint, who'd worked for their grandfather even before Davis took over the operation. Despite his age, Clint's hold on Conner was steely, and Brody, restrained by Juan Manuelo, another long-time employee, was in the same fix.

"Just like the old days!" Juan crowed, delighted. "Eh, Clint? Remind you of Davis and Blue, when they were kids?"

"Sure does," Clint agreed, with a husky chuckle. Then, closer to Conner's ear and much more quietly, he said, "You promise me you won't go after Brody, and I'll let you go."

Conner's neck and face were hot; he was aware of the truck drivers and the other cowboys looking on, and he felt like he was sixteen again, and stupid in the bargain.

A few feet away, Juan and Brody seemed to be having the same kind of exchange.

"All right," Conner finally said, rolling his shoulders when Clint released his hold. "But if he comes at me—"

Brody neither advanced nor retreated. He looked around for his hat, spotted it lying flat in the dirt and shook his head in disgust.

The noise had abated a little, anyway, since the first two trucks had been unloaded and the third one hadn't been maneuvered into position yet.

"What the hell do you think you're doing?" Conner finally ground out.

"Easy," Clint counseled, from just behind him.

"I'm unloading *my* livestock on *my* rangeland," Brody retorted, peevish. "And that was a damn good hat. You *owe* me, little brother."

Conner shifted his weight, doubled up one fist.

"Don't even think about it," Clint said easily.

Conner wrenched off his own hat and flung it at Brody, who caught it in both hands and pulled it on so hard that it was a wonder he didn't lower his ears a notch or two.

"If you're not going to lend a hand," Brody growled, "then get out of the way, Conner. I've got *work* to do!"

"Have at it," Conner said generously, grinning because he knew that would get under Brody's hide, and quick.

It did just that. If Juan hadn't been so fast on his feet, and gotten Brody by the bends in his elbows before he could take a second step, the fight would have been on. And this time, there would have been no breaking it up.

After that, Brody got on with it, while Conner watched from alongside the fence as that crazy mix of bulls and broncos and thick-legged cows spread out over the range in all directions. He gave an affable nod as Brody passed by, on horseback now, to do some herding.

Clint and Juan got on their horses, too, and rode out, and for a while the whole thing was like a scene out of a modern-day *Lonesome Dove*. The truckers unloaded the third rig—just cattle in that one—and once the last cow was through the gate, Conner secured the gatepost with the customary barbed-wire loops.

Rodeo stock.

Trust Brody to come up with a fool idea like raising bad broncos and even badder bulls, on the same range with beef cattle.

Conner splayed the fingers of one hand and shoved them through his hair, now damp with snowflakes and matted with dirt, and pointed himself toward the barn, where the usual chores awaited.

If Brody thought for a New York nanosecond that he was going to stick his "little brother" with the responsibility for any or all of that extra livestock when the urge to roam came over him again, as it inevitably would, he was sadly mistaken.

Conner walked around the three semis, feeling the

cold bite into the back of his neck, and he was clear inside, out of the weather, before he realized that he was grinning fit to split his face in half.

CHAPTER THIRTEEN

"I'VE MADE LISTS for the movers," Natty said, bright and early on Tuesday morning, standing in the middle of her coffee-scented kitchen and holding up a clipboard. The sky was blue and the ground was bare of snow, but there was a wintry nip in the air, too, one that made Tricia shiver in her jeans and wooly sweater.

Once Natty had announced her intention to move herself and Winston in with Doris and the Pomeranians in Denver, things started happening at a breakneck pace, it seemed to Tricia.

Except for a few personal belongings—clothing, books, photographs and special pieces of jewelry, mostly—Natty wasn't taking much along with her. Tricia was to have her pick of the furniture, dishes, quilts and a myriad of other items, and the rest would be boxed up by moving men and hauled to a storage unit, there to await donation to next year's rummage sale/chili feed.

Sasha was scheduled to fly home to Seattle the next day, and Tricia was going with her. For no reason she could pinpoint, she hadn't called, texted or emailed Hunter. She'd gone so far as to change her screen saver for a shot of herself and Rusty, posing in front of a long-ago Christmas tree, both of them smiling amid stacks of wrapped packages.

Seeing Rusty's image flash onto her computer

monitor still threw her a little, especially when she was thinking of the million and one things on her to-do list, but underneath was a sense of healing. The grief was beginning to subside at last, leaving a sweet, quiet joy behind.

Now, confronted with Natty's clipboard, not to mention the outfit, a tiny red running suit with white racing stripes down the pant legs, topping off a matching pair of high-top sneakers, Tricia wedged her hands into the pockets of her hooded sweatshirt and grumbled, "Okay."

"You'll have to keep an eye on them," Natty warned, shaking an index finger at Tricia. "The moving men, I mean. Make sure they put things in the right boxes and label everything properly—"

"I'll see that they do the job right," Tricia promised glumly.

"I'm counting on that. When Esme Smithers went into assisted living, her children hired movers, and her entire teapot collection went missing—she swore she saw her grandmother's Wedgwood on eBay!"

Tricia sighed, bent distractedly to pat Valentino's head. He seemed to sense change coming on, and he stayed close to her when he wasn't following Sasha around.

"You don't think you're, maybe, *rushing into things,* just a little?" Tricia asked diplomatically.

Natty drew on her apparently inexhaustible supply of timeworn clichés for a reply. "Make hay while the sun shines, that's what I always say," she chirped, pursing her lips as she studied the papers on her clipboard. "Last week, I felt terrible. *This* week, I'm just *full* of energy. Heaven only knows why that is, but I'm taking advantage of a good thing while it lasts."

"Right," Tricia said. There was no use in urging Natty to take it easy. If she wasn't bedridden, she was bustling from project to project.

Natty looked up from the clipboard and narrowed her twinkly blue eyes. "Are you coming down with something, dear?" she asked. "You aren't your old self."

No, I'm not my old self, Tricia thought crankily. *And I'm not at all sure who the new self is, either.*

"I'm just tired, I guess," she said, in belated response to Natty's question.

"Where's Sasha?" Natty asked, checking off an item on her list.

"She's upstairs, in my kitchen, sitting in front of the computer and exchanging instant messages with her dad," Tricia answered, crossing to the table and plunking down in a chair.

"There's coffee," Natty said. "Or would you rather have a nice cup of tea?"

"Nothing for me, thanks," Tricia replied, as Valentino, still at her side, laid his muzzle on her knee and gave a shuddery canine sigh.

Natty took a chair opposite Tricia's, setting the clipboard aside with a matter-of-fact motion of one hand. "I never thought I'd say this," the older woman began, "but I think a trip to Seattle might be just what you need right now. You could use a change of scene, a fresh perspective."

Tricia stroked Valentino's head. He liked Conner, and she suspected he would adapt to the change of households quickly, but she dreaded saying goodbye to the dog. It made her throat tighten painfully every time she considered the prospect.

"You may be right," she agreed halfheartedly. She *was* looking forward to spending time with Diana and Paul, though of course they'd be busy making preparations for their upcoming move, and she planned on checking out some potential gallery spaces and condominiums, too. She wanted to do some shopping as well—her wardrobe had dwindled to jeans and casual tops since she'd moved to Lonesome Bend. She hoped to reconnect with some of her friends and possibly hit a favorite restaurant or two.

"Tell me what's the matter, then," Natty insisted quietly. "You're *moping*, Tricia. Does this mood of yours have something to do with that—that man you were seeing, before you left Seattle?"

Tricia frowned. "Hunter?"

"Yes," Natty said. Her tone wasn't exactly disdainful, but it was crisp. "That's it—*Hunter.*"

Tricia nodded. "Have you ever been very, very sure of something," she began, "or of *somebody,* only to find out, when push came to shove, that you're not sure after all?"

Natty giggled, and that broke the tension. "No," she said, "I haven't. I was sure of my Henry from the day I first set eyes on him to the day we laid him to rest, God keep his fine and honorable soul. But we're not discussing me, are we, dear? We're talking about *you* and—Trooper."

"Hunter," Tricia corrected wryly.

"Whoever," Natty retorted, with a wave of one hand.

Tricia couldn't help smiling a little, sad sack that she

was these days. "Stop it," she said. "You know perfectly well what Hunter's name is. There's nothing wrong with your hearing or your memory."

"All right," Natty conceded sweetly, with another wave of her hand. The huge diamonds in her wedding and engagement rings caught a flash of sunlight through the window. "Hunter, then. I take it he's the 'thing' you were 'very, very sure' about and now—not so much?"

"Not so much," Tricia confessed, with regret. While she wasn't sure how she felt about Hunter, she knew now that she *should* be sure, or at least have some idea. The only certainty here, as far as she could say, was *un*-certainty, but she had figured out this much: she wasn't going on a romantic cruise with one man when she'd so enjoyed being kissed by another. Even if that kiss was bound to lead nowhere.

Deep down, she knew she had to make a clean break with Hunter—and soon. "I think," she went on softly, and at some length, "that I've been in love with love all this time. I didn't want to let go of the *concept,* even though the reality might never have existed at all."

Natty smiled and got out of her chair, very spry for a woman getting ready to downsize practically every area of her life. "I'm making that tea," she said firmly, "and don't try to talk me out of it."

Tricia chuckled, feeling better. Valentino stretched out at her feet, let out a sigh and went to sleep. "I know better than to try to talk Natty McCall out of *anything,* once she's made up her mind. Or *into* anything, either, for that matter."

Natty busied herself with the process of brewing tea from scratch, something she could probably have done in a catatonic state, she'd had so much practice over the years. While the loose-leaf orange pekoe steeped in a china pot, Natty got out cups and saucers to match, and brought them to the table.

Once the teapot had been transported, too, Natty sat down with a happy sigh. "Now," she said. "Where were we? Oh, yes. You were telling me that you only *thought* you were in love with this Hunter person, but now you realize that you're meant to spend your life with Conner Creed instead."

Color flared in Tricia's cheeks. "I don't realize anything of the sort," she replied, not unkindly, but in a rather terse tone that she instantly regretted. She drew a deep breath and let it out very slowly. "I'm willing to admit that I'm attracted to Conner," she said, changing her approach. The kiss replayed itself in her mind yet again—it was on a loop, evidently—and the reverberations spread into every cell of her body, causing her to blush even harder.

She held up a palm when Natty's eyes began to dance with joyful mischief. "I said I was *attracted* to the man, not madly in love with him. And, anyway, we're moving in different directions—Conner and I. He'll get old and die on that ranch of his, content to live out his days within a stone's throw of his hometown. I, on the other hand, want a city bustling around me, 24/7. I want sidewalks and bright lights and malls and bookstores and *people*. I want to go to operas and symphonies and get season tickets to the theater—"

"Denver has all those things, and it's only an hour's drive from here, when the roads are clear," Natty was quick to point out. "And while I certainly wouldn't describe you as antisocial or anything, you aren't at all fond of crowds. They wear you down, remember? Sap your energy. I know you're young, and you've probably felt pretty isolated here in Lonesome Bend over the last couple of years, but—"

Tricia raised an eyebrow. Poured tea for her great-grandmother and then for herself. "But?" she prompted.

"It wouldn't be wise to do anything drastic," Natty said, her brow knitted with concern. "For heaven's sake, Tricia, give yourself a chance to *think* before you go rushing off to things you've *already left behind*."

"You're a fine one to talk," Tricia pointed out, thinking that she'd never loved her spunky great-grandmother more than she did right at that moment. She huffed out a breath. "You were *born* in this house, Natty. You were married here, you raised your son and your grandson here. Now, all of a sudden, you're moving to Denver—and that isn't *drastic?*"

"It's not sudden," Natty said, though she didn't deny the "drastic" part, Tricia noticed. "Doris and I have been talking about sharing her house for years. It's smaller and more modern—much more manageable, for two old women especially—than this one. For a long time, I couldn't face the idea of living anywhere but here. Now, well, there's just too much to worry about—plumbing that might freeze, heating bills that are higher with every passing year and then, when spring comes around, there's the yard, and the flowerbeds—" Natty stopped, and her beautiful blue eyes filled with tears. "I'm *tired,* Tricia—tired of being weighed down by *things,* and commitments and responsibilities."

Tricia nodded, took a sip of tea. It gave her an almost instant lift, and she wondered, very briefly, if the sweet old lady sitting across from her in a red running suit might have laced it with some kind of fast-acting antidepressant.

"I just want you to be happy, Natty. That's all."

"I want the same thing for you, dear," Natty pointed out. Her gaze dropped to Valentino, sleeping peacefully on the floor. "What's the plan for the dog?" she added, in a whisper.

Before Tricia could reply that Conner would stop by the house and pick Valentino up in the morning, after she and Sasha left for the airport, Sasha strolled into the kitchen, all smiles.

"Dad had to go offline," she told Natty and Tricia. "He and Mom are checking out of the hotel in a little while, then they're going to have dinner, and *then*—" Her eyes sparkled with excitement and anticipation. "And *then* it will be time for them to leave for the airport so they can board their flight back to Seattle—where you and I will be waiting!"

Tricia smiled at Sasha's happiness—it was catching—and slipped an arm around the child's waist, holding her close.

But Sasha pulled free, and reached into the deep pocket of her pink sweater to bring out Tricia's cell phone. "You left this on the counter upstairs," she said. "And it rang a couple of times."

Tricia thanked her, took the phone from her hand and checked for messages.

Carla, her real-estate agent, had called twice, clicking off the first time but leaving a message the second. "Tricia? I'm assuming you're at home, even though you didn't answer your phone, and I'm on the way over there in a few minutes. I know who the competing buyers are, and you are never going to believe it—I have to see your face when I tell you."

Tricia didn't bother to call Carla back; it was already too late. She saw the woman's big car bounce past Natty's kitchen window as she sped up the driveway.

"Land sakes," Natty said, alarmed. "If you could see your expression. What on *earth* is going on?"

Tricia didn't answer; she just went to the back door and opened it.

Valentino roused himself to give a couple of lackluster barks before settling down again.

Carla, a small woman with a short pixie haircut and big sunglasses, was just getting out of her car. Her teetery high heels sank into the soft ground, and she carried a smart leather portfolio under one arm. "I have the papers and a check for the earnest money right here!" she sang out, beaming.

Although strangely nonplussed herself, Tricia certainly understood Carla's delight in making a deal. Besides the reclusive movie stars and upper-echelon executives who occasionally bought or sold ridiculously large houses hidden away in copses of aspen trees, at the ends of long, long driveways, she didn't have all that many clients. In Lonesome Bend, properties tended to be passed down from one generation to the next, without ever sporting a single For Sale sign.

To Tricia, and most of the other people in town, those VIP mansions were hardly more real than the village of Brigadoon. The owners evidently came and went under cover of darkness; no one ever saw them walking along the streets of Lonesome Bend, like the locals, and they certainly didn't socialize.

"Aren't you going to ask about the buyers?" Carla trilled, coming up the steps of the back porch.

Tricia stepped back to let her in, nearly tripping over Sasha as she did so.

She didn't get a chance to say anything, though, because Carla entered talking.

"Both Brody and Conner Creed put in bids," she said, nodding to Natty and eyeing Valentino with a degree of trepidation. Given that he was sleeping, the trepidation was brief. "Conner withdrew his offer this morning, but Brody is prepared to close the deal at any time. *And* he's willing to pay your asking price, if you recall."

Tricia just stood there, not knowing *what* to think.

Conner had wanted to buy the campground, the RV park and the Bluebird Drive-in? Why?

Carla laughed merrily at Tricia's look of consternation. "Who would have thought Brody Creed would ever show his face in Lonesome Bend again after—" She looked at Natty, then at Sasha. "After what happened," she finished.

"What happened?" Sasha asked.

"Never you mind," said Natty, watching Carla but speaking to the child. Then, for Carla's benefit, she added, "Besides, all of that was a long time ago, wasn't it?"

Carla gave another of her tinkly, music-box giggles, but it sounded tinny this time around. "Yes," she said. "What's done is done. Water under the bridge, and all that."

"Precisely," Natty said. Then she turned a warm smile on Sasha. "Dear, would you mind carrying in some of that nice firewood Conner brought by while I was in Denver? I think a cozy blaze would be just the thing, on a cold day like this."

Sasha hesitated, clearly aware that she was getting the bum's rush so the adults could talk freely, but in the end she was too well-mannered to object. She gave an eloquent sigh and pounded upstairs to get her jacket. Carrying wood in from the shed out back would be chilly, splintery work.

"All you have to do is sign on the dotted line, accepting Brody's very generous terms, and we can get this thing rolling," Carla said, slapping her portfolio down on Natty's tablecloth and slipping out of her stylish coat.

"Why were they so secretive in the beginning?" Tricia asked, barely scratching the surface of what she wanted to know. "Brody and Conner, I mean. You said the offers came through corporate attorneys."

"They did," Carla said, taking a chair and briskly unzipping the portfolio, taking out a sheaf of documents. Again, Tricia had that disturbing sense of everything speeding up, reeling out of control, like some carnival ride gone berserk. "But each of them was trying to keep the other out of the loop—they weren't out to deceive us in any way."

"But—"

Sasha reappeared, wearing her coat, and headed outside to get the requested firewood, closing the door hard behind her.

Both Natty and Tricia smiled.

Carla merely started slightly and shook her head. Her expression said, *Kids.*

"Did Brody happen to say why he wants River's Bend and the drive-in?" Natty asked mildly.

Carla smiled an oh-happy-day kind of smile, tapping

the already tidy stack of papers against the table. "Does it matter?"

Tricia thought about her dad, cutting the grass out at the drive-in for years after it closed, picking up litter over at the campground, teaching her to fish at the edge of the river. "Yes," she said, very quietly. "It matters."

Carla reddened slightly. Hesitated.

From the woman's expression, a person would have thought Brody Creed intended to turn River's Bend into a dumping ground for toxic waste.

Carla held out the pen.

Tricia ignored it.

Outside, chunks of firewood could be heard striking the back porch.

Carla sighed. "Brody wants to make the properties part of the Creed ranch," she said, her eyes darting between Natty and Tricia. "That's all."

Tricia kind of liked that idea. She'd always known, of course, that the old movie screen would have to come down; it was an eyesore. It was nice to imagine cattle and horses grazing there, meandering down to the riverside to drink.

"Why did Conner try to buy it?" Natty asked.

"You know how those two are," Carla said, with another anxious little smile. "They—compete. It goes all the way back to—well—that scuffle over Joleen."

"Ancient history," Natty said.

"I guess so," Carla agreed, uncertainly.

"Joleen used to come here for piano lessons," Natty recalled fondly. "Every Tuesday, after school. She was a spirited girl, there was no denying that, and she enjoyed playing games, too, always pushing the envelope when it came to flirting and boys. But she wasn't cut out to marry Conner Creed, or live in Lonesome Bend for the rest of her life, and everybody knew it."

Everybody except, maybe, Conner, Tricia thought, with rising despair. Had Conner wanted to buy her land because he knew she meant to leave town as soon as the ink was dry on the contracts?

"And we're talking about seven figures, here," Carla reminded everyone.

Tricia sighed. *Ah, yes. The money.* Until she'd learned what Brody's plans were, she'd been secretly afraid a housing development might be going in where the campground and the drive-in were now or, God forbid, one of those sprawling big box stores.

"Right," she said, knowing how pleased Joe would be that his long-range plans for his daughter's financial well-being had paid off so handsomely. For him as much as for herself, Tricia picked up the stack of documents and read every word on every page.

Sasha came through the back door, her little arms full of wood. "Can I come in now?" she asked. Her lower lip was protruding slightly, and her gaze was fiery. She didn't like being sidelined. "It's *cold* out there, you know."

"Yes," Natty said, with a tiny smile. "You may."

Tricia read on. Everything seemed to be in order as far as Brody's offer was concerned; he wasn't asking for any improvements or upgrades and he was prepared to close at any time. Satisfied, Tricia signed beside each of the little stick-on arrows Carla had put in place ahead of time.

Carla all but snatched up the documents, as if she thought Tricia might change her mind and cancel the deal. Only after the woman had tucked the papers into her portfolio and zipped the zipper did she speak. "Well, then, that's done," she said, clearly relieved. Rising, she stuck out a hand to Tricia. "Congratulations."

"Thank you," Tricia murmured. Because her head was spinning a little—even considering taxes, the last of Joe's debts and Carla's commission, she was a wealthy woman—she didn't get out of her chair.

"I'll just be on my way. I'll call you with a choice of dates for the closing," Carla said. Putting her coat back on proved an awkward enterprise, since she was evidently unwilling to lay the portfolio down and free both hands at once.

"I'll be out of town for a little over a week," Tricia recalled. "Starting tomorrow. But you can reach me on my cell phone."

Carla smiled. "Eventually, yes," she said.

And, moments later, she was gone, back in her big real-estate agent's car, driving away.

Tricia frowned.

"You don't seem very happy," Natty ventured, watching her.

"I'm *happy*," Tricia lied.

One stubborn woman recognizing another, Natty didn't press the point.

CONNER WAITED UNTIL he was sure Tricia and the little girl had left for Denver the next morning, before stopping by to get Valentino.

Natty, busy lording it over a crew of moving men, paused long enough to smile sadly and say, "We are going to miss that dog."

"I'll take good care of him, Natty," Conner answered. Sure, he'd been meaning to get a dog for a while, but he was doing somebody a *favor* here, wasn't he? So why did he feel guilty, like he was kidnapping the critter or something?

"I know," Natty said softly, patting his arm distractedly. "I really thought Tricia would want to keep more of this stuff," she confided. "Turns out she only wanted family photos and some of the china. She's not much for *things,* though."

Word was all over town about Natty's move to Denver, so Conner wasn't surprised to find her sorting her belongings. Still, she *was* shedding a lot of memories, it seemed to him, right along with the figurines and the needlepoint pillows and the like. And she wasn't wasting much time doing it.

"What's the big hurry, Natty?" Conner asked, without planning on saying anything of the sort.

"Once I make a decision," Natty replied, "I like to move on it. There's nothing to be gained, in my opinion, by dillydallying." She paused. "Don't you agree?"

"I don't reckon it's my place to agree or disagree," Conner hedged. The dog, soon to be rechristened Bill, leaned heavily against his leg.

Natty sighed and put her hands on her hips. She looked a little quaint, standing there in a flashy gold lamé running suit and sequined shoes. *Bring on those big-city lights,* her getup seemed to say. *And let's party!*

She also looked annoyed. "I declare, Conner Creed," she said, causing him to rock back slightly on his boot heels, "for an intelligent man, you can be remarkably obtuse!"

He blinked and, knowing all the while that he'd live to regret it, asked, "What are you talking about?"

Natty looked back over one shoulder, probably making sure the moving men were doing what she'd hired them to do, but her blue eyes had a chill in them when they landed on Conner again.

The dog sighed and sat down.

"I'm talking about Tricia," Natty said, in a stage whisper. "And if you weren't such a lunkhead, you'd have known that without asking!"

Conner felt that sinking sensation again. It was as though the floor had suddenly turned to foam rubber. "What *about* Tricia?"

"You know darned well *what about Tricia,*" Natty lectured. "Are you really, *truly* going to stand by and do nothing while she makes the biggest mistake of her life?"

They were standing in the entryway.

The moving men were listening in.

So Conner took Natty lightly by the elbow and escorted her into the small parlor, where there were still plenty of chairs.

Valentino slogged resolutely along, apparently resigned to go with the flow. There was something sad about that, to Conner's mind—as if the dog knew he was being ditched and had decided not to fight it.

"Sit," he told the animal.

"I beg your pardon?" Natty demanded, feathers ruffling right up.

Conner chuckled. "I was talking to Bill, here," he said.

Natty frowned. "Bill?"

"The canine formerly known as Valentino," Conner explained.

Natty sank into a prissy little chair. Now, there were tears in her eyes.

Conner's heart skittered up into his throat, because he hated it when women cried. He never knew what to do, or say.

"It's all so sad," Natty said, after a short silence.

Conner dropped to one knee, ruffled the dog's ears to let him know he'd be okay, but he kept his gaze fastened on Natty McCall, an institution in Lonesome Bend. "What's sad, Natty?" he asked, very quietly. "Leaving this house? If you don't want to go, just say so, and I'll have those guys packing up your stuff out of here in no time—"

Natty interrupted him with a shake of her head. She dabbed at her eyes with a lace-trimmed hanky plucked from the pocket of her sparkly jacket. "It's time for me to go," she said.

Something in her tone gave Conner a chill. "I hope you didn't mean that the way it sounded," he said carefully.

"To *Denver,*" she clarified, with a moist giggle. "Conner, I'm an old woman, but I'm not so far gone that I don't know passion when I see it, that I don't know *love.*"

"Whoa," Conner said gravely. "Passion? Love? You've lost me again."

Natty shook her head, set her very small jaw. "Men," she scoffed, her tone mild but her eyes fiery. "Are you just going to let Tricia move back to Seattle without even giving the two of you a *chance?*"

Tricia's plans to leave were never too far from his mind, but the facts had a way of pouncing on him when

he wasn't paying attention. He got to his feet, after murmuring a few soothing words to the dog.

"I can't make Tricia stay in Lonesome Bend, Natty,"
he said quietly. "She's a grown woman, with her own
plans." He paused, cleared his throat, remembering the
ski-guy in the screen-saver picture. "Anyway, there's
somebody else in her life. Somebody she wants to get
back to."

Natty waved a hand at him. "Nonsense," she said.
"Tricia is attracted to *you*, Conner. She told me so, just
yesterday. In fact, she went so far as to confide that
she's been fooling herself about having a future with
Hunter."

Conner didn't know what to say to that. Tricia had
responded to his kiss, he knew that, and every time they
were in the same room, the air crackled. So they were
attracted to each other? That was a far cry from being in
love, and if all Conner had wanted from a woman was
good sex, well, hell, there had never been any shortage
of that.

The problem was that Conner wanted a lot more than
a bedmate. He wanted a full partner, a confidante, somebody he could trust with all those dusty old dreams of
his. He wanted kids and dogs running every which way.
He wanted a *family*.

And he wasn't willing to settle for less, even if it
meant being alone for the rest of his life.

"Bill and I had better get going," he finally said, his
voice gravelly. "We're burning daylight."

With that, he crossed to Natty's chair, bent and kissed
her lightly on the forehead.

"Goodbye, Natty," he said. "If you need anything,
anything at all, you just let me know."

She put a small hand on his coat sleeve, held on for a moment then let go.

His last image of Natty McCall was of her sitting there in that slipper chair, dressed up like Elvis, her eyes that much bluer for the sorrow they held.

CHAPTER FOURTEEN

TRICIA HAD BEEN IN SEATTLE for three full days when Diana finally shamed her into contacting Hunter.

"If you won't call or email the man," Diana said, one morning when the two of them were sitting in her sunny kitchen, chatting and drinking coffee, "then go and see him in person. You can't go on like this, Tricia."

Tricia sighed. "Like what?" she stalled. Since her and Sasha's plane had landed on Wednesday afternoon— they'd waited only an hour for a jet-lagged Diana and Paul to arrive via Air France—it seemed as though every minute of her time had been occupied.

While catching up, she and Diana had shopped for groceries, picked up dry cleaning, cooked together and pored over about a million digital photos of the new house in Paris.

After much discussion, the couple had decided to put most of their things in storage and lease out their lovely suburban home in Seattle, rather than sell it. That meant sorting stuff, stuff and more stuff.

"You seem—confused," Diana said, after thinking about Tricia's response for a few moments. "Or *down*, or something. For nearly two years, all you've talked about was Hunter this, and Hunter that, and I'll bet you haven't said three words about the man since you got here. That spells *A-V-O-I-D-A-N-C-E*, my friend. On top of that, you're about to be debt-free and rolling in money, but you haven't looked at a single storefront for that gallery you've wanted to open for as long as I've known you, or even checked out a condo, for that matter."

"We *have* been a little busy," Tricia pointed out.

"Tell me I'm right," Diana said, undaunted. "You've seen the error of your ways. You're about to dump the biggest loser. That's why you've been so preoccupied, isn't it? That and the cowboy Sasha can't stop talking about?"

Tricia sighed, raised and lowered her shoulders in a slow semblance of a shrug. "It's just that so many things have happened lately," she said, hoping Diana wouldn't press the Conner issue.

Fat chance.

"Sasha says she saw him kiss you," Diana said. "The cowboy, I mean."

"His name is Conner," Tricia said. "And the kiss was just—a kiss. An impulse. We lost our heads."

"Sure you did," Diana said, with a saucy little smile.

Tricia blushed. "Okay, so maybe I enjoyed the kiss, all right?"

Diana laughed. "Nothing wrong with that."

"There *is* something wrong with it," Tricia argued, after looking around to make sure Sasha wasn't within earshot, "if you're technically involved with *someone else*."

"'Involved'? You and Hunter? Give me a break. When was the last time you even saw the man, let alone had sex with him?"

"Shhh!" Tricia scolded, color stinging her cheeks. "What if Sasha had heard that?"

"Sasha," Diana replied, "is in the garage helping her dad decide which set of golf clubs he wants to take to Paris." She leaned forward slightly, her green eyes twinkling as she studied Tricia. "What about Conner? Come on, 'fess up—have you been to bed with him?"

"Of course not," Tricia said.

"Pity," Diana said. "You want to, though, don't you?"

"Diana."

"Don't you?"

Tricia groaned. "Okay," she admitted grudgingly. "Yes. Maybe."

"'Yes, maybe'? Now there's a definitive answer. Either you want to hit the hay with this Conner dude, or you don't."

Tricia looked away.

"You do!" Diana exulted.

Tricia forced herself to meet her friend's gaze. "All right, I do," she said. "Maybe."

"Maybe nothing," Diana said. "You want him. And from the way Sasha described that kiss, he definitely wants you. So what's the holdup?"

"What's the holdup?" Tricia echoed, frustrated and embarrassed. She felt as shy as she ever had as an adolescent. Any minute now, her teeth would sprout braces and her skin would break out. "I told you. I have to clear things up with Hunter first. And even if I—even if I *do* end up—" she lowered her voice to a near whisper "—going to bed with Conner Creed, it might not change anything."

"Oh, it'll change something, all right," Diana teased. Then she stood up, walked over to the desk in the corner, and came back with her purse. She rummaged through it and laid a set of keys on the table in front of Tricia. "As a general rule, I like to keep certain observations to myself, but this time, I'm making an exception. You're acting just like your mother, Tricia."

A pang of recognition struck Tricia in that moment, so she went into immediate denial. "Oh, right. My mother is at an emotional remove from everything, including herself. She's afraid to care about anything other than a natural disaster of some kind."

Diana simply sat back in her chair, folded her arms and said, "Isn't that why you stuck it out with Hunter all this time? Because you could keep your distance and still enjoy the fantasy that you were in a real relationship?"

Tricia blinked. "No," she replied, but it took a beat too long. "For heaven's sake, Diana, you make me sound like one of those women who marries a guy serving life in prison—"

Diana arched an eyebrow, gave her head a slight shake. "I wouldn't go that far," she said. "But you're scared of really *connecting* with a man—especially a man who, unlike Hunter, won't settle for anything less. My guess is, the cowboy terrifies you."

"That's preposterous," Tricia sputtered. But gears were turning in her mind. *Was* she like her mother? Was she incapable of opening her heart and her life to another person?

Diana smiled. Pushed the car keys closer. "Here. Take my car and drive yourself to Hunter's studio and tell that egomaniac what he can do with his romantic cruise to Mexico, not to mention all those promises. That will be a start, anyway."

Tricia swallowed hard. It didn't seem like a start to

her, but the end of a safe and comfortable and, okay, *boring* time in her life.

In the next instant, another possibility occurred to her. "Is there something you should have told me?" Tricia asked, very quietly. But she did reach for the car keys. "Diana, what do you know about Hunter that I don't?"

"I'm your best friend," Diana said, with equal amounts of frustration and affection. "If I had any kind of goods on the guy, I'd have told you in a heartbeat. It's just a feeling I have, that's all—that he's not good enough for you. He's sort of—shifty."

"Shifty." Tricia sighed. "I'll be back," she said.

A few minutes later, she was driving toward downtown Seattle in her friend's sporty blue BMW, keeping the comparison Diana had drawn between Tricia and her mother at bay by rehearsing what she'd say when she got to Hunter's studio.

I'm sorry I didn't call first. I know it's rude to just show up like this.

Trouble was, she didn't feel like apologizing. After all, she hadn't done anything wrong.

There's this guy in Lonesome Bend...I barely know him, you understand, but I'd like—love—to explore the possibilities.

No, that wouldn't do, either. What might or might not happen between her and Conner was flat-out none of Hunter's business, once they'd agreed to see other people.

Let's face it, Hunter. We haven't been a couple in a long time.

"Excellent," Tricia said, out loud and with scorn.

She took a wrong turn at the next light and, since

downtown Seattle was composed of one-way streets, she had to drive even farther out of her way just to backtrack. By the time she pulled into the parking lot in Pioneer Square, she was no closer to deciding what to say to Hunter than she had been when she'd left Diana and Paul's place.

And it was only then that she realized she hadn't even checked her lipstick, let alone done anything with her hair.

She was decently dressed, though, since she and Diana were planning a trip to the mall later that day. She'd replaced her usual Lonesome Bend garb of jeans and tops—T-shirts in spring and summer, sweatshirts in fall and winter—with a pair of black jeans and a simple white top.

Breaking up, she decided, marching herself toward the brick building where Hunter lived and painted in an elegantly rustic loft, shouldn't be all *that* hard to do.

The converted warehouse boasted a doorman, as well as a stunning view of Elliott Bay and the Olympic Mountains, and Tony recognized her right away.

His eyes rounded. "Haven't seen you in a while," he said awkwardly. "How have you been, Ms. McCall?"

"I've been fine, Tony," Tricia said, stepping into the elevator. "I'll see myself in, thanks."

Tony blinked and, as the door slipped closed, Tricia would have sworn she'd seen him lunge for the intercom.

Sure enough, when the elevator reached the top floor, Hunter was standing right there, waiting for her.

He was good-looking, she thought offhandedly, in a game-show-host kind of way. All teeth and hair.

"Tricia!" he said. "I wasn't expecting—"

"I'm sorry," Tricia said, forgetting her firm decision not to apologize. "I should have called."

Hunter sighed, shoved a hand through his hair. He didn't seem to know what to do or say and, once or twice, he glanced back at the half-open door leading into his loft. "Well," he finally stammered out, "I guess there's no harm done."

"Good," Tricia said. Puzzle pieces were falling into place.

What an idiot she'd been, she was thinking. What a naïve, romantic *idiot*. Hunter wasn't alone, and he probably *hadn't* been, from the day she left for Colorado, intending to settle her dad's estate and return right away.

She smiled. If she'd cared about Hunter, she might have said something catty, like, "Aren't you going to ask me in?"

If she'd cared, she'd have been hurt and angry, because she knew in every fiber of her being that there was a woman inside, probably listening at the door. Maybe dressed and maybe not.

Instead, she felt a tremendous sense of relief. And she *laughed*. "It's okay, Hunter," she said. "I just came by to tell you I won't be coming along on that cruise, but thanks anyway."

Hunter's eyes narrowed, and his mouth dropped open for a moment, before he regained control. Enormously successful in just about every area of his life, he wasn't used to rejection.

A face appeared in the opening between the door and the frame. Hunter's guest was pretty, with spiky blonde hair, and way too young for him.

"What cruise?" Lolita asked, pouting.

"Oops," Tricia said, amused.

Hunter reddened. "Monica has been doing some modeling for me," he said.

Along with a few other things, Tricia thought.

"Monica," Hunter snapped, "go back inside."

"I want to know about this cruise," Monica said.

"It's all a big mistake," Tricia told the young woman cheerfully. "I must be in the wrong building."

"Oh," Monica replied, still confused but willing to be mollified. With that, she retreated, and closed the door to Hunter's loft.

"It's just that you were gone so long," Hunter said, miserably. Then he brightened. "But now that you're back—"

Tricia smiled and shook her head. "I'm not back, Hunter," she told him. "Not the way you mean, anyway."

"If you'll just give me a chance—the cruise—"

"No cruise," Tricia said, turning to push the down button that would summon the elevator again. "Goodbye, Hunter. Have an excellent life."

She truly meant those words.

It was over.

She was *free.*

"Wait," Hunter protested. "What about all our plans? What about the gallery we were going to open together? What about—?"

The elevator doors swished open. It hadn't gone anywhere.

Tricia stepped inside. Waggled her fingers at Hunter in farewell and mouthed the word *Over.*

And that was it.

Tony, the doorman, was waiting anxiously when she

emerged into the lobby seconds later. He was probably used to women coming and going, used to scenes.

Tricia's smile obviously took him aback.

He opened his mouth, closed it again, then scrambled to hold the lobby door for her. "You're all right?" he asked meekly.

"Oh, I'm better than all right," Tricia answered. *And I am not emotionally distant, like my mother. Much.*

THE DOG RAN AWAY TWICE before he figured out that he didn't live in town anymore.

Both times, he went straight to Tricia's place, and both times Conner found him sitting on the landing outside her door, waiting in vain to be admitted.

The sight choked Conner up a little, and not just because the critter looked so pitiful. He knew how that dog felt, because he missed Tricia, too. Missed her more than he'd ever thought it was possible to miss a woman, especially when he'd never done anything more than kiss her.

"Tell you what," Conner said gruffly, after hauling the dog bodily down the stairs and setting him in the passenger seat of his truck. "We'll go back to calling you Valentino. No more Bill. How would that be?"

Valentino licked Conner's cheek and settled himself for the ride back out to the ranch, looking straight out through the windshield.

It started to rain right after that, and Conner succumbed to the low mood that had been trying to drag him under ever since Tricia left for Seattle. At home, he did the usual chores, keeping one eye on Valentino while he worked. The dog sat in the open doorway of the barn, his furry back turned to Conner, cutting a forlorn figure against a backdrop of gray drizzle.

Later, Conner built a fire in the stove in the kitchen and grilled up a good-size T-bone steak for supper.

He and Valentino shared the meat and a couple of cans of beer.

When Brody wandered in out of the storm, around eight that night, Conner was damn near glad to see him.

"Guess I've thrown in with a somber outfit," Brody drawled, shrugging out of his wet coat and hanging it up, along with his hat. "I don't know which of you looks more down in the mouth, little brother—you or the dog."

"His name is Valentino," Conner said, resting his booted feet on the chrome ledge around the stove. He'd changed and showered after he was through with the chores, but he couldn't seem to get warm.

Brody chuckled. "Valentino? I thought it was Bill or something like that."

"Bill didn't work for him," Conner admitted. "So it's back to Valentino."

"Oh," Brody said, moving to the refrigerator. He sighed, once he'd seen the contents. "I thought I smelled steak."

"You did," Conner said. "We ate it."

Brody hadn't closed on the property he'd bought from Tricia yet, and Carolyn was still staying up at Kim and Davis's place, so the brothers had been sharing the main house. Giving each other lots of room and speaking only when it couldn't be avoided.

"Kim called today," Brody said, taking a carton of eggs from the fridge and moving on to the electric stove.

"They're coming back early—her and Davis, I mean—and there'll be a crowd for Thanksgiving. Boston and his pretty wife and the kids will be here."

Boston was and always had been Brody's name for Steven.

"That's good," Conner said. Brody was in an unusually chatty mood, it seemed to him. Maybe he'd shut up, if Conner kept his responses to a word or two.

A cast-iron skillet clanged onto a burner, and Brody started cracking eggs.

"You hungry?" he asked.

"No," Conner answered.

Right about then, thunder tore open the sky, and hard rain lashed against the sturdy walls of the house, pattered on the windows.

Valentino scooted closer to Conner's chair, and Conner reached out to stroke the dog's head.

"Weather like this chills a man to the core," Brody remarked, with an audible shudder. "There ain't much I wouldn't give for a nice, warm woman right about now."

The statement rankled, though Conner couldn't have said why. Not without giving it some thought, anyhow. He decided it was the *ain't* that got to him.

"What's with the yokel routine?" he grumbled. Brody had a college degree, just as he did.

Brody laughed. "I was waxing colloquial," he said. "Making conversation."

"Well, don't," Conner snapped.

"Don't wax colloquial?"

"Don't make conversation."

Brody gave a heavy sigh. "This isn't about Joleen, I'm guessing, " he said.

"Nope," Conner agreed.

"Then what? The land I bought from Tricia McCall?"

"Why would I give a damn about that?"

"Got me," Brody said. The words had a built-in shrug. "Maybe you figure Tricia goes along with the deal."

If it wouldn't have scared the dog, Conner would have been on his feet, across the room and closing his hands around Brody's throat, all in the space of a heartbeat.

"Tricia's got better sense than to take up with the likes of you," Conner said, still in his chair in front of the stove. *Or me,* he added silently. "She plans on moving back to Seattle pretty soon. That's why I have the dog."

"I do believe that's the most you've said to me in ten years," Brody commented, rattling utensils around in a drawer until he found a spatula to turn the eggs. "You like her, Conner?"

"She's all right," Conner said.

All right? Kissing her had practically turned him inside out. God only knew what would happen if they ever made love. Fireworks, probably.

Meteor showers.

Earthquakes, without a doubt.

Again, Brody laughed. It gave Conner that old feeling that he and Brody could see inside each other's heads.

"I don't have designs on Tricia," Brody said. He'd stacked the eggs onto a plate like a pile of pancakes, and he was headed for the table.

"None of my concern if you do," Conner said.

"Like hell," Brody responded, busy digging in to the eggs. "You think you know all about me, brother, but you don't."

"Is that right?" Conner asked, wondering if it meant anything that Brody had just said "brother" instead of the usual "*little* brother." Deciding it didn't.

"Fact is," Brody reflected, looking at Conner now, "I'm more like you than you'd care to admit, and you're more like me than anybody else knows."

Conner absorbed that statement, swallowed the immediate urge to refute it. Even in friendlier days, he and Brody had lived to disagree with each other—he supposed it was because they'd needed, as kids, to establish separate identities. In most people's eyes, they were practically interchangeable, each of them only half a person without the other.

"Where have you been all this time, Brody?" Conner asked, taking himself by surprise. It seemed he was always saying something he hadn't *meant* to say, lately. To Brody and to Tricia, anyway.

"Around," Brody said.

"Come on," Conner said, in an angry rasp, turning his chair around so his back was to the stove now, and he was facing Brody, who was still sitting at the table, though he'd stopped eating. Valentino adjusted himself to the new arrangement, sticking close enough to rest his muzzle on Conner's right boot.

"Just around," Brody reiterated. "For now, Conner, that needs to be enough."

Conner didn't answer.

Brody wasn't finished, though. And that was strange, given that this time he'd been the one to pull his punches. "I'll tell you what I told Boston, back when he asked me the same question," Brody said. "I wasn't in jail, or anything like that. There's no big secret—but there is some stuff I'm not ready to talk about. Fair enough?"

"Fair enough," Conner replied.

Brody left the table, carried his plate and his silverware to the sink, set them down. "I'll be out of town for a few days, as of tomorrow," he said, as though it mattered. "But I'm coming back to Lonesome Bend, for sure. Soon as I close on that real-estate deal, I'll be living in that log building at the campground and you'll be rid of me."

"Whatever," Conner said.

"Yeah," Brody said hoarsely. "Well, good night, little brother."

"Night," Conner ground out.

When he and Valentino were alone in the kitchen again, the dog lifted his head off Conner's instep and gave an inquiring little whine.

"We might as well turn in, too," Conner said.

Tired as he was, sleep eluded him for a long time.

TWO DAYS LATER, Conner awakened to a loud pounding at the back door.

Grumbling, he rolled out of bed, pulled on a pair of jeans and padded out into the kitchen.

Dawn hadn't even cracked the horizon yet, but the porch light was on, and he could see Tricia standing out there, hands cupped on either side of her face, peering in through the window beside the door.

Conner's heart did a funny little spin, right up into his throat.

Valentino, at his side as ever, gave a happy little yelp.

"I want my dog back," Tricia said, first thing, when Conner had pulled open the door. With that, she dropped to her knees, right there on the threshold, and hugged

Valentino, laughing as he licked her face in welcome. "Oh, buddy, I've missed you." she crooned, burying her face in the dog's ruff.

Conner rubbed his bare chest with the heel of one palm. "You mind coming inside?" he asked, in a tone that would have led some people to believe things like this—women showing up at his house in what amounted to the middle of the night—happened to him all the time. "So I can shut the door?"

She got to her feet, smiling, and stepped into the house.

Conner pushed the door closed, looking her over.

He saw her eyes widen as she registered that he wasn't wearing a shirt. "Hold on," he said, heading into his old room, the one Brody had taken over, and grabbing the first garment he got his hands on.

Turned out to be a T-shirt with a lot of holes and a lewd slogan on the front.

"I guess I woke you up," Tricia said, sounding chagrined. She'd already hunted up Valentino's leash, and she was bending to attach it to his collar. He supposed it should have galled him, her certainty that he'd just give back the dog and say nothing about it, but it didn't.

"Bound to happen," Conner observed dryly, glancing at the stove clock, "at three forty-five in the morning."

She had the good grace to blush. "I'm sorry," she said. "I took a red-eye from Seattle to Denver and all the way home, I was thinking about Valentino—"

Conner tried to remember the last time he'd been jealous of a dog and came up empty. Besides that, his sleep-drugged mind got snagged on the word *home*. Since when did Tricia McCall consider Lonesome Bend "home"? All she'd wanted was to get the hell out of there.

Just a figure of speech, he decided, rummy but waking up fast.

"He's still your dog," Conner said, folding his arms. Drinking in the sight of her. For somebody who'd been up all night, Tricia looked good—deliciously so. "Took off twice, after you left, and both times, I found him waiting on your doorstep. Coffee?"

Tricia blinked, probably at the conversational hairpin turn—Conner was prone to those, since his brain moved a lot faster than his mouth. "I couldn't impose," she said.

Conner laughed. "As if. This from a woman who couldn't wait till daylight to reclaim her dog?"

She blushed. She looked damn good, with color blossoming in her cheeks and that shine in her eyes. It would be interesting to see what a nice long orgasm did for her.

"I'm sorry," she repeated.

"Sit down," Conner said, moving on to the coffee-maker and starting the brew. Once it was percolating, he turned around to look at her again. She'd taken a chair, and the dog was standing there with his head resting on her knees, his eyes rolled up at her in frank adoration.

Conner could identify.

"I thought you'd decided Valentino was too big a dog to live in the city," he ventured. That was as close as his pride would let him get to asking her what her plans were, but he sure as hell wanted to know.

"We'll adapt," Tricia said, stroking Valentino lovingly.

Conner reminded himself that it was stupid to envy

a dog. "So," he responded casually, turning away to get cups from the cupboard, "you're still going back to Seattle?"

"I haven't decided," she answered. "There's no hurry, after all."

Conner looked back at her. "What about ski-guy?" he asked, and then could have kicked himself. Now she'd know he'd seen—and remembered—that snow-globe picture of her and the boyfriend on her computer screen.

She smiled. "Hunter? That's over." She said this lightly, in the same tone she might have used to say she'd once believed that the moon was made of green cheese, but now she knew it was just one big rock. "Actually, it's *been* over for a while now, but it took me some time to notice."

He got real busy with the cups, even though the coffee was a long way from being ready to drink. "I see," he said, when the silence had stretched to the breaking point. Of course, he *didn't* see. He was damned if he could figure out how a woman's mind worked, some-times. Especially *this* woman.

She looked around. "Where's Brody?" she asked. Then she colored up again. "Sleeping, I suppose."

"I doubt that," Conner replied. "He's out of town right now."

"Oh," Tricia said, squirming a little on the hard seat of that wooden chair. Not quite meeting his eyes.

Hot damn, he thought. Was it possible that she was there for another reason, besides fetching her dog?

Whoa, dumb-ass, he told himself silently. *Don't go jumping to conclusions.*

Conner needed something to do, so he went ahead

and pulled the carafe from the coffeemaker, even though it wasn't done doing its thing. The stuff sizzled on the little burner and scented the air with java.

He filled a cup for Tricia and one for himself and finally joined her at the table.

"Sugar?" she asked.

Holy shit, he thought, as a zing went through his whole system. But then the request penetrated his thick skull and seeped into the gray matter.

"Sure," he said, getting up to find the sugar bowl and get her a teaspoon so she could stir the stuff into her coffee. "You want cream, too? I've got some of the powdered stuff, I think."

Tricia shook her head and concentrated on doctoring the contents of her mug. "No, thanks," she said.

He sat down again.

The dog, he noticed, had positioned himself halfway between the two of them, and he kept turning his head from one to the other.

Tricia's spoon rattled in her cup.

Conner sipped his own coffee and mused.

Finally, she looked up at him, and he was amazed to see tears standing in her eyes. "I can't believe Natty won't be there when Valentino and I go back to the house," she said.

So that was it, Conner decided. She didn't want to face her great-grandmother's empty rooms—not in the dark, anyway, and not after a long and probably uncomfortable flight, followed by the drive from the airport.

"You could stay here," Conner said. Might as well put it out there in the open. All this pussyfooting around was getting them nowhere. "Go back to Natty's place after the sun's up and you're feeling a little stronger."

She blinked and, with a subtle motion of one hand, wiped her eyes. "Would you mind?"

Mind? Would he *mind?*

"I could sleep on the sofa, I suppose," she said in a thoughtful tone.

"You can have my bed," Conner answered. There were guest rooms in the house, of course, but none of them were made up, and he couldn't bring himself to put her in Brody's, empty though it was. There were probably cracker crumbs on the sheets, anyhow. "I'll just get an early start on the chores."

Tricia bit down on her lower lip, finally nodded. She used both hands to pick up her coffee mug this time, and they shook visibly.

"Okay," she said, looking at him over the rim. "My—my suitcase is in the Pathfinder—"

"I'll get it," Conner said, on his feet immediately. Over by the door, he paused to pull on a pair of boots and his denim jacket.

"Thanks," she said, after clearing her throat.

He braved the cold, retrieved the suitcase and hurried back inside. By then, she was standing at the kitchen sink, rinsing out her cup.

"This way," he told her, and the words came out sandpaper-gruff.

They followed him, the woman and the dog, through the old-fashioned dining room, into the hallway beyond. Conner flicked on a light when he passed the switch, thumped on the door across from the one leading into his room.

"That's the bathroom," he said.

Then he pushed open his own door, where the bed-side lamp was still burning; he'd turned it on earlier, when she knocked. The bed, a massive four-poster, dated back to the 1800s, when Micah Creed had brought his mail-order bride home to a much smaller version of this house. According to legend, old Micah wasted no time bedding the woman, and she hadn't minded.

Tricia peered around his right shoulder, taking in the natural rock fireplace, the bowed and leaded windows that formed an alcove of sorts on one side of the room.

"Wow," she breathed. "It's like going back in time."

"Except for the 3D TV, yeah," Conner agreed.

Tricia swallowed. "This is—very kind of you."

"Don't mention it," he said, with a partial grin.

"Oh, believe me," she replied, with a nervous laugh, "I won't. Not to anyone. You can just imagine the talk."

"Hadn't thought about it," Conner said, and that was true.

"Of course you haven't," Tricia said, seeming to loosen up just a little. "You're a man."

Oh, yeah, Conner thought. *I'm a man, all right. And I've got the hard-on to prove it.* He carried her suitcase in and set it on the antique bench at the foot of the bed, then crossed to the bureau to take out fresh clothes. "Make yourself at home," he said, heading toward the door.

Valentino settled himself on the rug in front of the fireplace, even though the hearth was bare, yawned and shut his eyes.

"You, too," Conner added, speaking to the dog, and then he and Tricia both laughed.

There was something intimate in the exchange, ordinary as it was. Laughing with Tricia felt good, but when it was over, they were both uncomfortable again.

"Holler if you need anything," Conner finally said.

And then he left the room without looking back, careful to close the door behind him.

CHAPTER FIFTEEN

ONCE SHE WAS SURE she wouldn't run into Conner—she'd heard the back door shut smartly in the distance—Tricia took her last clean sleepshirt out of her suitcase, left over from the trip to Seattle, along with her toothbrush and a tube of toothpaste, and ventured into the bathroom.

The shower was huge, and there were plenty of thick, thirsty towels. Tricia leaned inside the stall and turned the spigots, planning to adjust the spray, but pleasantly warm water flew out of a dozen different showerheads, placed at all levels and angles. With a little shriek of surprise, she jumped back, laughing, and started peeling off her now-soggy clothes.

What followed wasn't a mere shower, it was an *experience,* like being massaged by a hundred industrious Lilliputians. Although she most definitely *had not* come to the ranch to seduce—or be seduced by—Conner Creed, the warmth and the soap lather and the dance of the water against her naked skin *was* sensual.

Okay, Tricia admitted to herself minutes later, as she stood on the lush-plush bathmat, drying off, if she was perfectly honest, maybe coming here was a *little bit* about having sex with Conner. She didn't seem to be in any big hurry to put on her nightshirt, after all.

As the steam fog cleared from the big mirror above

the long vanity, with its artfully painted ceramic sinks and ornate copper-tile backsplash, Tricia assessed her wild-haired image. She had a pretty good body, compact and firm where firmness was an advantage. She turned in one direction, studying her profile, and then the other.

Finally, since goose bumps were starting to crop up all over, she put on the nightshirt, brushed her teeth thoroughly and crossed the hallway to Conner's room.

There was a nice blaze crackling in the fireplace grate now, and Valentino, still lounging on the rug, had rolled onto his back in an ecstasy of warmth, all four paws in the air.

Tricia smiled at the sight, but only after she'd scanned the room and made sure that Conner hadn't stuck around after building the fire.

He hadn't.

This was, as it happened, both a major relief and a disappointment.

Too tired to consider the implications—there would be plenty of time for that in the morning, when she was over her exhaustion and this crazy sense of ending one chapter of her life to begin another—Tricia crossed the room and climbed into the bed, stretching out on sheets that smelled woodsy and fresh-air clean. Like Conner.

She bunched up a pillow, snuggled down.

The bedframe was probably old, but the mattress was definitely modern, made of some space-age material that supported her softly, like the palm of a huge and gentle hand. She yawned, closed her eyes and promptly conked out, tumbling into a dreamless sleep, deep and sweet.

Hours later, upon awakening to a stream of sunlight

and a cheerful yip from Valentino, Tricia stretched deliciously before turning onto her side and seeing Conner on the other side of the room.

Fully dressed, his honey-gold hair damp and recently combed, he was just turning away from the fire. He'd added wood, and the flames leaped and popped behind him, framing him in a reddish glow.

"Hey," he said. His grin flashed. "All rested?"

"Yes," Tricia said, as the inevitable sense of chagrin settled over her. She jerked the covers up over her head, so he couldn't see her face. "Don't look at me," she added.

Conner laughed. "That's asking a lot, don't you think?"

"I could *just die,*" she said, the words muffled.

"No need to go that far," he replied. The echo of laughter lingered in his voice.

"I'm *in your bed!*" she pointed out, through layers of cloth.

"Yes," Conner answered easily. "I know that." A pause, a circumspect clearing of his throat. "Believe me, I know. And I'll admit this isn't exactly how I pictured things turning out—sure, I imagined you in my bed, lots of times—but I sort of expected to be right in there with you."

No way she was coming out from under the covers now—or maybe ever. "You pictured me in your bed?"

"I'm human," he said. Apparently, Conner considered that an answer.

"Please leave the room," Tricia said. "Before—"

"Before what?" Conner's voice was throaty.

She felt a distinct tug at the covers. And a need to breathe freely.

Tricia lowered the blankets just far enough to peer over the edge and suck some air in through her nose.

Conner's face was an inch from her own.

"I have a theory," he drawled. His gaze rested on her lips, made them tingle with the anticipation of illicit things.

"W-what theory?" Tricia ventured, suspicious and wary and hot to trot, all at the same time.

"That you want to make love as much as I do."

Her eyes widened. "What makes you think a thing like that?"

How did you know? Am I that obvious?

"I said it was a theory," Conner murmured, and by then his mouth was almost touching hers.

When he actually kissed her, Tricia couldn't help responding. The demands of her body instantly overrode conscious reasoning; the wanting raged through her like fire, swift and fierce, devouring every doubt, every hesitation, every fear in its path.

Her arms went around him, her fingers splayed across the hard expanse of his shoulders. The walls and floor and ceiling of that room seemed to recede, leaving in their places a void that throbbed rhythmically, like an invisible heart.

By the time that first consuming kiss was over, Conner was on top of Tricia, his hands pressed into the mattress on either side of her, being careful not to crush her under his weight.

"Hold it," he murmured, gasping for breath, and for the life of her, Tricia couldn't have said whether he was addressing her, or himself. "Hold on a second."

She looked up at him, her very cells drinking in

the hardness and heat, the blatant, uncompromising *maleness* of him.

A fragment of that milestone conversation with Diana flashed in her fevered brain, and a part of Tricia acknowledged that, yes, she was afraid to open herself, body, mind and soul, especially to this man. For all that, her need of him felt ancient, a cell memory, a part of her very DNA.

There was, she knew, no turning back. However advisable that might be.

"Conner," she said, softly but clearly, "make love to me."

His eyes were so serious, and so impossibly blue, as they searched hers, took in every nuance of her expression. It was almost as though he could see inside her mind, see past her desire, past her every defense, to the essence of her being, where all her deepest secrets were stored.

"Are you sure about this?" he asked.

She nodded. "Yes," she said, and it was the purest truth she knew in that moment.

Still, Conner hesitated, pushing back from her, standing up. She felt afraid then, afraid he would turn his back and walk away.

Instead, he hauled his shirt off over his head, without bothering to unbutton it first. He opened a drawer in the nightstand and took out a packet, set it within easy reach of the bed, his gaze fixed on her, blue and hot, missing nothing. After a few moments, he was out of his jeans and gently sliding Tricia's nightshirt up and then off over her head.

He lowered himself to her, kissed her again. Wherever her skin made contact with his, it seemed to Tricia, they fused, one to the other.

She felt dazed and, conversely, powerful. She was more than herself, more than an individual woman with a name and a heartbeat and a collection of disparate emotions—she was *womanhood itself,* as ferociously feminine as a she-wolf taking a mate. She wanted him inside her.

Now.

But Conner moved at his own excruciatingly slow pace, every nibble or touch of his tongue designed to heighten her need and, at the same time, delay the gratification she craved with her whole being.

His lips traced the length of her neck, returned to her earlobe, shifted to her collarbone and then the rounded tops of her breasts.

When he finally took one of her nipples into the warmth of his mouth, Tricia cried out in throaty, wordless welcome, and arched her back out of pure instinct and incredible need.

Still, Conner savored her.

She alternately flailed and writhed under his mouth and his hands, gasped his name. Pleas spilled out of her, intertwined with desperate commands.

Conner Creed wasn't taking orders—or dispensing mercies.

He ran the tip of his tongue around her navel, leaving a fiery little circle blazing on her skin, building the sweet, terrible pressure inside her, then easing off.

Tricia clawed at his shoulders, trying to pull him up from her belly, draw him onto her, *into* her.

But still Conner would not be swayed, would not be

hurried. Conquer her he would, that was plain, but on his own terms and in his own time.

He moved farther down her frantic body, parted her legs and then raised her by the strength of his hands, took her softly into his mouth.

She gave a strangled, exultant sob, and her legs went around him, because her arms couldn't reach. She repeated his name, over and over again, like some litany offered in delirium, now begging, now cajoling, now crying out in ecstasy.

The first orgasm was long, *endless,* with peaks and valleys, slow descents followed by rapid trajectory to an even higher pinnacle than the one before it. It wrung every last ounce of passion from Tricia, that continuous climax, causing her mind and soul to buckle and seize right along with her body. She was breathless when Conner finally let her rest, trembling, against the sheets.

Speech was impossible; she'd forgotten the language. She'd been transported, catapulted out of herself and then flung back in at the speed of light, and yet she felt every delicious thing Conner did to her. She was alive, and responding, on every level—physical, spiritual, mental and emotional.

He asked her again if she was sure; she barely made sense of the question. But she nodded.

Felt the shift of his powerful body as he put on the condom.

And then it happened, the hard, deep thrust as he claimed her.

Had her thoughts been coherent, Tricia might have wondered how Conner could possibly have aroused her to such a state of need, so soon after satisfying her so completely. As it was, she could only marvel, flexing wildly beneath Conner, hungry for release, fighting for fulfillment.

The pace, so slow before, was a rapid, powerful lunging now. The whole of life seemed to be concentrated in their coupling bodies. Tricia at once yearned for relief and wanted to burn in the fire of Conner's lovemaking forever.

When they came, they came simultaneously, with low, hoarse shouts of nearly intolerable pleasure, slamming together hard, as though to become one and stay that way for all eternity.

Afterward, they clung together, hard against soft, warm pressed to warm, both of them breathless.

Tricia drifted, finally settled slowly inside herself, like the feather of some high-flying bird riding the softest of breezes back to earth.

Then Conner left the bed, returning long minutes later to stretch out beside her.

"Tears?" he asked gruffly, sliding the side of one thumb across her cheekbone.

Tricia hadn't realized she was crying until then, and she had no explanation to offer, no way of sorting through the tangle of nameless emotions he'd stirred to life within her.

"Tricia?" Conner pressed, sounding worried. "Did I hurt you?"

She could only shake her head *no.* She slipped her arms around his neck, though, and held him close, unable to tell her own heartbeat from his.

He watched her, a gentle frown in his eyes. And he waited.

How could she tell him, in words, that he'd opened

up new places inside her, broken down barriers she had no recollection of erecting in the first place? How could she explain that their lovemaking had altered her, possibly for all time, in ways that were beyond her power to define—ways that made her feel both triumphant and dangerously vulnerable?

"Hold me," was all she could manage to say.

But it was enough.

Conner did hold her, and closely, his chin propped on top of her head, his shoulder smooth and strong under her cheek, his arms firm but gentle around her.

There was no telling how long they might have stayed like that if Valentino hadn't suddenly stuck his cold nose between Tricia's bare shoulder blades and given a plaintive whimper.

She started and cried out, and Conner chuckled.

"And now back to the real world," he said, pulling away from her, sitting up, throwing back the covers to get up.

Tricia listened, keeping her eyes closed, as Conner got dressed, spoke a few gruff but reassuring words to the dog and finally left the room.

As soon as she heard the door close, Tricia bolted out of bed, grabbed her clothes and raced, wobbly-legged, into the bathroom. There, she locked the door and started water running for a shower.

And now back to the real world.

Was *that* ever true. She'd landed smack-dab in the center of reality, with a bone-jarring *thunk,* too, like a skydiver whose parachute had failed to open.

Of course, her body still hummed liked the strings of a recently tuned violin, and that only made everything worse. She'd given herself to Conner Creed in haste, and now, as the old saying went, she would repent at leisure.

What would happen now?

Tricia couldn't say, of course, but she was sure of a few things, anyway. She'd crossed some invisible line, entered some uncharted territory, a place she'd never been before. She didn't speak the language, and she didn't know the rules. She was adrift.

And worse? There was no going back.

TRICIA DIDN'T JUST LEAVE.

She *fled* that venerable old ranch house, muttering some lame excuse about a forgotten appointment in town, remembering to take the dog with her but leaving her suitcase behind.

Conner watched through the window over the kitchen sink, a slight smile crooking his mouth up at one corner, as the Pathfinder sped off down the driveway toward the road. Once the rig was out of sight, he poured himself some coffee and fired up the right-front burner on the stove to cook some scrambled eggs. He made toast and sat down to enjoy his solitary breakfast, feeling strangely peaceful, though he supposed Tricia's quick exit wasn't an especially good sign.

After he'd eaten, Conner headed to the barn to feed the horses and then turn them out into the corral for some exercise. Brody's rodeo stock was way out there, on the range, and against his better judgment, Conner worried. There was plenty of water, since the river flowed clear across the ranch, but the grass was getting skimpy, now that it was November.

And Brody wasn't back from wherever it was he'd gone. Fuming a little, Conner strode to the equipment shed, rolled up the high, wide door, and drove the flat-bed truck out, leaving it to idle beside the barn while he climbed into the hay mow and began chucking bales down. When he had a load, he got behind the wheel again and made his way through a series of gates and out onto the range. He attracted a crowd of hungry cattle right away, though the horses kept their distance at first.

Methodically, silently cursing his twin brother the whole time, Conner drove from one part of the ranch to another, cutting the twine around the bales with his pocket knife, flinging the feed onto the ground so the livestock could get at it. After he'd dropped the last pile, he drove back toward the house. All the while, he was conscious of the heavy gray clouds overhead, promising snow. Maybe a lot of it.

What he tried *not* to think about was making love to Tricia McCall. Yes, he acknowledged silently, he'd enjoyed the experience. But it had left him shaken, too, and more than a little confused.

He'd been with his share of women in his time; the mechanics were the same. What *wasn't* the same was the way he'd felt, before, during and after. He supposed it could be compared to dying a good death at the close of a long and happy life, or being knocked off a horse on the road to Damascus by a Light so irrefutably real as to be utterly transformative.

He was thinking all those crazy, un-Connerlike thoughts as he pulled up next to the barn, shifted gears and shut down the truck's big engine. There was no point in putting the rig away in the equipment shed; knowing Brody, he, Conner, would be out there feeding cows, bulls and bucking broncos again, all by his lonesome, come morning.

A light rain, mixed with snow, began to fall as he stepped out onto the running board and leaped to the ground. A sound, or maybe a flicker of movement, drew his attention to the back door of the house, and there was Bill—*Valentino*—sitting on the step, looking as though his last friend had just caught a freight train for points south.

He walked quickly toward the dog, noting as he approached that the animal's hide was damp and streaked with mud. Judging by the way Valentino sat, instead of getting up to greet Conner, he was footsore, too.

"Hey, buddy," Conner said, crouching in front of Valentino and looking straight into those expressive, dog-brown eyes. "What brings you all the way out here?"

Valentino gave a low whine, but he didn't move.

A chill trickled down Conner's spine, like a drop of ice water. He glanced around, but there was no sign of Tricia or her Pathfinder.

So he reached out gently and ruffled Valentino's floppy ears.

Valentino whined again and raised his right foreleg slightly, prompting Conner to examine the dog's paw. It looked swollen, maybe a little bruised, but there was no blood.

Conner frowned. "Okay," he said, partly to himself and partly to the dog. "Let's get you inside. Give you some water and let you rest up a little."

Valentino permitted Conner to hoist him into his arms, carry him into the kitchen. He set him gently on the bed he'd improvised when the critter first came to stay with him, then headed for the phone.

A glance at the wall clock above the stove surprised him with the realization that it was barely 10:00 a.m. Conner could have sworn he'd lived a lifetime since Tricia had left the house on a dead run.

It occurred to him that he didn't know her number, either the landline or the cell. So he dialed Kim and Davis's place and, as he'd hoped, Carolyn answered.

Conner identified himself and asked for Tricia's number.

Maybe it was something in his voice. Maybe it was just woman's intuition. In any case, Carolyn was instantly worried, and there was some intrigue there, too. "Is something wrong?" she asked.

"Probably not," Conner said, after indulging in a long sigh that wouldn't be kept inside him. "I'd just like to make sure, that's all."

Carolyn hunted up the number, then recited it to him.

Conner thanked her and hung up, but before he could punch in the appropriate digits, the phone jangled in his hand. The unexpectedness of it made him flinch.

"Hello?" he rasped.

"It's Tricia," came the answer, at once shy and anxious. "Conner, have you seen Valentino? I took him for a walk, and everything was fine, but when we got home and I unhooked his leash from his collar, he took off like a shot. I've looked everywhere, but—"

"He's here," Conner said, closing his eyes. Bracing himself against the wall by extending one hand, palm out. "Tricia, are you all right?"

She hesitated before answering. "I'm—I'm fine. What's Valentino doing all the way out there?"

Conner chuckled, though inside, he was quaking with

relief. Nearly sick with it. He opened his eyes, straightened his spine. "I guess you'll have to ask *him* that. I went out to feed the range stock and, when I got back, Bill—er, Valentino—was waiting for me."

"Is he okay?" Tricia sounded anxious.

"I think his feet might be a little tender," Conner allowed, glancing at the dog. "Must have been quite a hike, from Natty's place to here."

She was quiet for so long that Conner started to think the connection had been broken. "Maybe Valentino would rather be your dog than mine," she said, at long last.

The words bruised Conner's heart in some deep and private places. "I could bring him back," he offered, after a long time.

"Conner—"

He sighed. Shoved a hand through his hair. "Look, if you regret what we did this morning, Tricia, I can deal with that. What I *won't* do, under any circumstances, is pretend that nothing happened."

She was silent for a while, but this time Conner knew she was still on the line, because he could hear her soft breathing. "I'm—I was vulnerable last night, and I didn't mean—I don't want to—"

"It's *all right,* Tricia. If you don't want things to go any further than they already have, I'm okay with that. But, as I said before, I won't accept business as usual, either. We *did* go to bed together. It was better than good. Beyond that, you can put any spin on this that works for you."

Again, she didn't answer right away. "Lonesome Bend is a small town," she said, finally. "If you—well, if you kiss and tell, Conner—"

He huffed out a snortlike chuckle, a sound completely devoid of amusement. "If you think I'd brag about our getting together, Tricia, you don't know me very well."

"Exactly," she said, after a long time. "I *don't* know you very well, Conner. And you just said you weren't going to pretend—"

"With you," Conner clarified, annoyed. Even a little hurt. "I'm not going to pretend *with you.* But neither do I have any intention of announcing to the whole town that we slept together."

A low whistle of exclamation made Conner whirl in the direction of the kitchen door.

There stood Brody, wearing a grin as wide as the Mississippi River. His timing, as always, was rotten.

Conner swore under his breath, roundly and with considerable creativity.

Tricia, being a woman, instantly took offense. "I beg your pardon?"

"I wasn't talking to you," Conner told her, so calmly that he amazed himself. He glowered at Brody, who ignored him, crossed to Valentino, and crouched to stroke the dog with a sympathetic hand. "Listen, Tricia—I'll bring your dog home in a little while. We'll talk then."

"What if I don't *want* to talk to you?"

"Well, I guess that's your prerogative. I could always keep Bill. Obviously, he likes it here."

"Who's Bill?" Tricia wanted to know.

"Bill," Conner replied patiently, "is what I called Valentino before you decided to take him back."

"Oh," Tricia said.

"Yeah," Conner said. *"Oh."*

On the other side of the room, still on his haunches

beside the dog, Brody chuckled and shook his head. "God almighty," he told Valentino, in a voice just loud enough to carry, "no *wonder* my little brother can't score with a woman. He has all the subtlety of a Brahma bull at a church social."

"What if you bring Valentino back and he runs away again?" Tricia asked, her voice soft and sad, echoing faintly with losses he knew nothing about. "He could be hit by a car, out there on the road, or attacked by coyotes—"

Trying to ignore Brody, who was still inspecting the dog for injuries, Conner thrust out a sigh. "Here's the problem, Tricia," he said quietly. "The road goes both ways. He could just as easily take a notion to take off for your place."

"What are we going to do?" Tricia asked.

"Keep an eye on him," Conner answered, wanting to offer her solutions but having none to offer. "That's all we *can* do, right now."

Brody, getting to his feet and ambling over to the refrigerator, where he no doubt hoped to find that his favorite foods had materialized by magic, had evidently gotten the gist of the conversation by listening in on Conner's end of it. And he jumped right in there with his two cents' worth, unasked, like always.

"That poor dog," he said mildly, "will run himself ragged going back and forth between the ranch and town. If he's with you, Conner, he misses Tricia. And vice versa. He's only going to be happy when both of you are under the same roof."

Brody's remark made a certain amount of sense, to Conner's irritation.

"Stay out of this," Conner said, adding, at Tricia's indrawn breath, "Brody."

Brody shrugged. He'd shaved recently, and his hair was still fairly short. Furthermore, he was either wearing Conner's clothes again, or he'd gone to a Western store and outfitted himself with similar ones.

What the *hell* was going on with him, anyhow?

"So," Tricia interjected, "are you bringing Valentino back or not?"

"Might as well," Conner said lightly. If Brody hadn't been right there, he'd have reminded her that she'd left her suitcase behind, though he was pretty sure she must have realized that by now. "I've been feeding my brother's livestock," he added, putting a point on his words and raising his voice a notch, "so I have to shower and change first. See you in about an hour?"

"Yes," Tricia said, rallying audibly from some distraction all her own. Her tone and her words were formal. They might have been business associates, or mere acquaintances, the way she talked, instead of two people who'd been wound up in a sweaty tangle together just a few hours before. "Yes, that would be fine."

Frowning, Conner said goodbye and hung up.

Brody was still rummaging through the fridge. "Don't you ever buy food?" he complained.

"Don't you?" Conner countered.

Brody closed the refrigerator door briskly. His jaw tightened as he studied Conner, but then mischief twinkled in his eyes.

"You slept with Tricia McCall," Brody said. "Little brother, I'm proud of you."

Conner gave a ragged laugh, but he wasn't amused. "Brody?"

"What?"

The dog lifted his head off the blanket-bed and looked at them curiously.

"Stay the hell out of my private business."

Brody leaned back against the counter, in that old, familiar way, folding his arms, tilting his head to one side and planting the toe of his right boot on the other side of his left one. "Thanks for feeding my stock," he said idly. "But it wasn't necessary. I made arrangements with Clint and Juan before I left, and I figured on being back in time to haul out a load of hay this morning. Which I was."

Conner was still annoyed, but the subject they were on was better than kicking around what had gone on between him and Tricia—by a long shot.

"Well, I didn't have any way of knowing that, now did I?" he asked.

Brody sighed, looking put upon and sadly amused, both at once. "Those critters belong to me," he said. "And I'll take care of them. If I need your help, Conner, I'll ask for it."

Conner cleared his throat. Looked away. Momentarily, and with a stab of pain so sudden and so fierce that it nearly stole his breath, he wondered what things would be like by now, between him and Brody, if Joleen had never come between them.

"I want to get along, Conner," Brody said, surprising him. "But you're not exactly making it easy."

"Imagine that," Conner snapped, but the truth was, the grudge was starting to weigh him down. He was getting tired of carrying it.

Brody huffed out another sigh. "I'm heading for town to pick up some grub at the grocery store," he said. "If you want, I could drop the dog off at Tricia's and save you the trip."

Conner felt a whisper of distrust, fleeting and foolish.

He wanted to see Tricia again, and any excuse would do, but he knew she needed space, and time to think.

"Okay," he said, secretly pleased to see that Brody had expected him to refuse the offer out of hand.

Conner crossed to the dog, crouched beside him. "You be good, now," he told the animal. "No more running away."

CHAPTER SIXTEEN

THE OLD VICTORIAN HOUSE literally echoed all around Tricia, whenever she made the slightest sound.

Natty was gone. So was Sasha. Even Winston and Valentino had bailed on her.

She finally sat down in front of her computer, sorely in need of distraction, but when she booted up, there was Rusty, filling the screen saver, grinning a dog-grin. And there was her younger self, still shy, but with luminous eyes, full of hopeful expectations.

Her eyes scalded, and she swallowed. Touched the image with the tip of one finger, watching as pixels spread out in a tiny radius, like still water disturbed.

Instead of sorrow, though, she felt a soft surge of happy gratitude for Rusty, and for his devoted friendship. He'd bridged the gap in some important ways, she realized, between her and her feuding parents.

She smiled and clicked her way online. Her inbox was full, and she spent a few minutes weeding out once-in-a-lifetime offers, then scanned the list of incoming messages.

Two from Diana. One from Sasha. *Seven* from Hunter. And, finally, one from her mother.

Her mother?

Tricia couldn't resist opening that one. She and her mom weren't close, so they didn't chat or swap instant messages and silly forwards. When one of them made the effort to get in touch with the other, there was a reason.

She opened the message and was surprised to see her slender, blonde mother smiling back at her from a photograph taken in front of some jungle hut.

Beside Laurel McCall stood a handsome man with a receding hairline and wire-rimmed glasses. He was beaming, too, one arm around Laurel's waist.

Tricia gulped, flicked a glance at the subject line above the picture.

"Meet Harvey, your new stepfather," Laurel had written, the phrase supplemented by half a dozen exclamation points.

"My new—?" Tricia whispered. She was feeling something—all kinds of things, actually—but she couldn't have said what those things were.

A knock sounded from downstairs; someone was at Natty's front door. Conner, bringing Valentino home? No, Tricia decided. He would have come up the outside staircase and, besides, he knew Natty was off in Denver.

Strangely jittery, Tricia closed the message without reading her mother's long missive, pushed back her chair and went to the living room window to look out at the street. Conner's truck was parked at the curb.

The knocking, though still polite, grew more insistent.

Tricia hurried downstairs, worked the stiff locks and pulled open the door.

Her gaze dropped to Valentino, sitting there on his haunches, panting and looking up at her, all innocence and unconditional canine love.

"You," she told the creature fondly, "are a bad dog."

She forced herself to look up and meet Conner's eyes. He'd said they weren't going to pretend, and she knew he'd meant it.

The man standing before her looked like Conner—*exactly* like him, in fact—but this *wasn't* Conner. It was Brody.

What was going on here? Tricia wondered, glancing past Brody's shoulder at Conner's truck. Was this some kind of immature twin trick? The old switcheroo?

"Hey," Brody said, and it was clear from the laughter lurking in his Conner-blue eyes that he'd picked up on her thoughts. "Brought your dog back."

"Thanks, Brody," Tricia said, stepping back. On the one hand, she was glad she didn't have to face Conner quite yet, because she wasn't ready, after the way she'd carried on in his bed and then run out of his house in a stupid panic. On the other, she felt his absence like a physical ache. "Come in. I'll put on a pot of coffee."

Brody's grin was crooked, identical to Conner's, and yet—*different*. "I guess you can tell my brother and me apart," he said, following Valentino over the threshold. Taking off his hat and holding it respectfully in one hand, cowboy style. "Most people can't, when we're trying to look alike."

Tricia, headed for the inside stairs, looked back over one shoulder. "Did you set out to fool me, Brody Creed?" she asked bluntly, but with a touch of amusement.

"If I did," he allowed good-naturedly, "it didn't work, did it?"

She shook her head.

"Ready for the closing tomorrow?" he asked, when

they'd reached the upper floor and her apartment. The place was too quiet without Sasha. Without Natty. But Valentino was back. That was something.

It took Tricia a moment to remember that Brody was buying her property, hence the mention of a closing.

Thanks to him, she was suddenly presented with a plethora of choices. Go or stay. Take a chance on a flesh-and-blood man or run for the hills.

Decisions, decisions.

"All ready," she answered, at last. But she was frowning slightly as she moved toward the coffeemaker. At a nod of invitation from her, Brody pulled back a chair and sat down at the table, resting his hat on the floor.

Valentino, meanwhile, plodded over to his bed, sniffed his blue chicken a few times and laid himself down with a loud, contented sigh.

"Crazy dog," Tricia said, shaking her head.

Brody shifted in his chair, taking off his denim jacket, setting it aside, with the hat. And grinning. "If I didn't know better," he said, "I'd be convinced that that critter is trying to play matchmaker."

Tricia turned her back to Brody, because her cheeks were suddenly warm and probably pink. Her heartbeat quickened a little, and she wondered exactly how much he knew about her relationship with Conner.

But Tricia shook her head an instant later, in answer to her own unspoken question. Conner wouldn't kiss and tell.

Brody chuckled to himself and didn't press her for a verbal reply.

"You'd be good for Conner," he said, after a long and thoughtful silence, just as Tricia was turning away from the coffeemaker. He looked, and sounded, totally serious, and there was something gentle in his eyes. "He's been alone too much, for way too long," Brody finished.

Tricia averted her eyes, ran her suddenly moist palms down her blue-jeaned thighs. She was blushing again, and this time, there was no hiding it. Still, she couldn't bring herself to speak.

"I walked in on that conversation you and Conner had this morning, over the telephone," Brody explained kindly. "And I overheard a pertinent detail."

He stood up, leaned to draw back a chair for Tricia.

She sat, still not looking at him, or saying anything.

He sat, too.

The coffeemaker chortled and hissed, and Valentino started to snore.

"Like I said," Brody told her finally, with a smile in his voice, "I think you'd be about the best thing that ever happened to my brother."

She met his eyes. Bit down on her lower lip, searching her brain for a sensible answer, discarding every prospect she managed to come up with.

Finally, she settled on, "I'd rather not talk about Conner."

"Okay," Brody said, with an agreeable nod. "Then let's talk about River's Bend, and the old drive-in." He paused, chuckled. "I have some great memories of that place. By my calculations, half the kids in Lonesome Bend must have been conceived there, back in the day."

Tricia was beginning to relax a little—she was comfortable around Brody in a way she wasn't with

Conner—probably because she and Brody had never been intimate. She smiled, let out her breath.

"Are any of them yours?" she asked, with a twinkle.

He laughed. "Not that I've heard," he replied. But then a new expression flickered in his eyes, and Tricia read it as uncertainty. She'd certainly touched a nerve, and now she wished she'd held her tongue.

She got up and poured them both a cup of the still-brewing coffee. Took a careful, steadying sip before turning the conversation back to her late father's properties.

"I guess you'll be getting rid of the screen and the speakers and stuff, out at the Bluebird," she said.

There was an easing in Brody. He'd made some kind of internal shift, away from whatever had been bothering him. His grin was companionable, his manner brotherly. "Yes," he answered. "Does that bother you?"

Tricia pondered the question—not for the first time, of course—and then shook her head. "No," she said. "Things change. What about the campground and the 'lodge,' as my dad used to call it?"

Brody shifted in his chair, looked down into his coffee cup as though he saw some benevolent scene playing out on the liquid surface. A moment later, though, he met her gaze. "Come spring," he said, "I plan on clearing that land and building a house and a barn. Putting up some pasture fences and the like."

She recalled that Carla, her real-estate agent, had mentioned Brody's intention to make the newly acquired land part of the Creed ranch, but hearing it directly from him made it real, took the idea outside the nebulous realm of local gossip and speculation.

"Will it seem strange," she began, "living somewhere besides the main ranch house, I mean?" The Creeds were a legend in Lonesome Bend and for miles around, probably. Natty's house, historical monument that it was, was new by comparison to the one Brody and Conner had grown up in.

Both the house and the ranch had been passed down from father to son for generations.

Too late, Tricia saw that her question had pained Brody, at least a little.

He cleared his throat, but his voice was still gruff when he said, "As you're probably aware, Conner and I don't get along very well. We inherited the ranch in equal shares, and that includes the house, but since he stayed put all this time, while I was off roaming the countryside, I figure it's only fair to let him have the place."

Tricia nodded, understanding. "It's too bad," she said, meaning it. "That you don't get along, I mean."

"I agree," Brody said, with quiet regret. "But what's done is done. Once Conner makes up his mind to write somebody off, the person might as well be dead. When he's finished, that's it."

The statement saddened Tricia, and frightened her a little, too. If Diana had been there, she probably would have said that was the reason for Tricia's history of arm's-length relationships—the fear of caring too much about someone, and then being tossed aside, forgotten.

"Because of Joleen," she said, without meaning to say any such thing.

"Because of Joleen," Brody confirmed grimly. "Or,

to be more accurate, because of what Conner thinks happened between Joleen and me once upon a time."

A combination of remembered pleasure and potential pain washed over Tricia; it was completely ridiculous, but she hated the idea of Conner making love to any other woman—past, present or future.

"It didn't happen?" she asked, her voice small. She was treading private ground, she knew, and yet she hadn't been able to keep the question inside.

Brody shook his head. "Nope," he said. "But there'll be no convincing Conner of that."

She recalled the day of the trail ride, when Joleen and Brody had come racing across the range together, bent low over their horses' necks, laughing. They'd looked like a couple in love, Brody and Joleen had—particularly to Carolyn.

How *was* Carolyn, anyway? She needed to find out.

"Have you tried?" she asked. "Convincing Conner, I mean?"

Brody gave a raspy, raw chuckle, the kind of sound it hurts to make—and to hear. "He knows the truth, somewhere in that hard Creed head of his. The thing is, Conner resents me for a whole other reason, one he might not even be aware of."

Tricia waited, desperate to know what that reason was, but unwilling to pry any more than she already had. She was way out of bounds as it was.

"Being an identical twin can be a great thing," Brody mused, looking off into some other place, beyond Tricia and beyond her kitchen. Maybe even beyond Lonesome Bend itself. "Or it can be a bad one. Sometimes, it's like you're one person, the two of you, but split apart. Believe it or not, you forget sometimes that you've got an exact double, and then you look up and see *yourself* standing on the other side of the room. It can be unnerving."

Tricia nodded again. The revelation was highly personal, but Brody had been the one to put it out there. She hadn't pried. "Is it true," she asked carefully, "that if one of you gets hurt—thrown from a bull at a rodeo, say—the other one feels pain?"

Brody nodded. "It happens. With Conner and me, the connection tended to manifest itself in other ways, though. As kids, the teachers used to separate us on test days, even put us in different rooms, because they thought we must have worked out a way of signaling each other—the answers we gave were always the same, no matter what they did to keep us apart." He paused, chuckled at the memory. "Even the wrong ones."

Tricia smiled. "I didn't go to school in Lonesome Bend," she said, "but I remember the fuss everybody raised when you two switched places."

"Those were the days," Brody said. He'd finished his coffee, and now he pushed his chair back, ready to leave. Retrieved his jacket and his hat and put them on. "Guess I'd better get back to the ranch. Shoulder my share of the load, and all that."

"I'll see you tomorrow, at the closing," Tricia said, rising. "Thanks for bringing Valentino home."

She opened the kitchen door, and he stepped out onto the landing. The wind was chilly, laced with tiny flakes of snow, and it ruffled his hair, caused him to raise the collar of his jacket and shiver slightly.

"Thanks for the company," was Brody's belated reply.

He didn't move to descend the outside stairs, and Tricia didn't close the door.

"You *were* trying to fool me, showing up in Conner's truck," she finally said. "Why?"

Brody looked away into that private distance of his again, then looked back. Gave the faintest semblance of that infamous Creed grin. "I wasn't expecting to pass myself off as my brother, if that's what you're thinking," he replied. "I just wanted to know for sure what I already suspected, since you and I ran into each other at the big chili feed that weekend—that you're one of the few people in this world who sees Conner as one person, and me as another."

Of course she remembered the encounter. She'd said, without any hesitation at all, "Hello, Brody."

She reached out now, touched his arm. "See you," she said, just as the landline rang behind her.

Brody grinned, raised one hand in a wave, and took his leave.

Tricia closed the door, turned, and leaped for the phone. Maybe it was Conner calling.

She hoped so.

She hoped *not*.

"Doris and I are going on a cruise," Natty announced, without preamble. "And I need someone to look after Winston while we're gone."

Tricia smiled, forgetting, for the moment, all the complications in her life. A new stepfather was just the beginning, though, of course, she had no intention of laying that on Natty.

"I'd be happy to do that," she told her great-grandmother. "I've missed Winston almost as much as I've missed you."

"I miss you, too, dear," Natty said. "In truth, I wasn't sure you'd still be in Lonesome Bend. I know Seattle beckons."

"Seattle," Tricia said, "is right where I left it. It will keep. Where are you and Aunt Doris going on this cruise of yours?"

"Everywhere," Natty responded happily. She sounded like a teenager instead of a woman in her nineties; living with her sister was clearly good for her. "We sail to Amsterdam next week, out of New York, and then from one Baltic port to another, all the way to St. Petersburg."

"That sounds wonderful," Tricia said, pleased.

"You could come with us," Natty mused. "But, then, I don't know who would take care of Winston if you did. Doris leaves her dogs at a local kennel, but I think my poor cat has had enough to get used to lately, without being sent to some strange place."

Tricia smiled. "Not a problem. How long will you be away?"

"Three weeks," Natty said, after a little pause. "Is that too long?"

"No," Tricia said, thinking of all the times Natty might have gone traveling if she hadn't chosen to stay in Lonesome Bend and help look after her great-granddaughter every summer instead. "Of course it isn't too long. Take all the time you want." She looked over at Valentino, who had lifted his head to take it all in. Did he know, somehow, that his feline sidekick was coming back for a visit? "Shall I come to Denver to fetch Winston?"

"No, dear," Natty replied, revving up again, in that old familiar way. Full of excitement and anticipation. "Doris's friend's oldest son, Buddy, drives a delivery truck to Lonesome Bend and the surrounding area five days a week. He'll bring Winston directly to your doorstep."

"Okay," Tricia answered. "Good."

"There is one other thing," Natty said.

Tricia felt her shoulders tense up slightly. It was something in her great-grandmother's tone—a certain hesitancy. "What?"

"Carolyn Simmons is moving in downstairs," Natty said. "She's my new renter. Housing is at such a premium in Lonesome Bend, and with Kim and Davis Creed coming home early, she doesn't have anywhere else to go. I didn't think you'd mind, since the two of you seem to like each other."

"I don't mind," Tricia confirmed. What she found hard to accept, though, was the sudden and certain realization that Natty really wasn't planning to come back home. Ever.

"I kept thinking of how *abandoned* that house would be, especially if you left. It's never been empty since it was built, you know. Not for any length of time, anyway. Even when Mama and Papa went to Europe on their honeymoon trip, my grandmother and great-grandmother were there to keep the home fires burning." Natty stopped to draw a breath, then rushed on. "What to do, what to do. That's what I wondered. You can just imagine. And then, all of the sudden, inspiration! I could offer that nice Carolyn Simmons a sort of home base. Everybody needs that. In any event, I knew she was housesitting for Davis and Kim, so I called her there, and she said she'd just love to stay in a beautiful house like mine and look after the plumbing and such, but she *insisted* on paying rent."

Tricia smiled. If she did decide to move back to Seattle—or elsewhere—at any time, she wouldn't have to worry about Natty's house. Even when she was minding someone else's place, Carolyn would keep an eye on the lovely old Victorian.

"I'm glad you found someone," Tricia said.

"Not that you need to be in any kind of hurry to leave, dear," Natty was quick to say. "After all, one day the place will be all yours."

"Not too soon, I hope," Tricia replied. She hadn't told her great-grandmother about the breakup with Hunter—she hadn't had the chance. And she certainly wasn't going to mention the latest development with Conner.

If it *was* a development.

Sex meant more to a woman than it did to a man, after all. She had to be careful not to read anything into that one incident.

I think you'd be good for my brother, she'd heard Brody say.

"How was your trip to Seattle?" Natty asked. She'd mentioned a few times that her husband had dubbed her Chatty Natty, and it was easy to see why.

"It was fine," Tricia answered, smiling again. "Diana and Paul are busy getting ready to leave for Paris, and of course I enjoyed getting to spend more time with Sasha. I did some shopping, too. Bought some actual *clothes*."

"Did you see Trooper?"

"Hunter," Tricia corrected, with amused patience.

"Hunter, then," Natty conceded, with good-natured *im*patience. "Did you see him?"

"Yes," Tricia said. "I saw him."

"And?"

Tricia laughed. "And we decided to go our separate ways," she answered.

"My dear," Natty told her, "you and Hunter went your separate ways a *long* time ago."

Tricia closed her eyes for a moment. Thought of her mother. And it spilled out of her then, without her ever intending for it to happen. "Do you think I'm like Mom?" she blurted.

Natty was quiet, an unusual situation in and of itself. "In what way, dear?" she asked, at long last. "Physically, you've always been more like your father—"

"You're stalling," Tricia accused. "Diana said I was only interested in Hunter because he was unavailable, and therefore *safe,* and that allowed me to keep my distance and still claim to be in a relationship. Is that how it was with Mom and Dad?"

Again, Natty hesitated. Then she spoke decisively, but with her usual gentleness. "Your father *was* available. That was the problem, for your mother. I don't think she was comfortable being close to another human being."

Including me, Tricia thought, rueful.

"You mustn't blame Laurel," Natty said quickly. "She was doing the very best she could. She was raised in foster homes, remember. Joe always said she tried, and I believed it, too."

Tricia, standing all this time, made her way to a chair and dropped into it. Shut her eyes tightly against the memory of all those lonely days and nights, when her mother had been working, working, *working,* while her daughter made do with nannies and babysitters and housekeepers.

"Her best wasn't all that terrific, Natty."

"I know that, sweetheart," Natty replied softly. "And

it's unfortunate. Nevertheless, there is only one way to deal with something like this, and that's to make up your mind to do better, in your turn, than poor Laurel did."

By that time, Tricia could only nod. She wasn't crying, but she was definitely choked up. She'd resented her mother for so long, yet now she felt sorry for her.

And happy about Harvey.

Once the conversation with Natty was over, Tricia returned to her computer. Made her way back into Laurel's effusive email.

Harvey was a doctor, Laurel had written. He was funny and strong and she loved him with all her heart. They'd gotten married on a recent and apparently brief sabbatical in Barcelona and sincerely hoped Tricia wouldn't mind that she'd missed the wedding.

It had all happened so quickly.

Tricia smiled as she studied the photo for a second time. Then she hit reply and began her response, starting with, "Congratulations!"

After that, well aware that she was procrastinating, Tricia read Diana's emails, both of which were comfortingly mundane, and then Sasha's. The child reported that she was already learning French, so she could start making new friends right after the family arrived in Paris.

Finally, Tricia turned to Hunter's emails. She considered deleting them, unopened, but decided that that would be cowardly. They weren't enemies, after all. Just two people who didn't belong together.

The first message contained a long and involved explanation of how lonely he'd been, after she'd left Seattle. Tricia nodded as she read.

Six more emails followed, all of them much shorter,

thankfully, and progressively less woeful. In the final one, clearly an afterthought, he said he wished her well and hoped they could get together for a friendly dinner if and when she returned to Seattle.

Tricia sent off a lighthearted reply and went offline.

Glancing up at the window, she saw that the snow was coming down harder and faster, the flakes feathery and big. Later, she'd walk Valentino again, she decided, and this time, she'd be careful not to let him off his leash before they were safely inside the apartment again.

One thing was for sure, she thought, with a sigh, looking around her small, well-organized kitchen.

She needed something to *do.* The leisurely life was not for her.

It gave her too much time to think.

HIS TRUCK WAS GONE.

Conner stood in the driveway, Tricia's forgotten suitcase at his feet, shaking his head in consternation.

Damn Brody, anyhow. It was just like him to take off in somebody else's rig, without so much as a howdy-do, and leave his own rusted bucket of bolts behind in its place.

Conner picked up the suitcase and gave Brody's old pickup a rueful once-over. The tires looked low, the back bumper was held in place by grimy duct tape, and the rear window was so cracked that the glass was opaque.

He swore under his breath. Brody wasn't a poor man, no more than he was. He could afford to drive a decent vehicle—he was buying the McCall properties for a huge chunk of cash, after all—but, no. A modern-day saddle bum, Brody liked to look the part.

Except when he was heading for Tricia's place, bringing back her dog. He'd wanted *Conner's* truck for that. Conner's clothes and haircut, too.

The realization stung its way through him like a jolt of snake venom. Made him swear again, but with a lot more vehemence this time.

Brody knew he was interested in Tricia. Was it happening again? Was that even possible?

"That's crazy!" Conner said out loud, but he tossed Tricia's suitcase into the back of that beat-up old truck just the same and, seeing that Brody had left the keys in the ignition, he plunked down behind the wheel. After a few grinding wheezes, the engine started, and he pointed that rig toward town.

The drive was short, but it gave him enough time to cool down.

Brody wasn't above betraying him, as history proved, but Tricia was another kind of person entirely. She wasn't like Brody and she wasn't like Joleen, either—she had her share of hang-ups, like everybody else on the planet, but she didn't play games with people's heads.

Or their hearts.

He knew that much about her, if little else.

When he pulled up in front of Natty's place, there was no sign of Brody or of Conner's truck. But Tricia and the dog were in the front yard, Valentino was on his leash and Carolyn was there, too, smiling, with both hands shoved into the pockets of her coat. Flurries of snow swirled around both women, like capes in motion.

Conner sat for a moment, before shutting off the engine and getting out of Brody's sorry-looking rig.

Carolyn and Tricia had been engaged in conversation before, but now they turned to look at him as he crossed the sidewalk and stepped onto the lawn. The difference in their expressions was something to see—Tricia looked shy but pleased, Carolyn stunned. She even took a step backward.

Conner recalled how she'd split herself off from the rest of the people on the trail ride Sunday afternoon, out at the ranch, and realized that she thought he was Brody—probably because of the truck.

He started to speak, wanting to put the woman at ease by identifying himself, but before he got a word out, Valentino broke free of Tricia's grip on his leash and bolted toward him, barking gleefully, the strand of nylon dragging through the dying grass behind him.

Three feet shy of slamming right into him, the dog leaped through the air like a circus performer and Conner barely had time to brace himself before twenty-plus pounds of squirmy canine landed in his arms.

He laughed, scrambling to hold on to the dog so it wouldn't fall. The wonder was that *both* of them didn't hit the ground.

Tricia hurried over, her eyes shining, her cheeks the same shade of pink they'd been after she'd had the umpteenth orgasm that morning, in his bed. "Valentino!" she scolded lovingly. "Bad dog!"

Conner set Valentino down and shoved a hand through his hair. In his hurry to reach Tricia, he'd forgotten his hat and, come to think of it, his coat, too.

She was exuding a glow that warmed him, though. Through and through.

"I'm sorry," she said, sputtering a little. "I guess Valentino was glad to see you."

"Guess so," Conner agreed.

By that time, Carolyn had reached them. Her hands were still balled up in her jacket pockets, and her eyes were narrowed as she peered at him through the thickening snow.

"Conner?" she said.

He gave her a half salute and a slight grin. "That's me," he affirmed.

Carolyn studied him, studied the old truck at the curb. "I thought—"

"Common mistake," Conner said. He was having trouble looking at anybody or anything besides Tricia.

Damn, she was hot. He wanted her all over again.

He was about to go back to the truck and hoist the suitcase out of the back, but it came to him that such a thing as that could be misunderstood. So he wedged his hands into the pockets of his jeans, like some kid with a confidence problem, and waited to see what would happen next.

"I'd better be going," Carolyn said, breaking the silence. "I'm expecting Kim and Davis at any time, and I want to have a special meal waiting for them when they get home."

Tricia nodded, but she was looking back at Conner. It was as though their gazes had snagged on each other, like fleece on barbed wire, and neither one of them could pull free.

Tricia managed it first. Handing Valentino's leash to Conner, she hurried to catch up with Carolyn, who was already making her way toward her car, head down against the cold wind.

"I'll be in and out tomorrow," Conner heard Tricia say to Carolyn. "Because of the closing and everything. But you have a key, right? When your furniture gets here, you'll be able to let the movers in?"

Carolyn nodded and gave some response Conner didn't hear, over the noise of the worsening weather. Then her eyes slipped past Tricia, past Conner, and touched briefly on Brody's old truck.

Conner couldn't remember the last time he'd seen a sadder look on anybody's face. Someone had done one hell of a number on Carolyn Simmons, and that someone was most likely Brody.

CHAPTER SEVENTEEN

NATTY'S FRONT DOOR STOOD AJAR, since Carolyn and Tricia had been inside, moments before Conner's arrival, discussing where to put various items of furniture once Carolyn's things had been delivered the next day.

Tricia was definitely looking forward to having a housemate again.

"Let's go in," she told Conner, as Carolyn backed out of the driveway and drove away, giving a jaunty toot of her horn in parting. The woman had obviously been shaken by Conner's arrival—she'd mistaken him for Brody at first, and had all but gone limp with relief when he identified himself. "It's cold out here."

Snowflakes rested on Conner's caramel-colored hair and on his eyelashes. He'd gotten an early start on his five o'clock shadow, too.

Tricia felt the same bone-deep, visceral attraction she had on previous encounters with this enigmatic man. Maybe, she reflected, inviting him into the house hadn't been the best idea; she was still assimilating aspects of that morning's wild lovemaking, emotionally *and* physically, and she needed more time, but she was dangerously amenable to a repeat performance, too.

Conner Creed had a way of making her nerves dance, with no discernible effort.

He handed her Valentino's leash and, for one awful

moment, Tricia thought he was about to tell her he couldn't stay, that he'd just turn right around and leave again.

While that probably would have been the ideal scenario, given her ambivalence about getting romantically involved so soon after cutting Hunter loose, the thought of Conner's going blew through her like a cold and desolate wind.

Did she love Conner, or did she love the *idea* of loving him? Was she ready to be fully present in a relationship, as she *hadn't* been with Hunter, or any of the other men she'd dated over the years?

There were just too many questions. And way too few answers.

But then, in the midst of her private dilemma, Conner gave that tilted grin that warmed her all the way to her toes, and the very landscape of her soul seemed to shift, powerfully and with a series of aftershocks. "You forgot your suitcase when you left this morning," he said. "You and Valentino go on inside, and I'll get the bag out of the truck."

Tricia hesitated, then nodded, and went up the porch steps. Valentino stopped at the top and sat down, looking back at Conner. The animal made a low, mournful sound in his throat.

She thought of Brody's offhanded theory—that Valentino might be doing a little canine matchmaking by running back and forth between her house and Conner's—and sighed. She'd dismissed the idea as silly before, but now she wasn't so sure. Of anything.

She gave Valentino's leash a gentle tug. "Hey, you," she said. "Be a good dog and come inside with me."

But Valentino didn't budge until he saw Conner

turning back, coming up the walk, grasping the handle of Tricia's heavy suitcase and carrying the thing as though its weight could be measured in ounces instead of megatons.

The dog gave a happy little yelp as Conner reached the porch, shifted the suitcase to his left hand and pressed the palm of his right to the small of Tricia's back, guiding her gently but firmly through the doorway.

Now, of course, Valentino cooperated. He was all bright eyes and lolling tongue and wagging tail. Everything was right in his world—because Conner was around.

Tricia sighed. She knew where the dog was coming from on that one.

Standing in the entryway, Conner took in the large, empty parlor where Natty's belongings had huddled together in lace-trimmed little groups for decades.

Tricia stood beside him, feeling a lump gather in her throat. The wallpaper was faded, and speckled with bright spots where paintings and photographs had hung. If Tricia recalled correctly, her great-grandmother had once confessed that she hadn't redecorated since 1959, but it hardly mattered. Carolyn, thrilled that her mail would be coming to an actual address instead of a box at the post office, planned to paint several rooms and sew new curtains for the kitchen windows.

"You sew?" Tricia had asked, impressed.

And Carolyn had laughed and retorted, "Yes. It's not brain surgery, Tricia."

For me, it might as well be, Tricia thought now.

Conner nudged her with an elbow. "Missing Natty?"

"The way I'd miss a severed limb is all," Tricia

answered, with a roll of her eyes for emphasis. Since the front door was safely shut now, she leaned down and unfastened Valentino's leash. "Guess what she's up to now."

"I couldn't begin to," Conner said, as the two of them started up the inside staircase. It was narrow, so he paused to let Tricia step in front of him, and Valentino gamely brought up the rear.

"Natty and Doris," Tricia said, stepping into her kitchen and turning to wait for Conner and Valentino to catch up, "are going on a three-week cruise. They leave New York next week, sailing to Amsterdam and then beyond, through the Baltic Sea. They're even going to *St. Petersburg.*"

Conner's voice was gruff and arguably tender when he replied, "Is that something you'd like to do, Tricia? See the world?"

She considered the question. "My mother has the travel bug," she said, "but I think it skipped me entirely. I'm more like my dad, I guess—something of a homebody, really." She bit her lip. "Color me boring," she finished, blushing a little. She hoped it was true, what Natty had always told her about blushing—that it was good for the complexion—because she'd sure been doing a lot of it lately.

"I guess it's a matter of perspective," Conner said, looking around for a place to put the suitcase down and finally just setting it on the floor beside him. "There's a lot to be said for home, if it's a good one."

Tricia didn't know how to answer that. "I could make coffee," she said.

You're a conversational whiz, McCall, mocked a voice in her head.

"I really just stopped by to drop off the suitcase and make sure the dog had stayed put," Conner said.

Tricia's gaze dropped to the bag. "Thanks for not sending it with Brody," she said, and promptly wished she hadn't. Conner didn't react overtly to the mention of his brother's name, but she would have taken it back anyway, if that had been possible.

Conner gave that crooked grin, but the usually vibrant blue of his eyes had darkened to a stormy gray. It wasn't that he looked angry—just unhappy. He started to say something, then stopped himself.

"And for not bringing it in when Carolyn was here," Tricia added quickly, because the moment seemed oddly tenuous. "I wouldn't want people to get the wrong idea."

Conner's grin didn't waver. "Like that we slept together?" he countered.

A small, nervous laugh escaped Tricia. "We *slept?*"

That made him chuckle. "Not that I recall," he said.

They stood looking at each other then, neither one moving or speaking.

Valentino finally wedged himself between them and tilted his head back to gaze up at them in frank adoration.

Conner grinned. "He likes us," he said.

"Ya think?" Tricia teased. Her voice came out sounding small and breathless, though. Even with the dog between them, she felt things stirring around inside her, in response to Conner's nearness.

She took a quick step backward.

His grin softened to an understanding smile. "No pressure, Tricia," he said quietly.

Tricia swallowed. "Right," she said. "No pressure."

He started for the outside door. Valentino trailed after him, making that whimpery sound again. The message couldn't have been clearer if that dog had suddenly developed the capacity for speech: *Don't go. Please, don't go.*

Conner turned, leaned slightly to pat the top of Valentino's head and muss up his floppy ears a little. "Hey, now," he said, in a low rumble of a voice, "no fair playing the heartstrings, buddy."

It touched Tricia, the way Conner acted with Valentino. The way he seemed to care so much about the animal's feelings.

Tricia held her tongue, afraid she'd say something foolish if she allowed herself to speak just then. Conner lifted his head and looked straight at her. And that was when the something-foolish tumbled out of her mouth, despite her best efforts.

"Stay," she said. Then, flustered, she clarified, "F-For lunch, I mean."

"All right," he replied, after a pause. "But if we're having grilled cheese sandwiches, I'd better make them."

Tricia laughed, relieved. Ridiculously happy. "No worries there," she said. "I'm fresh out of cheese. And butter. And bread. Basically, I'm out of *food*."

"Well, then," Conner answered, with a smile in his eyes, "I reckon we'll have to go out. Maybe hit the drive-through, since the dog's bound to raise a fuss if we leave him behind so we can sit in some restaurant."

"Unthinkable," Tricia said, practically diving for her purse and coat. She hadn't been this excited about fast food since—well—*ever*.

"Assuming that old rattletrap Brody calls a truck can make it to the other side of town," Conner replied, "we're on our way to grease-burger heaven."

Valentino barked happily then, as though he'd understood, and turned in joyous circles, making it a challenge for Tricia to fasten his leash to his collar. Conner finally had to take over the job.

The snow was coming down in earnest when they got outside, already dusting the sidewalks and the road and frosting the limbs of trees. For Valentino, it was an adventure—all the way to the pickup he leapt at the flakes, trying to catch them in his teeth.

Brody's truck, being so old, had a single bench seat.

"Hope it starts again," Conner said, after hefting the dog into the cab of the vehicle. "Valentino is going to be pretty disappointed if we don't go someplace, now that he's gotten his hopes up."

"We can always take my car," Tricia pointed out, but she got into the truck on the passenger side and made Valentino scoot over a little so she could fasten her seat belt—the old-fashioned kind that didn't have a shoulder harness.

"Let's see what happens," Conner responded, and shut the door behind her.

Once he'd walked around the truck and climbed behind the wheel, he cranked the keys in the ignition and the motor started with a lusty roar. Tricia cheered, and Valentino joined in with a string of short barks that would probably have translated as, *Let's go, let's go!*

They made it to the burger place, Conner ordered at the drive-through, and a clerk handed out a grease-blotched paper bag, along with two cups of cola, and

Valentino was practically beside himself at the smell of that food.

Eating in the truck would have been impossible, with the dog crammed in between them, so Conner suggested that they head for River's Bend. If it was too cold to eat outside at one of the picnic tables, they could take refuge in the office.

Tricia agreed, though her feelings about returning to a place that wouldn't be hers anymore, after tomorrow, were decidedly mixed. On the other hand, a visit seemed fitting, a sort of goodbye.

Since both the wind and the snowstorm had picked up some momentum, even in the short time since they'd left Natty's, they ended up going inside. It was only marginally warmer there, so Conner built a fire in the stove before the three of them tucked into their meals. Except for the snapping of that blaze and the sounds Valentino made, snorking up a rare treat—his very own cheeseburger—the office was quiet. In fact, with the snow falling, the whole *world* seemed quiet, in a luminous kind of way.

Tricia, who managed to chew and swallow about a third of her monster burger before she was full, rose from the desk chair where she'd been sitting and walked over to look up at an old map of Lonesome Bend, hand-drawn and colored, the campground marked with a lopsided star.

She'd made that map herself, the summer she turned eleven, sketching it out carefully on butcher paper, making the river vivid blue and the land a pale, milk-paint green. There were little trees around the campground, and outsized fish in the water, and in the lower right-hand corner, she'd carefully inscribed, "To Dad, from Tricia."

She touched the chipped wooden frame, remembering her father, how proud he'd been of her, of that drawing, of River's Bend and the Bluebird Drive-in. The original people-person, Joe McCall had enjoyed dealing with campers and moviegoers from late spring until early fall, and even though he'd never made much money, Tricia knew he'd considered himself a success, particularly as a father.

So had she.

"I asked my dad, once upon a time, if he'd ever wished I'd been a boy," she mused quietly, aware that Conner was watching her and listening in that focused way he had, as if everything a person said was important. "And he said he wouldn't trade me for a thousand boys."

"You miss him," Conner observed, standing behind her now, resting his hands on her shoulders.

She nodded. She *did* miss Joe McCall, but she'd done her grieving, reached a place of simple gratitude that he'd been her father. She could celebrate the part he'd played in her life, celebrate his humor and his steadiness and the easy constancy of his love.

Partly because she'd always been so sure of Joe's affection, she was strong enough to let go. Strong enough to move on. Just as he would have wanted her to do.

"I suppose I ought to take all these pictures down," she said, reaching up to lift the map off its hook. She'd be leaving behind all the furniture and office equipment, such as it was, but she wanted to keep the framed photos. So, primarily because she thought she might cry, and she was *sick* of crying, she set the map on the floor, leaning it carefully against the wall, and reached for the shot of Joe on the dock, with the kayak.

Conner let her take down and stack half a dozen dusty frames before he stopped her, turned her gently around, and pulled her close.

"Shh," he said, even though she wasn't making a sound.

She rested her forehead against the hard flesh of his shoulder—his shirt was still damp from the snow—and slipped her arms loosely around his lean waist. Let out a long, shuddery breath.

"I'm okay," she said, but she didn't pull back out of Conner's embrace. "Really."

Conner curved a finger under her chin and lifted, looking directly into her eyes. "If you want to do this now," he said, indicating the photographs with a slight nod of his head, "I'll help you. If you don't feel up to it, that's okay, too. Brody will understand."

I love you, Conner Creed.

The words rose so suddenly and so vividly in Tricia's mind that, for a split second, she was afraid she'd said them aloud.

She trembled, tried to look away.

But Conner cupped her face in his hands now—she loved the calloused roughness of his palms, in contrast to the near-reverent gentleness of his touch—and held her gaze.

"Tricia?"

"I-I'd rather make a clean break," she said, and was immediately caught up in a backwash of regret. "With River's Bend, I mean," she added anxiously.

Conner chuckled, and his hands remained where

they were. "That's a relief," he said. And then he kissed her.

The kiss was deep, and it sent a tingling rush of sweet, vibrant energy through Tricia, from her head to her feet, but it wasn't the same as the passionate, near-frantic kisses they'd exchanged in Conner's bed that morning.

No, this kiss wasn't a prelude to lovemaking. It was an assurance, a promise, as if Conner were telling her, without words, *I'm strong. And I'll be here, when you want somebody to lean on.*

He was the one to end the kiss, as it turned out. He went on holding her, though, and there wasn't any need for words.

After a minute or two, they separated. Conner disappeared into the storage room and returned right away with a couple of large, empty boxes.

They were both quiet as they took down all the pictures, one by one, wrapping them in old newspaper, also from the storeroom, and setting them carefully inside the boxes.

Valentino, meanwhile, lay curled up in front of the stove, blissfully content to be warm, full of cheeseburger and in the presence of his two all-time favorite humans.

TAKE IT SLOW AND EASY, you big dumb cowboy, Conner told himself, an hour later, after he'd delivered Tricia and Valentino back home and lugged in both boxes of pictures, along with the framed map.

He wanted nothing more than to spend the night right there in Tricia's apartment—in her *bed,* actually—making love to her. He knew she'd let him stay—it was in her eyes—but he also knew she'd be going against her own better judgment if she did.

"I need time," she'd told him, while they were rattling back from River's Bend in Brody's clunker, the dog looming like a hairy mountain between them. "You know—to figure things out."

"Okay," he'd responded, his hands tightening on the steering wheel. *What* kind *of things?* he'd wanted to ask. Hell, he'd wanted to *demand* an answer. But he'd restrained himself, because this was important.

Tricia was important.

This was no time to go off half-cocked and ruin everything.

So he stood there, coatless, in Tricia's kitchen, with one hand resting on the doorknob, looking his fill of the woman, memorizing the dark, silken fall of her hair, the flushed smoothness of her skin, the glow in her eyes, as hungrily as if the memory would have to last him for a long, long time.

I love you, Tricia McCall, he thought.

She glanced over at Valentino, who was stretched out on his dog bed, with his blue chicken tucked under his muzzle, ready for a nap. So much for Brody's matchmaking theory.

When Tricia's gaze returned to Conner's face, he felt as though the floor had gone soft under the soles of his boots.

"You could stay," she said, very softly.

He wanted to do just that, big-time. But there was a delicate process going on here and, whatever it was, he wasn't about to complicate the situation.

Besides, he was a rancher.

"I've got horses and cattle to feed," he said.

Tricia nodded. They were standing a few feet apart, and he was tempted to backtrack far enough to kiss her, but he didn't give in to the urge, because he knew that if he did that, if he touched his mouth to hers, there would be no leaving after that.

And the livestock *did* need to eat. Six generations of Creeds would roll over in their graves if he let the animals go hungry, even for one night, and he sure as hell couldn't depend on *Brody* to make sure the work got done.

"Go out to dinner with me tomorrow night?" he asked, opening the door a crack to remind himself that he had to leave, whether he wanted to or not. "Without the dog?"

She smiled one of those light-up smiles. "I'd like that," she said.

Pleased beyond all reason, Conner nodded, promised to call her the next day, and forced himself out of the warmth of her home and her presence and into the bitterly cold twilight of a wintry day.

The snowstorm was beginning to look more like a blizzard as Conner nosed that old truck toward home. Though it had worked just fine earlier, when Tricia and Valentino were riding with him, the rig choked and lurched and backfired its way along the nearly invisible highway.

It died at the bottom of the driveway, just inside the main gate, and Conner, wishing he'd remembered his coat, put his head down and slogged uphill toward the light glowing from the ranch house windows.

Brody was in the kitchen, frying up chicken, when Conner came inside, soaked to the skin and shivering.

"Thanks for taking off with my truck," he said,

through chattering teeth. He reached for his warmest coat, the leather one lined with sheepskin, and jammed an arm into one of the sleeves. "Yours just gave up the ghost, by the way. Down by the road."

Brody lifted the lid off a pot and peered in at whatever was cooking. "Spuds are almost ready," he said, as though Conner hadn't said anything about the dead truck. "Take off your coat and stay awhile, little brother. I've already done the barn chores. Clint and Juan and I fed the range stock, too."

Conner knew how to be irritated with his brother, but he'd forgotten how to deal with the rough-edged kindness Brody sometimes showed—always at the most unexpected times, of course. The minute a person got to expecting anything from Brody Creed, he'd shoot off in the opposite direction, just to be contrary.

Slowly, stuck for an answer, Conner took off the coat. Hung it on its peg again.

"Davis and Kim got back a little while ago," Brody went on. "You ought to see our old uncle with those two pint-sized dogs they bought. He's crazy about them, right down to the pink bows in their topknots. Even lets them ride in his coat pockets."

Brody was working at the electric stove, but the woodstove was going, too, and Conner went over to it, to warm himself up a little.

"That must have been a sight to see," he said.

"It was." Brody laughed, shook his head, went on turning pieces of chicken over in the skillet. The food smelled half again better than good. "Kim's complaining that they're supposed to be her dogs, not Davis's."

There was a brief silence.

"Since when do you cook?" Conner asked.

This was as close to a civil conversation as he could remember having with Brody since before Joleen. It felt fragile, like something that could break apart at any time.

"I like to eat," Brody replied. "Therefore, I cook."

Conner felt his back molars clamp together. He unclamped them so he could talk. "Why'd you take my truck?" he asked for the second time.

Brody looked at him over one shoulder. The chicken sizzled and the pot lids rattled and the whole setup was homey as all get-out.

"I wanted to see if Tricia could tell us apart," Brody replied, his tone easy, like his manner.

Brody's blunt honesty could be as much of a surprise as his kindness, and Conner was taken aback.

"She can," Brody added, with a wicked grin. "Fancy truck or no fancy truck, she knew I wasn't you."

Conner swallowed hard, warning himself to be watchful, not to let himself be suckered in. His brother was, after all, a master at hooking fools and reeling them in for the kill. Still, it made something leap inside Conner, hearing those words. Knowing that, to Tricia at least, he wasn't interchangeable with his twin.

"What if she *hadn't* known?" he finally asked. His teeth had stopped chattering, but he sounded hoarse, like he was coming down with something. "What if Tricia had thought you were me? What would you have done?"

Brody pushed the skillet off the burner and turned to face Conner squarely. "Nothing," he said, quietly but with a tinge of anger. His jaw worked, then he ground out, "*Dammit*, Conner, you're my brother."

"You were my brother when I thought Joleen and I

were going to get married and raise a family together," Conner heard himself say, his tone mild and matter-of-fact. "How was that different?"

"I was a kid," Brody growled. "So were you, and so was Joleen. But she knew, even if you *didn't,* little brother, that both of you were too young to think about marriage, let alone making babies."

Conner wasn't cold anymore. He walked over to the table, hauled back a chair, the legs scraping loudly against the floor, and sat down. His shirt and jeans felt clammy against his skin, and he would have sworn that even his socks were wet.

"I trusted you," he said, without looking at Brody.

"And you were *right* to trust me, brother, because I didn't sell you out. Not with Joleen or anybody else."

The truth of that hit Conner like a wall of water. *Cold* water.

"All this time, you let me think you and Joleen—"

Lightning fast, Brody took hold of the front of Conner's shirt and yanked him to his feet. They were practically nose to nose, Brody already furious, Conner getting there fast. In a moment, they'd be tying into each other, right there in the kitchen, butting heads like a couple of rutting bulls.

"You believed I'd do something that low-down and chicken-shit," Brody seethed. "So don't go talking to me about selling out!"

Conner knocked Brody's hand away, but the fight had gone out of him and it must have been plain to see. He felt that old-time sensation of having switched bodies with his brother, of seeing himself through Brody's eyes. "You could have denied it!" he rasped.

"I was too *insulted* to deny anything!" Brody yelled.

"I shouldn't have *had* to deny it, because you, Conner, *you of all people,* ought to have known what the deal was!"

"You didn't go to bed with Joleen," Conner said, in a slow, let-me-get-this-straight voice.

"I sure as hell didn't," Brody snapped, breathing hard but no longer yelling. He paused, shoved a hand through his hair in exactly the same way Conner had done, and then he grinned. "Not back then, anyhow," he clarified.

Conner laughed.

Brody laughed.

"Let's have ourselves some fried chicken," he told Conner. Then he frowned. "Maybe you ought to change clothes, first, though. It would be a hell of a note if you came down with pneumonia just when we're getting so we can stand to be in the same room."

Conner nodded his agreement and left the kitchen for his room upstairs. The bedcovers were still tangled from his and Tricia's lovemaking, and he caught the faintest scent of her skin as he headed for the bureau.

Armed with a pair of jeans and a warm sweatshirt, he went on to the bathroom, set the clothes on the counter, stripped off what he was wearing, and stepped into multiple sprays of hot water, coming at him from every direction.

Because he was hungry, because there was so much to tell Brody and so much to ask him about, Conner made quick work of his shower, dried off, dressed again and swiped a comb through his hair a couple of times.

By the time he got downstairs, he was beginning to think he might have imagined the confrontation with Brody, but there was his brother, with the table set properly and the food steaming fragrantly in the middle.

"All you need," Conner told Brody, in order to lighten the moment a little, "is a ruffled apron."

Brody chuckled, hauled back a chair. "Don't push your luck, little brother," he said. "I might have decided to let you live, but the jury is still out on whether or not I kick your ass from here to next week."

Conner sat down at his own place, picked up his fork and stabbed three pieces of chicken onto his plate. "You're welcome to try that at any time," he said affably. He looked the whole meal over again, and shook his head. "You even made gravy and mashed the spuds," he marveled. "What else can you do, brother? Darn socks? Make curtains out of flour sacks?"

"Keep pushing it," Brody drawled, but there was laughter in his eyes.

For a while, they ate in silence. This was the first real meal Conner could remember having at that table since Kim and Davis moved to their own place up the road.

"You've been in prison all this time," Conner speculated. "And they put you on kitchen duty. That's the big mystery."

"There *is* no big mystery," Brody said, and now his eyes were solemn and his tone was serious. "I was on the rodeo circuit, I told you that."

"I follow the rodeo circuit," Conner pointed out, considering a fourth piece of chicken and deciding against it because he was full to the gills. "I saw your name once or twice, Brody, but not often enough to account for *ten years* of being gone."

Brody sighed. "You are not going to leave this alone, are you?"

"No," Conner said. "I'm not."

That was when Brody told him about the woman, and the boy, and the accident that had taken their lives.

CHAPTER EIGHTEEN

THE NEXT DAY, in the small conference room at Lonesome Bend's one and only bank, Tricia held the cashier's check in both hands and stared at it in awe. All the papers had been signed and witnessed, and now River's Bend and the RV park and the Bluebird Drive-in belonged to Brody Creed.

Suddenly, she was free. Suddenly, she had *so many choices.*

Of course, she had to settle the few debts Joe had left behind, and pay off the small balance on her one credit card, and there would be taxes to pay. Even so, she was *rolling* in it.

Possibilities flashed through her mind—none of them were new, but they were all more substantial, now that she didn't have to live from hand to mouth.

She thought about Paris, about not only visiting the City of Light, but living there for a while.

She thought about Seattle, that bustling, busy place where something was *happening,* everywhere and all the time.

She thought about a gallery, with her name over the door in elegant gold script, a small but tasteful storefront full of vibrant art of all sorts and mediums.

But mostly she thought about Conner.

There were two worlds in Tricia's personal universe

now, it seemed—one with Conner in it, and one with-out. Should she choose the world her brain wanted—freedom, counterbalanced by the inevitable times of loneliness—or summon all her courage and follow her heart? Allow herself to take the terrible risk of loving and being loved in return?

Tricia shook off the nagging questions. She had things to do, starting with depositing the funds that would change everything, no matter *what* she decided to do in the end.

Brody, dressed to the nines in a perfectly tailored gray suit and a spiffy tie, looked wan and a little hollow-eyed as he watched her tuck the check back in its envelope and slip that into her purse.

"Buyer's remorse?" she asked, with a little smile.

"No," Brody replied, shoving his hands into his pockets. "Nothing like that."

She should get going. Head back to Natty's and help Carolyn supervise the placement of her furniture and unpack. Figure out what to wear for her dinner date with Conner that night.

Oh, and what to do with the rest of her life. Add *that* to the list.

But she liked Brody Creed, and she was grateful to him, so she tarried.

"Thanks," she said, putting out her hand to Brody.

He smiled and shook it, very businesslike.

She squinted at him. "Are you all right?" she asked, very quietly, so the bankers and Carla, still chatting in the conference room, wouldn't overhear.

Brody gave a raspy chuckle. "Conner and I were up pretty late last night, talking things through," he explained. "It'll be a long road back, but at least we're on the way."

"That's good," she said, remembering their conversation at her kitchen table, after Brody brought Valentino home from the ranch. She knew it troubled Conner, maybe even grieved him, to be estranged from his only brother, though he hadn't talked about it much, at least to her.

"It's good," Brody agreed. "But we went over some rough ground, my brother and me." He paused, and the smile drained out of his eyes, replaced by a dark expression she couldn't put a name to. "It's some consolation to know that Conner feels like he's been dragged backwards through a knothole, just as I do."

Tricia stood on tiptoe, kissed his cheek. "Give it some time," she said. "Things are bound to get better if you don't give up."

"If you say so," Brody joked, but the change in his eyes indicated that something else was going on beneath the surface here.

"Are you moving in over at River's Bend today?" she asked, hoping to lighten the mood.

"Yeah," Brody replied. He smiled again, but there was an edge to it. He nodded, as if to say goodbye, and half turned away from her, only to turn back. "Tricia?"

She waited. Glanced past him to the door of the conference room; she could see Carla's shadow through the frosted glass. Any moment now, the others would join them.

Brody gave a deep, ragged sigh. Ran a hand through his hair. "I might be way out of line here," he said hoarsely, "but there's something I need to say. About you and Conner, I mean, and whatever is or isn't going on between you."

Inwardly, Tricia stiffened. Outwardly, she probably appeared calm. "What's that?"

"Don't hurt him," Brody said. With a nod, he indicated the purse she held, an oblique reference to the cashier's check inside, most likely. "You have a lot of options now. If your plans don't include Conner, then I'd appreciate it if you'd back off and leave him alone."

Heat suffused Tricia's face. Carla, still chatting with the bank officials who'd overseen the closing, started to open the door.

"You were right before, Brody," Tricia said evenly, careful to keep her voice down. "You *are* out of line. By a country mile."

With that, she turned on her heel and stormed along the corridor, practically erupting into the main lobby, where the tellers stood at their windows, between customers and therefore watching her with interest.

Tricia stopped, took a deep breath, released it slowly.

Be calm, she told herself.

Then she marched over to the nearest teller, opened her purse and took out the envelope with the seven-figure check inside.

"I'd like to make a deposit, please," she said.

Brody caught up to her outside, several minutes later, as she was about to get into her Pathfinder.

"Tricia, wait," he said, and he looked pained.

She glared at him. This was one of the biggest days of her life so far, and he'd nearly spoiled it by implying that she might be jerking Conner around, encouraging him when she had no intention of following through. "What?" she snapped, begrudging him even that one word.

"I might not be the most tactful person in the world," Brody said.

"Maybe not," Tricia agreed, settling herself in the driver's seat and fastening her seat belt with a noisy click. She couldn't have shut the door if she'd wanted to, because Brody was in the way.

"I'm sorry," he said.

"Oh," Tricia mocked, with a sweeping gesture of one hand, "*well, then.* That changes everything!"

"Give me a chance, here," Brody responded. "I'm trying to look out for my bullheaded brother, that's all. Lonesome Bend is a small town, Tricia, and there's a lot of talk going around. Is it true that you're heading back to Seattle as soon as that check of mine clears the bank? That there's some guy waiting for you there?"

All the steam went out of her.

"There's no guy," she said softly. "Not anymore."

"What about leaving town? Is that what you mean to do?"

Tricia was quiet for a long time. Then she turned the key in the ignition, switched on the heater. With the door open to the cold, much of which seemed to be coming from Brody rather than the environment, the benefits were limited. "I don't know," she finally said. "There are a lot of things to consider."

"Here's another one for you," Brody said evenly, gripping the framework of the door and leaning in a little way. "Conner cares about you. It might be a while before he gets around to admitting that, to himself *or* to you, but, believe me, he *does* care. He's a good man, through and through, and he's smart as all get-out, but game playing is something he just doesn't understand—when he falls for somebody, he falls hard. He's rock-solid, the original straight shooter, the kind of guy most women think isn't even out there anymore."

"Are you finished, Brody?" Tricia's flippant tone was a bluff. Hurting Conner in any way, shape or form had never crossed her mind, but it *was* true that she might leave Lonesome Bend. After all, without River's Bend to oversee, she was pretty much at loose ends. Money or no money, she needed something to occupy her days or she'd go crazy.

"Just one more thing," Brody finally answered, stony-faced. "If you break Conner's heart, he'll be alone for the rest of his life, because he's not the sort to settle."

With that, Brody stepped back.

Trembling a little, Tricia shut the door.

And then she just sat there for several minutes, waiting until she felt calm enough to drive home.

CONNER SPENT THE MORNING on the range, with Clint and Juan and some of the extra hands Brody had hired on, setting up feed stations for the cattle and horses. Just before noon, he rode back to the ranch house, his coat collar raised against the icy wind, his hat pulled down low over his face. The sky churned with low-bellied clouds, gunmetal gray and, in his opinion, fixing to give birth to the perfect storm.

Kim and Davis drove up in their going-to-town car just as Conner was dismounting in front of the barn. He waited, speaking quietly to the horse, and grinned wide when his uncle eased his big frame from behind the wheel and got out, settling his hat on his head as he approached.

Two tiny dog faces looked out of the deep, wool-lined pockets of Davis's coat, bright-eyed and clearly enjoying the ride. And damn if they didn't have little pink bows on the tops of their heads, just as Brody had said.

The sight was so incongruous that Conner had to laugh. Kim, glowing with happiness as usual, looked Conner's way and shook her head with amusement.

Davis, so comfortable with his own masculinity that it probably wouldn't have occurred to him to be embarrassed to be seen with a pair of pink-bowed pocket dogs, grinned. He and Conner shook hands, their customary way of greeting each other after a separation of any length. "I hear Brody went ahead and bought Joe Mc-Call's property," Davis said.

Conner nodded. The chill bit at the edges of his ears, even with his hat on, and he cast a wary look up at the fitful sky. "He's in town finalizing the deal right now," he said. Tricia would be at the closing, too, of course. He was glad for her, glad for Joe, who had held on through thick and thin, having set his heart on leaving something behind for his "little girl."

"Is the coffee on?" Kim wanted to know, reaching into Davis's pockets, one by one, and collecting the dogs. Holding them up to her face to nuzzle them between their perked-up ears. "If not, we'll make some, won't we?" she asked the pups.

Davis rolled his eyes, but his love for his wife was almost palpable.

He watched her fondly as she headed for the house, being as much at home there as she was at the other place, then walked alongside Conner as he led his horse into the barn and removed the animal's saddle and bridle inside the stall.

Davis brought a couple of flakes of hay and tossed them into the feeder, while Conner gave the gelding a quick brushing-down. It was an ingrained habit, something he always did after a ride and rarely thought about.

That day, though, he was jumpy as a five-year-old on Christmas Eve—he'd be taking Tricia out for dinner that night—so he made short work of the grooming.

The other horses nickered companionably as he and Davis left the barn. A few enormous flakes of snow were drifting down.

Conner squared his shoulders, adjusted his hat again.

Inside the kitchen, Kim had all the lights on, and she'd started a fire in the cookstove while the coffee was brewing. The little dogs peeked out of a bottom drawer in the china cabinet, keeping a close eye on the proceedings.

"Are you sure those critters are dogs," Conner teased, grinning at Kim, "and not some kind of fancy rodents?"

Kim made a face at him, then laughed. "They're Yorkshire terriers," she said.

For as long as Conner could remember, she'd been like that, lighthearted and easy to get along with, full of mischief and uncomplicated joy, taking things as they came and making the best of the bad as well as the good.

It must have been a disappointment to Kim, Conner thought now, that she and Davis had never had a family of their own, but if it was, she'd never let on. She'd loved him and Brody and Steven full-out, like any mother.

Davis chuckled and hung up his hat, then his coat. "Wait till you hear their names," he told Conner.

The pups spilled out of the bureau drawer and trotted over to sniff at Davis's boots. They were pretty damn cute, all right, but Conner was worried that he might step on them. To make sure that didn't happen, he crouched and scooped them up, one in each hand, and both of them commenced to licking his face as though he'd used gravy for aftershave that morning.

"One's called Smidgeon," Davis went on, "and one's called Little Bit." His tone was teasing, for Kim's benefit, but there was a certain pride in his gaze, too. The look on his uncle's face reminded Conner of Steven, when he'd brought Melissa and Matt and the babies to the ranch to show them off.

"Smidgeon and Little Bit," Conner mused, with a wink for Kim. "Isn't that redundant?"

"Your uncle," Kim said dryly, eyes still twinkling, "wanted to name them Puffy and Fluffy. I had no choice but to intervene."

Conner put the dogs down carefully and looked over at Davis. *"Puffy and Fluffy?"*

Davis colored up a little, under his jawline. "I haven't had a lot of practice at naming dogs," he said. "The last one already had a name when we got him."

Conner laughed.

The dogs explored the kitchen, inch by inch, then leaped back into the bureau drawer, snuggled up in a furry little pile and went to sleep.

Kim poured coffee and the three of them sat at the table, sipping the brew, letting the heat thaw the marrow of their bones.

They talked, mainly just about catch-up stuff. Sure

enough, Kim confirmed, Steven and Melissa were coming home for Thanksgiving, and of course they were bringing the kids.

Brody showed up, driving Conner's truck because his own was still down by the gate, the engine deader than a doornail, just as Davis and Kim were about to take Smidgeon and Little Bit out of the drawer and head for town. Kim thought they ought to stop by the supermarket and stock up on nonperishables, in case the storm turned out to be a humdinger.

"Was it something I said?" Brody joked, looking on wryly as Davis tucked the yawning pups into his coat pockets.

Kim laughed and kissed his cheek before stepping back to give him the once-over. "That's quite the suit," she remarked. "If Conner hadn't told us you were at the bank, sealing a real-estate deal, I'd think you were about to get hitched."

Brody chuckled, but the look in his eyes was out-and-out somber. "I can't wait to get out of it," he said, and disappeared into his bedroom.

When he came out, wearing jeans and a T-shirt, Kim and Davis and the pups were gone, and Conner was standing at the sink, a fresh cup of coffee in one hand, watching the snow come down.

The flakes were thick as goose feathers, and there wasn't much space between them now. In fact, he could barely see the barn.

Brody drained the carafe of the coffeemaker into a mug and sighed. "Damn," he said. "I could do without a blizzard right now."

Conner turned his head. Studied his brother's grim profile. "Join the club," he said, with a halfhearted effort at a chuckle. "We've got months of feed-hauling ahead of us, if we want to keep the range stock alive."

Brody met his gaze. "You're gonna kill me," he said, out of the blue.

Conner frowned. "Maybe," he allowed solemnly, "but I guess I'd like to know why before I go ahead and do it."

Brody tried for a smile, but it didn't work. "I meant well," he said.

Conner felt a small muscle bunch up in his cheek, then wriggle itself loose again. He knew this speech had something to do with Tricia, since Brody had just been with her at the bank.

"What?" he rasped out.

Brody gave a heavy sigh and made his way to the table, hobbling a little, as if he'd been thrown from one too many bad-ass bulls during his rodeo career. Which he probably had.

"Sit down, Conner," he said, still gruff.

Conner nearly tipped his chair over, pulling it back from the table. But he sat.

Brody was across from him, but still within throttling distance if it came to that. "As I said," he reiterated, "I had the best of intentions."

Conner didn't say anything. He just waited, flexing his fingers into fists, relaxing them again.

Brody plunked his elbows on the table and splayed his hands over his face long enough to bust out with a loud sigh, as though he were the beleaguered one.

"I might have interfered in your—relationship," he finally confessed.

Annoyance sang through Conner, electrified him.

"What the hell is *that* supposed to mean?" he demanded, his voice dangerously quiet.

"I told Tricia not to hurt you."

Conner slammed his palms down hard on the table. It was a good thing those little dogs were gone, because he was about to go off like a geyser. They'd have been scared right out of their rhinestone collars and their itsy-bitsy hair ribbons.

"You did *what?*"

Brody looked chagrined, but if a fight broke out, he'd hold his own, Conner knew, as always. "You know how people talk—"

"Brody, I swear to God—"

"Joleen's mother heard it at Bingo Friday night," Brody said. "All about how Tricia has been seeing this yahoo in Seattle for years, just waiting to unload Joe's property so she could get the hell out of here—"

"Joleen's mother heard it at Bingo Friday night," Conner repeated, in a tone that didn't begin to express his disbelief.

"Okay," Brody allowed, "so maybe I overreacted a little."

"Maybe you should have kept your nose out of my business," Conner speculated, after unclamping the hinges of his jawbones.

"I'm sorry," Brody said. "I wish I'd stayed out of it, but I was afraid—after the way you took the breakup with Joleen, I was afraid you'd never take a chance on a woman again, if things went wrong with Tricia—"

Conner swore. And that siphoned off some of the fury.

"I was a *kid* then, Brody. Yeah, I thought losing Joleen was the end of the world, especially losing her to you.

But I also thought professional wrestling and Jeanine Clark's boobs were for real."

A grin tugged at the corner of Brody's mouth, and he didn't look quite so grim as before. "Jeanine Clark's boobs weren't real?" he asked, widening his eyes a little.

Conner gave a snort of laughter, but his amusement didn't last any longer than the rush of anger had. He felt—numb.

Neither one of them spoke for a while. They just breathed, and drank their coffee, and occasionally glanced over at the snow tumbling past the windows, thicker and thicker. Wood crackled in the antique cookstove, and the lights flickered and Conner wondered if he'd be able to get to Tricia's place on anything but cross-country skis or a snowmobile.

The county workers wouldn't start plowing the roads until they were sure the snow was going to stick, and even when they did, they'd be working on the far side of Lonesome Bend, keeping the main highway clear.

He pushed back his chair and stood. "If I don't get back in time," he told Brody, "feed the horses and make sure the water doesn't freeze up out in the barn."

Brody opened his mouth, shut it again.

Conner crossed to the row of pegs by the door and put on his hat and coat. "Keys," he said, since Brody had been the last one to drive his rig.

"In the ignition," Brody answered, rising from his chair.

"Figures," Conner muttered, on his way out.

He was halfway to his truck when Brody called to him from the doorway. He turned just in time to catch his flying cell phone in one hand.

There couldn't have been more than twenty feet between them, and yet Brody was just a shape, framed in a big square of light.

"Be careful," he said, in a low shout. "And call if you need help."

Conner nodded, dropped the cell into his coat pocket, smiling briefly because it made him think of Davis and the dogs.

Once he was inside the truck, though, with the engine going and the windshield covering over with snow between every swipe of the wipers, he was getting worried—and not just about Tricia.

Were Davis and Kim on the road? He didn't figure they'd had time to wheel a cart through the supermarket, load up the groceries and get home again, but he supposed it was possible, if they'd decided to hurry. Practically every winter, somebody ran off the road when the snow was heavy or the roads were iced over or both, and there wasn't always a happy ending.

Conner fumbled for his phone. Calling either Davis or Kim was always a crapshoot—Davis thought cell phones were more hindrance than help, as he put it, and Kim's was usually in her other purse. That is, the one she wasn't carrying.

Covering about a foot a minute, because of limited visibility, Conner keyed in his uncle's number. He got voice mail.

He tried getting in touch with Kim. Ditto.

He called their house, hoping they'd changed their minds about going to town and driven home. Voice mail again.

He swore under his breath and told himself the last thing the world needed was another fool out driving around in this weather, but he kept going, stopping now and then to reorient himself to the disappearing road. It was a good thing he'd lived in that country all his life, driven across it thousands of times.

Nearly an hour passed before Conner got to town, a trip that rarely took more than fifteen minutes, even in a hard and slippery rain. When he spotted the bright lights of the local supermarket off to one side, he cranked the wheel in that direction.

He cruised up and down the rows of cars and pickup trucks until he came to Kim and Davis's rig. Davis had the window rolled down, and fumes billowed from the tail pipe, but the tires wouldn't grab and he wasn't going forward or backward.

Conner pulled up alongside, pointed in the opposite direction, and buzzed down his own window. A whiff of burnt rubber met him, along with a face full of snow.

"I knew we should have brought the truck!" Davis grumbled.

Conner laughed, shoved open his door and held his hat on as he approached. Bent to look across at Kim, who looked as worried as he'd ever seen her, the two tiny dogs huddled together on her lap, shivering.

Kim brightened at the sight of him. "We're saved," she told the dogs. "Conner's here."

Davis was indignant, probably at the suggestion that any woman or critter in his care would need saving by Conner or anybody else. "Hell, Kim," he growled, "we're in the middle of town, not out on the range somewhere."

"Can you take us home?" Kim asked Conner, ignoring her husband. "Davis can stay here *in the middle of town* if he wants to, but Smidgeon and Little Bit and

I want to take our kibble and our canned goods and hightail it for the ranch."

Conner answered by going around to the other side of the car and helping Kim out. She'd tucked the dogs inside her coat, and they looked out over the folds of her lapels, transfixed by the snow.

By the time Conner had settled his aunt and her pups in the backseat of his extended-cab truck, Davis had given up on getting the car moving and opened up the trunk to transfer the groceries.

Neither he nor Conner said much while they hustled the bags into the back of Conner's rig—they'd have had to yell to hear each other over the howl of the wind, and there was no point in that—but Davis had plenty to say once they were inside again.

"I told Kim before we even left our place that we ought to take the truck, because I didn't like the looks of that sky, and there were already a few flurries coming down, but *no*. She said her car hadn't been started up in a while, what with our being away from home and all, and we ought to take that to town, blow the cobwebs out of the motor—"

"Oh, Davis," Kim said sweetly, from the backseat, "do shut up."

The air seemed to throb inside that truck, as if there were going to be an explosion, and Conner braced himself for it.

Instead of blowing up, though, Davis just laughed. "Sometimes," he joked, "I wonder if this relationship is going to last."

"You're stuck with me, cowboy," Kim told him, leaning forward to pat her husband's shoulder.

Conner let out his breath. It was no big revelation—

married people argued, even when they loved each other—but it struck him as a good thing to remember.

He took Davis and Kim as far as the main ranch house—the road to their place was all uphill and it was narrow. Too treacherous to travel over in the dark.

Brody came out to help unload the grub from the back of the truck, and Davis hustled Kim and the pups toward the house. When Conner started back to his truck—the snow was up to his knees now—Brody objected.

"Tricia's *all right*." He probably shouted the words, but the wind carried them away.

"I need to know that for myself," Conner yelled in response.

"You could call her, you dumb-ass!" Brody hollered, looking as though he might try to physically restrain Conner from getting into that truck and heading back down the road toward Lonesome Bend. "Did you ever think of that?"

Conner *had* tried to call Tricia, both on her landline and her cell. No luck with either one. And he wasn't going to take the time to explain, because the storm was getting worse, not better.

He shut the door and backed up, the tires grabbing as the ones on Davis's car had earlier, in the icy parking lot.

And Brody jumped right onto the running board and pressed his face to the window.

Conner lowered the window.

"Are you crazy?!" Brody demanded, the instant he could. "You're damn lucky you made it to town and back the *first* time—"

Conner planted one hand in the center of his brother's chest and pushed.

Brody went sprawling backward into a snowbank, came up ready to yank Conner out of that truck and pound on him, but the tires finally got down to solid ground and grabbed, and Conner was on the move.

It took twice as long to get to town this time, and the lights were out in the supermarket as he passed. Except for Davis and Kim's car, the lot was empty.

He made his way over buried roads to Natty's place, working mostly from memory because he could hardly see.

The old Victorian house was dark, like all the others he'd passed, and Conner thought about the wood he'd delivered, hoping Tricia had at least built a fire to keep herself and Valentino warm.

The wind fought him all the way to the outside stairway. The steps had already vanished beneath an even layer of snow, a perfect, gleaming slant of white.

"Conner!"

He turned, looked behind him, on the off chance that he'd heard correctly, over the screech of the wind. Sure enough, Tricia was standing on Natty's porch, a flashlight in her hand.

"This way!" she shouted, beckoning.

Conner headed to the porch steps, which had been covered, like the ones leading up to the apartment, and slogged his way up them. In the entryway, Valentino was waiting to greet him, wagging his whole rear end instead of just his tail.

"What are you doing here?" Tricia asked, setting aside the flashlight to peel Conner's coat off him.

He was wildly glad to see her, find her safe. "We had a date," he quipped, shaking off his hat before hanging it on the doorknob behind him. "Remember?"

She pushed at his chest with both hands, but she was smiling and her eyes glistened in the near darkness. Inside Natty's former parlor, a fire blazed on the hearth and there were a few candles burning here and there, on top of boxes and what looked like teetery TV trays.

He remembered that Carolyn was moving in, looked around for her as he headed for the fireplace. "Where's your roommate?" he asked.

"Staying at the Skylark Motel," Tricia answered, glowing like a goddess in the light of the fire and the candles. "She called about two seconds before the phones went dead—her car couldn't make it through the snow, and she decided not to risk freezing to death by trying to walk here."

"Good decision," Conner said. He was starting to get the feeling back in his fingers.

Tricia came to stand beside him. Rested her head against the outside of his upper arm. "I can't believe you were idiotic enough to drive all the way here in this god-awful weather," she said.

"Actually," Conner replied, slipping an arm around her waist, "I was idiotic enough to do it twice. Davis and Kim got stranded at the supermarket, and I took them back to the ranch."

She pulled away just far enough to look up at him. The firelight danced in her eyes and sparkled in her hair. "And then you came back here? Why?"

He bent his head, tasted her mouth. "Because you're here," he said, breathing the words as she melted against him. "Nothing could have kept me away."

CHAPTER NINETEEN

BECAUSE YOU'RE HERE. Nothing could have kept me away.

Those words, like Conner's kiss, reverberated through her. She rested her cheek against his chest when it was over, sighed softly. His arms were around her, easy and safe.

It came back to her then, some of what Brody had said to her that day, at the bank. *Conner cares for you—when he falls for somebody, he falls hard—he's rock-solid, the original straight shooter, the kind of guy most women think isn't even out there anymore.*

Conner propped his chin on top of her head. "I hear you had a little run-in with my brother this morning," he said, as if he'd been reading her mind.

She tilted her head back, looked up Conner. "I'm over it," she said honestly. "Brody loves you. I realized pretty quickly that he was only trying to look out for you."

Conner chuckled. The sound echoed through Tricia, just as the kiss had, just now. "Yeah," he agreed. "I figured that out, after I got past the desire to do him bodily harm."

Tricia laughed, still gazing into that strong, handsome face. Conner was integrity and commitment personified; if the man signed on for something, he was in for the duration.

Tricia's doubts about a future with Conner Creed had been slipping away all day, the victims of quiet logic, but as she stood there, drinking in the sight and the feel of him, Tricia said goodbye to the last of her hesitancy.

As frightening as it was, she loved Conner. Furthermore, she would *always* love him. He was literally part of her, and while she would certainly survive without him, possibly even thrive, she'd still be shortchanging herself, settling for less than she might have had. Less than she might have *given.*

"What do we do now?" she asked him.

But Conner wasn't taking the long view, as she was. Not yet, anyway.

"Lay a blanket or two on the floor in front of this fireplace and make love like a caveman and his woman in mating season?"

Again, she laughed, a throaty sound, tinged with mischief. "I thought we had a *dinner* date," she said. "Not one for hot, wet, unbridled sex."

He chuckled, held her closer, nibbled at her lips again. The fire burning on that hearth had nothing on the one Conner had ignited inside her. "With any luck," he murmured, "our dinner date would have evolved into 'hot, wet, unbridled sex' anyhow."

"But we haven't *had* dinner," Tricia stalled, just to prolong the anticipation a little.

Conner was already unbuttoning the practical flannel shirt she'd put on after she returned from the closing, in order to help Carolyn with all the moving-in chores. With the storm getting worse by the moment, she'd written off the date with Conner as a lost cause.

And now here he was. Seducing her. Making her

want him—*need* him. Her heart raced, and her breath grew so short that she was afraid she'd hyperventilate.

He moved the shirt back off her shoulders, weighed her lace-covered breasts gently in his rough, rancher's hands before deftly popping the front catch of her bra, setting her free. Her nipples hardened instantly, not from the chill, but in response to Conner's hungry appreciation of her partially unveiled body.

The bra went, too, after that, sailing off into the surrounding darkness.

Tricia turned her head, overwhelmed by this new and deeper vulnerability. She and Conner had made love before, of course, but this was different. As fantastic as the first round of sex had been, she'd been responding physically but struggling the whole time not to respond *emotionally*. She'd held back some vital part of herself, even at the frenetic height of satisfaction. Now, she was offering him everything—not just her body, but *everything*.

She was gloriously terrified, like an astronaut about to step out of some craft into deep space, except that, in this instance, she had no special NASA-designed suit to sustain her, no line to tether her to the last vestige of a world she knew and understood.

"Conner," she whispered, closing her eyes, letting her head fall back as he toyed with her nipples, chafed them with the sides of his thumbs, preparing them, preparing *her* for incomprehensible pleasure. "Oh, Conner."

He kissed her again, lightly this time around, the tip of his tongue exploring the corners of her mouth, promising a deeper, wilder conquering, moments from now. Or minutes, or maybe even hours.

"Wh-what about—protection?" she asked.

Conner was unsnapping her jeans, unzipping them, pushing them down, right along with her panties. He dropped to one knee, worked off her shoes and socks, freed her from the last of her clothing.

She stood bare before him. *Cavewoman by firelight,* she thought fancifully, breathlessly, fully aware of Conner in every part of her.

Aware, too, of the question suspended between them.

"Conner," she repeated, with the last of her resistance, the last of her strength.

"I brought something," he said, and then he took her into his mouth and suckled, and she was utterly, completely, deliciously lost.

Long before Conner allowed Tricia to reach that first, desperately needed orgasm, her knees threatened to give out, and he lowered her to the rug, consumed her with his mouth, his hands, his eyes.

At some point, he must have shed his own clothes, though Tricia had been too delirious to notice until he was kneeling astride her, magnificently naked, his erection huge.

She watched, dazed, as he put on a condom and lowered himself to her.

"I love you, Tricia," he said, and even though both of them were trembling with need by then, his voice was even, his words clear.

Aroused to a state of primitive need, Tricia answered him with all the honesty in her. "I love *you,* Conner Creed."

He delved inside Tricia, wringing a shout of hoarse, welcoming joy from her. "Will—you—marry—me?"

he gasped, punctuating the sentence with hard, deep strokes.

Tricia, already teetering on the verge, came then, laughing and sobbing and shouting, "Yes!" all at once.

After the lovemaking—*long* after the lovemaking—Tricia and Conner dined on peanut butter and jelly sandwiches, partially dressed and sitting cross-legged in front of the fire, facing each other.

Valentino, hoping for a bite of one of their sandwiches at first, finally settled for a ration of kibble and went back to sleep.

"Some dinner date," Conner said, his eyes twinkling.

Tricia smiled, raised her shoulders in a slight shrug. She was wearing Conner's shirt, with only a few strategic buttons fastened. "I'm not complaining," she said.

He laughed, raised his iced-tea tumbler, a third filled with wine he'd rummaged for upstairs, in the dark, and clinked it against Tricia's jelly glass. "Me, either," he replied.

Tricia took a sip of wine, set her glass aside, and gazed sidelong into the fire. "About that marriage proposal—"

Conner stilled. "Second thoughts?" he asked, and while his tone was light, she knew the answer mattered to him.

She met his eyes. "When I said yes, I *meant* yes," she said.

He let out his breath. He looked like Example A of the perfect man, sitting there, clad only in his jeans, with the flickering fire giving him a light side and a dark side, like the moon. "Is this going somewhere?" he asked, with no sarcasm at all. He really wanted to know.

Tricia blushed, searching for words. They were about as easy to capture or even herd in one direction as a flock of frightened chickens.

"We were—making love at the time," she began, feeling her way.

"Yeah," Conner agreed. "I'd say that's the understatement of the century, but, yes, we were making love when I asked you to marry me."

She was too flustered to be diplomatic. "Did you mean it?" she blurted out. "Or was it just—?"

"I never say anything I don't mean, Tricia," Conner said, his expression tender and serious now. "I love you. I want to marry you and make babies together and all the rest of it."

Her heart soared. "Really?"

His mouth crooked up at one corner. "Yeah, really."

"When?"

Conner chuckled, reached over to give her braid a light tug and then slip it behind her shoulder. "When do we get married, or when do we start making babies?"

She blushed. "Take your pick," she said, gasping a little when he slid his hand from her hair to the inside of the shirt, cupped it around her breast. The nipple pulsed against his palm.

He eased her down onto her back. "You're the bride, so you can set the wedding date. Next week, next year—I don't care, as long as I can do this whenever I want to—"

To demonstrate his point, he laid the shirt open, baring her to the firelight and his gaze and drawing on her with a combination of tenderness and lust that instantly awakened all the previously satisfied forces within her.

At his own leisurely pace, he attended to her other breast. "And this," he said, kissing his way downward now. "And, of course, *this*—"

A soft, sweet climax seized Tricia instantly, made her body ripple like a ribbon trailing in the wind. Instead of crying out, she crooned, surrendering to the slow, luxurious pleasure.

She sighed, when it ended, trembled with contentment.

Conner kissed his way back up to her mouth. "Now, the babies," he began, as if there had been no break in the conversation, no fiercely delicious orgasm to fuse together all the broken places inside Tricia, "might not be as easy to time."

He was stretched out on top of her now, wanting her.

And she wanted him. Again. Already.

"Why's that?" she murmured, her hips already beginning to rise and fall of their own accord, seeking him.

He chuckled, the sound a sexy rasp, low in his throat. "Because," he said, "there was only one condom."

"Uh-oh," she purred.

"Yep," he muttered, kissing the length of her neck.

"You're sure you only had one?" The question came out on a series of ragged breaths.

"Positive," he lamented, back at her breast.

She cried out and arched her back. Grasped his face in both her hands and demanded, "Did you mean it when you said you love me, Conner Creed? When you said you want us to have babies together?"

He nodded.

"Then have me," she whispered.

And he did.

"GOD BLESS THE POWER COMPANY," Tricia said, hours later, when the electricity set things to clunking and then whirring all around her and Conner. The lights came on in her kitchen, and the furnace roared to life two floors below, in the basement. Exquisite curlicues frosted the glass in her bedroom window.

Warmed by each other, four quilts, two blankets and one dog, Tricia and Conner slowly began to untangle their limbs.

"I think we ought to stay here until the house warms up a little," Tricia said.

Valentino, curled up at their feet, gave a doggish sigh.

"Or a lot," Conner agreed. "Is that my leg, or yours?"

Tricia laughed. "If it's hairy, it's yours," she teased.

He put his arms around her, held her close against his chest.

"Now, I *know* that isn't my hand," he said, with a grin in his voice. And the slightest groan of renewed lust.

Valentino yawned broadly, jumped down off the bed, and padded out into the kitchen. Moments later, he was lapping up water from his bowl. Next, he crunched away on his kibbles.

Conner gave a strangled chuckle and groaned again.

"I've decided on a wedding date," Tricia told him.

"I—can't wait—to hear about it—" Conner choked out, rolling onto his side and then poising himself above her.

"I think we should get married right away," Tricia said, getting a little breathless now herself, as Conner began to caress her with slow promise. "As soon as we can round up Natty and your family."

"Umm," Conner muttered. "You don't want a regular wedding?"

"Weddings—take too long to—*oooooh, Conner*—plan. There's the dress—the cake—the invitations—the—oh, God, *do that again*—"

He grinned. And did it again.

Valentino came back into the bedroom, collar tags jingling, and made a low, whining sound, almost apologetic.

"He needs to go out," Conner rasped. "Now. Of all times." He groaned loudly.

Tricia sighed, resigned to the inconveniences of pet ownership. "Yes," she said. "Now, of all times."

Conner rose, grumbling, and scrambled into his jeans. Reclaimed his shirt from the floor, where it had fallen the night before, soon after they came upstairs, and put it on. Looked around for his boots, which were still downstairs.

Tricia started to get up.

"Stay there," Conner told her. "The dog and I will head downstairs and try to tunnel our way out the back door."

The room was brutally cold, without Conner to keep her warm. It would be a while for the furnace to overtake the chill. So Tricia huddled inside the bedcovers, with only her head sticking out. Before she could protest that Valentino was her dog and therefore her responsibility, both of them were gone.

Tricia spent a couple of minutes trying to work up

her courage to climb out of bed; the least she could do was woman-up and get out there in the kitchen to put the coffee on. Conner, after all, was braving postblizzard conditions; he'd need the hot brew when he came back inside.

The soles of her bare feet nearly stuck to the floor, and goose bumps leaped out on every square inch of her skin.

Teeth clattering together, hugging herself, Tricia hip-hopped to her dresser, snatched a pair of black sweat-pants and a blue woolen hoodie from a drawer, and plunged back into bed. She hid there, waiting for the chills to subside, and began squirming into the clothes, still under the covers, when she heard Valentino coming up the inside stairs, with Conner.

She got tangled in the sweatpants and then the sheets, and as she struggled on, she heard a familiar masculine laugh from the doorway.

"No fair starting without me," Conner said.

Tricia fought her way into her clothes. Her voice muffled by layers of covers, she replied, "This is *not* funny."

Again, he laughed. "Of course it is," he said. "It's a hoot. If I didn't know better, I'd say there was a wres-tling match going on under those quilts."

"Just for that," Tricia said, dressed at last, "you can make your *own* coffee."

"Is this what it's going to be like when we're mar-ried?" Conner teased.

By the time she tossed the blankets back, she was smiling. "Probably," she said, glancing at the window, which was still opaque with frost. "What's going on outside? Is it still snowing?"

Valentino squeezed past Conner in the bedroom doorway and shook himself, hard, sending icy moisture flying in every direction.

"No," Conner said, after a pause to enjoy Tricia's consternation over the impromptu christening, "but there must be two feet of the stuff on the ground. The sun's out and the sky is clear and blue enough to break your heart."

Tricia stroked Valentino's damp head, looking around for her slippers. Then she remembered—she'd donated them to the rummage sale.

She got out a pair of socks and sat down on the edge of the bed to pull them on.

"I suppose you have to go and feed cattle or something," she said, because this intimacy—taking the dog out, making coffee—was in some ways more profound than making love. It was a reflex, that attempt to establish a distance between them, however slight.

Conner nodded. "Yep," he said. "I'm a rancher, Tricia. That's what we do."

"What if the roads haven't been plowed?" she asked reasonably, slipping past him to enter the kitchen.

"That truck will go anywhere," he said. "I'll put chains on the back tires and then roll."

She reached for the coffee carafe, filled it with water at the sink. Through the kitchen window, which hadn't frosted over, she could see the pristine shimmer of a snow-whitened world. It looked almost magical, but Tricia's feelings were bittersweet. On the one hand, she was glad the storm was over, at least for now, so people could start digging themselves out and get on with their daily life. But on the other, she didn't want Conner to leave.

"You could ride along, as far as the ranch house, anyway," Conner ventured, his voice quiet and a little gruff. "Keep Kim and those little dogs of hers company while Davis and Brody and I go out and check the herd."

Tricia hesitated long enough to push the button on the coffeemaker. Sighed. "I'd better not," she said. "Winston—Natty's cat—is supposed to arrive any day now. I have to be here to take delivery if, by some miracle, the truck gets through."

Conner approached her, pinned her gently against the counter in front of the coffee machine. "You could call the delivery company to make sure," he said. "Unless, of course, you're set on putting some space between us."

Tricia blinked up at him. She was getting aroused again, starting to ache in needy places. "Why would you say that?"

"Because you've seen my soul and I've seen yours," Conner replied, kissing her forehead. "If you're like me, you're happy, but you're scared, too." He drew back just far enough to hook a finger under her chin and lift, so that she had to look at him. "We love each other, Tricia," he reminded her. "We'll have to find our way forward from there, like everybody else, but we'll make it. One step at a time, we'll make it."

Tricia relaxed, with a soft sigh, and put her arms around Conner, let herself lean into him. Her cheek rested against his heart; she could feel the strong, steady beat of it. "You're right," she said, thinking of her parents, and their ill-fated union. "Nobody gets a guarantee, do they?"

He stroked her hair, coming loose from its usually

tidy braid. "Nobody gets a guarantee," he agreed. "But we can stack the odds in our favor, Tricia."

"How?" she asked, thinking that if she loved this man any more than she already did, she'd burst from it.

"Davis told me one time that he and Kim have stayed married all these years mainly because neither of them was willing to give up on the other. They scrap once in a while—they're both strong-minded people—and they've had their share of disappointments and setbacks, too, but they don't quit."

Tricia nodded, loving the feel of Conner Creed, the scent of him, the warm strength of his arms around her, the pressure of his chest and hips. "Natty adored my great-grandfather, Henry, but according to her, the secret of a good marriage is not expecting to be happy all the time, because no one is. Whenever she and Henry went through tough times, Natty said, they made sure they were on the same side, stood shoulder to shoulder and took on whatever came their way."

"Natty's a pioneer," Conner said, with amused admiration.

Out on the street, a mighty roar sounded, and Valentino tilted his head back and howled once, like his distant ancestor, the gray wolf.

"Snowplow," Conner told him. "Take a breath."

Valentino went over to his bed, sighed, and lay down on top of his blue chicken, resigned.

After coffee and a couple of slices of toast, Conner took a quick—and lukewarm—shower, got dressed again and, after giving her a kiss and a promise that he'd be back no matter what, headed for the ranch.

Tricia waited until the water was hot before taking her own shower.

She dressed warmly, in jeans and a bulky blue sweater, found Doris's Denver number in her address book and dialed. Tricia figured the great-aunt-and-grandmother combo might already have left for New York, where they would board the cruise ship, but it was worth a try.

Doris answered on the other end, greeted Tricia in her fond but businesslike way, and called out, "Natty Jean! It's for you."

Tricia smiled to herself as she waited

"Did Winston get there yet?" Doris asked, while both of them waited for Natty to made her way to the phone. "Buddy stopped by and picked him up this morning. He said the highways were clear all the way to Lonesome Bend, thanks to a whole night of plowing."

"No sign of Winston yet," Tricia answered, smiling, "but I'll be sure to call and let you know when he arrives."

"That's good," Doris said. "Natty Jean frets about him, you know."

"I know," Tricia said gently. "But Winston will be fine here, with Valentino and Carolyn and me."

Doris didn't get a chance to respond; Natty must have wrested the handset from her, because the next voice Tricia heard was her great-grandmother's.

"Is Winston there, dear?"

The smile was back. "No," Tricia said, "but I'm expecting him anytime now. Shall I tell him you called?"

Natty laughed. "Yes," she said. "Right after you call *me* to say he's safe and sound."

Tricia repeated her promise.

"So the old house is still standing, then?" Natty

inquired. "Phew! I haven't seen that much snow fall in one night since the blizzard of 1968. You wouldn't remember that, of course."

"The house is as sturdy as ever," Tricia said. "Will the weather be a problem for you and Doris, cruise-wise, I mean?"

"Heavens, no," Natty informed her, and her tone made Tricia think of Conner's words, earlier that morning. *Natty's a pioneer.* "The airport is already open again and, anyway, we don't leave until day after tomorrow."

"Send me a postcard?"

"Of course, dear," Natty said. "At least one from every port."

Tricia's heart warmed. "There's something I need to tell you, before you go jetting off to board the QE2, or whatever your ship is called."

An indrawn breath. "I presume it's something good?" Natty murmured.

"Very good," Tricia said, feeling so happy in that moment that her throat thickened and her eyes burned. "You were right, Natty. About Conner being the right man for me, I mean."

Natty's voice was fluttery—and loud. "Doris!" she called, making Tricia wince and hold the handset away from her ear for a moment. "Doris! It's happening—just like I told you it would—" A pause, with Doris muttering unintelligibly in the background. "Well, *of course* I mean that Conner and Tricia have fallen in love! What else would it be?"

Tricia chuckled. "We're getting married," she said.

More delight on Natty's end, followed by, "Oh, dear,

that's *wonderful*. When, though? Not before Doris and
I get back from our trip, I hope."

"Not before then," Tricia promised. "I couldn't get
married without you there, Natty."

"I should hope not," Natty said stoutly. Then, brightening, she went on to ask, "Are you planning on living
in sin in the meantime, dear?"

"Maybe not *living* in sin, but it's safe to say there
might be some dabbling."

This time, it was Natty who laughed. "Henry and
I lived in sin for a whole week," she confided. "Hush,
Doris, it's true and you know it. Don't be such a stick-
in-the-mud."

"You and great-grandpa *lived in sin?*" Tricia couldn't
help being intrigued, though a part of her pleaded silently, *Don't tell me!*

"Well," Natty said, after clearing her throat and lowering her voice to a confidential tone, even though Doris
had obviously gotten the gist of the conversation and,
thus, the proverbial horse was out of the barn, "we didn't
move in together, like young people do today, but we *did*
run off to get married. We were so busy honeymooning
that we forgot all about the wedding, though, and Papa
showed up and made a terrible scene before he dragged
me back home. Mama was furious, and when Henry
came looking for me—he was very brave, my Henry—
she met him at the front gate and told him she'd shoot
him with an elephant gun if he didn't make an honest
woman out of me. I'll never forget what he said to her.
'Eleanor,' he told Mama, just as bold as you please, *'I
can't make Natty an honest woman, because she already is one. But I'd be proud to make her my wife.'*
Isn't that what he said, Doris? Don't deny it, you were

hiding behind the lilac bush the whole time, and you heard everything."

Tricia smiled, imagining the scene. She'd probably never pass through the gate out front again without thinking of her spirited great-grandparents and the romantic scandal they must have created, back in the day.

Some things, she thought happily, never change.

Downstairs, the doorbell rang.

Tricia carried the phone into her bedroom, which was at the front of the house, and wiped a circle in the thawing frost covering the window. A large brown truck was parked at the curb, undaunted by the high snowbanks.

"I'm pretty sure Winston is here," Tricia announced.

"Well, then, you go and welcome him, dear. Doris says they have computers on the ship, so I'll be in touch after we set sail."

"Natty?" Tricia said, moving through the house, toward the inside staircase.

"Yes, dear?"

"I love you."

Natty gave a pleased little chuckle. "Well, I love you, too, dear. Take good care of Winston."

"I will," Tricia promised, disconnecting and laying the handset on the wide windowsill in the entryway so she could open the door.

"Meow," Winston complained peevishly, from inside his plastic carrier.

The driver, presumably the aforementioned Buddy, wore earmuffs as well as a stocking cap, a heavy scarf and a quilted uniform to match his truck.

"Tricia McCall?" he asked.

"That's me," Tricia said.

"Reoooooow," Winston insisted.

Buddy handed Tricia the electronic equivalent of a clipboard, so she could sign for the cat.

"He's been doing that since we left Denver this morning," Buddy said. "Miss Natty gave me all his gear, but that's still in the truck. Maybe you ought to take him inside, though, while I fetch it. I wouldn't want the noisy little feller to catch a cold or anything."

"Good idea," Tricia said. She stepped into the house, set the carrier down on the floor and opened the little gate.

Winston shot through the opening like a furry bullet and made a dash for the stairway.

Valentino gave a brief, happy bark of welcome, already partway down the stairs.

Just as Buddy was handing over the pet-store bags filled with cat toys, a fluffy little bed, a new litter box, a five-pound bag of cat food and three cans of sardines, Carolyn drove up.

She passed the retreating Buddy on the as-yet-unshoveled walk, high-stepping it toward the porch.

"I see you survived the storm," Carolyn called, her voice sunny.

Tricia thought of the chain of tumultuous orgasms she'd enjoyed, first on the floor in front of the downstairs fireplace and then *up*stairs, in her bed. *Survived* was hardly the word, but for now, she'd keep that to herself.

"Come in," Tricia said, smiling at her friend. "Before you freeze."

Winston zoomed past, evidently running off some of his excess energy.

Carolyn laughed and raised one eyebrow in good-natured question.

"That's Winston," Tricia explained. "When he calms down, I'll introduce the two of you. In the meantime, the coffee's on upstairs, and you look like you could use a cup."

Carolyn nodded, and the two of them climbed the stairs.

In Tricia's kitchen, they settled themselves at the table, their steaming cups in front of them. Tricia was bursting with her news, but she wanted to tell Diana first, now that Natty knew.

Carolyn took on a serious expression. "I think you should know about Brody Creed and me," she said.

Surprised, Tricia studied her. "That's not necessary," she said carefully.

"It is for me," Carolyn said. "I know you and Conner have something going, and he's Brody's brother, of course, and—well—it will just be too awkward, keeping secrets."

"Okay," Tricia said, drawing out the word, wondering if, as curious as she was, she really wanted to hear this story.

Carolyn took in a long breath and let it out very slowly, in a here-goes kind of way. Her high cheekbones were pink, partly because she'd been out in the cold, certainly, but mostly because she was embarrassed.

"A couple of years ago," she began, "I was housesitting for Davis and Kim, while they were on the road. One night, Brody showed up—I thought he was Conner, of course, but I realized my mistake as soon as I got a good look at him, standing there under the porch light. I told him the Creeds weren't home, and he said that was just his luck, or something like that. He looked so tired and discouraged and—well, sort of *scruffy*—that's mainly how I knew he wasn't Conner—he said he'd spend the night in the barn and head out in the morning." Carolyn stopped, sipped her coffee, swallowed in a way that looked painful. "He didn't leave in the morning," she said finally. "And after that first night, he didn't sleep in the barn, either."

Tricia waited, knowing there was more.

"I thought—" Carolyn paused again and gave a bitter little laugh, shaking her head, "I thought I meant something to him. We talked about so many things—he told me about growing up as an identical twin, and all about his falling-out with Conner—but there was one thing he left out."

Again Tricia waited. The moment was too delicate not to.

"He was about to marry another woman—and she was carrying his baby."

Tricia ached for Carolyn, and for Brody and the unknown woman and the baby. It was a lose-lose situation, all the way around.

"That's pretty much it," Carolyn said, her eyes filling.

Tricia reached across the table and squeezed her hand. "Let's have one more cup of coffee," she said, "before we go downstairs and start taking your things out of boxes and putting them away."

"I—" Carolyn cleared her throat, blushed harder. "I wouldn't want anyone else to know—"

"Don't worry," Tricia replied. "As my dad used to say, mum's the word."

Carolyn laughed, wiping away tears at the same time. "Mine used to say that, too," she said.

Tricia smiled.

Winston jumped unceremoniously into Carolyn's lap and settled himself there, purring loudly. Valentino, standing nearby, looked a little envious.

Carolyn stroked the cat's back, smiling down at him.

"I guess I've made another friend," she said.

EPILOGUE

New Year's Eve
The Brown Palace, Denver

CONNER SWEPT HIS WIFE of two full hours up into his arms and kissed her soundly, outside the door of Room 719.

They'd been married at her great-aunt Doris's place, with Natty giving the bride away and Brody serving as best man, while Davis and Kim and a very quiet Carolyn looked on. Tricia's mother and stepfather had been there, too, via webcam, as had Diana and Paul and a very excited Sasha, the three of them tuning in from their apartment in Paris.

Yep, it was a high-tech world, all right. Fit to boggle a cowboy's mind.

And speaking of scrambling a man's brain...

"I love you so much," Tricia said, after Conner had managed to jimmy open their hotel room door and carry her over the unusually high threshold.

Champagne awaited, nestled in a silver ice bucket, and the bed had been strewn with delicate white rose petals, a touch Kim had suggested. Now, seeing the effect, Conner was glad he'd called the florist and had those flowers sprinkled around.

He kissed Tricia, letting his mouth linger on hers. The

first of many lingering kisses, he thought, with a rush of grateful anticipation. "And I love you," he answered.

Then he set his lovely bride on her feet.

She wobbled a little, not used to high-heeled shoes. At home on the ranch—she'd moved in with him at Thanksgiving, bringing Valentino with her—Tricia wore boots and jeans most of the time. Although she and Carolyn were cooking up a plan to open some kind of shop on the first floor of Natty's house, the newest Mrs. Creed seemed to love living in the country.

Seeing her in the fancy pale blue dress she'd bought for the wedding was quite a change from every day. To Conner, she always looked amazing, no matter what she was—or wasn't—wearing.

Flakes of snow glistened in Tricia's hair and on the shoulders of her coat as she stood there looking at him, her heart in her eyes. He doubted a lot of things in his life, but there was no doubting her love for him.

"It's almost the new year," she said. At times, the old shyness overtook her, even with him, but it never lasted long.

He touched her cheek gently, wanting to put her at ease and, at the same time, wanting to get her naked on that flowery bed and drive her out of her mind with a whole constellation of explosive orgasms.

"New year, new life," he said, helping her out of the coat, watching as she kicked off the shoes. Wriggled her toes and sighed with undisguised relief.

A few moments after that, she moved close, slipped her arms around Conner's neck, and nibbled at his mouth, her eyes dancing with sultry mischief now.

"Make love to me, Mr. Creed," she murmured.

He gave a throaty laugh, a little raspy, a little raw. It

was terrifying to be so happy, to fly so close to the sun. "It would be my pleasure, Mrs. Creed," he replied.

Tenderly, Conner turned Tricia around, unzipped her wedding dress, and eased it off her perfect shoulders, down over her arms and her hips, letting it fall into a patch of glistening blue on the floor.

She faced him, a vision in her white lacy bra and panties, no longer shy.

She was flushed, from the curve of her breasts to her hairline, but her eyes blazed with passion and confidence and the power to turn him inside out and then put him right again.

"Your turn," she said.

Conner grinned. He took off his coat, tossed it aside.

Tricia moved in to loosen his tie, open the first few buttons of his shirt. She made a soft cooing sound as she touched her lips to the skin at the base of his throat, and he could feel his heart beating there.

And somewhere else, too.

"It's our first time as husband and wife," she murmured, baring more and more of his chest, putting her hands under his shirt, fingers splayed and searching. "Let's make it wild."

Conner gave an exultant laugh. "Good idea," he said, just before he kissed her. All the while, he was peeling off the last stitches of fabric keeping him from her. He lifted her off the floor, and her legs, with their sexy pull-up stockings, the only things she was still wearing, went around him.

They kept kissing.

Tricia moaned.

Conner used his tongue, foreshadowing what would happen in the very near future.

He laid her sideways on the bed, and the rose petals settled around her, softly fragrant.

Conner straightened, one knee on the mattress, took his time rolling down one of Tricia's stockings, then the other. She gasped and moved her head slowly from side to side as he stroked the insides of her thighs, the soft mound of her belly, her firm breasts.

Her nipples hardened against his palms, and she cried out for him, grabbed for him, trying to pull him down on top of her.

"You wanted it wild," he reminded her.

She nodded, her eyes closed, making that low, come-hither sound she always made when she needed him inside her. "And *fast*—" she told him breathlessly.

But Conner draped her legs over his shoulders, one at a time.

Tricia bit down on her lower lip, but she couldn't contain the soft, choking cry his touch elicited.

He bent his head to the crux of her, nuzzled his way through warm silk, and took her greedily into his mouth.

She climaxed almost instantly, in a wild, writhing fury of surrender, but when it was over, when she settled, sighing with satisfaction, into the cushion of rose petals, clearly, she expected Conner to take her then.

Instead, he started her on a second climb, this one long and slow, to heaven.

* * * * *

Look for Linda Lael Miller's next original novel,
THE CREED LEGACY